# THE
# SPLINTER
# SOUL

JEREMY THOMAS FULLER

# BOOKS BY JEREMY THOMAS FULLER

## THE METALWOOD SAGA

### SEASON ONE

*The Metal Wood*

*The Stone Flame*

*The Death Edge*

*The Fatal Cure*

*The Prime Trees*

### SEASON TWO

*The Absent Memory*

*The Crystal Curse*

*The Silent Binds*

*The Twin Fury*

*The Splinter Soul*

## STANDALONE

*Attention Deficit*

# THE SPLINTER SOUL

## THE METALWOOD SAGA
### BOOK 10

JEREMY THOMAS FULLER

STARMIST ENTERTAINMENT

STARMIST ENTERTAINMENT

166 Geary Str STE 1500 #1259
San Francisco, CA 94108
United States

*jeremythomasfuller.com*
*instagram.com/jeremythomasfuller*
*facebook.com/jeremythomasfuller*
*bsky.app/profile/jeremythomasfuller.com*

Cover designed by Maria Spada
Author photo by Zack Griset
Set in Stix Two

STARMIST ★
ENTERTAINMENT

Out of all the wonders of ancient Valaralda, perhaps the most impressive and enigmatic are the pyramids that dot the desert. Akhenaten was legendarily secretive about their purpose—what was considered a series of tombs may in fact have had some other use.

No one but the erstwhile archaeologist Tarathiel has ever explored the inside of the pyramids. But rumors abound—not of magic, but of the haunting of souls.

*Excerpt from*
  *"A History of Valaralda"*
  *by Fyliaster Magnus,*
  *High Historian,*
  *Ilyrion Council of Mages*
  *99,705 A.A.*

# PART ONE

# ONE

THERE WAS an army of souls in the desert.

Quynn stood, not quite slack-jawed, and watched them come. Millions of ghostly people were streaming out from burning Trees which had appeared out of nowhere in the sand. They milled about almost randomly, with no particular purpose or intent. But despite their ghostly appearance, they seemed real enough—he could see them kicking up sand, sliding down the dunes, even fighting with each other.

They were real and yet not real, as if the dead were coming back to life.

What could they be? What source of magic was this? Quynn didn't know—and unless these strange souls decided to attack him, he realized he didn't care.

He was far more interested in the monsters standing right in front of him.

"Greetings," one of the wolf-man things said. The voice sounded like a cross between a growl and a cough, but the Eldrim language was surprisingly recognizable, nonetheless. "My name is Falgr."

He held out his hand, claws and all.

Something about the creature seemed familiar to Quynn. Not that he'd seen anything like it before, just that he'd *heard* of it. He pictured jungles, a walking stick. Magona, her blind eyes everywhere.

Oh. Of course. Saul had described the very figure standing before him. It was called a rylak, and it had been the intelligent life on Eryn, before the Sundering there.

Not an *it*, then. More like a *he*.

"Greetings," Quynn said. Evidently this Falgr wanted to shake his hand, but the razor sharp claws would prove quite dangerous. Surely these creatures didn't shake each other's hands in the human tradition? They must have picked the habit up somewhere. He thought it through, the gesture hanging in the air.

Then he reached for the rylak's hand.

Falgr withdrew his claws just as Quynn's hand met his own. Quynn thought he caught an expression of some kind flicker across the wolf-man's face—respect? He didn't exactly know how to read the man.

The handshake was firm and brief, then Quynn stepped back. "How are you here?"

"Cariel," Falgr said. "She took us from Ambarhal and led us here. She kept us on Tanomar for millennia, breeding us like rats. None of us remember our home, but we have kept the stories alive."

"Damn," Quynn said. "I've been to your home world. Eryn is beautiful, if you like jungles."

"Cariel kept us training, kept us sharp. She wanted us in fighting shape for when her...war...started."

"Is that why you're here in the desert?"

"Yes, though the war never actually happened. All we had was a short fight against a few small elves. Then they defeated Cariel, and her control of us ended."

"You're not interested in killing elves?"

"All we want," Falgr said, "is to go home."

"That's all I want," Quynn said. "Perhaps we can be of some use to each other."

"I managed to send a message before her soulbind made me come here," Falgr said. "It was a word of warning. I believe I sent it to you. Are you Tarathiel?"

Quynn almost said no, but then he realized that the answer would be wrong. Quynn *was* Tarathiel—albeit half of him. Perhaps there would be something to gain for owning up to his original self. He didn't want to reintegrate with Trey— he would *never* do that—but it couldn't hurt to be honest, here.

"I am Tarathiel," he said. "Thank you for the message." He hadn't read the message, of course, but he might as well play the part.

"We have heard that Tarathiel knows great magic," Falgr said. "We had hoped you might be able to grant us our return."

"Great magic," Quynn said. "Yes. Yes, I believe I can help."

Magic was what had brought everyone here. Magic was what had created all this conflict. It was why Quynn was half a person—the better half, but still not whole. Magic and splinters were dangerous toys, perhaps not best played with.

A new rylak appeared suddenly, stepping in from some-where to Quynn's right. He looked bedraggled, possibly injured, and he hadn't been standing with the others. The figure towered over him, teeth bared, claws extended.

"Ah," the new rylak said, "I see you have finally come to pay us a visit. My name is Talon."

Quynn narrowed his eyes. Something about Talon didn't seem right.

ELANIL HADN'T SLEPT. How could she? So much was wrong with the world. New San Francisco had been destroyed. The Twins were still on the loose, and no one was any closer to locating this Imprisoner they were so keen on finding. Worse, the Twins couldn't be defeated. Not with ordinary magic, anyway, or any technology they had. Only a mysterious power that no one understood had affected Nelenor, and that same power had killed Beam.

Rylan was gone.

He had hurt her, and he had left her. He was too dangerous to contain.

But all his magic was gone now.

So much was wrong with the world.

So she sat, huddled beneath a tree, shivering. It had rained, but she had let it fall, soaking her to the bone. She couldn't bring herself to do anything more.

Rylan was gone.

"Elanil?" a voice said, and she looked up to see Phoenix approaching. The woman's eyes were red, her hair wet and bedraggled. She looked like she hadn't slept, either.

"Ho," Elanil said, weakly.

Phoenix sat beside her. "I can't believe he left."

Elanil was silent, trying not to cry.

"What did he mean in his note?" Phoenix asked. "What was he apologizing for?"

"He..." Elanil wasn't sure what to say. Could she really tell his mother what had happened between them? What had *almost* happened? "His magic is—was—out of control. He mindmastered me. He started to make me do things I...did not want to do."

"Oh, no," Phoenix said, her voice filled with dread. "No, no, no."

"He didn't mean it," Elanil said. "The magic was just too much for him. He said the Aspects all bleed together."

"It sounds like emotion got the better of him," Phoenix said. "Perhaps there are still things left that I can teach him."

"I would like that," Elanil said, laying her head on Phoenix's arm. "I wonder if Nelenor has killed him yet."

"Shush," Phoenix said. "We have to stay positive. There's a reason he went to Nelenor, and it wasn't just to get away from you."

"It may have been."

Phoenix put her arm around Elanil. "He loves you," she said. "I've seen it on his face. He left so he could protect you."

"I don't *want* him to protect me."

"I know. But I think he has another plan. He might actually have a way to stop this Twin from hurting us."

"Do you really think so?"

"I hope so," Phoenix said, squeezing her. "I hope so for all our sakes."

Another face materialized in the gloom, stepping out of the trees. Imra.

"Couldn't sleep either?" she asked, coming over to sit beside Phoenix.

"I can't believe the city is just *gone*," Phoenix said. "What else could these Twins do, if they had a mind? Are entire planets within their reach?"

"Their machine created magic," Imra said. "There's no end to what they can do."

"All those underkids," Elanil said. "Who will answer for their deaths?"

"We will," Imra said. "We who couldn't stop what was coming."

"I hate magic," Elanil said.

"I started hating magic a long time ago," Phoenix said.

They were silent for a time. Birds began to wake up around them in the forest, sparrows and starlings twittering. A pair of squirrels moved about overhead, scolding each other. The sun was beginning to rise, the camp stirring. There was still life down here, Elanil knew. The world had not yet ended. Why, then, could she only think of death?

"I miss him," she said.

"I miss him, too," Phoenix said.

"I don't understand what that red magic was," Imra said. "How could the Soul Tree just kill Beam like that?"

"It hit me, too," Phoenix said. "I could feel it inside me, as if it were tearing at my soul."

"What even *is* a soul?"

Phoenix shrugged. "I don't know, but apparently it powers all this magic."

"There were souls in that Tree," Elanil said. She shivered —both from the cold and from the memory.

"Poor Beam," Phoenix said. "To lose two people she loved in so short a time. I can't imagine what that must have been like. I hope she's happy, wherever she is now."

"Do you think there is a beyond?" Imra asked.

"There was, before the Twins were released. But now? Now I don't know."

"I guess we'll all find out, sooner or later."

"Maybe sooner," Elanil said. "If Rylan isn't successful."

"Elanil," Phoenix said, "are you okay? Did my son hurt you?"

"He almost killed me," Elanil said, remembering how the branch had felt piercing through her body. "But I'm stronger than I appear. I can heal myself without any primewood now."

"You soulbound a Tree."

Elanil nodded. "Rylan made me do it, before we left. I guess he's the reason I'm okay now."

"Emotions run strong in our family," Phoenix said.

"How well did you know his father?"

"Not well. And anyway, the person I knew wasn't Quynn —it was an illusion. He was putting on an act."

"I knew him," Imra said. "A little, at least. I watched him fight. He was vicious. Evil. Selfish."

"Wasn't he working for Lorelei?" Elanil asked.

Imra nodded. "And Lorelei was working for Tarathiel, in the end—even if she didn't remember it."

"Weird," Elanil said. "Strange how it comes full-circle. But how do the Twins factor in?"

"What do you mean?" Imra asked.

"I mean, why are they here? What do they want, besides the Imprisoner? They must have arrived here for a reason, back when they were imprisoned."

"I don't think anybody knows," Imra said. "If they did, it's been lost to memory."

"Maybe that's Rylan's plan," Elanil said.

"What is?"

"Maybe he's going to ask them what they want."

"What should *we* do?" Phoenix asked.

"You should come with me," a man's voice said, and Orym stepped out of the shadows.

# TWO

"WHERE HAVE YOU BEEN?" Elanil asked Orym. "In case you didn't notice, a lot of people are dying."

Everyone was standing in a clearing in the forest outside Lusvunub. The sun was up, and Elanil could see the six remaining sky cities floating above them, disconnected in the air. The birds were still singing in the trees, unaware of the destruction that had occurred all around.

Orym stood taller than usual, back held straight. His eyes held a new confidence, as if he had found new knowledge. His blond hair was slicked back as it usually was, and he was dressed in flowing clothes of tans and browns. He looked like he belonged in a desert.

"I was figuring out how to stop the Twins," he said.

Dill stepped forward, clasping his father's hand. "It is good to see you, Father."

"I am glad you're safe," Orym said. "I'm glad you all are."

"Father," Dill said, "do you know who this Imprisoner is?"

Orym shook his head. "I do not."

"Nelenor was looking for his kin. I think it's me."

Had Elanil caught a look of alarm flashing across Orym's

face? She couldn't be sure—it was gone too quickly, if it had been there at all.

"That doesn't make sense," Orym said. "Unless...no. It couldn't be."

"What?"

Orym's eyes got sad. "Your mother."

"My...*mother*?"

Elanil had never heard anything about Dill's mother. She glanced at Phoenix, saw confusion in the woman's eyes.

"Tiala was always enigmatic," Orym said. "When she left, I—"

"You never knew the reason."

Were those tears in Orym's eyes? "I didn't want her to go," he said. "She was *everything* to me."

"She wasn't a hundred thousand years old."

Orym looked at the ground. "Who knows? I never thought I was as old as I am. Neither did Trey, or Arra. Or Lorelei. There could be many other ancients walking amongst us, and we would never know."

"Mother wouldn't have done this," Dill said. "Even if she were that old, she wouldn't have imprisoned the Twins. Hell, how would she have done it? What magic must that have required?"

Orym took a step forward. "Do you think you knew her?" he asked, his voice suddenly dangerous. "Do you know what went on inside her head? She was a passionate woman, your mother. She was unpredictable, independent. There's a reason we never got married."

"She left you, Father. She didn't like the man you were becoming. *That's* why you never got married."

"How *dare* you," Orym said, his voice shaking. He almost seemed to grow bigger before Elanil's eyes, his skin darkening. "Tiala *loved* me."

"Orym," Phoenix said, "tell us how we're going to defeat the Twins."

Orym glared at Dill for another moment, then stepped away. His form seemed back to normal now. Perhaps Elanil had only been imagining it.

"Simple," he said. "It's the pyramids."

Elanil frowned at him. He glanced at her, his eyes flicking away nervously.

"Explain," Phoenix said.

"In Tarathiel's research, there was something called the Defense Mechanism. He thought Edrafen was the key to enabling it, but he was wrong. It turns out the *pyramids* are the Mechanism."

"And you know how to turn it on?"

"I'm still working on it, but I think I'm close." He looked up at the sky, at the cities wheeling overhead. "What happened here, anyway?"

"New San Francisco was destroyed," Elanil said. "Along with tens of thousands of underkids from all seven cities."

"Shit," Orym breathed. "Nelenor did this?"

Elanil nodded. "The cities had to break apart afterwards. They only just finished dropping the husk of New San Francisco somewhere to the south."

"That's…incredible," Orym said. "I had no idea the Twins had that much power."

"There must have been a reason we worshipped them as gods."

"It is such a shame. Such a waste. That was the only San Francisco we had left."

He didn't look sad. He wasn't shedding any tears. Hadn't Orym had any *friends* up there, any other family, anything that he would actually be sad to lose? He'd helped *create* the cities, or at least that's the story Elanil had been told. He'd lived up there the entire time.

He was taking this awfully stoically.

"Where's Nelenor now?" Orym asked.

"We don't know," Elanil said.

"With Rylan," Phoenix said.

"That's interesting," Orym said. "What does the boy hope to accomplish?"

"We don't know," Phoenix said. "He seems to think he can do something to affect Nelenor's actions."

"He'll probably die," Orym said.

Elanil felt anger growing inside her.

"Sorry," Orym said. "I didn't mean to put it that bluntly. It's just—I mean, if Nelenor destroyed an *entire city*, I'm not sure what Rylan can accomplish. But maybe he'll surprise us."

"He already has," Phoenix whispered.

"What?"

"Never mind."

"How did you get here?" Elanil asked.

Orym looked at her. "I gated."

"But aren't you—"

"A fallfoiler, yes. But now I'm apparently a Prime Mage."

"How?"

"Atlantis. The traps there—I think they broke through whatever was blocking me. I can tell you the story when this is all over."

"Another Prime Mage," Phoenix muttered. "Soon everyone will be."

"Would that be so bad?" Imra asked.

"I don't see how it could be good."

"Isn't gating dangerous?" Elanil asked. "I thought it caused memory loss."

"Just so," Orym said. "Though I've recently discovered a trick to that. You can make a gate to nowhere."

"You can?"

Orym nodded. "Just visualize a gate that leads to nothing. Put that around yourself, then put another gate around that, going to where you need to go. And just like that, it's safe."

"I've never made a gate before," Elanil said.

Orym smiled. "You'll get the hang of it, I'm sure."

He didn't ask her how she was alive, how she was suddenly a Prime Mage. He didn't seem to care anything about her, even though he hadn't seen her or any of the others in a long time. Hell, he hadn't been surprised to see Phoenix alive, either. Was he really so focused on the Twins that he couldn't spare a thought for the people in his world?

Or did Orym have more knowledge than by any right he should?

"Listen," Orym said, "I have to go. Some of you have radios, yes?"

Phoenix and Dill nodded. Rylan had one too, Elanil knew. Maybe they should try calling him on it.

"Good," Orym said. "I have one that will connect with yours, even when we're on opposite planets. I need to head back to Valaralda now, to see if I can get this Mechanism working. I'll call you all once I figure it out. Sound good?"

Something about the whole thing was ringing false to Elanil, but she couldn't put her finger on it. Orym seemed too callous, too inured to what had happened. He was focused on defeating the Twins, which was good—but Trey had been wrong about the Mechanism once. Who was to say that Orym had the right of it?

But he *was* the scientist in the group. Perhaps his knowledge was superior to Trey's.

"Agreed," Phoenix said.

"Be safe, Father," Dill said. "What should we be doing?"

"Join me on Valaralda when you can," Orym said. "You have the secret of the gates now. You can go anywhere you want."

And without another word, light flashed around him and he disappeared.

ORYM FLASHED into existence in his Nekhrumetian palace, a smile on his face. It had been startlingly easy to hide the truth from those idiots on Earth—they hadn't even suspected. Except for maybe the girl—he would have to watch her. She seemed far too smart for her age.

Perhaps he shouldn't have given them the nowhere gate trick. But really, what harm could it do? Now they could move around more quickly. It only meant that they could help him more easily, when the time came. They would arrive when called upon, like lambs to the slaughter.

This was all way too easy.

He hadn't expected Dill's revelation, though. The Twins somehow saw their souls, knew that he was Orym's son. How were they doing that? It must be related to Guruthos, somehow. The device operated via sparkthreads, he knew. Maybe that was the trick he was missing.

He ached to get his hands on it.

Bringing up Tiala had been a good deflection on his part. Even now, after all this time, it still hurt to think of her. He and she had had a fling that lasted for more than a century, and in the end it had all gone down in flames. She had known, he was increasingly sure. She had known that he was really Aten, what he was really capable of.

What he really wanted out of life.

Did that make him evil? He wasn't evil. He was still the same scientist he'd always been, going after bigger and brighter things. Wouldn't the greatest Earth scientists have done the same thing, if magic had appeared before them? Wouldn't Einstein, Hawking, Newton have wanted to experiment, to see what this new power could do? Guruthos violated every law of physics he knew—what was the crime in studying it?

He wasn't a bad man.

He was sure of it.

And once he had Guruthos in his hands, he would prove it to the world.

# THREE

"GREETINGS, LITTLE HUMAN," Nelenor said, moving to a seated position on the ground. The Anubis figure looked strange, twenty feet of torso atop crossed legs.

He didn't seem dangerous at all.

"Ho," Rylan said, taking a careful step forward. He'd seen what the Twin could do. He'd seen New San Francisco in flames. He knew that one wrong move would mean the end of his life.

And yet he had to try. He had no choice.

He had to do this for Elanil.

"I hope you aren't come to fight me," Nelenor said. "It would be a shame to have to kill a superuser."

"I'm not a superuser anymore," Rylan said. "And besides, you already tried to kill me once."

Nelenor seemed to sigh, shifting his weight slightly to one side. "You people are so quick to judge," he said. "Humans and elves alike, all so eager to see us meet our doom. Yet do you know us? Have you taken the time to talk to us at all?" He pursed his Anubis lips. "You'd think you were not, in fact,

Seeds. I would have expected better from sons and daughters of Starmist."

"We don't know anything about Starmist," Rylan said. "We're just trying to survive."

Nelenor dipped his head. "You are succeeding better than I had anticipated, truth be told."

"We haven't even made a dent!"

"You dented me. Or that Soul Tree did. I am still not sure what that was."

"Wait," Rylan said, taking another step forward. "*You* don't know what the Soul Tree was?"

Nelenor shook his head. "The souls here do not work the way we were used to on Starmist Prime. There, our own souls communicated with the devices directly—something almost none of you can seem to do. But you are young, and untrained—perhaps you simply need more time."

"You didn't use Trees on Starmist Prime?"

Rylan took another step forward into the clearing, staying wary for any sudden moves. Nelenor seemed content to talk, for now. Perhaps the Twin just needed a friend.

"We did not have Trees on Starmist Prime," Nelenor said, "at least not in the same manner as you. Perhaps our climate engineering was to blame. Perhaps it was the near-immortality our scientists were able to achieve for humans and elves alike. But I don't think that was it. Actually, I think it was the dragons."

That had been a lot of new information. "Humans *and* elves?" Rylan asked.

"Both species were on Starmist Prime," Nelenor said. "How else do you think we Seeded you both?"

"And dragons?"

"Another species of sentient life. Large winged creatures, reptilian in nature."

"I've heard of dragons, but only in myths. A book Con had—it showed pictures of them. But they aren't real, at least not on Earth."

"We did not Seed all species to all Seed Planets. The rylak, for instance—we did not wish them to coexist with the other races. Their propensity for violence was too high, especially in the absence of advanced mitigation technology. It took us many millennia on Starmist Prime to bring them into a fruitful relationship with the other peoples."

Rylan had seen rylak before, on Valaralda in the desert. "It seems to me that you harbor a great love of life," he said. "Why exterminate so much now? Why are you so violent?"

Nelenor gave a great sigh. "Sometimes even the most enlightened beings succumb to emotions. Even the most powerful make mistakes. *Especially* those."

"I was one of those," Rylan said. "I was too powerful."

"You just needed to learn control. Given time—and far less time than you think, for one with such ample aptitude as you—you will be fine."

"Will?"

"Xyclami," Nelenor said, "please reinstate user 69327A49Z7."

Rylan felt power flowing into him almost instantly.

*Welcome to Xyclami*, the machine's voice said in his mind. *Your blood sugar is below recommended norms for your species.*

"I—" Rylan said. "I think I need to eat something."

*Transmuting is one of the granted power divisions*, Xyclami said. *Please activate your sparkthread with instructions.*

"Uh," Rylan said, and he Willed a branch on the ground to turn into a can of baked beans.

It worked.

*Caloric content: 307. Protein: 18 grams. Subject will require further sustenance after approximately 93 minutes, subjective time.*

"I'd almost forgotten how much I hate being a superuser," Rylan said, bending to pick up the can of baked beans. "Do you have anything to open this with?"

Nelenor gestured with his hand, and the top of the can flicked open. "Why do you hate it?"

"Xyclami," Rylan said, digging into the can with his fingers. "It talks way too much."

"That's an easy fix. Xyclami, please enter low verbosity mode for user 69327A49Z7."

*Low verbosity mode activated. Responses to direct queries only, life-threatening situations excepted.*

"Damn," Rylan said. "I could have done that the whole time?"

"You missed basic training," Nelenor said. "There is much I can teach you, if you do not fight me."

Rylan ate another bite of beans, fishing them out with his bare fingers. They tasted good, if a little cold. He was starving, as it turned out. He'd just been too nervous to notice.

Things with Nelenor were not quite going as he had expected.

"Where are the dragons now?" he asked.

"I'm afraid I do not know," Nelenor said. "Some pieces of our reality were lost during the escape, and the machine we built to reintegrate them has disappeared out of our sight. Perhaps we misunderstood its function."

Another machine. Another device with technology far beyond anyone's wildest dreams. Was it as powerful as Guruthos? Did it create a form of magic, a power that mere mortals could barely comprehend? Rylan shuddered, thinking about it. Guruthos was bad enough. Magic was powerful enough.

He thought perhaps reality should win.

"I wonder why we have myths of them here," he said. "Dragons, I mean."

"The original Seeds must have retained that memory," Nelenor said. "I would guess that all Seed Planets harbor with them imagery of dragons, whether or not the species itself actually exists."

"You seem different," Rylan said.

Nelenor shifted his position slightly. Rylan flinched, but the Twin was only getting comfortable on the ground. Was it his imagination, or had the Anubis figure grown smaller as they talked?

"Different how?" Nelenor asked.

"Nicer. You're just speaking with me—no violence or shouting. Don't you still want to find the Imprisoner?"

"I grow weary of fighting," Nelenor said. "But yes, I still do very much want to find the Imprisoner." He cocked his head to the side as if listening to something. "Ah! Velion has felt him on Valaralda. I must go."

"You can feel the Imprisoner?"

"He is hiding himself, somehow. Only rarely, when he lets his guard drop for a moment, do we feel him. His soul is connected to ours, you see. His and the one who unlocked us."

"Trey."

"Yes. Those two will always share reality with us, connected across time. That is what the Prison magic does."

"I see." He didn't see. But it seemed good to keep Nelenor talking, to extract as much information out of him as he could—even if he didn't understand it all. "So you're leaving?"

"Yes. I must find this Imprisoner, and make him pay."

"Why? Are you really the vengeful type?"

"I—" Nelenor actually seemed at a loss for words. "I must go."

"Is the Imprisoner named Orym?"

Nelenor nodded. "A woman named Lorelei told us this."

So it *was* true. If Orym was the Imprisoner, it meant he had to be at least a hundred thousand years old. It *also* meant that he was a very different sort of person than anyone had known.

But as Rylan thought of it, he realized that perhaps it wasn't so unexpected. Orym always had been callous, focused on science and discovery to the exclusion of everything else. He'd never been particularly nice to anyone. And hadn't Dill said that sometimes there was a little too much of his father in him? That his mother, Tiala, had left because of it?

Pieces were beginning to fall into place.

"Are you coming?" Nelenor asked.

"Will you tell me about the Imprisoner?" Rylan asked. "What happened between you so long ago?"

Nelenor sighed. "I will tell you, little one, but then we must be away. I only do this because you are a superuser, and so you are owed certain rights and privileges."

It seemed as if Nelenor might even *respect* him a bit. That was certainly the last thing Rylan had been expecting.

*Xyclami*, Rylan thought as Nelenor began telling him the story, *can you send my friends a message?*

*Affirmative.*

Rylan kept an eye on Nelenor, wondering if the Twin had heard his exchange with the machine. It seemed, for the moment, that he had not.

# FOUR

ELANIL'S RADIO suddenly burst to life, causing her to jump in surprise.

"Dance," it said, in a voice that was not Rylan's, "Nelenor is about to gate back to Valaralda. I'm coming with—end of message."

"What in the—" Elanil said.

"That sounded like a computer," Dill said.

"A what?"

"Could that have been Guruthos talking to us on behalf of Rylan? Who is Dance?"

Elanil felt herself blushing. "That's me. He calls me Dance, and I call him Wind."

"That's cute," Phoenix said. "I'm so glad he's okay."

"It sounds like he was cut off mid-sentence," Dill said. "He may be okay now, but if he's with Nelenor he's still in a great deal of danger. At least the Twin hasn't killed him outright."

"Not yet," Phoenix said. "Should we go to Valaralda, too?"

"If that's where Nelenor is going, then yes," Dill said.

"I want to find Rylan," Elanil said. "Maybe there's a way to rescue him."

"Then it's agreed," Dill said. "Imra? Allain? Erodar? You coming with us?"

They all nodded. "I'd like to see this through," Imra said.

"So would I," a new voice said, and Lorelei stepped out of the woods.

"JUST BEFORE HE locked us away for a hundred millennia," Nelenor was saying, "Aten made us look like this." He gestured to himself. "He said we reminded him of dogs, always willing to serve. Which, I am ashamed to say, was true: we were far too nice, too willing to go along with whatever he did."

"You weren't used to the culture," Rylan said. "It sounds like Starmist was far more advanced."

"It was. And it is true: the Seeds appear to have devolved considerably. Which is to be expected, given the fact that we did not seed any technology whatsoever. We left each world to fend for themselves, to evolve society as they saw fit. It should have been no surprise to us that things ended up the way they did."

"Being nice isn't a bad thing," Rylan said. "My whole life I've been around the worst of people. It would have been nice to have some kindness around."

Nelenor smiled at him. "I see it within you," he said. "Perhaps that is why you are a superuser. You grew up hard, but inside you are soft."

"I think it comes from my mother," Rylan said.

Nelenor's smile grew wider. "This is what we came to find," he said. "One hundred thousand years ago, we were searching for our family. Our sister—who is still here, I might add—was the most important thing left to us. We desperately wanted to be reunited with her."

"You are all-powerful," Rylan said. "Why couldn't you just find her immediately?"

"We are limited by the technology. Sifting the spark-threads takes time, even for us. Even with a device as powerful as Xyclami. Our sister's strand is here, somewhere. We will find it."

"I hope you do," Rylan said. "I will help you, if you will allow it." He stepped close to Nelenor, holding out his hand.

Nelenor's Anubis eyes twinkled. "I would like that."

And his appearance changed. His muzzle shrank, flattening into his face. His ears grew smaller as well, their high points becoming the familiar tips of elven ears. His body grew smaller, more lithe, more graceful. Long, blond hair grew out of his head and his eyes became thinner, slightly angled, sparkling blue. In just a moment a beautiful male elf was standing before Rylan, dressed in clothes of flowing white, reaching out to clasp his hand.

"Greetings," Nelenor said. "I trust I will have no further need of that illusion."

"Ho," Rylan said. "It's very nice to finally meet you."

"ORYM IS THE IMPRISONER," Lorelei said, striding out of the forest. A woman Elanil had never met was trailing behind her, looking distinctly out of place.

"Are you sure?" Phoenix asked.

Lorelei gave her a cold stare. "I was there. I helped imprison one of the Twins myself."

Everyone gasped, herself included. "But that means—"

"It means *you're* the Imprisoner," Dill said. "Or one of them. You said you helped?"

"Myself and Cara—Cariel—helped," Lorelei said. "And many others. But it was all Aten's doing. Orym. It was his idea. He wanted the power of Guruthos for himself."

"I don't believe you," Dill said. "My father is not that old. And even if he were, he doesn't have that much evil inside him."

"He designed the sky cities," Lorelei said. "He imprisoned *millions* of people."

"Acting on *your* orders."

"I fully acknowledge my role in all of this."

"He was *fighting* you at the end," Elanil said. "We all were. He was there the night you shot me. He was trying to help us get rid of you and your kind."

Lorelei looked at her, and for a moment the old Lorelei was back. The hatred, the anger was back there in her eyes. The desire to get her way, to kill anyone that was trying to stop her. But Elanil met her gaze calmly, cooly, and after a moment the woman softened.

"We were young, back then," she said. "We all wanted power. Aten thought that by imprisoning the Twins, he would have longer to study the magic. What he didn't know was that the Department of Magical Research had already sent Guruthos away. He didn't mean for them to be imprisoned that long—none of us did."

"Then he should have released them," Elanil said.

"I still don't believe you," Dill said. "I think you're covering up for yourself, for your sister. It *can't* have been my father who did this. It can't have been."

Lorelei shrugged. "You'll have to see for yourself, then. Does anyone know where he is?"

"Back on Valaralda," Elanil said. "That's where Nelenor is going, too."

"Then we should go."

"Very well," Phoenix said. "Everyone, grab your supplies —we may need these tents on Valaralda. We'll go as soon as everything is packed. I'll gate us over myself." She fingered the fireblade at her waist.

"It's not him," Dill said. "It can't be."

"I'm sorry you had to find out this way," Lorelei said. "I'm sorry all of this happened."

LORELEI WAS TIRED OF INACTION. Even now, Aten was on the loose, committing who knew what atrocities in the name of power. And while that was happening, these elves were doing nothing but *pack*.

Still, Orym had been alive for a hundred thousand years without doing much harm. Lorelei herself had been the more dangerous one, in the end. Lorelei and her sister. She shuddered to think of Cariel, how she had looked at the end, bleeding out on the forest floor.

A spider crawled across her forearm suddenly, and Lorelei jumped, almost shrieking, brushing it off as quickly as she could. It wasn't that she was afraid of spiders. It was just... okay, she was afraid of spiders. It wasn't like one to just jump on her like that. She looked around, saw a few more of them climbing on a nearby tree. It seemed strange, but she wasn't sure why.

"Never seen you jump like that before," Allain said, approaching with a crooked smile on his face.

"It just scared me," Lorelei said.

"Never liked spiders much myself. You doing okay? It's been a while since I saw you."

"I'm fine," Lorelei said, hearing the iciness in her tone. Still, she had to admit that it was nice to be asked. Nobody else in this place had given a care for how she was doing. "Sorry—I've been out of sorts, lately. For a very long time, to be honest." She tried on a smile. "I'm frazzled. Haven't slept enough. I'm worried about Aten. What will he do if he succeeds in killing the Twins?"

"You think that's what he's planning?"

"I'm sure of it. Back when we imprisoned them, he said he wanted to find a way to force them away from Guruthos. Something tells me he figured out that way."

Allain stepped closer, gray eyes on hers. "You look good," he said.

"Thanks."

That was a forward comment, but in the short time she'd known him he'd always been like that. It was how *she* was, come to think of it. Forward, with an edge. She didn't meet many others like that. Quynn had been the last one.

Allain was young, to be sure. Just turned fifty, she believed—finally an adult. But he was handsome, if a bit rough around the edges. He had a great body, though many young elves did. But it wasn't his body that was drawing her in as he stood there, watching her. Okay, maybe it *was* his body, but there was something else. Something in his eyes. Some kind of mystery there, a bit of adventure. They shared something, she realized then.

If only he weren't so young.

"Almost ready!" Imra called. "Lorelei, Allain, you guys good to go?"

"We are," Lorelei said, still meeting Allain's eyes.

"Let's do it," Allain said, giving her a smile.

Lorelei couldn't help the little blush that touched her cheeks.

"WE DID MAKE ONE MISTAKE," Nelenor said. "When we shaped the Fourteen powers, we experienced minor difficulty with the final one."

They were still in the forest outside Lusvunub, and apparently Nelenor was seeing fit to give Rylan another training lesson. He didn't mind—the longer he could keep Nelenor talking, the more time the others would have to figure out how to stop the Twins.

"Which power is that?" Rylan asked.

"Gatesending. It was a novel use of the dimensional rift, something the original creators of Xyclami did not necessarily intend. The problem we uncovered is that the soul is wrenched too quickly across dimensions. Sometimes this can result in pieces of reality being lost, as happened when we fled from the Starmist system."

"You said you had some kind of device to retrieve these pieces of reality?"

"It is lost to us," Nelenor said. "Luckily, there is a trick. If you hold a gate to nowhere around yourself, then put *that* gate through another gate, your soul's reality remains moored. We could alter the Fourteenth to make this technique automatic, but it would require rebuilding the Powers from scratch—something that requires an immense amount of energy and would leave us vulnerable during the process. The Imprisoner is hot on our tails, most likely—if he finds us before we find him, our existence could be threatened. We know his plan was to separate us from Xyclami, though we know not how. If he has discovered a method for this, we are in grave danger. So for now, just remember to use the double gate trick. Your soul will thank you."

"Why tell me all this?" Rylan asked.

The elven form of Nelenor shrugged. "All magic users have a right to know. We didn't intend for gatesending to have this dangerous side effect."

"So much would be different if it didn't."

Nelenor eyed him for a moment. "Let us go. You are accompanying me to Valaralda?"

"Am I free to make up my own mind?"

"You are not my prisoner, young Rylan. You may go where and how you please, so long as you do not attack us."

"Very well," Rylan said. "I'm going with you."

Whatever was about to happen, Rylan needed to be there when it did. His fortune had held this far—perhaps he could talk the Twins out of whatever misfortune they had planned.

"Excellent," Nelenor said.

Light crashed over them, and the world of Earth disappeared.

# FIVE

ARRA STEPPED into the halls of the Eglaria with trepidation. The last time she'd been here, she'd been convinced the whole place was a cover for something dark and sinister.

Now she was sure of it.

Faranel led them through the dark and dingy halls, torchlight revealing the tapestries hanging from the walls. The Eglarian True Spirits looked down on them with malice in their eyes, dinosaurs and wolves and strange birds with red beaks. Arra tried not to breathe the musty air too deeply as they passed, their feet clicking on the dusty cobbles.

The room in the back was just as austere as Arra remembered: stone walls with a huge stone slab of a table in the middle, looking like some kind of sacrificial altar. There were no wall decorations or even any torches—the room was lit by two dozen candles on the table. Arra was suddenly sure they were going to die in here, surrounded by the strange shadowmen that roamed the halls.

Trey took her hand, and she willed her breathing to slow. It would be okay. They could protect themselves. They could protect each other. The Twins were on the loose, which was a much greater threat than this place.

Whatever this place was.

"Please," Faranel said, "sit."

Chairs were arrayed about the table, huge high-backed things made out of thick wood, ornately carved. Arra, Trey, Lashel and Cresius sat awkwardly, looking at each other in the flickering candlelight. Why were they here again?

Faranel came around to his side of the table, pulling up his chair with a loud scraping sound. He sat with his elbows on the table, fingers steepled together. "Greetings," he said, his eyes partially lidded. "I had not thought to see our friend from the Department here today. What brings you to the Eglaria?"

"Information," Trey said.

"I'll tell you what I can." He was still looking at Cresius.

"Who are the Twins?"

Faranel finally turned his gaze to Trey. "The Twins?"

"This room does echo."

"Funny. Why do you think I know anything about the Twins?"

"Don't play dumb," Trey said. "The Eglaria is—was—a religious organization, was it not? Surely the Twins entered into it at some point."

Faranel frowned. "We are not the Devout."

"I didn't ask about the Devout. Tell me what you know about the *Twins*. They destroyed Ilyrion, or didn't you hear? That storm outside is their doing."

"The storm has just stopped."

"It—really?"

"Can't you hear?"

"We're inside layers and layers of stone. How could I *hear* anything?"

"Oh," Faranel said. "I forgot how sensitive one's hearing becomes from spending years inside this place. The storm stopped mere moments ago. Something has just changed."

"Could one of the Twins have been hurt?" Arra asked.

"They may have simply changed their minds," Cresius said. "Who knows what their intent was?"

"I'll tell you what I know," Faranel said, "if Cresius tells me what I want to know."

"Deal," Cresius said.

"You don't even want to know what I'm going to ask?"

"I have no secrets from you," Cresius said. "The Department is an open book."

"It was not ever this way."

"No. But times have changed, my old...friend. We're engaged in a war for our very survival."

"Are we? I am not aware of any fighting taking place."

Cresius slammed his hand down on the table suddenly, causing everyone to jump. The sound echoed several times around the dark chamber. "Dammit, Faranel, why must you always be so pig-headed? We went to University together, or have you forgotten? Were Akhenaten's teachings so seductive to you that you renounced all laws and customs in this land?"

Faranel didn't look shaken at all. His face was still impassive, his fingers steepled. "First," he said, "Akhenaten founded *both* our orders. And second, the laws and customs you refer to were created by *you*, or by the faction you represent. No darkprime magic. No gatesending. No practicing the Gifts of the Soul. No research into other worlds. These restrictions fly in the face of the very man who created our orders, who wanted us to exist. He wanted *research*, man, or have you forgotten? He wanted us to progress."

"And we have," Cresius said. "And as I said, my book is

open to you now. I will gladly show you the DMR research facilities. You can even see the Elite in action."

Faranel actually got a smile on his face at that. "You drive a hard bargain," he said. "Very well—I'll tell you everything I know. It will be a long story, though." He snapped his fingers, and an attendant entered the room. "Wine for everyone, please, and meat and cheese. We will be in here for a while."

Arra settled back in her uncomfortable chair, wondering what kind of story she was about to hear.

"The Eglaria is an ancient order," Faranel said. "Aten founded several such societies in the years following the Awakening: the Corps of Astronomers, the Department of Magical Research, and the Eglaria. He even created this rich city of Nekhrumet, that all its citizens may live in peace and prosperity out here near the river Iteranu. With his beautiful and kind mistress Selenia, he ruled over the denizens of the desert for hundreds of years."

"Wait," Arra said. "*Selenia* was his mistress?"

"Of course," Faranel said. "You have not heard the tales of the jewel-tongued Mistress of the Desert?"

"I believe I have not," Arra said. "But I know this Selenia. How *old* is she?"

"Long dead," Faranel said. "But if she were alive today by some happenstance of immortality, she would be over one hundred thousand years old."

"Cariel," Arra said.

"Yes," Trey said. "It's interesting that she kept the name Selenia for so long."

"It's more interesting that she was affiliated with Aten. Could he still be alive, somehow?"

"Doubtful," Cresius said.

"He is not alive," Faranel said. "Aten died by his own hand in 300 A.A."

"Then was resurrected in 500 A.A.," Cresius said.

"That is a disputed fact," Faranel said. "Akhenaten may have borne a striking resemblance to Aten, but there is no reason to believe it was the same person. How could it have been? No one comes back from the dead." A smile grew on his face as he said it, and Arra was completely sure that he was lying.

"It doesn't matter," Trey said. "Continue with your tale."

"Very well," Faranel said. "As I said earlier, both the Eglaria and the Department of Magical Research were formed for the same reason: to conduct research into magic. Except our order was to study the side of magic not often talked about or understood: the Fourteen Gifts of the Soul."

"What I saw in the forest," Arra said. "That was your order. You were *resurrecting* people."

Faranel bowed his head slightly. "You have the right of it, I'm afraid. Though this may be difficult to hear, one of the Fourteen Gifts does indeed grant us the ability to resurrect souls in the service of the Twins. They are henceforth known as shadowslaves, beholden only to the gods."

"Disgusting," Arra said.

"They have no free will of their own?" Trey asked.

"No," Faranel said. "Truth be told, you or your friends doubtless encountered one or two of them in your travels. One brought Quynn to Valaralda, for example. It was not entirely at our behest."

"You were working with Cariel."

"Very astute. Yes, we were working with Cariel. I understand that now she is dead."

"I killed her myself," Arra said. "So that proves it: we can't trust you. Trey, we need to leave."

"Peace," Faranel said. "We mean you no harm. We were

working toward immortality—a gift only the Twins can bring. We did not desire power over others."

"Immortals have *great* power over others," Arra said.

Faranel smiled. "I have heard that you are, in fact, one of these immortals which you seem to hate."

Arra sat forward in her chair. "I'm a Prime Mage," she said, "and don't you forget it."

"Very impressive, I'm sure," Faranel said. "But you did not answer my question."

"We're immortal," Trey said. "Or we're *extremely* long-lived, if there's a difference."

"Ah," Faranel said. "Then you see, we have no reason to work for or with Cariel now. It seems this immortality we seek is within our reach."

"All you need to do is die," Trey said, his teeth flashing in the candlelight.

The room was silent for a moment.

"He's not kidding," Cresius said. "You literally need to die. On a tree, from what we've surmised. Killed by a Talented mage. Oh, and you need to be Talented as well."

"You picked all that up already?" Trey asked.

Cresius shrugged. "I'm in charge of the Department of Magical *Research*, Trey. I'm a quick study."

"Does this technique still work?" Faranel asked.

Arra and Trey exchanged a look. "It may not," she said. "With the Twins released, Ambarhal may not function as it once did."

"Ambarhal," Faranel echoed, the sound multiplying in the chamber. "We have many tapestries devoted to this."

The attendant arrived again, bearing with him a tray with two stone pitchers and five glasses. The glasses were beautiful, made of what appeared to be crystal and polished to a glorious shine. They reflected the candlelight in myriad directions, lending a hypnotic effect to the room. Arra found herself salivating as the red wine was poured. She hadn't had wine in a very long time.

"To our health," Faranel said after everyone had been served. "And to the rightful end to this conflict."

"To the rightful end," Trey echoed, and Arra murmured her assent.

They clinked their glasses together, the crystalline sound echoing strangely in the dark chamber.

It wasn't until after she'd taken a sip that she realized the wine may have been poisoned.

But she was a Prime Mage now. She had soulsoothing magic at her fingertips. She pulled a piece of light birch out of her pouch just in case, the wood warm on her skin.

Nothing happened. The wine was fine.

"I'm not here to kill you," Faranel said. "Let me continue the story. To really understand the Twins, you must go back a hundred thousand years."

# SIX

"TALON," Quynn said, reaching out his hand. "I'm guessing you took that name yourself."

The big rylak raised his hand with claws out, clasping Quynn's hand with his own. Quynn kept his face impassive as the sharp edges sliced into his skin.

"The rylak are a proud people," Talon said, withdrawing his claws as he withdrew his hand. Quynn's blood dripped to the desert sand. "We do not suffer the leadership of elves lightly."

The leadership of elves? Quynn stared at Talon, trying to ignore the great pain in his hand. He wasn't talking about Quynn, that much was sure.

Realization finally dawned.

"Magona."

"She was known as Cariel on our world," Talon said. "But yes—Magona was one of her favorite personas. She controlled us for *millennia*. I wanted nothing more than to see her dead, her corpse strewn across the ground."

"And did you get your wish?"

"She is dead," Talon said, "though not by my hand. We all

felt the bond disappear." He looked around at the other rylak, who nodded in return.

"Then you are free," Quynn said.

"Yes."

Quynn's attention was distracted by the ghostly souls in the distance. They were still amassing, filling up the desert with their shimmering, otherworldly bodies.

"Do you know what they are?" he asked.

Talon turned to survey them. "They are souls," he said, his voice a growl. "Taken from Ambarhal, as we all were."

"But you seem real enough."

Talon unsheathed his claws. "Cariel wrenched us from that place, bringing us through the Trees. We were alive, there, or as near as we could be. These souls—they were Sundered. It is different."

Oh. They were from the Sundering? But that meant— "They didn't die?"

"They're dead," Talon said. "But souls can never die. They form here now because Ambarhal can no longer hold them."

"I don't like this," Quynn said.

"I'm not sure I like *you*. Who are you, anyway?"

"Quynn—Tarathiel. I'm—well, I'm nobody, really."

"Then kindly get out of my way, nobody."

"I didn't sunder those souls."

"I don't care. We're going home."

"How?" Quynn asked. "There are no spaceships left."

"We will gate."

"You do realize how dangerous that is, right?"

Talon took a step forward, his chest outthrust. Quynn tried not to wince as he saw the man-beast's claws unsheathe. "Do not speak to me of danger, slick-skinned child," Talon said. "I have seen more danger than you can possibly know."

Quynn swallowed, deciding how to play this. He could

acquiesce and simply leave, allowing this monster to go about his business in peace. Or he could fight back, antagonize him, put him in his place. He had no reason for the latter, but something told him Talon might make a useful ally.

And this ally needed a show of strength.

So he lifted a finger, poking it into Talon's chest fur.

Hard.

"I can see that Cariel has muddled your mind," he said, adopting a growling tone of his own. "Or have you grown soft? You fight, then flee as the moment strikes you. Go if you wish. I care not."

Talon growled, the sound deep in his throat. "You play a dangerous game, puny elf. Do you wish so badly to die? We have only just met, but I will gladly help you meet that purpose."

"As I said," Quynn said, "I care not. You don't seem that useful, anyway."

He turned, careful to show a look of disgust on his face before he did, and began to stride away.

The slashing of claws came just as he'd expected.

But Quynn was burning dark oak. The claws flew right through him, mergemelding magic rendering his body into nothing in the air.

Then he turned, switching to light oak, feeling strength enter his arms, feeling his body grow. He strode back to Talon in one step, and hit him across the face.

The rylak went flying, claws and anger wheeling in the air. The other rylak surged around him, letting him fall, threatening faces glowering at Quynn. Rumbles erupted all around. Talon was on his back in the sand, the other rylak hiding him from view. For a moment, Quynn was sure he'd have to fight every single rylak right here, in hand-to-hand combat.

Then Talon started laughing.

"You are strong," he said, getting to his feet. The other rylak moved out of his way as he approached. "I see the glory of the Hunt in you. You say you have been to our home world?"

"I have," Quynn said, relaxing his magic. He pulled his hand out of his pocket, making sure to keep a piece of dark oak between his fingers just in case. His hand was still bleeding painfully. Not for the first time, Quynn wished he was a soulsoother. It was perhaps the one bad thing about being a splinter—Trey had gotten all the healing magic.

"Has it changed?" Talon asked. "Is it still as wild as before?"

"It is wild," Quynn said. "I think you would like it there."

"You say these gates are dangerous."

"They cause memory loss, more often than not. You might arrive on Eryn not knowing who you were."

Talon growled. "That would undo all our millennia of existence," he said. "I thank you for your warning." Then he smiled, slyly. "Of course, I knew all that. I was in charge of a place called Memory, after all. I know better than anyone living how gates affect the mind."

"This was a test?"

"One which you passed," Talon said.

Other rylak growled around them, and Quynn looked to see what was the matter. Hadn't he just resolved things with Talon? Then he saw it, and he clenched the oak harder in his fist.

While they'd been distracted with each other, the strange, ghostly souls had completely surrounded them in the desert.

# SEVEN

ORYM HAD HAD new cushions and pillows brought into his palace, along with a plate of grapes and wine. He found himself missing his cheetah as he lounged, thinking through his plan. He found himself missing Selenia.

But no. Selenia—Cara—had been treacherous, in the end. She'd wanted power as surely as he had, and she was at least as cunning as he. She had been a worthy opponent—and a worthy partner in bed. He did miss her.

But he missed Tiala more.

She had been like Selenia in intellect if not in looks. Yet she was the opposite in manner: she was peaceful, engaging, the kind of person who liked to learn what others wanted and then helped to make that happen. She was a facilitator, a friend. Her personality was Orym's opposite in every way, which perhaps explained why it had all gone down in flames.

But no matter. No more. He needed to stop thinking about past lovers. He needed to focus on the future.

The Pyramid Offensive System. Step one was eliminating the Soul Tree. He was sure it stood over Nekhrumet even now, invisible to all, watching over the world with malevolent eyes. He was sure that it was the reason his great soul magic did not work. The Tree captured souls, after all—and when it was destroyed, it disgorged them upon a weak and unsuspecting world.

He knew how to destroy the Tree. Unfocused, wild Destroyer Aspect magic would make it happen. He was not a superuser like Rylan, or a sensitive like Phoenix. But he *was* a forcefinder now, and he knew the trick Phoenix used. He could do it, he was sure. He could eliminate the thing standing in his way.

But when he did, pure hell would rain down on Nekhrumet. Thousands would die. The city would be plunged into chaos, and if he wasn't careful, he might take the blame. And so, it seemed, he needed to time things right. He needed to destroy the Tree just before he was ready to activate the System.

And *that*, he knew, required gaining access to the Control Center. It utilized a rotating gate, using a formula he no longer remembered. Three gates led into the Control Center, but each were active only at a specific time. If you went through the right gate at the right time, you'd end up inside the Control Center, ready to activate the System. But if you went through at the wrong time, well—you would likely never be seen or heard from again.

It was the last and final defense he had arranged, intended to keep Selenia away from his magic. And it had worked for all these years—only now it was also working against him. He didn't remember the formula for the gates.

Luckily, that problem held an easy solution.

He needed to gather his friends together. Trey and Arra would be first to volunteer, he knew. They held no suspicion of him like the ones on Earth had held. They would go where he bid, like lambs to the slaughter, eager to rid the world of the threat of the Twins.

Yes. It was all so easy. He simply needed to find out where they were.

He directed his gaze down off his high balcony, down to where the Eglaria Temple rose up from the city streets. It was a gorgeous stone building, domed and gilded, set off with colored tile and intricate carvings. He had loved that building when he had first commissioned it, and he had to admit he loved it now.

That was when he realized where Trey might very well be.

"IF ATEN IS LONG DEAD," Trey was saying, "why are the Twins asking for the Imprisoner?"

Arra took a sip of wine, wondering why they were still sitting here, talking. Talking was not going to stop the Twins from destroying both their worlds. Talking was just delaying the inevitable. Sure, it was interesting to hear about the history of all of this, but Arra was failing to see how any of it was actually *useful*.

"He must still be alive," Cresius said. "We just don't know who he is."

The attendant came in again, whispering in Faranel's ear. "Ah," Faranel said. "Send him in." The attendant left. "It would appear one of your friends has arrived."

Orym strode in a moment later, dressed in strange, flowing garments made of brown and tan. The flickering light of the candles gave his face an eery appearance, as if he were a part of some dark ceremony. Arra couldn't help but be reminded of the resurrections she'd witnessed in the woods. She shivered.

"Greetings," Orym said. "I hoped I'd find you here."

"Where have you been?" Arra asked. "We haven't seen you since you appeared in Ilyrion, when the Twins were released."

"I was on Earth for a time," Orym said, pulling a chair over from where it had sat against the wall. "New San Francisco is no more."

"*What*? What happened? Is Pano Sylrantheas okay?"

"It was Nelenor's doing," Orym said. "The city foolishly decided to reverse the device—Fennas Elenathon—sending energy down to the Twin. It did nothing but anger him, of course. It happened over Louisberg. Pano Sylrantheas is fine."

"Jesus," Trey said. "*All* of New San Francisco was destroyed?"

"Just so. The other six cities survived, but they're disconnected now. I do not think they will unite again. But that's not all I've been doing. I've also been researching the Defense Mechanism."

"It's real?" Trey asked. "I thought the Mechanism was a lie to convince me to unleash the Twins. It worked."

"It's real," Orym said, "only you got the name wrong. It's actually not a *defensive* mechanism, so much as an *offensive* one. It's called the Pyramid Offensive System."

"Oh," Trey said. "And what does it do?"

"As I'm sure you can surmise, it should defeat the Twins."

"Should?"

"It may not kill them," Orym said. "From what I've read, it may in fact simply separate them from their device—from Guruthos."

"Rendering them powerless."

"Just so."

"And where did this...System...come from?" Arra asked.

"Aten built it, a very long time ago. He foresaw the return

of the Twins, and did all he could to ensure we would survive the experience."

"I see," Trey said. "What do we need to do?"

"We at the Eglaria have heard of this System," Faranel said. "It is rumored to be impossible to control. There is a gate in three parts, spread to the far reaches of this land. It is written that entering the wrong gate means death."

"That matches my reading," Orym said. "Only I believe I have uncovered the secret."

"Then what are we waiting for?" Trey asked. "If this will stop the Twins, we need to do it now."

"The timing is tight," Orym said. "I need to send people to all three gates, ideally in pairs in case something happens to one."

"We'll take one gate," Trey said. "Or at least I will. I don't want to presume."

Arra smiled at him. "I'll go with you. We need to see this through."

"I'd like to accompany you," Lashel said. "That is, if it's not uncomfortable."

"We'd love to have you along," Trey said. Arra could almost see Lashel's chest swell with pride.

"I will return to the Department," Cresius said. "If this plan fails, we will need to attempt our original plan of luring the Twins to the Salt Spires."

"Very well," Trey said.

"I can radio the others," Orym said. "Perhaps you three would like to visit Thylmanas."

"I've always wanted to conduct a dig there," Trey said. "Elven civilization got its start in Thylmanas."

"We don't have time for a dig," Arra said. That familiar look was back on Trey's face, and it wasn't a bad thing. It was his curiosity, his love of adventure. She hadn't seen that look in a long time. "But it will still be good to see."

He gave her a grateful glance and sat back in his chair.

Orym was fiddling with his radio. "Dillon?" he said.

There was silence for moment before a voice came through in response. "Dad? Where are you?"

"Nekhrumet," Orym said. "We were just discussing the Pyramid Offensive System."

"Oh," Dill said. "Did you figure out how it works?"

"Just so. But I need your help—can you and one or two others come here, to Valaralda?"

"Already here, Dad. Should we meet you in Nekhrumet?"

Orym glanced around the room briefly. Was that a guilty expression on his face? Arra wasn't sure. "I need to leave again," Orym said, "but Trey and Arra are here. Perhaps they'd like to see you."

"Where do you need me to go?"

"Tanomar," Orym said. "It's an island to the south of Ilyrion. I'll radio the directions. There's a gate on the island that leads to the Control Center."

"Sounds good. We'll gate into Nekhrumet now."

"Stay safe, son."

"You too, Father."

Orym clicked the radio off.

"Who will be the third group?" Arra asked.

Orym stroked his bare chin. "I think I have an idea for that. I'll be in contact, folks. Thank you for your help."

And without a further word, a gate flashed over him and he disappeared.

"Should he be doing that?" Trey asked.

"We deregulated all magic yesterday," Cresius said. "But no, he shouldn't be gating. He could lose his mind."

"How did he even do it?" Trey asked. "Orym isn't a Prime Mage."

"Maybe he is," Cresius said. "You both were, and you didn't know it."

"It's called a soulblock," Faranel said. "One of the Fourteen Gifts."

"Doesn't sound like much of a gift to me," Arra said.

"Mages newly risen from Ambarhal are often soulblocked," Faranel said. "Without a soulshaman to guide them, many remain that way forever. It usually takes some kind of big, important event to lift the block—something that shakes the person to the very core."

"Callan almost dying," Trey said.

"Elanil getting shot," Arra said.

"Orym was on an expedition," Trey said. "He mentioned traps. His block must have lifted then. Still, it seems strange he didn't mention it."

Strange was right. Something was odd about the entire situation. Arra took a sip of wine, trying to piece things together and failing.

She felt there was something critical that she was missing.

# EIGHT

THE ARMY OF SOULS had completely surrounded Quynn and the other rylak. They were just standing there, salivating, holding makeshift weapons in their hands.

"What do they want?" Quynn asked.

"Anger," one of the souls said.

"Hate."

"Fear."

Then, as one, they all attacked.

Quynn had no weapons. Just a bleeding hand, and several more shards of primewood.

Well, at least he was a mage.

The horde of angry souls pressed inward, blades and fists swiping at him indiscriminately. Were they even real? Could they even hit him? They looked ghostly, partially transparent —surely they could do no harm.

The first sword that sliced his skin proved otherwise.

He yelped, feeling blood trickle down his shin, pulling a piece of primewood from his pocket. It was oak—the light kind. Very well.

He burned the wood, Willing himself to become stronger,

bigger. His eyesight grew sharper as the magic took effect, sounds growing louder in his ears. He felt his muscles responding to his commands, reflexes improving, synapses firing faster. The world went into slow motion as the strengthshaping magic took effect.

He could really get used to this.

Six souls came at him at once.

But they were moving slowly, languidly, thanks to his heightened perceptions. And so it was easy to punch the first one in the neck, sweep his elbow to the right, taking two more out, then follow up with a head butt to the fourth. All four souls sailed away as if they'd been hit by a wrecking ball, faces and neck completely crushed. Despite the fact that they looked like ghosts, they acted and reacted exactly like humans.

The remaining two souls advanced with weapons raised: swords, both of them. Quynn didn't know where they'd gotten swords, nor why or how the swords glimmered with an otherworldly light, semi-transparent. Whatever was happening here, clearly the whole thing was playing by an entirely different set of rules.

But strengthshaping magic continued to ripple through him. He stepped inside the grasp of the first soul, reaching in and simply snatching the sword right out of his grip. The move was too quick for the soul to track, and in short order Quynn had used the captured sword to parry the other blade.

They sparred, once. The soul was just too slow. It took but a moment for Quynn to lop its head off with his blade, then follow up with pierce to the last one's heart.

Six down—what must be *billions* more to go.

The rylak around him weren't faring as well. Newly awakened from their millennia of control, none of them appeared to have magic available. Or weapons, other than their claws.

Luckily, their claws were *deadly*.

He watched them dispatch souls by the dozens, rending them limb from limb without even breaking a sweat. Did rylak sweat? They were covered in hair—of course they didn't. They must be *hot*, Quynn realized, especially in this desert. He was. He wished there was something he could do to help.

More souls were coming from all around. And while the rylak certainly were deadly with their claws, the numbers were not on their side.

They were being quickly overwhelmed.

Quynn moved in to slash at more souls, catching an arm here, a leg there, two heads with one strike. He pierced three of them in the heart one after another, and that was all it took for them to die. Did they go somewhere when they died? Weren't they already dead? He didn't understand what was happening, here. This metaphysical shit wasn't what he was used to dealing with. Still, he had to acknowledge the danger of the situation.

There were just too many of them.

They piled forward, overwhelming the rylak, over-whelming him. He tried to slash again, but his strengthshaping magic ran out and the strike turned weak, too slow, glancing off the edge of one soul's blade. The sword flashed inward, narrowly missing his temple, Quynn barely able to duck in time. He needed more wood.

But he was out. Out of light oak as well as dark. That meant strengthshaping and mergemelding were impossible, and they were his two most powerful abilities.

"Shit," he said to no one in particular, doing his best to fend off the strikes of four more souls. It was much harder to do without strengthshaping magic flowing through his veins.

And the souls were still coming.

He got another nick on his arm, blood welling to the surface. That made three wounds, and he knew that more would come. This army was just too strong, too numerous, and he didn't have enough magic to counteract them all.

He needed to escape.

So, gatesending, then. He could do that. He had the wood. But he knew that gatesending had that perilous side effect, and he just couldn't risk it. He didn't want to lose any more of who he was.

Strengthshaping gone. Mergemelding gone. Could he mindmaster these souls? Might as well try.

He burned dark poplar. He only had one chip of it, but if he could Will it strongly enough, he might be able to manage a full quelling. He exercised the magic, seeing the familiar cloud of purple extending out over the army, suffusing their etherial beings.

And nothing happened.

He grimaced, gritting his teeth, Willing the magic to grow stronger.

But it was useless.

Ghostly souls, it would seem, could not be coerced by mindmaster magic.

Which left but one power. One power, because he was only half a mage. Because Tarathiel had split his soul into two parts, and now he was only half a man. Half a deity. Half a person. The better half, sure, but the lack of power was a problem, here. Now, for the fleetest of seconds, he wished he had reintegrated with Trey.

But no. Banish the thought. He wanted to remain *himself*, the Quynn he wanted to be. Sure, it meant sacrificing some of the magic he knew was his to wield. But it made him purer, more himself. It made him the man he was.

He liked it.

If only he could fix this situation.

He saw Talon go down in a flurry of limbs and teeth and fur, the blades of five souls chopping down at him relentlessly. He snarled and growled, claws flashing out, incredible strength evident in his lunges. But it didn't matter—there were just too many souls against him. Were they feeding off emotion? It almost seemed that way. The worse the fighting got, the stronger the souls seemed to become.

All of this was very strange.

The rylak were going down everywhere, overwhelmed by the number of souls surrounding them. They were like Quynn, fighting with what they had. They were brutal and ruthless and strong. They were ugly, by elven and human standards. They were beautiful.

And they were losing, despite their strength. They just wanted to go home, which was all Quynn wanted. They were tired of being controlled. Quynn could relate to that—for the past many hundred years, everything he'd done had been at Lorelei's behest. She was beautiful, yes, but she was not his master any longer. It was finally time to strike out on his own.

He wasn't so different from these rylak, he realized. They had no home. They didn't belong here. And neither did Quynn, if he was being honest. He had always been the outsider, no matter what he did, no matter how strong he kept himself. He'd gotten things done, sure, but he'd never actually been *loved*.

Not even Phoenix had really cared for him. Maybe for one instant, for one hour. When she thought he was someone else, sure—she'd liked him well enough. But love? No. And Lorelei had been no better.

But then again, Quynn had never really loved himself.

Maybe these beasts, these strange werewolves in the desert—maybe they would be the chance he finally needed.

So he struck out with the one power he had left: fallfoiling. Only he didn't move anybody *up*. He didn't move anybody at all.

He moved the sand, in a vast circle all around them, leaving a single path outward to the north.

He moved the sand *down*.

A massive sinkhole formed in the desert, souls falling by the tens of thousands. Quynn heard them screaming as they fell, grappling at the sand and failing to find any purchase there.

"Come on!" he shouted at the rylak. "We have to go!"

He ran, leading the way, feeling the ground shake beneath his feet as the sand continued to sink. The souls just fell and fell, swallowed up by the desert, shrieking and scrambling, waving ghostly swords. And Quynn ran, glancing back to see the rylak in a herd behind him, thundering across the narrow strip of sand he'd left for them to use. It was beginning to collapse as well, the edges of it falling off into the endless abyss that he had made.

Not all of the rylak were going to make it.

Talon was at the back, flailing about as he tried to balance on the shifting sand. Several souls had managed to latch onto him, grasping him with limbs made of ghostly flesh. Talon slashed at them to no avail—they were pulling him off balance, pulling him closer to the edge.

Quynn kept running, a piece of dark maple in his hand. He turned and caught Talon's eye as he ran, as the rylak toppled off the edge into the unknown.

Quynn caught him with his magic.

"Quickly!" he shouted, gesturing for the rylak to continue following him away from the sinking, circular abyss. The army of souls was distracted by it now—the ones who hadn't sunk were milling about the edges of the pit, unsure of what to do.

Talon was floating in the air.

Quynn cursed his stupidity. With only fallfoiling magic at his disposal, the only thing he could do with Talon was raise or lower him. He couldn't bring him nearer, grant him escape from the writhing army that was still falling to its death.

Talon was reaching for something. Quynn kept running, leading the rylak away from the falling cliffs of sand, racing through the hot sun toward their escape. Was Talon shouting something at him? He couldn't quite hear it.

Then Talon held up some wood in his hand, and Quynn finally understood.

He dropped his magic, allowing Talon to fall.

But Talon didn't fall. Instead, he sailed neatly over to Quynn, joining him on the ground. His legs seemed a bit rubbery when he landed but he managed it, running beside Quynn at the head of the rylak army.

"You're a Prime Mage," Quynn said.

"Couldn't get to my damn wood before," Talon said. "Thanks for the quick save. I guess these souls really took us all by surprise."

"Let's get away from them," Quynn said. "The further the better. Maybe if we quiet our emotions, they won't follow."

Talon barked a laugh. "Rylak, quiet their emotions? You really don't know us at all."

But his muzzle flashed a smile as he said it, if Quynn was reading his expression right. And Quynn realized that he hadn't just escaped certain death. He hadn't just saved hundreds of rylak from a strange, ghostly sort of doom.

He had made a friend.

# NINE

"SOMETHING STRANGE IS GOING ON," Arra said.

"What do you mean?" Trey asked.

The attendant arrived just then, speaking yet again in Faranel's ear.

"Oh," Faranel said. "Sure, sure, send them in. And get us some more chairs."

"What now?" Arra asked.

"It seems more of your friends have just arrived. You—or the Eglaria—are very popular today."

Arra was frowning at the door, wondering who else was going to interrupt them, when Elanil walked in.

"Lani!" Arra shouted, jumping up and running over to grab her in a big hug.

"Arra," Elanil said, a bit breathlessly. "It's so good to see you."

Arra put her down, just in time to see others filing into the room. Imra was there, giving her an unreadable look in the dark. And Lorelei, and Allain, and Erodar, and Dill. There was a woman she didn't recognize, with long, brown, curly hair. But the last person to enter the room was the biggest surprise.

It was Phoenix.

"I—but you—" Arra said.

"Ho," Phoenix said. "You look well."

"So do you," Arra said. "How are you alive?"

"The same way your sister is."

"You're a Prime Mage now," Arra said, and Phoenix nodded. "But you were soulburned!"

"I was," Phoenix said. "It seems that soulburning is not the final sentence everyone thinks it is."

"Interesting," Faranel said. "I would be keenly interested in hearing more. We have never encountered a soulburned person before...in the flesh."

Several Eglarians entered the room just then, bringing more of the heavy, wooden chairs. Soon they were all seated around the big stone table, wine poured and faces dimly lit.

"This is Elasha," Lorelei said, introducing the woman Arra hadn't recognized. "She went with Orym on his expedition to Atlantis."

"Nice to meet you," Arra said, and the others nodded their agreement.

"Quite the gathering we have here," Cresius said. "More Prime Mages in one place than have been assembled in many, many millennia."

Arra realized she should introduce the people on her side. "This is Donar Cresius XXV," she said, "Research Director for the Department of Magical Research."

"Pleased, I'm sure," Cresius said. "This is Lashel, for those who don't know."

"Where's Rylan?" Arra asked.

Elanil looked like she was about to burst into tears at that. "He went to Nelenor," she said. "We haven't seen him since."

"Do you know if he's still alive?"

"He was as of a few hours ago. He used Guruthos to send us a message on the radio."

"He used…what are you talking about?"

"It's a long story," Elanil said. "Rylan is a superuser now."

"You wouldn't believe us if we told you," Phoenix said, which was quite a thing to say. Arra had seen Phoenix do things *nobody* else could do. If Phoenix thought her son was doing the impossible, it really must be true.

"How did you know where to find us?" Arra asked.

"Orym told us," Dill said.

"How'd you get here so quickly?"

"We gated."

"You can't be serious."

"Orym taught us a trick to gating safely," Elanil said. "Just hold a gate to nowhere around yourself, then gate that somewhere else."

"A gate to nowhere?"

Elanil nodded. "It's easier than it sounds."

"Interesting. Did Orym seem…strange…to you?"

"He's the Imprisoner," Lorelei said.

"I don't believe that," Dill said, shooting her a glare. It was difficult to read their facial expressions in the dim candlelight. "You must be mistaken, somehow. Maybe Cariel put false memories in your head."

"That's not possible," Lorelei said, glancing at Faranel. "Is it?"

"We've attempted it," Faranel said. "As to whether it succeeded, that I cannot say."

"Shit," Lorelei said. "Just when I thought I'd gotten my life back."

"Something was definitely off about him," Arra said.

"Phoenix," Trey said, "we've never officially met, but I've heard the stories about you."

"Everyone keeps saying that," Phoenix said. "I hope they were good."

Trey dipped his head. "They were. But I have something to tell you now. Something I'm not sure you'll believe."

Oh. Shit. Arra had already almost forgotten about all that. She gripped the hand rests of her chair, waiting for what was about to happen.

"I'm Quynn," Trey said. "Quynn is half of me. We soul-splintered thousands of years ago."

"Quynn," Phoenix said. "Eric. I heard he's still alive."

"Yes," Trey said.

"But how are you the same person?"

"Ah," Faranel said, "now *this* is a juicy bit of news. The power to soulsplinter is one of the Fourteen Gifts. We have studied it extensively."

"So have we," Cresius said.

"Interesting. It would seem our groups have something in common, at long last."

"It's mistweaving," Allain said to Phoenix. "When you make an illusion of yourself, if you do it strongly enough, that other person becomes real."

As if to emphasize his point, Allain2 popped into existence, standing behind Faranel. Almost everyone in the room jumped, startled.

"Ho, idiots," Allain2 said.

A wide smile grew on Faranel's face.

"When you splinter," Allain1 said, "part of your soul gets split. Right now Allain2 has three of my Aspects, and I have the other three. We both retain the Seventh, though it is diminished."

"Well put, young one," Faranel said. "Well put, indeed."

"So you and Quynn did this," Phoenix said. "Thousands of years ago? But can't it be undone?"

"Sure," Allains said, and Allain2 disappeared with a sucking sound.

"We didn't know," Trey said. "Not until yesterday. We didn't know we were the same person."

"Phoenix," Arra said, laying a hand on her knee. She was the closest to her, with Imra seated on the opposite side. "That means Trey is also Rylan's father."

"I—" Phoenix said, shaking her head as if trying to clear it. She was just as gorgeous as Arra had remembered, seemingly unchanged from the events five years before. Defeating a volcano had not dampened her spirit, it would seem. She would make a wonderful mother for Rylan. "I'm not sure what to say."

"Let's table it, for now," Trey said.

"Does Rylan know?"

"Not yet," Trey said. "We haven't seen him since we discovered it ourselves."

"Where is Quynn now?"

"He escaped when we landed here. We don't know where he is."

Phoenix pursed her lips, glancing at Imra as if for support. Imra laid a hand on her other knee, giving her a little squeeze. Arra watched the exchange with interest, removing her own hand.

"The Gifts are strong," Cresius said after a moment. "Perhaps we should have studied them more. Cariel certainly caught us by surprise—her power was more than we had anticipated any mage having."

"We should have combined forces," Faranel said. "Though in truth, the Eglaria had been working *for* Cariel. Surely you knew that."

"We suspected as much," Arra said.

"We wanted power," Faranel said, "as did she."

"Were you behind the attack on Mirra's shack?" Trey asked. That sandstorm had almost obliterated them all. The sandstorm of Arra's own making.

"No," Faranel said. "The Devout ever were of their own mind about these things. Truth be told, we committed very little violence against anyone."

"It doesn't matter now," Trey said.

"Soulbinding," Arra said, looking at Faranel. "One of the Gifts."

"Yes."

"Is there a limit to how many soulbinds one can make at once?"

Faranel frowned. "In our testing, certainly. Most people can't form even one soulbind, in fact, and those that can are often limited to a mere handful, sometimes only one."

"Cariel had *far* more than that."

"Thousands," Cresius said. "According to my mages, she was controlling an army of beasts from Eryn, an army of rylak from somewhere on Valaralda, and an army of Remnant from Mar."

"And insects," Trey said. "Thousands of them. And at least one wildcat, several birds. Probably many more things."

"Plus her Trees," Dill said. "She had soulbound those, too."

"Incredible," Faranel said. "The world will never see her like again."

"Could she have...I don't know...*moved* her soul?" Arra asked.

"What do you mean?"

"Could some part of her still live on, despite her body's death? She was in *thousands* of others, after all."

"Not anymore," Trey said. "The soulmirror ended all her binds."

"She could have made more."

"It's possible," Faranel said. "But even if she were to live on in something else, I doubt that she could ever regain her true self again. She would be fragmented, only part of herself. Animals and insects can't hold an entire elven soul—they must leave room for themselves, too."

"They retain their own souls?"

"Of course. Their energy remains, waiting to be unleashed when the foreign invader leaves."

"What about the Soul Tree?" Phoenix asked. "Nelenor said other souls were trapped in it. It killed Beam."

"Beam is dead?" Arra asked, and Phoenix nodded. "I'm sorry to hear it. What is this Soul Tree you speak of?"

Phoenix told her, briefly, while Arra sipped her wine. It seemed a strange interaction of magic, something even more esoteric to add to the list. Elves had thought they'd known everything about the powers that surrounded them. How wrong they were.

"The souls of the dead," Arra said when Phoenix was done. "Who knew they could have such power?"

"Nobody knew suicide could cause so much death."

"I wonder," Arra said. "If the souls of the dead could do that much harm, how much more harm could the souls of the *living* do?"

Nobody answered that. Perhaps nobody understood her line of thinking. She wasn't sure she did, either. There was a thought there, but it was yet unformed. She felt another missing piece dangling in the air.

There was so much to consider. So many people sitting in this room. So much power was brimming beneath the surface of the dark, ready to be unleashed. Yet it was all useless, powerless against the Twins. Only Orym's mysterious System seemed to be the solution.

She didn't like it. She wanted the power in her hand. She wanted destiny to be hers alone. She didn't like depending on the unknown.

But she looked around the room, seeing the faces of her friends. Some old, some new, some young and some old. Some had died, and had returned. Some had begun powerless, and had emerged with power beyond belief. And some, like Imra, had been there supporting her the entire way.

She reached out to Trey, grabbing his hand in her own. "We'll do this together," she said. "Everyone. I'm so glad you're here."

"Together," Phoenix said, raising her glass.

"Together," Elanil echoed, giving her a smile.

They gestured at each other, and drank, and for a moment Arra's heart swelled. She had friends. She had family. With them she knew she could withstand anything.

The attendant entered the room again. Arra was starting to think she should get his name. He whispered in Faranel's ear, and the man's eyes got wide.

"Ah," he said, "my new friends have finally arrived. I must say, this will be an auspicious meeting indeed. Are we through with this candlelight yet? My eyes grow tired."

He touched a section of his desk, and bright fluorescent lights turned on overhead. Arra squinted in the sudden whiteness, putting down her wine glass in surprise. What the hell was going on?

A door opened in the back of the room. Not a stone door, like the others. It was metal, sharp and chrome, and it opened smoothly and silently on perfect hinges.

Jalnab stepped through, followed by his son, Martan.

Both were dressed immaculately, wearing black, three-piece suits. They strode in, Jalnab smiling broadly.

"Good afternoon," Jalnab said in a perfect British accent, his voice sonorous. "I trust your day is going well."

"Hi," Martan said. "Long time no see."

# TEN

NOBODY MOVED FOR A MOMENT. The room was silent, pregnant with confusion.

That had not been Jalnab's voice.

"What's going on?" Arra asked, her tone cool.

"Ah," Jalnab said, stepping further into the room. "I debated how to broach this particular topic, but in the end I could not think of anything that would be less surprising. With you all in one place, I deemed this the best moment."

"You speak English," Elanil said. "Perfectly."

"And with a British accent," Trey said. "I've heard it in old TV shows, from before the Sundering."

"That is correct," Jalnab said. "In fact, we have a lot to discuss."

"How long have you spoken English?" Arra asked. If she'd had hackles, they would have been up.

"For about 417 years," Jalnab said. "I'm not sure at what age exactly I started talking."

None of this was making sense. "You're an elf?"

"No. I'm quite human, I assure you. All the People are, barring Segena, I suppose. However, I must confess that those you deem the 'Remnant' have not always been completely truthful with you. In fact, our language is a sham, designed to keep you from understanding us. It is not a devolved version of English. It is, in fact, an invented language. A fabrication. I should know, because I'm the one who invented it."

Arra narrowed her eyes. It was almost too much to believe. This man had been alive for over four hundred years? He'd invented a false language to confuse others? And in all that time, through the Sundering and the death of humanity, he had never told another person outside the Remnant?

"You'd better explain," Trey said, "and you'd better do it quickly."

"Of course," Jalnab said. "For starters, my name is not Jalnab. It's John Ronald. I met my first elf when I was but sixteen, before the war. That was before I was a Prime Mage, you see. As it happened, that encounter would change my life —and the lives of many, many others. May I sit?"

Faranel motioned to two empty chairs that the attendants had just brought in, nodding. Jalnab—John—sat alongside his son, on the other side of the table. The uncomfortably bright lights somehow made his face look even more sinister than Arra had expected. She longed for the soft glow of candles.

"My son's name is not Martan, of course," John said. "It's Martin."

Arra caught the boy and Elanil sharing a glance. What must this realization be like for her sister? To know that the boy you'd liked was not the person you thought he was? A lot of people in this room had that in common, she realized. So many identities had been hidden, whether on purpose or through happenstance.

Perhaps she should not be so surprised that there was one more revelation yet to learn.

"The elf I met—a young lady by the name of Lúthien—was the most beautiful creature I had ever laid eyes on," John said. "She was three years older than I, and the wrong religion besides, and so my father forbade me speak or write to her until I was twenty-one, a ruling which I obeyed, despite my objections. To the humans of the world, like me, Lúthien went by the name of Edith. She was the light of my life.

"She was only eighty-two when she died—far too young for an elf. In fact—and this is something I and my family have labored long to hide—Edith was killed. Murdered by an elf with no Talent. And thus I went to avenge her, in my ripe old age, and so was killed myself. But the elf who killed me was Talented indeed, and as it happened so was I, and thus began my short stay in the realm of the Twins.

"It was there that I beheld the Valar, and the True Trees Telperion and Laravon, and I knew that all the stories I had heard and retold in my past life had elements of truth. Those things which I had written, that had entertained the world, were in fact stolen tales, apprehended visions. But I could not help myself. I had encountered *elves*, had fallen in love with one, had experienced what their lives and society were like. And I could not in good conscience keep what I had learned to myself.

"So I obfuscated it. I invented languages—but not all. High Eldrim itself was the foundation of my text, but fragmented, splintered into three. I used my training in philology and my interest in the myths and fantasies of this world, and crafted something that resonated for the world as surely as my Lúthien did for me.

"For quite some time, I was very happy."

"Who *are* you?" Trey asked.

"I am John," John said. "John Ronald Reuel Tolkien."

# ELEVEN

TREY SUCKED in a sharp breath of surprise. John Ronald Reuel Tolkien. He *knew* that name. Or he knew the initials.

It was J. R. R. Tolkien.

He had written *The Lord of the Rings*. The man had practically *invented* elves. Hadn't Arra mentioned that he'd met elves and lived to tell the tale? It seemed she had been right about that.

The one thing Trey hadn't expected was for the man to still be alive.

"I've read your books," Trey said. The response seemed somehow inadequate, but it was all he had.

"I'm glad," John said. "Did you like them?"

"Very much. I think I knew there was an inkling of truth in them when I read them. What I didn't know was that *I* was an elf."

"There are days I wish I was."

"So what happened?" Trey asked. "How did you survive the Sundering? What secrets are the Remnant hiding? And are you the only human Prime Mage?"

"Rylan is half-human," Phoenix said. "It would stand to reason that there would be more."

"There are," John said, "though they are very rare. Talented humans themselves are exceptionally rare, and nearly all of them are now concentrated in the sky cities. Almost everyone else was wiped out in the Sundering. I will tell you my story, and I will endeavor to keep it as brief as possible."

Trey settled back in his chair, wine completely forgotten. His literary hero was alive, sitting there in front of him! He couldn't wait to hear what he was going to say.

"I am the founder of what you call the Remnant," John said. "It was started as a society of sorts, at King Edward's School where I was a student. We called it T.C.B.S—Tea Club and Barrovian Society. We used to drink tea in the school library and, increasingly, in Barrow's Stores nearby. I had only recently met my first elf, but I would soon meet more. Edith introduced me to her family, who did not of course agree with her divulging this information. Elves had remained hidden for tens of thousands of years, after all—why should Edith suddenly break with this tradition?

"But we were in love, you see, and sometimes love has a way of defeating even the strongest dragons. I gained a certain knowledge of the elves through her, and what I saw amazed me to no end.

"But I was also very frightened by it. For I had also learned that magic was real, and carried with it very real consequences for the world.

"I was distracted for a time, by wars and teaching and family and other things. But in the quiet hours of the morning, when I would write verses or tinker with lexicons, the fear would return to gnaw at me. I felt it as the spiders of the Mirkwood, trapping me with its callous embrace.

"I realized as I wrote my books that with such great power, there had to also be great evil. That such evil must remain hidden for it to flourish, and that such great evil would beget greater evil still. I became convinced that my Sauron was an allegory for what might truly exist in this world—the dark side of the elves.

"As it happened, I was right.

"It took me many decades, but I finally uncovered the elves' own secret society: the Cothellon. I did not infiltrate them—how could I, as a human?—but I finally found an elf who did. An elf who is long dead now, who has no name or place in anyone's history. But it was through him, long after my wife's death and my return to reality, that I learned of the Sundering.

"That was when my plans began in earnest. I re-founded my Society, filling it with the smartest, most successful, most literate and intriguing and lovely humans the world held. No elves, for elves had shown the great evil that was inside them. We could not let even the elves we trusted inside the Society, lest we risk exposure. And so it was with great sadness that I reconciled myself to a life amongst the humans, without the wife I had loved so dearly.

"We could not fight magic. We had none of our own, save mine, and I was not yet aware of my true nature. I had not ever even utilized magic, nor suspected its existence in my blood. I had wandered the violet world and its Trees in ignorance, and upon my return I wandered even more.

"We could not fight magic. All we had was our technology, which was vast, but technology could not defeat a power as strong as the Sundering.

"But we *had* learned of a weakness. The magic was directional, of a certain height. We knew it would not reach the cities in the sky, which at that time had yet to be launched, but would be soon. We knew humanity was about to be wiped out. And so we did the only thing we could do, to preserve our knowledge and our faculties.

"We went underground.

"We distributed ourselves in sites around the world, including one under Lusvunub. There we prepared in secret, and waited out the death of the planet's people.

"We called ourselves the True People.

"We devised our own culture, our own language. We worked hard to make ourselves seem antiquated, useless, skill-less. And after the Sundering, as the centuries passed, many that remained on the surface were, in fact, as useless as they seemed.

"We are divided now. The one percent of humanity that was left after the Sundering is still on the surface of the planet, populating outposts such as Gulthurub and others. The True People live mostly underground, continuing their research, developing new technologies. But we remain a secret to this day, for the elves have not yet left us alone, and magic still presents far too great a threat.

"With the Twins unleashed now we are finally coming forward. We may not be able to offer much assistance in the battle to come, but we wish to do what we can. Perhaps by working together, we can overcome this great threat. Perhaps now elves and humans can *truly* be united."

He stopped, then, as if that were his entire story. Questions filled Trey's mind, but he wasn't sure where to start.

Faranel spoke first. "When Mar translated into the Persephone system," he said, "members of the True People reached out to us on Valaralda. They found the Eglaria, as fate would have it, and in us they found a likeminded group. We are similar outcasts, researching forbidden things in the dark."

"Those pins you used," Phoenix said. "The golden pins that let us understand you. Was that magic?"

"No," John said. "In fact, the talismans did nothing but signal the People who saw them to switch to English."

"That can't be true. So you all speak English, and you just refuse to do it?"

"That is the way of it."

"You lied to us."

"For our own protection."

"I'm not an elf, dammit," Phoenix said. "Beam wasn't an elf! You didn't need to protect yourselves from us."

"You came to us from the elven stronghold in the sky," John said. "We could not trust you, though I argued that we should."

"John," Phoenix said, "you *fought* the elves, and I helped you do it. How do you justify that? You said you *married* one."

John's face grew cold. "The reason we gave you was as right then as it is now: the elves destroyed humanity. They destroyed the world. They *deserve* to die, if vengeance is your aim. And Segena was nothing if not an influential person."

"I still don't understand why Segena wanted elves dead, either, if she was one of them."

"She was bitter for being stranded on Eryn," Arra said. "I think she wanted the entire world to burn."

"Not unlike the Twins do now," Dill said.

"Nothing new has happened since Rylan went to them," Elanil said. "Maybe he's actually managed to talk some sense into Nelenor."

"Or maybe he's dead," Arra said. "Sorry." Elanil's eyes had already teared up.

"You said you're here to help," Trey said. "I don't know that we can trust you, given everything you've said. The amount of lies you and your kind have perpetrated all this time—you are almost the equal of the Cothellon in this. Of the elves themselves."

"We had to be," John said, "if we wanted to survive."

"How do you propose to help?"

"As it happens," John said, sitting forward in his chair, "we might have a plan. We have hidden much from you and your kind over the centuries. Some of what we have hidden is right beneath your noses.

"The Under is not entirely what you think."

# TWELVE

ELANIL LOOKED around the room to gauge everyone's reactions. Phoenix and Dill looked the most shocked, of course. The others seemed less surprised, but perhaps they were just used to revelations such as this. Elanil wasn't sure if anything could surprise her now.

Still, John's statement *had* been unexpected.

John. Martin. Elanil was still having trouble grasping it. All this time and they both spoke English? They'd been *lying* to her all this time? What kind of relationship might she have had with Martin if she'd known? If John hadn't forbade her from seeing him, what might have happened? If the True People had shown their faces sooner, how might things have changed?

She couldn't blame them, she supposed. They'd just been trying to survive. But she *could* blame them for the deaths. The deaths of elves at Remnant hands. Gulthurub alone had been responsible for so many, and she wasn't sure if restitution would ever be met.

Still now was not the time. Luxuries like restitution could wait until the world was not in danger.

She sighed.

"Explain," Phoenix said. "I *lived* in the Under, in case you've already forgotten. How is it different than we think?"

"Have you explored it all?" John asked. "Mapped it all out?"

"Oh, shit," Dill said. "The mystery rooms. Shot told us that at least fifty percent of the Under was inaccessible during their last survey. Not just in New San Francisco, but in *all* the cities. They tried getting into the rooms, but failed. No one has any idea what they are for."

"I always thought the Under was bigger than it needed to be," Phoenix said. "Why were there roads for our undercars to take? Why was there so much empty space?"

"It was us," John said. "We couldn't infiltrate the Cothellon directly, but we *could* infiltrate the construction teams. All those cities in the sky? *We* built them."

"Because you knew about the Cothellon," Trey said. "Wow. And they had no idea about you."

"None that we know of."

"Impressive," Lorelei said. "I can assure you, the Cothellon was in the dark on this."

"So what did you do?" Trey asked. "What did you change?"

"We couldn't do anything obvious," John said. "We couldn't risk discovery, and we certainly couldn't change anything topside. But we were able to make many subtle changes to the floor plans of the Under, isolating vast sections of it. By then, of course, we'd already begun researching advanced technology, new metal alloys the elves hadn't yet discovered. So it took time, and a great deal of patience and care, but we were able to create our own Under inside the Under."

"What's it for?" Elanil asked. "What does it do?"

"We call it the Escape Module. It was never deployed."

"You wanted people to escape?" Phoenix asked.

"Exactly. We built it up over the past three centuries, adding to it and evolving it when we could. Unlike the elves, our research has not abated since the Sundering. Now we are quite advanced technologically, though we still remain hidden. For we have not yet found a way to counter magic."

"You need the ring," Trey said, a half smile on his face.

"If only it were that simple," John said, smiling back. Elanil had no idea what they were talking about. "The purpose of the Escape Module," he continued, "is to bring back the humans we lost to the elves. The Under is rigged to detach in hundreds of segments, carrying as many people away from the city as possible."

"I always wondered why construction on those cities took so damn long," Lorelei said. "You were there right under my nose the whole time."

John nodded. "We tried not to delay too much, but yes. Building the Escape Module took additional time."

"So it can fly?" Elanil asked.

"It can. And since the forcefields surrounding the cities are only one-way, leaving the city is not a problem. At the right time, the plan was to evacuate as many Citizens as possible into portions of the Under, then activate the Module and fly away."

"But surely you'd expect repercussions," Trey said. "The Cothellon would have fought you, brought their people back."

"Which is why we never enacted the plan," John said. "We spent the intervening years adding weapons, better propulsion and maneuverability. We felt we were finally at a point to fight the Cothellon directly about fifteen years ago."

"When Queen was in power," Phoenix said.

"Yes. She was initially allied with us, getting the Under

ready for evacuation. But then Quynn stepped in, and we realized we weren't ready. That in fact, we may never be. Because, again, of magic. Mindmaster magic."

"You're right," Trey said. "I was subject to that magic for a very long time. It's almost impossible to resist."

"I did," Phoenix said, her teeth gritted.

"The quelling that occurred that year really sobered us," John said. "Some people might be able to resist mindmaster magic, but certainly not all. So we felt the likelihood of success was low—too low to move forward."

"So you left everyone aboard the cities," Phoenix said.

"It worked out in the end."

Elanil supposed it had. But at what cost?

"Why bring it up now?" Trey asked.

"With the cities free of Cothellon influence," John said, "I believe that now we can use the Escape Module—not for its original purpose, but for a new one. We can turn it into a weapon."

"We tried that," Trey said. "Fennas Elenathon did nothing to Nelenor."

"I know," John said.

"You know?"

"I was there, watching. And you're right: it likely won't do anything. But if we mobilize the entire Module, it will be thousands of individual moving parts, pieces of high-tech machinery flying through the air. Every bit of it is outfitted with weaponry—advanced weaponry, Trey. We can do some damage, and if not, we can act as a distraction. The real beauty of it is it's all computer controlled—no lives need to be risked in the attempt."

"A distraction," Arra said. "Thats all you can offer?"

"It's all I have," John said. "You can use it or not, as you see fit. But if this fight returns to Earth, I submit that it may be the only chance we have."

"We still need to figure out how to actually defeat them," Arra said.

"Orym's System," Trey said.

"Orym's the Imprisoner," Lorelei said. "He's working against us."

"What if he's not?" Trey asked. "What if he *is* the Imprisoner, but he's had a change of heart?"

"He's not the Imprisoner," Dill said. "I know my father."

"I think we should do it all," Cresius said.

Everyone looked at him.

"I'm serious. Get John back to Earth with whoever he needs, get this Escape Module operational. Send people to these gates Orym mentioned, to activate the Offensive System. And mobilize the Army of Mages, draw the Twins to the Salt Spires, activate the traps."

"None of that will work," Arra said.

"Or all of it might. Does anyone have any better ideas?"

"The Prime Mages," Elanil said. "We left them in Ilyrion, underground."

"There are more Prime Mages?" Cresius asked.

"Yes," Elanil said. "Hundreds of them."

"Incredible," Cresius said. "If I pair them with my trained mages, we might actually stand a fighting chance." Excitement lit up his eyes.

"I want to find Rylan," Elanil said.

"As do I," Phoenix said.

"I'll go with you," Imra said.

"Orym needed me and Arra at Thylmanas," Trey said.

"I'm going to Tanomar," Dill said. "Who's coming with me?"

"I will," Allain said.

"Me too," Erodar said.

Lorelei emitted a little growl. "I'll go. I may be the only one left who can stop Orym, if it comes down to it."

"Then we're all set," Cresius said. "What will you do, Faranel?"

"I will mobilize the Eglaria," Faranel said. "We have hundreds of shadowmages that can fight. It may not be much, but we're close to the Salt Spires, here. Perhaps we may be able to help."

"Very good," Cresius said. "Then let us be about it, and may the Twins have mercy on our souls."

Everyone raised their glasses in a silent toast.

The Twins were no longer their gods, but mercy was still something they could grant.

Elanil felt that they would desperately need it in the times ahead.

# PART
# TWO

One of the indictments of civilizations is that happiness and intelligence are so rarely found in the same person.

— *William Feather*

# THIRTEEN

ORYM HOVERED FAR above the sand, careful to keep his nowhere gate around him at all times. It was difficult to do, with its dependence on primewood and Will. He couldn't do it forever, and lately he'd been slipping more and more.

He surveyed the sands. There was an army of ghostly beings arrayed out over a huge portion of the desert, filing out by the hundreds from a line of burning Trees. Near them but moving to the north, he saw a group of about a thousand rylak. And at the head of them, running across the sand, Orym saw a familiar face.

Quynn.

It had been a while since the two had spoken. Since New San Francisco, before the fall to Earth, before Orym had brought Trey into this mess. Quynn had been Orym's boss for a great long time, but now the tables had turned.

Perhaps Quynn could be useful to him now.

He floated down to the desert, ignoring the bristling claws that awaited him as he landed.

"Greetings," he said, looking at Quynn. "How goes your flight through the desert?"

"Poorly," Quynn said. "Why are you here?"

"I was actually hoping you could help me with something."

"Why would I help you? You betrayed me."

"I saved the world."

"Your boy Trey saved the world."

"*Your* boy, I think," Orym said. "Or was he not what you expected?"

Quynn narrowed his eyes, and for a moment Orym thought he was going to tell him something important. But then he just smiled. "What did you have in mind?"

"Killing the Twins," Orym said. "There's a device that'll do it, but I need your help to activate it."

Quynn looked at the rylak all around him. "I might be willing, if it means this madness can be put behind us."

"There's a gate," Orym said. "To the west. It leads to the Control Center. There we can activate the device that will defeat the Twins."

Quynn turned to the rylak standing beside him. "Well?"

"I just want to get off this planet," the rylak growled.

"I can help with that," Orym said, "if you help me."

Quynn turned to him, blue eyes flinty in the sun. "Very well. Send us in the right direction. And can you get us some food and water?"

"Of course," Orym said, a smile growing on his face.

WHEN RYLAN STEPPED through the gate, he found himself in yet another forest. This one smelled subtly different, though, and the trees looked a little bit strange. Sunlight filtered through the leaves around him, sending dappled shadows to the ground. A dozen birds burst up into the canopy upon his arrival, calling to each other in alarm.

"Ah," Nelenor said, stepping through and collapsing the gate behind him. "The Faedori Forest. Valaralda ever was a beautiful world." He brushed his long, blond hair back behind him in a distinctly feminine gesture, peering about at the forest with joy evident in his eyes. In that moment he didn't seem so much a god as just a person, out for a leisurely afternoon stroll.

Rylan swallowed hard. "I think the gate trick worked. My head feels fine."

"Good," Nelenor said. "Now where is—ah."

The forest shook, and a fifty foot tall Anubis figure appeared, pushing branches roughly aside as he moved.

Velion had arrived.

"Ho," Rylan said, craning his neck to look up at the other Twin. "How are you doing that, anyway? I thought the Anubis thing was just an illusion. But you're obviously actually as large as you seem. The ground is shaking."

Velion ignored him, looking at Nelenor instead. "Why have you changed?"

Nelenor shrugged. "The fictional form is unnecessary. We are simply playing into the Imprisoner's wishes with it."

"I disagree," Velion rumbled. "This form gives us power over our enemies."

"I have grown tired of it," Nelenor said. "Do you wish me to take it up again?"

"I wish you to be *strong*," Velion said, and for a moment Rylan almost thought they were going to come to blows.

"I have not lost my strength, dear Velion," Nelenor said. "I have simply changed my form. Is it not stronger to show the enemy my *true* self? Let them know me and fear me for who I *really* am: an elf, like them."

Velion crossed his arms, staring at Nelenor for a long moment. Then he turned his head to Rylan. "This form is not only mistweaving magic," he said. "I have also applied strengthshaping. When used at a strong enough power level, the body grows to be this size. It is also how my voice is so loud and low."

"Oh." Rylan should have figured that out, but strengthshaping wasn't a magic he was very familiar with. Which Aspect was it? Governor. White. The magic of pity and love.

Interesting that love could alter one's appearance so.

"We can't very well be called the Twins if we don't look the same," Velion said, sighing. "I suppose this form *was* getting a bit tiresome."

And he changed, growing smaller, his vulpine features morphing into elven ones. His hair grew long and blond to match his brothers, his body growing slim and graceful.

Then the hips filled out, and breasts grew, and in short order Rylan was staring at one of the most beautiful elves he had ever seen.

Velion was a *woman*.

"You—" he said.

"You are surprised?" Velion said, and sure enough: her voice was high and feminine. There was still an edge to it, though, as if she was not someone to be trifled with.

"Aren't you the one in charge of darkprime magic?" Rylan asked.

"That is indeed my side of Xyclami," Velion said. "Why?"

"Nothing," Rylan said. "It doesn't matter." For some reason it was hard to imagine a *girl* being the one controlling darkprime magic. Why, he had no idea. It just didn't seem right, somehow.

Velion smoothed her clothes out. She was wearing a white

sun dress, the cloth tight about the waist and flaring out around the thighs. Her eyes, like her brother's, flashed blue. And though he hadn't seen her smile yet, Rylan thought that it would probably be a sight to behold.

Velion was *beautiful*.

"Well, dear brother," she said, "shall we continue our pursuit?"

"Our sister is on Mar," Nelenor said. "I felt her presence when I was there."

"Why did you not go to her?" Velion asked. "We could be done with this."

"I could not be certain where she was. And besides—I was distracted. The elves and humans attacked me. Quite effectively, I might add."

"You killed a *lot* of people," Rylan said.

Nelenor turned to him, and for a moment Rylan thought he might attack. But he just stared, then returned his gaze to his sister. "We shall find the Imprisoner," he said. "Only then will our imprisonment be repaid. Only then shall we be free to find our sister and depart this place."

Velion stepped forward, taking both of Nelenor's hands in her own. "Very well," she said, a small smile flickering across her face. "Let us be about it, then."

# FOURTEEN

IT WAS strange making two gates at once. It was strange making *any* gate, actually, but Phoenix managed it. She was a Prime Mage now. She had to get used to making gates.

She stepped through into the middle of Ilyrion, ruins of the forest strewn out around her. Buildings lay toppled in the distance, smoke rising from fires that still burned. All was silent. Everyone was gone, having been driven away by the Twins. And the Twins were not there, either.

But Phoenix was not alone.

The others stepped through the gate behind her hurriedly, and Phoenix waited for them to arrive before she snapped it shut. Imra and Elanil stared out at the destroyed city alongside her, concern growing in their eyes.

It was not buildings that were on fire in the distance.

It was Trees.

Things were streaming out of the Trees, and this time they weren't mages. They looked like people, but they weren't quite solid—they were transparent, ghostly, looking like souls setting forth from Ambarhal.

Which, of course, is exactly what they were.

She recognized them now. She'd seen them by the billions underneath the violet sky, arrayed across the endless hills, a horde of people reduced to nothing but thought and wispy form. They weren't real. They couldn't be. But they were here, and they were heading right for the three women.

*Thousands* of them.

"The souls," Elanil said.

Phoenix glanced at her. "You've seen them?"

Elanil nodded. "When I was in Ambarhal. I wondered why they were there."

"This is the Twins' final retribution," Phoenix said. "Do you think they can hurt us?"

"Why would they be here if not?"

"This doesn't bode well," Imra said, drawing her bow. "Here they come!"

Souls came rushing at them by the dozens, flailing ghostly weapons in the air. Phoenix didn't have time to wonder where they'd gotten weapons before they were on her, transparent steel clashing on steel. The weapons, it seemed, were real enough to hurt.

She Willed fire into her blade, activating forcefinder magic Aspected into anger. Then she drove forward with it, slashing wildly at the souls that were in her way. They shied away at first, eyes fearful of the sudden flames. She decapitated one without much effort, its ghostly head rolling on the ground. The next she dispatched with a piercing thrust, the next with a slash to the groin. The souls could feel pain, it seemed, but she knew they could inflict it, too.

Elanil screamed from somewhere behind her.

Phoenix spun, blade up and ready, flames momentarily blinding her. She searched for Elanil, hoping the girl was okay. All she saw were souls and souls, and Imra, her bowstring slapping as she loosed shot after shot. She had plenty of arrows, but they didn't seem to be doing much damage to the souls.

Where was Elanil?

The girl screamed again, and then she rose in a shower of souls. Phoenix saw a great, gaping wound in her chest heal before her eyes, her shirt bloody and ripped where the gash had been struck. She grimaced as the healing overtook her, using the wood in her hand to thrust the souls away from her.

"It's a good thing I have that Palm," Elanil said, shivering as the soulsoothing magic finished its work. "Behind you!"

Phoenix turned just in time to parry the blow of another nameless soul, its eyes strangely hollow. It took two more strikes to kill it, but three more took its place. They weren't particularly skilled, but there were just so *many* of them. Phoenix didn't know how long they could survive.

"Together!" Phoenix shouted, backing up until she was next to Elanil. Imra moved back to them as well, and soon the three women were back-to-back in a triangle formation, facing out against the vast army of souls.

"Now what?" Imra asked. "These arrows aren't doing shit."

"At least you *have* a weapon!" Elanil said.

"Let's try something," Phoenix said, parrying a pair of blows. "Touch me."

Imra glanced at her, a wry smile on her face.

"Not like that," Phoenix said, blushing. "And keep your bow free. Touch me with your leg, or something. We have to work together."

"Okay," Imra said, bending her knee so it touched Phoenix's thigh.

"Now prepare to shoot."

"Do something quickly!" Elanil shouted. She was flinging souls away as quickly as she could, but they just continued piling in. Phoenix's fireblade was a blur as she dispatched them one after another, but it was no use. There were just too many of them.

"Now!" Phoenix shouted, and she invoked her forcefinder magic.

She didn't make a shield. She didn't use her sword. Instead she sent Destroyer particles into and around Imra's nocked arrow, just as the woman loosed it into the crowd of ghastly souls.

The souls exploded outwards in a shower of red light. Scores of them flew instantly away, shattered into pieces, bits of transparent bodies carried away by glimmering particles. It opened a huge gap in the souls, but more of them rushed in almost immediately.

"Twins," Imra cursed. "Why weren't you doing that with your blade?"

"It doesn't work like that for me," Phoenix said. "Something about your bladedancer magic, I think. I can't direct the particles as well as you."

"Well, let's keep doing it," Imra said.

So they did. Imra nocked another arrow, still touching Phoenix, and Phoenix Willed forcefinder magic into and around it. She added a little shield around the arrow in the air, making it intentionally unstable and filling the inside with as much magic as she could.

The arrow flew, and an even larger blast followed. Souls exploded into oblivion, the wind of their passing striking Phoenix in the face. She winced, hoping her magic wouldn't be close enough to hurt her, and loaded up another arrow.

This was almost kind of fun.

They fought like this for several minutes, loosing arrow after arrow into the oncoming horde. They killed souls by the dozens, by the hundreds, but still they came. Phoenix poured her magic into them, filling up the sky with sparkling projectiles, raining destruction upon them.

And still they came. There were far too many. Elanil was struggling at her corner of the triangle, her only weapon the magic in her hand. And Phoenix was beginning to tire now—this much magic was a lot to expend. And the souls kept coming by the thousands, streaming out of the burning Trees in the distance, running at them with faces full of anger.

Some of them were speaking, she realized with astonishment, loading up another arrow and watching it arc through the sky. She winced as it exploded, sending a shower of soul fragments in every direction. She heard words coming faintly from the crowd.

"Fear."

"Pain."

"Anger."

Emotion words. Red words. The souls were being drawn to them, she realized, drawn to her Destroyer magic. They almost seemed to be feeding off of it, even as they died by the hundreds.

It only incited more and more to come.

"They're drawn to our emotion!" Phoenix shouted.

"Why?" Elanil asked, fending off a pair of them with her bare hands.

"I don't know!" Phoenix said. "Why are they even here? Are they even alive?"

"They can certainly be killed," Imra said, firing off another arrow. It exploded in a shower of light, but the souls just surged back in. "I'm getting low."

She was, Phoenix saw. There were only three arrows remaining in her quiver.

They were running out of options.

"We can just fly away," Elanil said. "Or gate. Rylan's not here."

"If we don't stop these souls," Phoenix said, "who will?"

"We can't just stay here and die!"

"There must be *something* we can do! These souls will take over the entire planet!"

"We can't do anything," Elanil said. "Between this and the Twins, we're screwed."

# FIFTEEN

TREY WALKED down the streets of Errenmel, expecting everyone to be dead. Arra and Lashel were beside him, carrying primewood pouches and not much else. That's why they were here: to get supplies for their trip north. Thylmanas would be very cold this time of year. It was always cold up there.

Errenmel was intact. The buildings were all still there, and Trey could see people on the streets. Either the Twins hadn't visited the village, or they hadn't deemed it necessary to destroy. Perhaps they'd come back and ruin it all. Perhaps they'd moved on. Trey knew that as long as the Twins still lived, no one would ever know for certain what they would do.

The village was intact, but it was not quite the same as it had been before. There was a certain intensity to the air. The people walking along the street looked furtively over their shoulders, hands stuck in their pockets. It looked like they were fishing about for primewood, actually. Trey had done it himself enough times to know what it looked like.

"What's going on here?" he asked.

"They seem afraid," Arra said. "Maybe the Twins have paid them a visit."

"We'd know if they had," Lashel said. "I suspect this town would not have survived."

"Probably true," Trey said. "Then what could it be?"

They passed a sign that had been nailed to the wall of a wooden building. "Seventh Aspect For All," it said. Trey remembered seeing signs like that all over the place, before the Twins had arrived. It was something the Devout wanted: the deregulation of magic.

Which Cresius said they had done.

Sure enough, a gate appeared in the distance. Trey could see it swirling, orange light shining out like a beacon, clearly visible even in the afternoon light. He saw several figures darting through it, then it disappeared.

"It seems they haven't wasted any time," Arra said.

"They'll lose their memories that way," Trey said.

"Maybe they don't care."

"They're using darkprime magic," Trey said. "Which means..."

"Put up a forcefield," Lashel said.

"You read my mind," Trey said. He'd kept the Tree Ring Staff with him, luckily. He pulled it off the clasp on his belt now, hand automatically finding ash. A forcefield sprang into existence around the three of them, moving as they walked down the middle of the street.

As if on cue, a cloud of purple formed in the air in front of them.

"You see it?" Arra asked.

Trey nodded. "Mindmaster magic."

"Someone is up to no good in Errenmel," Lashel said.

"Maybe a lot of someones," Arra said. "We should get what we came for and get out of here."

"We might encounter some resistance," Trey said. "The Devout didn't like us much when we last encountered them."

"They don't have anything to fight for, this time," Lashel said. "We aren't about to invade one of their sacred tombs."

"They got what they wanted," Arra said. "They can use all the magic they want to now. Why would they attack?"

"Perhaps you should ask them," Trey said, motioning to the building on their left.

A sign was on it, bearing the word *Hauruite*. It was a general store, and there were four people on the roof, dressed in the desert robes of the Devout. They didn't have guns— instead, they wore primewood pouches slung low about their waists. All were staring at the three of them with malicious intent.

"They still hate us, apparently," Trey said. "No idea why."

"Might be the shining forcefield you just put up," Lashel said.

"Not a very sporting bunch, I guess. I wonder what they want?"

"Chaos, it would seem," Arra said. "Maybe they think to take advantage of the present situation with the Twins."

"Bunch of morons, if you ask me," Trey said.

"Will this forcefield hold?" Lashel asked.

"It should. Let's get inside this store, see if we can find what we need."

"Sounds good."

The Devout mages did nothing to them as they entered the store, perhaps sensing that their magic could not pierce the forcefield. None of them were mergemelders, evidently, or perhaps they just didn't know how powerful that particular power was.

*Hauruite* had been looted. Shelves were tipped over inside the store, their contents strewn about the floor. Lights flickered from the ceiling, giving haphazard illumination to the various items that remained.

"Shit," Trey said. "I guess Errenmel isn't as peaceful as it seems."

"Does it *seem* peaceful?" Lashel asked. "There are four Devout on the roof right now, ready to do us in."

"Let's try and get what we need," Arra said. "I don't see an owner or anything."

"Whoever did this left most of the stuff here," Trey said. "We need camping gear—warm stuff, including coats and sleeping bags. Flint and tinder, food, bags of water. Utility knives, plus any other useful weapons we see. Thylmanas will be *cold*."

"We're good on primewood, at least," Arra said. "Let's split up and look."

It took them the better part of an hour, but they eventually found everything they needed. They couldn't just gate to Thylmanas, having never been there before. Trey could use exploratory gates—that was how they'd Sent everyone to the other worlds—but he knew they came with a cost: significant time and power. It would be easier to gear up and just fly there directly, surviving in the cold until they found what Orym had sent them to find.

He just hadn't expected their supplies to be free.

"Ready?" he asked. They were gathered at the front of the store, new backpacks filled with gear, tents and sleeping rolls attached.

"They might attack us as we leave," Arra said.

"We'll have a forcefield up. Let's go."

They left the store, Trey channeling a forcefield from his Tree Ring Staff as they did. Walking was a whole lot harder with all the gear weighing him down. If he'd been more athletic, perhaps it wouldn't have bothered him at all. Quynn probably wouldn't have given it a second thought. He probably had all the athletic tendencies of the two.

"What has magic done?" Trey asked as they walked down the street, the sun once more beating down on them. A group of mages were fighting in the distance, light flashing as they wielded previously forbidden shockstriking magic.

"It's done a lot," Arra said.

"Yes, but what *good*? All we do is fight and kill. We lose people for millennia, all for passing through a gate. We send cities into the sky, but we forget *why*. We kill people to make the Trees, again and again and again. We posture and pontificate and vote, and all for what? What good has magic done?"

"You're the one pontificating," Lashel observed.

"I'm serious," Trey said. "Why does the world need magic?"

"Trouble brewing," Arra said, pointing up ahead.

More Devout had entered the area, running out into the street from wherever they'd been hiding. They were easily identifiable in their brown robes and head scarves, rifles slung back behind their backs and primewood pouches wrapped around their waists. Trey could only see their eyes, and each of them held nothing but malice. He had no idea why.

Soon there were ten Devout standing in front of them in the street, and Trey couldn't help but give a sigh.

"Don't they know we have bigger problems?" he asked.

But just then, his fingers slipped on the Tree Ring Staff, and the forcefield disappeared.

The Devout opened fire.

# SIXTEEN

THE SOULS WERE OVERWHELMING THEM. Elanil cast back and forth with leafrunning magic, throwing the ghostly beings violently away. Behind her, Imra and Phoenix continued shooting dazzling arrows infused with Destroyer magic, blasting the souls into fragments. They died by the hundreds, but more always appeared to take their place.

"I'm out!" Imra shouted.

"Shit," Elanil cursed, reaching into her primewood pouch and finding no more elm there. She could switch to other magics, but she was not as skilled with them. "I'm out, too!"

"This isn't good," Phoenix said, fireblade brandished in front of her face. "I can't hold them back much longer." She waved the blade, the women rotating, the fire keeping the souls at bay. Elanil knew it wouldn't last.

"Attack!" a male voice shouted suddenly, the sound loud in Elanil's ears. She was looking around to see who was there when suddenly hundreds of elves appeared, shooting upwards.

Through the ground.

"What—" Elanil began, but already the elves were amidst

the souls, battling with swords and magic flashing. She saw shockstriking magic flaring out, sending dozens of souls flying backwards, jerking as electricity arced through them. Other mages used leafrunning to throw the souls away, like Elanil had been doing. Still others were strengthshapers, using their arms and fists to dispatch soul after soul. It took her a minute of watching them before she finally realized who they were.

The Prime Mages had arrived.

They'd all used mergemelding to ascend from their position underground, and now they were there to battle the army of souls. They were glorious, blasting forth with every magical power at their disposal.

The only problem was, they were losing.

They weren't dying. She saw several mages heal themselves from mortal wounds, shrugging off sword blades as if they were nothing more than an inconvenience. Then those same mages struck back with devastating effect, destroying souls by the hundreds.

But it wasn't enough. The Prime Mages were strong, powerful, but there were only about two hundred of them. Two hundred mages against *millions* of souls, and they just kept coming.

There was no way to win.

And Elanil was useless. It wasn't only that she was out of elm—she was just so *weak* compared to Phoenix. She didn't have any of the sparkly force magic, any power over her emotions. She was just a fifteen year old girl, alone amidst a maelstrom of whirling, faceless souls.

She had no idea why she was here at all.

She watched the Prime Mages fight the endless waves of souls, knowing that the entire thing was pointless. Even with two hundred mages doing their best, there just wasn't enough power here. Magic wasn't good enough to defeat this threat. Elanil wasn't good enough.

"Greetings," a man's voice said, and Elanil jumped, startled. She turned to see a rather dashing man standing next to her, dark hair cut short and spiky on top. He had the fine features typical of elves, with flashing green eyes and a well-muscled body. He was probably triple her age at least, but she had to admit: he was pretty hot.

"Who are you?" she asked, her voice barely audible over the sounds of battle all around them.

"The name is Lightning," the man said. "I've been looking after all your friends. I brought something for you."

He pulled out two Books of Amplification.

"Found these in your ship," Lightning said. "Figured you'd want them back."

"Thanks," Elanil said, taking both Books from him. "Do you know what these are?"

"Not much of a reader, myself," Lightning said. "But I figured they had sentimental value for the three of you."

"They do," Elanil said, giving him a shallow smile. "They do. Hey—do you have any light elm?"

"Of course." He reached into his primewood pouch, pulling out a handful. "You're another Prime Mage, right?"

Elanil nodded. "A weak one. Phoenix is the strong one, here."

"I see," Lightning said. "Well, I'm sure you'll manage just fine. Shall we?" He turned to face the oncoming soul horde, primewood clenched between his fingers.

"Um," Elanil said, "would you actually mind calling off the Prime Mages?"

"What? But we need to fight!"

"There's something I want to try, but I don't want to hurt anybody."

Lightning surveyed her for a minute, as if trying to weigh her worth. Then he nodded, raising a whistle to his lips and blowing.

The harsh sound hurt Elanil's ears, but every single Prime Mage in the area stopped what they were doing immediately when they heard it. Lightning blew a series of short tones next, and the mages all raised their hands in a salute.

Then, as one, they sank into the ground.

"You've trained them," Elanil said.

"What little I could," Lightning said. "Now—your plan? We only have seconds left to live."

"Yes," Elanil said, looking out at the souls clamoring for them. Even now the gaps left by the Prime Mages were filling in, hundreds of new souls rushing in. The line of Trees were still burning in the distance, disgorging souls from Ambarhal. Elanil wondered how long they would stay there, and if they could be stopped.

Perhaps it was time to find out.

"Elanil?" Phoenix asked. She was fighting with her fire-blade, eyes anxious. Imra had been reduced to swinging with her bow, doing her best to knock out as many souls as she could.

Elanil took a deep breath. She could do this.

She handed one Book back to Lightning. "Hold this," she said. "I only need one."

"Now's not really the time for a leisure read."

She ignored him, holding the other Book in her left hand, some light elm in her right. Now was the time to finally see just what this Artifact was capable of. The souls filled the entire area, a sea of them, grasping for their emotions and their lives. Elanil was the only hope they had.

She Willed the magic to life.

She could feel it flowing through her, amplified by the

Book. It felt like a raging torrent, like the biggest river she'd ever seen, like an entire ocean of magic channeled through her mind. She could almost taste the power, feel it ripple beneath her fingertips. She could do incredible things with it, if she so desired.

So she did.

She waved her hand. It was a casual motion, almost uncaring. She didn't need to exert herself in the slightest to do what needed to be done.

The Book would do it for her.

Magic rippled out in a circle around her, pushing everyone and everything away. Souls erupted into the air, shot into the sky with the barest flicker of a thought. The circle grew and grew and grew, tens of thousands of souls ripped away like dust in the wind, flying further and higher than she'd ever seen before. The destruction rippled further and further, the remains of trees and buildings caught up in it. And then it hit the Trees—the burning Trees—and for an instant she finally felt resistance to her leafrunning magic.

She gritted her teeth and pushed through it.

The Trees ripped apart, splintering into pieces before the horrible onslaught of her magic. Wood and leaves and flame erupted into fragments, blasting outward and away. And still the souls kept going, moving and dying, screaming as her magic swept them into the sky and out into nothing. Soon they were miles away and still flying, most dead from the sheer force of her magical blast. The ones that had survived would fall to their death when she released her magic, she knew. But they deserved it. She felt no remorse.

The wood in her hand scintillated into dust, and she felt the torrent of power rolling through her abruptly disappear.

She slumped to the ground, barely able to keep her eyes open.

The woods were empty now. There were no souls, no trees, no buildings. Nothing. The center of Ilyrion had been blasted down to its bedrock, and all by one simple, small fifteen year old girl.

Elanil had saved the day.

"Never call yourself weak again," Phoenix said, bending down to help her up, a smile on her face.

"It wasn't me," Elanil said. "It was the Book."

"Still," Phoenix said, "thank you. You did well."

Elanil found herself blushing.

# SEVENTEEN

ARRA SAW the forcefield go out around them. She had light birch in her hand already, with other woods ready to go. Not for the first time, she wished she had a staff like Trey's, something that could provide primewood whenever she needed it, without running out.

The Devout opened fire.

Bullets flew through the air, but none of them hit Arra. She looked around, trying to figure out what had happened. Lashel seemed okay.

Trey slumped forward, blood appearing from a dozen wounds, the Staff slipping from his hands.

Arra darted toward him, but the Devout fired again—and this time they hit her. She felt metal slugs ripping through her body, excruciating pain filling her. She burned the birch in her hand, feeling ice ripple through her as the healing magic worked. Bullets forced their way out of her body, pinging to the ground in a clatter of spent metal.

And the Devout fired again.

She reached for her primewood pouch, feeling fear surging through her veins. One shot to the head would be all it took to kill her, she knew. Soulsoothing magic couldn't heal her if she were dead. Trey was on his knees, blood dripping from his mouth, eyes glazed. Lashel had scrambled for cover, cowering behind the corner of the store.

Arra heard bullets whizzing by her face, felt one hit her arm. It *hurt*, and she needed to heal Trey, and she couldn't seem to find any more birch in her pouch. She needed the magic, dammit. She needed to not be so bad at this.

Then she found it: birch. More bullets flooded the area, several of them hitting her. She winced—it never got easier to feel the pain of impending death, even when you knew you could heal it all away. But she had to heal Trey—he was near death, and for some reason he wasn't reaching for any wood. The Staff lay useless at his feet, even as more bullets pummeled his body.

He fell.

And Arra crouched over him, heedless of her own pain, reaching down to grasp him on the shoulder. Then she channelled the magic, sending soulsoothing surging through them both.

It healed them in moments, even as yet more bullets ripped through them. She reached down and picked up the Tree Ring Staff, placing it in Trey's hand.

"Use it," she said. "You have to snap out of this."

Trey shook his head, staggering to his feet, both hands on the Staff. "Sorry," he said. "The pain...it was just too much. Thank you."

She squeezed his shoulder, taking another piece of birch from her pouch. "Shall we?"

He smiled, turning to the Devout. "Hey!" he shouted. "Why are you shooting at us?"

One of them shook his head, but none of them said a word. They were busy reloading their weapons, no evidence of magic apparent. What did they want? Why were they here? Arra didn't know. Perhaps they simply enjoyed the chaos. Perhaps they desired to be like the Twins.

It made a sick kind of sense.

"This is getting us nowhere," Trey said, throwing up a forcefield as the Devout opened up fire again.

"We have to kill them," Arra said.

Trey sighed. "Fine."

He lashed out with something she couldn't see, and all ten of the Devout crumpled into the ground, dead.

The village was silent for a time.

"I hate this," Trey said. "Magic shouldn't be this powerful. It shouldn't be this easy for me to kill those people."

"They tried to kill us first."

"Because of *magic*," Trey said. "Because of the Twins. Magic is why this whole thing started. Magic is the problem."

"No," Lashel said, stepping out from where he'd been hiding. "*Religion* is the problem."

Trey regarded him. "When it comes to the Twins," he said, "magic and religion are the same damn thing."

Arra saw the pain on his face. He had hated killing those Devout, hated that he'd been forced into this position. He was a good man, she knew—a better man than Quynn. Better than he'd been when he was whole, though now he lacked certain dimensions of his personality. Could she love him if he stayed this way? She wasn't sure. But he was definitely better now.

She stepped toward him, wrapping her arms around his waist. "We can't stop magic," she said. "We just have to do the best with what we have."

He sighed again. "I know. I just wish there was something we could do."

He bent down to kiss her, and she moved her mouth to

meet his. He tasted of the honeybread they'd had for lunch, his little beard whiskers tickling her where they'd started to grow in. She pulled back, admiring his face, seeing the familiar intensity back in his eyes. He loved her, she could see. He was passionate about her. And about their quest, on an errand Orym had ordained. Were they following a madman? Should they be going to Thylmanas without knowing what was waiting for them there? Was magic, in fact, the root of all their problems?

She didn't know. All she could do was hold this man, and kiss him, and hope that everything was going to be okay.

She hoped they wouldn't have to murder too many more people they'd never met along the way.

# EIGHTEEN

LIGHTNING LED ELANIL, Phoenix and Imra down into his underground lair. The man walked with confidence, as if he'd seen the Twins and somehow not been intimidated. Perhaps that was how he'd been able to wrangle the Prime Mages so effectively.

Still, the mages hadn't exactly been effective against the souls. They were still uncoordinated, haphazard. Elanil had destroyed the Trees that were yielding the souls into this world, but she had a feeling it may not have been enough. There had to be more Trees, more souls, somewhere.

There had to be.

"Sundering magic is a terrible thing," Lightning said as he led them into a large, metallic chamber. It reminded Elanil of Memory a bit, what with all the metal walls and electronics. But the room was huge, easily large enough to hold the two hundred Prime Mages that were even now sitting at tables, eating.

"It killed a lot of people on Earth," Elanil said.

"Not just that," Lightning said. "It isn't just the deaths. No one knew that the souls of those who had been sundered remained, stuck in limbo for centuries. They were all in Ambarhal, just waiting to be released. Now they live a half-life, a not-life."

"They didn't seem like people to me," Imra said.

"I don't know exactly *what* they are," Lightning said. "All we know is that they can hurt you like real people can, and they seem drawn to strong emotion. We don't know what they want, other than to kill. Maybe that's it. Maybe they're trying to seek revenge for the way their lives were cut short."

"You've encountered them before?" Phoenix asked.

Lightning nodded. "Just a few of them, wandering in from the desert. There's a vast army of souls out there even now. Then the burning Trees appeared in Ilyrion, and you appeared along with them. Ah, here he is."

A man appeared, with long hair and a grizzled chin. "Greetings," he said. He was dressed in a robe of muted red.

"Alinar!" Elanil said. She remembered him from Tanomar. He'd gone hunting with her on the island, finding boar.

"Alinar has taken charge of the Prime Mages," Lightning said.

"I thought *you* were in charge?" Elanil asked.

Lightning smiled. "I'm just a poor radio operator now, and not much of a mage. No, Alinar is a much better leader of this motley crew than I could ever be."

"What have you been doing?" Phoenix asked.

"We started by finding food and supplies," Alinar said. "It was easy to do, what with Ilyrion emptied of all its people unexpectedly. We gathered everyone here, making sure we were all fed and clothed, giving out what weapons we could find. Then we delved into the darkprime stores."

"That was my discovery," Lightning said. "The black market was surprisingly forthcoming with where they kept their wood."

"I see," Elanil said. "So what's the plan, then?"

"Well," Alinar said, "we were hoping you could tell us. Here." He handed Elanil a radio made of black metal. It was heavier than she'd expected, and cold. "Turn this dial to set the channel, and hit this button to talk. This should let you speak with the others in your group. Lightning procured it for us—he's a bit of a radio expert."

"I caught wind of some of your transmissions earlier," Lightning explained. "It seems your crew has been quite active of late."

"We tried to kill Nelenor," Elanil said. "We failed."

"I surmised as much. He is back here now?"

Elanil nodded. An idea was beginning to form.

She hit the talk button on her radio.

"Hello? Is Cresius listening to this channel? This is Elanil."

She released the button, and nothing happened for a moment. Then the radio crackled, and Cresius' voice sounded over the tinny speaker.

"Cresius here," he said. "Where are you?"

"With the Prime Mages," Elanil said. "We're underground in Ilyrion, and everyone is ready to be of use."

"Excellent. Let me track your position—I'll be right there."

"He can do that?" Elanil asked Lightning.

"This is Donar Cresius XXV of the Department of Magical Research?" Lightning asked. Elanil nodded. "Wow. He's sort of an idol of mine. The tech they have up there at the DMR— yes, he can definitely track you here."

A gate appeared suddenly, and Cresius stepped through. The light was blinding for a moment, and then it disappeared as quickly as it had come.

"Greetings," Cresius said. "Boy, that's a rush."

"First time gating?" Elanil asked.

Cresius nodded. "Hope I did it right. That double gate thing is a bit strange. But my head feels fine."

"You've really never gated before?" Phoenix asked. "I find that hard to believe."

Cresius gave her a tight smile. "Fine. I admit it, I've gated plenty of times. It was all illegal, you understand, so I can't admit that to anyone. And I have to say, being able to gate without messing with my brain is really quite amazing."

He looked around the room, as if suddenly noticing how many people were in there. The Prime Mages had all stopped what they were doing, looking up at him from where they were sitting.

"Ah," Cresius said, a wide smile growing on his face. "This will be most excellent."

Elanil left him and Alinar to speak. She'd helped with this part, joining the Department with the Prime Mages. Now she needed to be about her real mission.

She needed to locate Rylan.

She hit the button on her radio again. "Rylan?" she said softly. "Are you there? Can you hear me?"

"He might be on a different channel," Phoenix said. "Try this one." She rotated the dial to the left, and Elanil tried again.

Nothing happened.

They tried every channel, one after another, sending out words into the air. But there was no response. Rylan wasn't there.

"We'll have to look for him some other way," Elanil said.

"We can comb the country," Phoenix said. "The whole world, if we have to. I want to find my son."

"Dance?" Elanil's radio said suddenly, and Elanil scrambled to hit her button.

"Wind? Is it really you? Are you okay?"

"I'm okay," Rylan said. "I'm in the Faedori Forest, with the Twins."

"*Both* of them?"

"Yes. They haven't hurt me. They gave me my magic back."

Elanil wasn't sure if she should feel happy or afraid to hear that news. He sounded hesitant, as if he were afraid to be speaking to her. "Can they hear this?" she asked. "Can they hear your radio?"

"I don't think so," Rylan said. "Not as long as I stay quiet. They're nicer than they seem, you know. The Twins. I don't think they are nearly as evil as everyone makes them out to be."

"Surely you can't believe that," Elanil said. "They killed *millions* of people in the past two days!"

"I know. It's just—you have to meet them, Dance. Then you'll understand."

"They might turn on you at any point," Elanil said. "Please, you have to believe me. You have to be careful."

"I will. I promise."

"Listen," Elanil said. "I know we need to talk about what happened between us. And I—I miss you, Rylan. Okay? We'll talk about it later. But right now there's something we need to do."

"What is it?"

"The Department of Magical Research has laid a bunch of traps in a place called the Salt Spires, north of the Thesserin Desert. We need to lure them there, somehow. We think we might be able to stop them."

"You want me to *lure* the Twins somewhere?"

"I mean...yes. If you can. It's our only shot."

The radio was silent for a moment. Then: "Give me a few hours."

Rylan clicked off, and Elanil found herself missing him even more intensely than before.

"I really hope he's okay," she said.

"Me too," Phoenix said. "He can't actually be *right* about the Twins, can he? They're *monsters*."

"I don't know," Elanil said. "I really don't know. Twins—I just realized how hungry I was."

# NINETEEN

THEY HAD FRESH MEAT, at least. Phoenix didn't ask how they'd gotten it—the elves on Valaralda were clearly far more advanced than anything she'd seen on Earth. The meat might not even be real, but she didn't want to think about that. As long as it nourished her and tasted good, that was enough for her. Meat was such a rarity in the Under.

She left Elanil eating with Lightning at one of the tables. Phoenix and Imra took their food and found a quiet corner to eat, sitting on the floor with their backs to a wall. It felt more natural to Phoenix, more like home. And though Phoenix knew that Imra was more used to forests and open air, she didn't complain.

Their plates had the aforementioned meat and also a few fried potatoes, a green bean-like vegetable, and bread. Even with the end of the world now upon them, apparently food was not difficult to find.

"This doesn't feel like the Under," Phoenix said around a mouthful of food.

"Why would it?" Imra asked, taking a drink of water from a tin cup she'd been given.

"We're under the city, here. I guess I just figured there would be some similarities."

"Do you miss it?"

Phoenix put her head back against the wall. "Sometimes. I think I miss the idea of it more than the reality, though. Being free to make your own choices, free to move about as you wanted. There was none of this 'save the world' nonsense down there."

"Were you ever really free?"

Had she been? Even during the best of times, Queen had still been in charge. Even when she'd surrendered herself to ecstasy with a forbidden man, he'd turned out to be some kind of evil liar mage. Even when she'd thought she'd had something special with Beam, it had all turned out to be nothing in the end.

She felt tears coming to her eyes.

Beam was dead. There was no going back to her now. No repairing what had been lost. No way to find out what had broken and why.

A tear tracked its way down her cheek, and Phoenix lifted the hunk of nameless meat to her mouth to mask the pain.

"I'm sorry," Imra said. "I don't really know you. I don't know what your life was like. All I know is you're this myste- rious underkid, come down with the Remnant to kill us all— then you suddenly change sides, and now you're fighting *against* them. You were strong. You *are* strong. Like her."

"Like Arra."

"She was always better at me than everything. Still is. I guess that's what happens when you're twenty fucking thou- sand years old."

Phoenix looked at Imra, saw the anger written on her face. It was hurt in the guise of anger, she knew. Hurt that she couldn't have the woman she desired.

"You're an incredible archer," Phoenix said. "At least as good as Arra. I saw you both, you know. You're deadly with a bow. We made a good team out there."

Imra blushed a little at that. "Thanks, even though I know you're lying. Arra has *always* been the better archer. And a Prime Mage now, and she has her man, and—"

"Hey," Phoenix said, putting down her plate and touching Imra's arm. "You have to stop doubting yourself so much. Stop thinking about Arra, okay? She has her life, and you have yours. You have to be your own person. I like you just the way you are."

Imra looked at her, then, green eyes swimming. "You're so pretty," she said, and then she turned away suddenly, embarrassed. "I shouldn't have said that."

"Nonsense," Phoenix said. "A girl likes to hear a compliment, especially when it's from someone as beautiful as you."

She reached up to touch Imra's chin, using her finger to bring her face back to her own. Imra really *was* beautiful: curly, dark hair framed a cherubic face, those startling green eyes blazing out like two beacons in the night. And her milky white skin, and her thick, red lips...Phoenix found herself becoming flushed.

They just looked at each other for a long moment, thoughts of food forgotten.

The world was coming to an end. The Twins might end everyone, everywhere. Her son might die. *She* might die. Phoenix *had* died, had lived for five aching years underneath strange, violet skies. And now her girlfriend, the mother of her child, was dead. Now the world was conspiring against her to bring unhappiness and pain. And all she could do was stare at this beautiful woman, this strong woman, this green-eyed girl who was hurting so much and felt so alone. They were from two different worlds, Phoenix and Imra. They were so different and yet already so much alike. And Phoenix knew that if she didn't take this moment, it might pass her by.

She leaned in, and Imra came the rest of the way.

When their lips touched, it felt like magnetism. As if the skies had parted for one small moment, and all Phoenix knew was the sun and Imra's taste and the feel of her cheek beneath her fingers. She pressed her lips into Imra's, relishing the feeling, their tongues intertwining effortlessly. It wasn't at all like kissing Beam—it was fluid, as if the two of them were the same person and yet different. As if their minds and lips and hearts and tongues worked only together, beating at the speed of harmony.

For a long, beautiful moment, Phoenix was transported to another world.

Then the moment ended, but Imra took her hand. She squeezed it, and stared at her with those gorgeous green eyes, and Phoenix saw that a wall had just come down. That Imra was her real, true self, finally and completely. Phoenix felt the heat of her face, the quickness of her breath, and she knew that in that moment she had found something, too.

The thing she didn't know that she'd been looking for.

"That was—" Imra said.

"You're—" Phoenix said.

They both laughed, nervously at first, then uproariously, together. Phoenix twined her fingers through Imra's, settling back against the wall, Imra leaning against her. It was soon. It was so soon after Beam's death, after Phoenix's own death at the hands of magic. And yet it *wasn't* soon, for either of them. It was perfect. It was right.

Even in the harshest desert, certain flowers grow.

They sat like that for several minutes. Eventually they picked their food back up, not quite looking at each other, just happy to be side by side.

"What did Arra say when you told her?" Phoenix asked.

"About how I feel?"

"Yeah."

"She said she didn't want to lose me. But it was perfectly evident that she had no interest in me. Not like that."

"Did it hurt?"

"More than I can describe." Imra leaned against her, their shoulders touching. "But I don't want to talk about Arra, anymore. What about Beam? What was she like? I barely knew her."

"Beam was hard," Phoenix said. "I think she wanted to be. She wanted to be in charge, be the best. I think that's why she liked me, in the beginning. I was someone she could control."

She knew she wasn't being fair, but it was how it had felt. Beam and her had grown more distant the moment Phoenix had met Dill. The moment she'd become a fire mage, able to put emotion in her magic.

And the moment Beam had succumbed to Queen, Phoenix had lost her, too.

It had only taken ten long years to figure it out.

"I'm sorry she died," Imra said. "Whatever she was, at least you had each other."

"Not anymore," Phoenix whispered. "I died, and Beam moved on. But I don't want to talk about her."

"Deep stuff," Imra said. "It's too much right now, I know. So ask me something."

"What do you want in life?"

Imra looked at her, green eyes close to her own. "Deep stuff, indeed. Twins, Phoenix. That's a tough question."

"You don't have to answer."

Imra looked away, toying with her food. "Peace, I think," she said. "For starters. I want this whole adventure to end. I want the world to emerge whole and unchanged, and I want to sit beneath a tree and kiss a beautiful girl, and for that moment I want nothing else at all to matter. Not archery, not magic, not Arra, not myself. I just want the forest and the sky, and I want to *matter* to someone."

"The forest is nice," Phoenix said.

"You think you could like it?"

"There's something Beam and I always used to say: we're not afraid of getting a little dirty. I think we meant adventure, but we also meant dirt. The Under is a cold place, Imra, and I don't mean the temperature. There are no friends, no food, nothing that really makes it *home*. Yes, it's where I'm from. And no, I didn't go topside when I had the chance. But I don't think I can go back there now that I've spent a new lifetime drifting amongst the Trees, lost in my own strange world. The Under for me seems like nothing but a distant dream."

"There's plenty of dirt in the forest."

"I know. And there's...well, there's you."

Imra grabbed her hand. "I can't believe this is actually happening."

Phoenix looked at her. "Why?"

"I just—well, I just *met* you, but it feels like I've known you my entire life."

"I know just what you mean."

"Phoenix, what was it like to die?"

"Megan," Phoenix said.

"What?"

"My real name is Megan."

"Oh," Imra said. "Thank you for telling me that."

"It didn't hurt," Phoenix said. "It felt...like a piece of me departed, I guess. Like I was seeking something, and I had finally found it. Like I was suddenly free. And then everything disappeared, and I realized I *wasn't* free. I was lost."

"I'm glad you came back."

"I'm glad, too."

They sat like that for several minutes, finishing their food. The sounds of the Prime Mages echoed in the chamber all around them, quiet conversation and clinking silverware and the occasional laugh. She didn't know any of the mages, but she could tell they were ready to fight. Her life of late had been a whirlwind of new faces and sights and violence and death, but she knew that she was ready to fight, too. She needed to see this through. She needed to find that peace that Imra had spoken about.

She wanted it for herself.

"Dance?" Phoenix's radio piped up, startling her. She almost dropped her plate. "Dance, are you there?"

"Wind!" Elanil's voice said over the radio. "What happened? Are you okay?"

"I did it," Rylan said. "The Twins are coming to the Salt Spires. Now."

"How'd you manage it?"

"It was easy," Rylan said. "I simply told them the truth."

# TWENTY

ELANIL FLEW OVER EVERYTHING, wind streaming through her hair. She and Phoenix and Imra had left the others behind, taking nothing but some food and water, Phoenix's fireblade, and the two Books of Amplification. If Elanil ever saw Rylan again, she would give him one of them. Then maybe they could be reunited, control of magic be damned.

Cresius and Alinar had stayed behind, saying they needed more time to get the Prime Mages integrated into the Department of Magical Research. It was a worthy operation, Elanil was sure—she just hoped it didn't take too long.

Or maybe the vaunted traps at the Salt Spires would actually do the job. Maybe they would be the thing that would finally kill the Twins.

Elanil wasn't holding her breath.

Rylan had told the Twins the truth, he had said. And their interest had been piqued: they wanted to see these traps for themselves. They controlled magic, after all, and Nelenor had been interested in elvenkind's creativity with the power. Perhaps that was why even now everyone was heading toward the Salt Spires, to see what sort of doom awaited.

They couldn't gate there, of course, because none of them had been there before. So they flew, carrying Imra between them, and for once Imra didn't even seem embarrassed. Something had changed between her and Phoenix, and Elanil had a good idea what it was.

Finally Imra had someone who cared about her the way she needed someone to.

Elanil smiled as they flew, sweeping across the arid desert, the sun at their backs. It was getting low, sending golden rays across the endless sand. She hoped the battle in the Spires didn't last too long—she didn't want to fight at night.

She hoped Rylan was still okay.

Then the Salt Spires finally appeared in front of them, and Elanil's mouth dropped open in amazement.

The desert turned into a massive pit ahead, miles and miles in every direction. The sand just fell down what must be a hundred feet at least, turning into blackness where she couldn't see the bottom. And inside that pit, where the sun didn't quite reach, hundreds and hundreds of tall spires rose up. Each was a brilliant white, glinting where they caught the light, tall and cylindrical and strange. Many of them had flat tops, and you could stand on them if you so desired. Still others were pointed or craggy, irregular shapes making strange silhouettes against the sand. The Salt Spires were an odd formation, indeed. Elanil wondered how they had come to be.

"What a strange place," Phoenix said as they neared the Spires. "I wonder what caused this to exist?"

"No idea," Imra said, "but I hope it does what everyone thinks it will."

WHEN QUYNN ARRIVED at the Salt Spires, he wondered if he was being played. The spires stretched out endlessly ahead of him, sharp tips of brilliant white against the sun. It seemed a pointless place, a place where nature had simply given up, doing the strangest thing it could imagine.

Of *course* Orym would like it.

"Is the gate supposed to be around here somewhere?" Quynn asked.

Talon shaded his eyes, looking out at the Spires. "I see nothing," he growled. "There are no places like this on our planet. What is it for?"

"I doubt it's *for* anything," Quynn said. "But since it's here, I bet someone wants to use it for something." He slapped at a bug that had landed on his arm.

"It is a terrible place."

"Strong words, coming from you. Well, at least we have water now. And weapons." Orym had seen to that.

"Surely this can't be where Orym intended us to go," Talon said.

"I think it is further to the west," Quynn said. "Shall we proceed? We can make it further before night falls."

"I don't like the look of this place," Talon said. "Let us continue on."

"At least we seem to have outrun that army of souls. We should count our blessings."

"I wonder, though," Talon said. "Where did they come from? It seems to me that whatever it was could happen again."

"Trees," Quynn said.

"What?"

"They came from Trees. Burning ones, like there." He pointed at a line of huge Prime Trees that had just appeared in the sand maybe a quarter mile away. The Trees were on fire, and already souls were pouring out of them by the thousands.

"I spoke too soon, it would seem," Talon said. "Do we run, or fight?"

"I'm surprised you would ask such a question."

"Why? I am no coward, but that does not mean I fight at every opportunity."

"It seems like that's *exactly* what you do," Quynn said.

"Fight, then."

"I'm not sure we have a choice."

More Trees had appeared to the west, blocking their passage to the gate Orym had sent them to find. They could fly, but moving the entire rylak army would take more energy than Quynn and Talon could muster. And he was loathe to leave them there to fend for themselves—he'd just befriended them, after all.

No, it seemed there was only one option in this situation: it was time to fight the souls yet again. This time, at least, they were well-armed and fed.

Quynn bared his teeth as the ghosts arrived.

ELANIL WATCHED as burning Trees appeared in the Spires. She and Phoenix and Imra were hovering near the northern edge, where the Spires turned into a rocky mountain range, complete with snow. The Trees appeared in a line right across the foothills, flames shooting from the tops. Souls immediately came issuing forth.

"Again?" Elanil asked. "Why do they keep appearing where we are?"

"They are drawn to emotion," Phoenix said. "Maybe they're drawn to me."

"There are *billions* of souls," Imra said. "We've only seen the smallest fraction of them. I wouldn't be surprised if there are eruptions like this going on all over Valaralda, and maybe even on Earth."

"The worlds can't handle billions of these," Elanil said. "All they seem to do is fight!"

The souls were pouring out of the Trees and into the Salt Spires as they watched. Many of them leapt directly onto the spires themselves, jumping astonishing distances through the air. They clung to the salt like ghostly spiders, leering upwards at the three women floating in the sky.

Elanil shivered. She hadn't expected them to jump like that. Hopefully none of them could fly. "I wonder if any of the souls are mages?" she asked.

"We'd have seen that by now, I would think," Imra said. "And it doesn't really matter—we can't keep hovering forever. Eventually we have to come down."

"Their numbers will overwhelm us no matter what we do," Phoenix said. "But still, we have to fight."

The souls were ranging out further onto the Spires, jumping from pillar to pillar as they went. Still more of them filed down from the mountain range, running directly between the spires along the ground. Soon the area was full of souls, brandishing weapons and calling to each other.

"Fear!"

"Anger!"

"Betrayal!"

"Let's do what we can," Elanil said. "We have to try."

"We should have gotten some sleep," Imra said.

"We'll just have to do the best we can."

So they flew toward the south, flinging what attacks they could down at the rampaging souls.

Elanil wondered if this fight would ever have an end.

QUYNN SLAMMED his sword into the nearest soul as hard as he could. Which was *extremely* hard, since strengthshaping magic was coursing through him at the time. The blow hit the soul and travelled on into the two souls next to him, those souls flying back and hitting the six souls behind them, and on and on. With just one wicked slash of his blade, Quynn took out well over a dozen souls.

But thousands more were coming.

He dodged a slash from his right, then burned dark oak to run right *through* another slash, the blade passing past his skin as if he weren't there at all. Then his body solidified once more, and he struck out at the souls with all his might.

This was actually kind of fun.

His Prime Mage powers had been blocked before, maybe for quite some time. Otherwise he was sure he would have been using strengthshaping magic more. It was powerful stuff, and didn't get nearly the credit it deserved.

Next to him, Talon was a fighting machine. The rylak was a full Prime Mage, not half of one like Quynn. And now that he'd had food and stocked up on wood, his full potential had finally been unleashed. Quynn couldn't help but admire his muscular form as he slashed through soul after soul, flipping through the primewood powers at random. Shockstriking magic burst into the souls, leafrunning magic adding force as they flew backwards, ghostly skin shimmering blue. Then he followed up with a wide swipe, claws out, strengthshaping magic giving him the power of twenty rylak at once. Quynn had to burn a hasty spurt of mergemelding just to get out of the next swipe's way, as Talon cut at the souls around him indiscriminately.

He was truly a force to be reckoned with.

But still the souls came. They were easy to kill. They were easy to avoid. There was nothing particularly deadly about them, as long as you were actually fighting and were a mage. But Quynn knew that eventually he would tire, and his primewood would run out. Even the rylak would find it difficult to fight forever. And the souls, Quynn suspected, did not need sleep. They did not need food. They would just fight and fight, and eventually they would have their way with the world. Eventually all would perish before their onslaught, Prime Mage or no.

There had to be another way to defeat them.


AT LEAST THE army of souls couldn't fly. It wasn't much consolation, but it was something. Elanil, on the other hand, could.

At least as long as she could still do magic.

She fragmented her leafrunning, using part of it to keep herself moving forward while using the rest to blast twenty souls hundreds of feet away. She wasn't sure if leafrunning was enough to kill them now—these souls seemed to have acquired the ability to jump and fall inhuman distances. Were they actually gaining new powers, or had they just never shown these ones before?

Perhaps she should switch to something else, like shockstriking. But shockstriking took a lot of energy to perform, even when it was your natural Alignment. She could hit a lot more souls at once with a little bit of leafrunning, even if it wasn't as fatal as it once had been.

"Where are we going?" Phoenix asked as they flew. Sparks were flying from her blade, formless red magic destroying souls by the dozen. Imra floated behind her, raining arrows down on the souls. Elanil and Phoenix were taking turns keeping the woman in the air.

"South," Imra said. "There's more fighting there—look."

She pointed, and Elanil followed the gesture. Sure enough, a large force of rylak were surrounded by thousands more souls, fighting at the southern edge of the Salt Spires. A familiar figure fought alongside the wolf-like monsters, cloaked in black and wielding his sword with great strength.

It was Quynn.

"Let's go see if we can help," Elanil said.

"Wait—is that *Quynn*?" Phoenix asked. "I don't know if I want to see him again."

"You'll have to face him sooner or later, if we make it out of this."

Phoenix sighed, the flames dying on her blade. "Fine. Let's go help them kill more of these infernal souls."

They floated down to where Quynn and the rylak were fighting, using leafrunning magic to clear a space. "Ho," Elanil said, borrowing the Under greeting. She missed Rylan.

"Oh," Quynn said. "Hi. Welcome to the fight." He eyed Phoenix nervously.

"Good to see you too, *Eric*," Phoenix said, raising her fire-blade. Flames raced over the surface of the metal.

"I see you remember your old tricks," Quynn said.

"I have many more tricks now," Phoenix said. "And you? Still raping people's minds?"

Quynn actually looked hurt at that. "I never raped you," he said. "Never that."

"We must fight," Talon said, the words coming out as a growl. "Now!"

The souls were pressing in all around them. Elanil pulled more primewood from her pouch, readying her soulbound Palm Tree on Tanomar in case she needed any healing.

The family reunion would have to wait.

# TWENTY-ONE

ALLAIN TRUDGED through the ruins of Ilyrion, wondering just what in the hell had happened. When he'd seen it last, sure—the city had been destroyed. But there had been buildings, or at least the remains of them. There had been Trees, bent and broken. There had been rocks and things.

Now there was nothing.

The center of the city was a massive, barren wasteland. It looked like a bomb had gone off, a bomb that inexplicably hadn't touched the ground. Everything in a circle was just *gone.*

The only explanation had to be magic.

"A leafrunner could have done this," Erodar said. "One of the Twins?"

"They're up north with Rylan," Allain said. "You heard the radio."

"Let's just do what we came here to do," Dill said. He and Lorelei and Elasha were taking up the rear.

"Are we sure we can trust Orym?" Allain asked.

"Yes," Dill said, at the same time Lorelei said, "No."

They looked at each other.

"Orym is the Imprisoner," Lorelei said. "He can't be trusted."

"For the last time," Dill said, "my father is *not* the Imprisoner! And even if he were, what does that even *mean*? You've seen what the Twins can do. They *needed* to be imprisoned."

"I was there," Lorelei said. "I know what he was back then. Power hungry. Mad for it. He imprisoned the Twins because he wanted Guruthos for himself—not to protect anyone. *He's* the reason the Twins are so angry with us now."

"Honestly?" Dill said. "All of that sounds a lot more like *you*. You were the one to imprison millions of humans in those floating cities, after all. You were the one who consolidated elven power, finding all the scientists, learning dark-prime magic. You were the one who almost destroyed an entire *planet*."

"Fine," Lorelei said. "I'm not going to argue any more, but I am coming along. Whatever this gate is that Orym wants us to find, it can't be good. We can't play into his plan. I'll stop you if I have to."

"I'm leaving," Elasha said suddenly.

Everyone looked at her. "Why?" Allain asked. "You just got here."

"I need to find Orym," Elasha said. "I think I—uh. I think I'm in love with him."

Lorelei snorted. "You knew him for what, a few days?"

"It doesn't matter," Elasha said. "I know how I feel. I'm going to find him."

"And do you even know where to look?"

"The desert."

"You'll die out there."

"I know how to survive the desert," Elasha said. "I've done it before."

"You'll die," Lorelei said, "because Orym will kill you."

Elasha's face looked stricken. "How *dare* you say that about him?" she said. "Orym is a kind man. An intelligent man. He would never hurt me."

Lorelei shrugged. "Suit yourself, girl. Now let's go. We have a stupid gate to find." She flashed a glance at Allain before moving on.

Allain felt his heart jump a little in his chest.

"You heard the lady," Erodar said, following.

Dill turned to Allain after they'd gone. "You really like her, don't you?" he asked.

Allain swallowed. "How could you tell?"

Dill clapped him on the shoulder. "Keep at it. I think she likes you, too."

He set out, leaving Allain bewildered. Really? Dill thought he actually had a shot with Lorelei? He felt his heart swell with excitement, his face flushing.

Then he realized he was being left behind.

THE DOCKS WERE INTACT, at least. So were the boats. There were two of them moored there, strangely silver and shimmering. "These don't look like they can sail," Allain said.

"They're called leafboats," Erodar said. "You're supposed to use leafrunning magic to move them."

"I'm not doing that," Lorelei huffed. "We'll have to find another way." She was the only leafrunner in the group.

"Why don't we just fly?" Erodar said.

"That leaves me out," Dill said. "I'm just a shockstriker, remember?"

"I'm not carrying him, either," Lorelei said.

Allain approached her, trying to discern what was wrong. Her green eyes were flashing, but they always did that. Her

mouth was set in a slight frown, full lips quirking at the edges
—but they always looked like that. Her chest rose and fell
with every breath, her breasts—

"Eyes up here," Lorelei said.

Allain blushed, returning his gaze to her face. "Sorry."

"You aren't the first," Lorelei said. Then she actually took
a step forward. They were standing close together, then,
Allain conscious of her lips and her breath. He felt his face
heating even further. "I don't want to do this," Lorelei said,
her voice quiet so that only he could hear. "Orym is just using
us out here."

"Using us for what?"

"To activate his Mechanism. To destroy the Twins."

"Isn't that what we want, too?"

Lorelei shook her head, luscious black hair waving as she
did. "He's going to take the power for himself. And when that
happens, the Twins will be a happy memory for us."

She stared into his eyes, and Allain knew that she really
believed what she was saying. And shouldn't *he* believe *her*?
She was a hundred thousand years old, after all, and the
strongest woman he'd ever met. He should at least give her
the benefit of the doubt.

"Say you're right," he said, stepping even closer. Their
faces were just inches apart now, but Lorelei didn't pull away.
"If Orym really is as powerful as you say he is, don't you
think he'd know if we defected? He probably has video
surveillance on us as we speak. He can probably hear this
very conversation."

Lorelei paled. "You're right," she said. "Shit, you're right.
We have to make it look like we're going along with his
request. Once we're out in the ocean, we can make a
decision."

"Dill wants to do what his father is asking."

"Maybe I can convince him." She glanced up at the sky, as if expecting to see a camera there.

"Alright," she said loudly, still just inches from Allain's face. "Let's get one of these boats in the water."

Allain smiled, and licked his lips, and really wished he could get Lorelei alone.

# TWENTY-TWO

THE AIR GREW COLDER AS they traveled north. Arra clutched her shawl around her, but it wasn't enough. "We should switch to the winter coats!" she called, and Trey and Lashel nodded.

They paused in the air, Arra hovering the three of them while they got their coats out of their large backpacks. It was awkward doing everything in the air, but it was better than being on the ground.

There were souls everywhere.

Lines of burning Trees kept appearing in random places, spewing out thousands of ghosts. They'd seen the souls attacking any elves they came across, and the results weren't good. So they'd avoided them as best they could, choosing instead to stick to the high ground. The air.

"It's amazing how quickly it gets cold as you go north," Trey said, shrugging into his thick woolen jacket.

"It's the altitude," Lashel said. He was carrying the two tents in addition to his other supplies, and he looked miserable. "The Thyl Mountains rise steeply here, even as the latitude increases. It's winter for long stretches of the year in these parts. Further north, we'll encounter permafrost."

"We're almost to Thylmanas," Trey said. "Come on."

They flew for another hour, shivering against the bitter wind.

"There it is," Lashel said, pointing down below them. "Thylmanas, or what's left of it after fifty thousand years."

Crumbling ruins lay as far as Arra could see. Bits of walls, half-formed statues, and the shattered remains of pillars filled the land, all covered in a blanket of brilliant white snow. There had been a city here once, Arra knew. A vast city, the height of civilization at its time.

Now it was gone.

They landed, shoes crunching in the snow. It was bitterly cold, and the wind blowing in from the east made matters even worse. Arra pulled her coat tighter. "What happened here?" she asked.

"You don't remember?" Lashel asked. "Weren't they teaching history when you were in school?"

Arra gave him a withering stare. "It's been a long time."

"Sorry. Well, I can tell you what I know."

They started walking, picking their way down what might have been a road in ancient times. Stones just a foot high indicated where walls might have been, where buildings may have housed families or patrons, where the old lines of the city had been drawn. It was just a shadow now.

There were no souls here, at least.

"Thylmanas is thought to be the seat of elven civilization," Lashel said. "It's where we all began."

"We evolved here?" Trey asked.

"Not that we know of. Some species on Valaralda have indeed evolved from precursor or primordial forms, but elves did not. Neither did many of our primary species—cows and horses, mosquitoes, many types of spiders—the list goes on."

"How do scientists know that?"

"The fossil record, or lack thereof. That was why Thylmanas was of so much interest to archaeologists, after it declined. We thought to uncover our prehistoric remains—proto-elves, so to speak. But no such remains were found. All fossilized remains here in Thylmanas match our modern genome, bone structure and brain size almost exactly."

"Why did Thylmanas decline?" Arra asked. She knew she'd been taught this stuff at the university, but now she couldn't seem to remember it. Was that gate magic at work, or just forgetfulness? She had been alive a long time, after all.

"It was at its peak shortly after the Great Awakening," Lashel said. They continued trudging through the remnants of the city, everything eerily quiet all around. "Magic unlocked the true wonders of civilization—especially here. At one point the Thylmanas Library was considered one of the wonders of the world. It burned to the ground during the War of Secession."

"That rings a bell," Arra said.

Lashel nodded. "It happened in 20,016 A.A., if memory serves. For millennia, Thylmanas had existed in close proximity to Ilyrion—not physically, but politically. The continent of Esara was united under common rule, and the seat of government was in Ilyrion. Thylmanas had representatives, of course: Senators, as well as members of the Council of Mages. But as time went on, the citizens of Thylmanas grew increasingly dissatisfied with the way of things. They thought their city was being treated unfairly, that Ilyrions couldn't possibly understand the needs of the people way up here."

"They weren't wrong," Trey said. "At least I don't imagine they were."

"They weren't," Lashel said. "But they underestimated how far Ilyrion was willing to go to keep the two cities connected. Thus began the War of Secession, which took ten bloody years to resolve."

"Why not just let them go?" Trey asked. "What did Thylmanas bring to the table? It couldn't have been agriculture, way up here."

He bent to pick up a piece of something from the ground, dusting off the snow and inspecting it. It looked like a pottery shard, a triangle of broken clay with intricate carvings on it.

"Two things," Lashel said. "Natural resources, and I don't mean food. The mines up here were legendary, yielding not only precious stones, gold and silver, but also rare metals, ingredients for advanced technology. Ilyrion knew that with Thylmanas an independent country, the economy could greatly destabilize. Thylmanas would be free to do whatever they wished in terms of trade—or simply not trade at all."

"What was the other thing?" Arra asked.

"Believe it or not," Lashel said, "the other thing was religion."

They stopped in front of a larger series of walls, arrayed at right angles. Arra could almost visualize the building that these walls had made: irregular stone formed the edges, with an angled, wooden roof on top. The peak of that roof would have towered above this portion of the town, ornate windows looking out on the citizens below.

"It was a church," Arra said.

"We don't know," Lashel said. "But yes, it could have been."

"What religion was practiced here?" Trey asked.

"The only religion this planet has known in the last hundred thousand years," Lashel said. "The Twins. Thylmanas was special because it was the birthplace of the religion: this is where the Eglaria was first formed."

"I thought it was formed in Nekhrumet?"

"It was moved there, shortly after Nekhrumet was built. But Aten founded the group as a religious one, and he did so here, in Thylmanas."

"But if it moved to Nekhrumet, why care about losing Thylmanas to the secession?"

"Religion is a funny thing," Lashel said. "It depends in large part on sacred things: objects, places, people. Once a thing gets latched into the collective consciousness of the faith, it can't be removed. Thylmanas had the First Church of the Eglaria. It also held the Eglarian True Spirits, the forms a soul is purported to take on its way to paradise."

"Obviously that's a load of bunk."

"Is it?" Lashel asked. "Do you remember the Spirits? They are depicted on the walls of the Eglaria Headquarters even to this day. You've seen them."

"Wolves," Arra said, remembering what the paintings looked like. "Dinosaurs. Strange birds with red beaks."

"Rylak," Lashel said. "Cavek. Sakul. They are all natives of Eryn."

"How did you—"

"How did I know? It was all over the wireless right after Eryn gated in. People jumped over almost immediately, took a look. Others found some old records that had been stored about the planet. It was one of the planets involved in the Sending, after all."

"You have an ocular implant?" Trey asked.

"Most people do. Is that a problem?"

"No. Of course not. You've just never referenced it before."

"I have a theory," Lashel said. "The Eglaria's mandate was to study the Gifts of the Soul. Their walls are plastered with depictions of animals native to Eryn. I think Cariel subverted the Eglaria, stole it right from under Aten's nose."

"Why does that matter?"

"It doesn't. The point is that the Eglaria started here, and here is where they developed their strongest mythology. Moving it to Nekhrumet didn't change that."

"Like the Catholic religion on Earth," Trey said. "Relics you can't replace."

"So what, then?" Arra asked. "Ilyrion feared some kind of religious rebellion if Thylmanas seceded?"

"Remember that religion here is more than just faith," Lashel said. "We've seen the Twins in the flesh. We know they're real. We know what they can do. We know that they control magic."

"Shit," Trey said. "Unlike on Earth, religion here is *real*."

"Worship of the Twins does not connote any real magical power," Lashel said. "So in that sense, no—religion is not 'real.' Yes, the gods we worshipped or swore to are most certainly real. But that wasn't the reason for the war."

They continued walking in silence for a minute, gazing at the snow-covered remains littering the area. Lashel turned them to the east, into the wind, and they walked a bit further. Soon they were standing in front of statue—one that had held together remarkably well over the millennia.

"An Anubis," Trey said. "I recognize this. It's part of Egyptian mythology."

"It's also what the Twins look like," Arra said.

"How did these images come to be?" Trey asked.

"From Aten himself," Lashel said. "He commissioned artists to create renderings of the Twins. The earliest surviving works that reference them show them in this Anubis form. We all assumed that's what they actually looked like. Now we've seen that it's true."

"So what was the real reason for the war?" Arra asked.

"Trees," Lashel said.

"What?"

"Prime Trees."

"I don't understand," Arra said. "There aren't any Prime Trees up here. Were they destroyed?"

"Not lightprime Trees. Dark."

"I—*oh*." They needed bodies to create darkprime trees. They needed murder. Death.

"You can't be serious," Trey said.

"It's never been proven," Lashel said, "but sources at the time believe that there was a hidden faction inside the Ilyrion government that *wanted* the War of Secession. It would have provided an abundant—and, most importantly, *legal*—way to create a great number of new darkprime Trees. At that time, you see, creating the Trees was already illegal."

"But why would Thylmanas go along with it?" Arra asked.

"They had no choice. They wanted to secede, and Ilyrion wouldn't let them. Thus, war. A war that killed tens of thousands of innocents, destroying families, ultimately wrecking civilization up here. Thylmanas would never go on to recover from the damage caused by that war—it faded. It took thirty thousand years, but the wound festered and the city died. And all for some spindly, horrible Trees."

"What hath magic wrought," Trey said.

Arra shivered. What hath magic wrought, indeed.

"What are we supposed to be looking for here, anyway?" Trey asked.

"A gate of some kind," Arra said. "Orym was cryptic as to where."

"He said he didn't quite remember. It's getting dark now, though. Let's make camp and continue the search tomorrow."

"Sounds good," Lashel said. "I'll be glad to get these damn tents off my back."

Trey looked at Arra. "You sure you're okay sharing a tent?"

"We're two adults," Arra said. "We'll be fine."

His face quirked a bit at that, as if she had wounded him. "Fine."

They set up the tents, not saying much else, waiting for night to fall.

# TWENTY-THREE

PHOENIX THRUST her fireblade out in front of her, red sparks showering into the nearby souls. They screamed as the magic hit them, reeling back in agony. But then they recovered, staggering forward, zombie-like in their movements. Phoenix felt the magic seeping out of her, energy funneling through the blade. There was a limit to how much longer she would be able to do this.

Eventually the souls would win.

An insect buzzed in her ear and she slapped at it, glancing at the spires behind her. Souls were still clambering across them, leaping from point to point with astonishing speed. They were already surrounding the group on the ground— Phoenix wasn't sure how much worse it could get.

They needed to leave now, or they were screwed.

Gates suddenly flickered into being all around them, figures pouring out to mix with the souls. Rough figures, with long, jata hair. Figures carrying machetes. Human figures.

The Remnant had finally arrived.

They yelled in defiance as they came, machetes swinging wildly, hacking into the souls with reckless abandon. Lightning appeared, grinning broadly, yelling at the Remnant to spread out and fight in threes. It seemed he'd been left in charge in Beam's absence. At least the Remnant hadn't been left entirely alone.

"Let's go!" she shouted to Elanil and Imra. The two of them nodded, forming up into a triangle formation. With hundreds of Remnant here to aid them, maybe they finally stood a fighting chance.

QUYNN DODGED a rapid slice to the throat, returning the blow with a strike of his own. The soul fell, but two more took its place. He prepared another strike, feeling the heaviness in his hand and arm. It had been ages since he'd wielded a sword. When had he learned it, anyway? His life stretched back so far—it could have been at almost any point.

He was just glad he still remembered the skill.

But he was growing tired now. This fight would need to end before too much longer. He could gate out, or fly, but it would mean leaving the rylak behind. And besides—he needed a way to actually *defeat* these souls. If there were more of them on Earth, he might not have a home to go back to.

There had to be a way.

He lifted his sword, muscles straining to make the move, when the two souls in front of him were suddenly struck down by an unseen blade.

A Remnant human stood in their place.

He grinned at Quynn, teeth bared in a feral expression, then turned to face the oncoming horde. Quynn found himself smiling in return.

Finally, some much-needed reinforcements!

He stepped up beside the nameless Remnant, the pair of them reaching out with their blades to cut down foe after foe. Quynn had killed many Remnant in the past, but he'd never thought to fight alongside one.

Times had certainly changed.

The Remnant made quick work of the souls. And the rylak, energized by the humans' sudden appearance, resurged into the fray. In moments they had cleared a huge circle in the souls. They were actually making progress! Perhaps this war *was* something they could win.

Another Remnant caught his attention. A woman, with the same long dreadlocks as the others. Her face was dirty, fierce, and there was something about her eyes. There was something about her muscles, too—she was *cut*, especially for a woman. But it was her eyes that had drawn him: they were a sparkling blue, an elven color, with an intelligence behind them that he hadn't expected.

And she was *strong*. Twins, she was strong. She dispatched soul after soul, charging into them without any hesitation. Quynn found himself lusting after her. Not since Phoenix had he felt this way about a human.

That was when a sword blade pierced his chest.

He lurched, pain spreading through his chest. He dimly saw a soul jeering at him, having somehow snuck up on him from behind. The world dimmed as he cursed his own stupidity.

A woman. It was always a woman that did him in.

ELANIL SAW the blade pierce Quynn, saw him start to go down. The soul behind him pulled the blade out, leering at him and cackling, not three feet from her.

She flung it away with elm, diving forward to catch Quynn as he fell. He was heavy but she managed it, using a bit of leafrunning to catch his weight. Then he was on the ground in her arms, bleeding out on the sand. Souls fought all around them, clashing with the Remnant and rylak forces. It was just Elanil and Quynn on the ground, and Quynn looked ready to die.

This was her chance to let him do it.

He had destroyed Sylrantheas, after all. He had killed so many people: her father, Fenian. He had worked for Lorelei, the woman who had killed *her*. And he was a Cothellon, an enemy elf, one of the imprisoners of humanity.

He was a very bad man.

But he was also Trey. The bad half, sure, but still half of him. And while that did not excuse the evil he had done, it did perhaps at least go partway toward explaining it.

But that wasn't the reason she was bent over him, touching him tentatively on the arm. It wasn't because of Trey that she called on the magic she knew he didn't have, pulling power from the Palm Tree far to the south.

It was because of her. Who she was.

She was not a villain. She was not evil.

She was not Quynn.

And so she healed him, feeling ice flowing out of her and into him, watching the wound repair, the bleeding stop. He gasped, eyes snapping to her own, and for an instant she saw something she never thought she'd see from this terrible, terrible man.

Gratitude.

# TWENTY-FOUR

RYLAN STOOD atop the tallest spire made of salt, feeling the sun beating horribly down on him. Nelenor and Velion were next to him, long blond hair gleaming in the desert light, watching the battle of the souls play out.

"The humans fight well," Velion said.

The Remnant were indeed fighting well—better than Rylan had ever seen Remnant fight, at least. These were different Remnant, he thought. Not the ones from Gulthurub. They fought together, more or less. They actually had skill with their weapons. He watched them kill souls by the hundreds, by the thousands, but they just kept coming.

"You should have seen them at Lusvunub," Nelenor said. "And not just these so-called Remnant—the ones from the sky cities also put up an interesting fight."

"The ones you killed," Rylan said. He was less afraid of them now. They were just people. Very powerful people, but people all the same.

"I had no choice," Nelenor said. "You think I should have let them kill me? Then Xyclami would be less one Operator, free to wreak its wild magic across the system."

150

"What would happen if just one of you died?"

"Xyclami was designed for two Operators," Velion said. "When only one is present, the power grows wild, chaotic— even more so than before. The device cannot be controlled by just one person. They would quickly be overwhelmed. Xyclami would take over for itself, becoming its own other controller, breaking down the Will of the sole Operator. Eventually it would be free to do as it pleased."

"Wait—you're telling me it would achieve *sentience*?"

"It already has," Nelenor said. "It is simply being kept in check by us. If the device is allowed to operate long enough without two Operators to bring it into check, it will devastate everything around it. It will become a power that is impossible to defeat."

"And you thought *we* were bad," Velion said, giving Rylan a smile. The expression looked strange, coming from her.

"You should not have created such a device," Rylan said.

"We were not the ones to do so," Velion said. "It was made by others far smarter than we. And Xyclami is not *nearly* the most dangerous device they made."

"Shit," Rylan said. He turned his gaze back out to the souls, trying to fit the pieces together in his mind. There was one thing that didn't make any sense, and he was staring right at it. "These souls," he said. "What are they?"

"Exactly that," Nelenor said. "Souls. The Thirteenth Power unmoored them from their bodies, transferring them instantly to Ambarhal in a process not unlike soulburning. We did not think Ambarhal could hold so many souls. Imprisoning us enlarged it greatly, which is probably why it happened. Ambarhal was not originally intended to hold the souls of the Operators themselves."

"Phoenix came back to life after being soulburned," Rylan said. "Why aren't they?"

"It is different. Sundering magic does not connect the souls to Xyclami—it simply throws them into Ambarhal, unmoored. As a result, they can never regain their physical form. They are stuck in a half-life, with no real Will or mind of their own."

"They seem dangerous enough."

"This is a poorly understood aspect of the magic, admittedly," Velion said. "As Operators, we are not trained for some of what occurred."

"Operators are not intended to be trapped inside the device," Nelenor said.

"You mentioned that," Rylan said. "So if they have no Will, what is driving them? And why are they here?"

"The imprisonment is ended," Velion said. "As such, they must be forced to leave Ambarhal. The burning Trees act as vessels for their departure, transitioning them out of the dimension and into this one. It is not a process we understand."

"And what drives them?"

"We do not know," Nelenor said. "It appears to be emotion."

"That makes sense, I guess," Rylan said. "If they don't really have conscious brains anymore, the only thing left to them would be emotion."

"Yes."

"So how do we stop them? And do you even want to?"

"We have no control over the souls," Velion said. "We could not stop them if we tried. And you must admit, they *do* form an excellent distraction for the ones who would otherwise be trying to kill *us*."

"They will overwhelm the world," Rylan said. "We can't just *leave* them here."

"We have no choice."

"There must be a way!"

"If emotion were to end," Nelenor said, "or perhaps dissipate—if the beings on this world did not hate and hurt and fear so strongly, perhaps the souls would themselves depart. We do not know."

"There's no chance of that happening," Rylan said.

"We must find the Imprisoner," Velion said. "He still hides from us."

"Please don't go back to killing my friends," Rylan said. "I thought you were past that."

"We cannot be past it," Velion said. "It is our mission now. We will find the Imprisoner, and then we will find our sister, and then we will leave."

"Yes," Nelenor said. "Orym must be out there somewhere. It is high time we reengaged the fight."

Rylan looked out once more at the battle of the souls, wondering if there was anything at all he could do to stop what was about to come.

# TWENTY-FIVE

LORELEI STOOD AMIDSHIPS, feet spread slightly, lips parted. Wind rushed through her hair, the westward sun shining on her as they sailed through the water. Well, they weren't *sailing*, exactly.

Lorelei was propelling them with magic.

It was exhilarating, in its own way. She had quickly gotten used to it, how it felt to keep the magic at a constant low level in the background, pushing the leafboat through the waves. It felt good to be out there on the ocean, smelling salt spray and relishing in the wind.

But she couldn't be happy.

Orym was out to kill them. She was sure of it. And not just them, but probably the *world*. The power he was after would do that, especially in his hands. And if there was one thing she'd learned about Orym over the many years she'd known him, it was that he always got what he wanted in the end.

The trouble was, nobody believed her.

So now she was stuck on a boat in the Airon Sea, heading toward an island she'd never been to, searching out a gate that would help Orym finally achieve his dreams. She was heading into the jaws of death, and she couldn't convince anyone to turn away.

At least she did enjoy the water. It had been far too long since she'd last sailed.

"You look unhappy," Allain said, coming up beside her on the deck. Dill and Erodar were somewhere toward the stern, exchanging stories about their respective city homes.

"I'm worried about Orym," Lorelei said. "And nobody here will believe me about him."

"I believe you," Allain said.

"Thank you."

She looked at him, at the way his jaw set, the way his eyes met hers. He really was well-muscled, much more so than she would have expected from a Sylranthean elf.

"What did you do in Sylrantheas?" she asked. "You're a mistweaver, so you must have been a Builder of some sort."

"I was a blacksmith by trade," Allain said, and she saw some kind of emotion flicker across his eyes. "Like my father."

"Is he—"

"Dead. Killed when Quynn attacked Sylrantheas. He was crushed by a pile of burning wood, saving the life of his friend."

"I'm—I'm sorry," Lorelei said. "He must have been a great man."

"He was," Allain said, and for a moment she saw something else in his face. Blame? Anger? Quynn had been responsible for that attack, not her. Still...

"I know I have a lot to make amends for," she said.

"You didn't kill him."

"I was in charge of the Cothellon. Quynn wasn't acting under my orders, but he *was* employed by me. So I suppose, in a way, I did have a role in killing your father. And for that, I'm sorry."

"I'm okay," Allain said.

Lorelei took a step toward him, conscious of the ever-present motion of the ship. The magic flowed through her fingers even as she continued the conversation with Allain.

"You're strong," she said. "Especially for your age."

He hung his head. She had hit a sensitive subject, apparently. He was worried about his age?

"My father died, too," she said, "when I was very young."

He regarded her curiously. "I'm sorry to hear that."

"My sister killed him."

"Twins."

"He deserved it, though. He murdered my mother in cold blood, right in front of me. Would have killed me, too, I'm sure. It was only a matter of time."

"I can't even imagine what that must have been like."

"Don't let your past define you, Allain. Twins know I have. Even when I couldn't *remember* my past, I let it define me far too much. Be who you want to be. Be your *best*. It sounds stupid, but that's the lesson I learned after all this time."

"I'm not sure if I know who that me is supposed to be."

She took another step toward him, bringing them close enough to touch. She laid a finger on his shoulder and left it there, unmoving. "You have a blacksmith's arms," she said, "but a carver's touch. There's art in the carvings you make, in the illusions you perform. And I think you have my smile."

Allain almost choked at that. "*Your* smile?"

"There's a certain mischievousness when I look at you. A certain darkness, I guess. An edge. It's what drew me to Quynn, I think. It's what's drawn me to a lot of men. You have that." He swallowed. "And don't worry about your age."

"Are you—uh—are you drawn to me?"

She gave him a smile. Honestly, she wasn't sure just yet. She couldn't deny that there was something about him that tantalized her, but she felt she didn't really know him yet. Still, that had never stopped her from getting in the sack before. And she'd fucked far worse specimens than this.

She drew her finger down his shoulder, tracing a line across his arm. "You'll find the answer to that soon," she said, smiling.

He swallowed again, his face growing red.

Men were so much fun to play with.

"So," she said, stepping away, letting the moment drop, "ask me something about me." She moved toward the bow of the boat, switching primewood chips to keep the motion going. Sometimes men had to be prodded along a little bit. She didn't mind.

"What was your Way?" he asked.

"Governor," Lorelei said. "Though the Cothellon mostly abandoned the Ways some thousand years ago."

"So you're a strengthshaper?"

"I'm a Prime Mage, but yes. That was my original Alignment. I killed my sister with that magic, one time."

"Cariel? But she—"

"The Twins healed her."

"Are you serious?"

"I was one of the first people on Valaralda to meet the Twins. They aren't who you think they are, Allain. They don't look like those Anubis monsters. They're just people, like us. Orym—Aten—is the *real* monster."

"I don't know how to convince Dill."

"It's going to take some kind of outside influence, I suspect. If he won't believe us, who *will* he believe?"

"You would have made a great Mentor," Allain said.

Lorelei found herself inexplicably blushing at that. "Why?"

"You just have that leadership quality. There's a certain urgency about everything you do, I guess. It's not magnetism, though you have that, too. It's sort of like...propulsion. Does that make any sense?"

"People think I'm a bully."

"People think that about me, too. They're not wrong."

"We're just misunderstood," Lorelei said. "It isn't that we hate people, it's just that we're impatient. We lack tact. At least, I assume that's the case with you. You've always been really nice to me."

"Arra never liked me very much."

"You two aren't a match," Lorelei said. "She's into nicer men, when she can get them. The more intellectual sort. But don't let that get you down—there are plenty of women who will be very interested in you."

"Really?"

"Come over here." She beckoned him to the side of the boat. He joined her at the edge, standing beside her and following her gaze out across the ocean. "This is how my life felt for thousands of years."

"What do you mean?"

"Like an ocean. Only waves, with no end in sight. It felt as if I were striving ever onward, with nothing but a flimsy rudder to guide me, never knowing if I would ever reach my destination."

"What *was* your destination?"

"Bringing Earth here," she said. "For a long time, that was my only goal. But I think my real destination is deeper. Earlier. It started when my parents died, when my sister disappeared. I struck out at the world, hoping it would strike back at me."

"You fought the world for the same reason I do," Allain said. "You just wanted to be loved."

She felt tears hit her in that moment, completely unexpected. His insight was startling in its simplicity. She had barely known him, and already he'd seen into the bright spot of her soul. Maybe they really were alike.

He placed his hand on top of hers on the silver side of the ship, the warm skin lending comfort. She glanced at him through watery eyes and saw the care reflected in his own. So she lifted her hand, taking her fingers and interlacing them through his. His hand was strong, his grip firm. He squeezed her hand, and the tears came even stronger.

"This isn't me," she whispered.

"You've been hurting for a long time," Allain said. "Let me help."

They stood like that for several minutes, hand in hand while the waves beat against the hull of the ship.

Some time later, she realized they were no longer moving. She extracted her hand from Allain's, pulling out more prime-wood and sending leafrunning magic flooding through the ship.

"Thank you," she said once they were underway.

"If you ever need to talk," Allain said, "I'm here."

"Blacksmiths can talk?" But she smiled when she said it.

He grinned. "We can do more than just talk."

She reached up and squeezed his bicep. "I bet."

He blushed.

There were benefits to being with one as young as Allain, she realized. His innocence was refreshing. "When we get out of this," she said, "you need to take me to a proper dinner. If there are even any restaurants left, anywhere." Her tears had cleared.

"I'd like that," Allain said. "I still can't believe I'm here with you."

"Don't press your luck," Lorelei said. "I'm a hot commodity!"

His face fell at that. So she leaned over and kissed him on the cheek. "So hot, everyone wants to kill me!"

"What?" Allain said, his face reddening again. "But you're on our side now. Nobody wants to kill you."

"Arra still might, given half the chance." She frowned. "No. That's not fair. Arra and I patched things up, I think, at least as well as we can. Now, things with Trey are a different matter entirely." She shook her head. "I still can't believe Quynn is actually Trey. It makes no sense, and yet it makes *perfect* sense."

"You were in love with him."

Love again. Always love. Did all elves focus on love?

Was she the one who was deluded?

"Yes," she said after a moment. "I think I *was* in love with him, from a distance, twenty thousand years ago. But no more. And never with Quynn. That man was too one-dimensional to ever be more than a toy to me. I guess I know why now. He wasn't an entire man."

"Perhaps it's time to start fresh," Allain said, reaching over and taking her hand. He was growing more forward by the minute.

She liked it.

"I think you're right," Lorelei said. "I would like that very much. Dating twenty-thousand-year-old men isn't quite what it's cracked up to be."

He squeezed her hand in response. They stared outward at the waves, watching the sky slip by. Lorelei wondered if there was a destination waiting for them, just beyond the far horizon. Perhaps it was the one she'd been waiting for her entire life.

Perhaps that destination was already standing next to her.

"Lovebirds," Dill said, coming up to stand beside them, "Rylan's on the radio."

Lorelei felt a flash of anger at the remark, but she clamped it down as quickly as it had come. She wasn't in love with Allain. She wasn't in love with *anyone*—not now. But why should the verbiage bother her? Maybe it was time to lighten up—*especially* about love.

"Guys," Rylan's voice said over the radio in Dill's hand, "Velion and Nelenor are about to join the battle at the Salt Spires. Whatever you're up to, do it quick. Oh, and in case you didn't hear: Orym is the Imprisoner. I've heard their story, and it sounds like he treated the Twins *very* badly when they landed here on Valaralda. He's not to be trusted. I have to go."

The radio went silent.

Dill gave a heavy sigh. "Dammit," he said, "I guess I need to start coming to terms with the fact that my father might in fact be a very bad man."

"Finally," Lorelei said.

# TWENTY-SIX

PHOENIX WAS STRUGGLING to stay alive. Alive and awake—she wasn't sure which of them was harder. Her fireblade slipped and her opponent managed to hit her with a devastating strike, pain shooting through her arm. She almost dropped her blade as she gasped, trying not to scream. It was all she could do to send some joy into the blade, green particles flowing out of it and surrounding her, healing her.

But it wasn't enough. She was too weak.

Then Elanil was there, Book of Amplification in one hand, her other hand reaching out to Phoenix. She felt soul-soothing flowing through her, her wound closing in a jolt of icy healing. Then she took a deep breath, feeling momentarily refreshed. She knew the feeling would not last long—this battle needed to end.

The souls would outlast them all.

"Oh, shit," Elanil breathed, and Phoenix looked up to see the sight she had been dreading.

The Twins had finally arrived.

They were no longer in their Anubis forms. Still, they were recognizable: larger-than-life elves, flowing blond hair streaming out behind them, faces incredibly beautiful. The sun was dwindling toward the horizon, but a kind of unnatural glow surrounded the Twins as they floated calmly in from somewhere to the east. They landed on a nearby spire, faces looking disdainful.

Everyone—including the souls—stopped to face them.

"Not good," Phoenix muttered.

"Get ready with a shield," Imra said.

"Greetings," the Twin on the right said. Was it a woman? Phoenix had thought the Twins to both be men. Her voice was amplified via strengthshaping, easily audible even from a distance. "My name is Velion. Please give us the Imprisoner. This will be your final warning."

Phoenix channeled pity through her blade. Strengthshaping magic coursed through her, amplifying her voice. "We do not have him," she said. "Orym is not here."

"Very well," Velion said, and she raised her hand to the sky.

Phoenix put a forcefield around as large a radius as she could.

Powerful, unformed magic struck them then, red particles blazing outward from Velion and impacting her shield. She had managed to protect all the rylak and most of the Remnant forces, though she could already feel the strain from channeling that much energy.

The magic ended as quickly as it had come. "You are very quick with those shields," Velion said. "But can you keep them up forever?"

"We're in trouble," Phoenix said to the women next to her.

"We can't attack them directly," Imra said. "Cresius said there were magical traps here, right? That's why we came to this awful place."

"That's right," Elanil said. "Maybe we can find one, lure the Twins to it?"

"But how?" Imra asked.

"I might have an idea," Phoenix said.

"I'LL SHIELD US," Elanil said, reaching into her pouch for some dark ash. "With the Book, I should be able to hold it for quite some time. You two do whatever your idea is." She looked around for Quynn. He was standing next to Talon, eyes looking tired in the twilight. "Are you okay here?" she asked him.

He nodded. "We can hold the souls. Go show those Twins a fight."

He seemed to respect her a little now. Or maybe she was just imagining things.

"Let's go," she said to Phoenix and Imra, and they took flight.

"Hello again," Nelenor said as they approached, flying toward him across the spires. All around them, the souls had resumed their battle. Elanil saw Remnant humans fighting side-by-side with growling rylak, fists and claws and machetes flying.

"You look better as an elf," Elanil said, dark ash held tightly in her hand. She also had dark maple and light elm, the magics that powered her flight. Part of her mind was holding herself and Imra in the air. The other part was focused on the Twins. "Where's Rylan?"

"There," Nelenor said, pointing. Rylan was standing on a different spire, alone. His face looked plaintive in the dimming light. "Perhaps if you'd given us the Imprisoner, he would not be here now."

"If you weren't so vindictive," Elanil said, "*none* of us would be here now."

"Bold words," Velion said, and she shot more light at them.

Elanil had a forcefield up just in time, strengthening it with the Book of Amplification. Velion's magic scattered harmlessly off the edge of the shield, but she could see a bit of humor in the female Twin's eyes.

She was enjoying this.

"Whatever your plan was," Elanil said to Phoenix, "do it now!"

Energy burst against the forcefield, pushing against it harder than Elanil had dreamed possible. She could feel it suffusing the shield, coursing through it, beating against it. She strained, using the Book to amplify the forcefield, barely able to keep up with Velion's strength as she ratcheted up her power bit by bit.

The Twins were *strong*.

"Follow me with that shield," Phoenix said. "I'm going to move."

Elanil nodded, teeth gritted as she struggled to maintain the magic. Phoenix was doing something with her blade: golden sparks were flitting out of it like fireflies, meandering about the air as if seeking a new home. Or as if they were looking for something hidden, which is probably what they were doing.

"Creativity," Phoenix said. "Not a state of mind I'm used to. But they had to be creative to make these traps, right?"

"Sure," Elanil said. Velion was still pummeling the force-field with bright red light.

"There," Imra said, and Elanil saw three glimmering golden sparks fly off in a different direction. The women followed, Elanil being careful to keep the forcefield centered on them in the air. Velion had an actual smile on her face now, hand raised as she casually sent torrents of Destroyer magic into Elanil's shield. Would the Twins ever tire? Somehow she doubted it.

Like the souls, the Twins would outlast them all.

"We have to draw them to us!" Imra shouted. The battle had moved out onto the spires, Remnant and rylak and souls jumping from tip to tip, striking at each other with whatever they had. The Twins, meanwhile, had not moved at all.

"Let me try something!" Elanil shouted, digging in her pouch for more wood. Then she flipped the forcefield one-way, shooting a burst of shockstriking magic out through it, heading toward the Twins, using the Book of Amplification to make it as big as possible.

A *massive* blast of bright blue light shot out at them, striking Nelenor squarely in the chest. He lurched backward in surprise, pain evident on his face.

"Well struck, young one!" he shouted across the battle-field, rising into the air as he said it. Velion followed suit.

Step one done. Now for step two.

"If you want us, you'll have to come and get us!" Elanil shouted, using strengthshaping to make herself heard. She shot another blast of shockstriking at them to make her point, then began moving in the air, following Phoenix. They chased the tiny golden globes, following them as they located the first trap. It didn't take very long.

Then the Twins were on them, both of them looming behind the women, looking like glowing, blond angels of death. Both were shooting fire at Elanil's shield, and it was all she could do to hang on. She flew just past where the glimmer had revealed the trap—it was positioned at the top of one of the spires. She was careful to skirt that spire, not flying directly over the top of it. Then she curved back around, leading the Twins in a straight line.

It worked exactly as she had planned.

She thought she saw the golden glimmer expand slightly just before the trap hit. Then something strange happened, and the entire world went wild.

The air *warped*, flexing as if being bent by an unseen force. Everything expanded out from a central point, blasting outward with incredible force. Elanil lost her forcefield in the confusion, and she felt the power of it slamming into her.

Everyone and everything flew outward violently, hurtling through the air. Spires shattered into fragments, flinging out in sharp segments, slicing through Elanil's skin. She heard screams and saw the Remnant flying, heads and bodies slamming into spires and falling to the ground a hundred feet below. She and Phoenix and Imra were flung several hundred feet away from the trap, the force of it enough to break bones. Elanil felt her neck strain, her head dangerously compressed from the strength of it.

And that had only been the first explosion.

It set off a chain from there, more traps triggering as the strange force hit them. Spire after spire disintegrated, motion pulsing outward from trap after trap. Nelenor and Velion were caught right in the center of it, their bodies flung around like puppets in the air. She heard them grunting audibly, but she was too distracted by the pain in her own body to make much sense out of what was going on.

She was very *very* injured.

So were Phoenix and Imra. So were scores of Remnant who had been caught in the blast. The spires had all been destroyed in a huge radius, and she could see bodies lying crumpled everywhere, groaning and struggling to move. She herself was barely conscious, the blast having pummeled her entire body with its hidden force.

Leafrunning magic.

That was what it was. It had to have been—the traps were magical, after all. Hadn't she done something very similar in Ilyrion, when she defeated the souls there?

The only trouble was, the trap had also acted against her side of the fight, decimating their numbers in one fell swoop. How could they have been so stupid? They needed to keep their troops away from the traps—but how? Nobody knew where the traps even were.

She was fading quickly. Everyone was dead or dying around her, and she was floating uselessly in the air. So she pulled magic in from her Prime Palm on Tanomar, sending soulsoothing magic through her with an icy shock. She felt better almost immediately.

It gave her an idea.

She clutched the Book of Amplification in her hand, channeling soulsoothing magic again. This time she used the Book, amplifying the magic as far as it would go, Willing everyone and everything in the vicinity to repair, correct, heal with the magic's touch. She didn't know if it would work. Soulsoothing required physical contact, after all. But wouldn't the Book do something different? Didn't it always stretch the boundaries of magic?

She was about to find out.

She saw it as it happened. A circle rippled out of her, green sparks scintillating across the spires. It touched everyone as it passed, sending backs arching and mouths wide. It caught Phoenix and Imra in its power, and she could see their wounds healing before her eyes. The magic rippled out and out, soulsoothing everyone who was still alive. It felt glorious, powerful, as if she could do anything! Joy suffused her as the soothing did its work, rippling across the spires.

Then it reached the Twins.

And they healed, too. Any damage the leafbomb trap had done was instantly nullified, fixed by Elanil's powerful tide of healing.

And just like that, everyone was back to the way they were before.

"Shit," Elanil swore.

Phoenix nodded. "We'll have to try again."

"Find another trap," Elanil said, "and this time we need to get further away from it, if we can. Lightning!" She spotted the man on the ground, getting up from her soulsoothing and shaking his head as if dazed. She swooped down to him. "Watch where we're going," she said. "Track our movements in the sky. We're drawing the Twins into magic traps, and you need to keep the Remnant away from us."

"Okay," he said. "Twins. I feel great now, but that *hurt*."

"Sorry," Elanil said. "I healed you as best I could."

"Thanks. I'll keep the Remnant away. Where are those damn Prime Mages? They should be here by now. We could really use the help."

Souls were already returning through the spires, streaming in from all directions. And the Twins were moving back toward Elanil and Phoenix, anger written on their faces. Elanil readied dark ash in her hand, preparing to put another forcefield up around them.

"Stay safe," she said to Lightning, and rose once more into the sky.

She hoped the other traps in this strange land were more useful than the first.

# TWENTY-SEVEN

PHOENIX SHOOK HER HEAD, trying to clear it. That succession of leafrunning blasts followed by Elanil's wide-area healing had felt like whiplash—one moment near death, the next feeling better than she ever had before. She knew it would only be a few minutes before the weariness set in again.

"Let's go," she said, watching as Elanil's forcefield returned around them. The Twins fired at them just as it did, multicolored blasts of unformed magic striking the shield with torrents of energy. "I'll draw them this time," she said to Elanil, and the girl nodded. Her jaw was set, her face flushed. She was so strong for a fifteen year old. Phoenix hoped things worked out between Rylan and Elanil—they were a good match.

"Let me help," Imra said, drawing an arrow.

Phoenix nodded, sending Destroyer magic out from her blade, winding it around the arrow. The Twins were near again, their faces a mask of rage. Phoenix held her hand on Imra's shoulder, keeping them connected while their magic did its work.

The arrow flew well, exploding on Nelenor in a shower of light. He roared in anger, moving toward them furiously.

Phoenix sent more golden sparks from the blade, watching them weave about the air. The sun was mostly down now, only a glimmer of it remaining. The golden sparks shone more brightly in its absence, curving and arcing as they sought other latent magic.

It only took them minutes to find the next trap, at the edge where the spires resumed. Phoenix helped Imra with another arrow, drawing yet more ire from the Twins. Elanil was struggling with the forcefield, she could see. They needed to wrap this up. Even with the Book, there was a limit to how much she could do.

Hopefully this trap did something useful.

"I see it," Imra said, keeping her voice quiet in case the Twins could hear. Phoenix glanced at Elanil, saw the girl nod, and flew toward the spire with the trap. She weaved around it at the last second, then put on a burst of speed. Elanil followed, bringing the forcefield with them as they moved. And the Twins followed all of them. All was proceeding according to the plan.

They were a hundred yards away when the trap triggered.

Cold air blasted outward from the spire, sending sleet and snow flying in a huge sphere. This time Elanil kept the force-field up around them, so they weren't affected. But Phoenix could see and hear the frozen storm shoot out in a thick wall of white, instantly freezing everything. It was stormwarden magic, stronger than she'd ever seen before.

But it was useless.

The Twins just powered through it, Destroyer fire instantly reversing the freezing effects of the trap. The sun finally dipped completely below the horizon as the Twins roared with rage, and Phoenix knew then that the situation might be hopeless.

She'd never seen anything like these magical traps. But for all their ingenuity and power, they were completely useless.

They would not defeat the Twins.

ELANIL WATCHED the souls pouring in from everywhere. The Twins were burning off the ice, swooping toward them with malice in their eyes. It had been another useless trap, but at least it hadn't hurt or killed anyone on their side in the process.

This was getting them nowhere.

"We need to try something else," Elanil said.

"Open to suggestions!" Phoenix said.

"I'm going to find Rylan. Maybe he knows how to stop the Twins."

"Don't you think he would have done it already if he knew?"

"I need to talk to him. Maybe the two of us can figure it out."

"Don't leave us, Elanil," Phoenix said. "We need your help with the shield. I'm too tired to do much more of this."

"Stay strong just for a little while longer," Elanil said. "Or run—there's no shame in that. This is a fight we can't win. Not with what we have, anyway. I'm going to find Rylan."

"Are you sure it's safe? You know what Rylan did last time."

"It's a risk I'm willing to take."

Phoenix flew over to her, placing a hand on her arm. "Be safe. I don't want anything to happen to you. And tell my son I want him back."

"I will," Elanil said. "Good luck."

She flew away, trying to remember which spire Rylan had been standing on.

Maybe he would know what to do.

# TWENTY-EIGHT

THERE WERE ONLY TWO TENTS, and the Thylmanas night was bitter cold. There was a moment of indecision—why had they only brought two tents?—but in the end they decided that the married couple should share, while Lashel slept on his own.

They had eaten a cold meal of salted venison—an Errenmel delicacy, apparently—and beans and a bit of wine Trey had managed to find from the store they'd ransacked. They'd sipped and talked underneath the stars for an hour or so, but the conversation felt hollow. There was a subtext to everything Trey and Arra said, feelings that needed to bubble to the surface.

So they'd said their goodnights and headed to their respective tents. Arra wasn't sure how she felt about the whole thing. Now she was stuck in close proximity to a man she wasn't sure about, forced to spend the night in a place she didn't want to be. Was there an expectation, here? Did Trey think something was going to happen?

She didn't know if she wanted anything to happen.

"You're different, today," Trey said after a few minutes.

They were laying in the pitch dark tent, sleeping rolls kept chastely several inches apart.

Arra took a deep breath. This conversation was not one she particularly wanted to have right now. "What do you mean?"

"You seem a little colder."

"It's cold up here, Trey."

"Toward me."

She gave a little sigh. "I know."

They were silent for a time.

"It's Quynn," Trey said. "Isn't it."

Arra didn't answer.

"Now you know who I really am," Trey said. "Who I could become, given half a chance. Now you're thinking back to all those times with me—those *bad* times—and you're remembering who I was when Quynn was still a part of me. And you don't like what you remember. Am I wrong?"

Arra paused before answering. Should she go down this road? There are some things you can't unsay. "You're not wrong."

He seemed to digest that for a moment. Maybe he hadn't actually expected her to respond that way. "The Quynn in me has always been too strong," he said. "Things have been easier with him gone—to a point. But my life doesn't feel complete, you know? Part of that was New San Francisco—" He stopped suddenly, and Arra thought she caught a note of grief in his voice. She turned toward him, straining to make out his face in the dark. She could just barely do it.

"Are you okay?" she asked.

"New San Francisco was my *home*," he said. "At least for a while. A long while. I walked those streets every day, with a book in my hand. I dusted my store. I had *friends*, Arra. I

175

almost had a family. I think I may have actually had love. Lorelei wasn't entirely dishonest about that much."

"I know." She couldn't help the hurt that crept into her tone.

"I'm sorry. I didn't mean to bring her up. It's just—I can't believe the city is *gone*. Just gone. And I wasn't even there to see it go."

He was crying now. She wanted to reach out to touch him, to comfort him, but she couldn't bring herself to do it. He wasn't hers to hold, anymore. She hadn't lived in that city with him. He had lived a fragmented life, even more than she. He had lived a lot of lies, and not all of them were of his making.

He had a lot of wrong to make up for.

But he had a lot of right, too. A lot of love. They had been in love, even up until the end. They had never lost that, even as their world crumbled down around them. Even as he railed and researched, she had still loved him. Deep down she knew that his energy was what had drawn her. That his need to discover the world had complemented her need to experience it. She'd known that he was strong, that he was inherently good, but that his impulses would get the better of him.

He had been strong in the wrong ways, in the end.

"Do you love me?" she asked. She knew the answer.

"Yes."

"Why?"

"I—" He paused. "It's your passion. Your sense of adventure. The way you approach every problem without hesitation."

"I hesitate a lot."

"Not like me. You actually get stuff *done*, Arra, while I—it doesn't matter."

"You love me because I get stuff done?"

"This isn't coming out right. You're beautiful, and strong, and intelligent, and—"

"You never thought I was very intelligent when you were doing your research."

"I was too focused on it, Arra. I know I didn't let you in. I know I made mistakes. I wish I could *remember* all of them—I'd apologize so much."

"I don't think it matters," she said, and she felt coldness seeping through her body.

"It matters. This matters. *You* matter."

"I don't think I do." She turned away.

"What would you have me do?" he asked after a moment.

She sighed. "We need to save the world. Worlds, I guess. We need to defeat the Twins and not die in the process. After that? I'm not sure. I feel as if I don't know who you are, Trey, and I'm not sure if you ever *really* knew me. Can a marriage survive twenty thousand years?"

"I'd like to try."

"I know. I'm just—" She'd given this a lot of thought over the past few days. She just didn't think he was ready to hear her answer.

"You *know* I love you," he said. "I couldn't bear to see you on that cross, dying for your mother's plan. Twins—I couldn't bear to see you with Fenian, but I want the best for you, Arra. I still think I'm the man for you, but if you don't..." He left the sentence hanging.

There are some things that can't be unsaid.

Arra wasn't ready for that yet.

She turned back to him.

"We were good together, in the beginning," she said. Her face was close to his. She could see the tears falling sideways from his eyes.

He nodded, smiling. "We were. Do you remember our first

date? You took me knife throwing. Knife throwing! Who even *does* that?"

"Sense of adventure."

"We did so much together, back then. Horseback riding, archery, gardening. Camping in the woods. We used to cook dinner together, but we could never get through it all."

She smiled at the memory. "We couldn't keep our hands off each other."

"Twins, Arra. You're the hottest girl I've ever met. Still."

He wasn't so bad himself. But instead she said, "You were always lusting after Leriaar."

"Never," Trey said. "Never, and you know that. Don't you? Haven't I always been honest with you? Yes, she's pretty. Twins—anybody can see that. But she's not the only pretty woman who isn't you. She doesn't have a monopoly on being hot. And besides—she wasn't a match for me. We would never have worked."

"But you *did* work. For three entire years."

She saw him wince at that. "She wasn't herself. She didn't even *look* like herself. She was a lot nicer to me than her real self is. She had to keep up the facade, you know? She had to get me to marry her. That was the game she and Quynn were playing."

"She and *you*, you mean."

"I—shit."

It sounded like he hadn't fully thought this through. She waited.

"Quynn represents my baser instincts," Trey said. "I think at first I had him under control, back when we were first married. But later, he got stronger. Too strong."

She thought back to the day of their wedding. To the look in his eyes as he had stared out at the setting sun. There had been a kind of darkness in his eyes, a burning passion she could not identify or explain. A passion that was not for her.

She had never been enough for him.

"What do you think will happen," she asked, "if you and Quynn reunite?"

Trey shuddered visibly. "He'll take over. I know he will. I'll be back to making the same mistakes I did before. The ones I made with you."

"Maybe you can keep him in check, this time. Have you grown stronger, being on your own?"

"I don't know. I don't think so. If anything, I've probably grown weaker without him around. I haven't had to fight my personality, my baser instincts. I've been walking around in a malaise. I've been aimless."

"Doesn't that make you want him back? You were never like that before."

"I was *too* driven, before. But I see your point. You're right, I guess. I should reintegrate with him. I should fight through that conflict. Maybe I'll end up a better man as a result. Or maybe I'll lose myself along the way."

She wanted to believe he'd make it through okay, but her history with him said otherwise. She couldn't tell him that, though. She couldn't tell him a lot of things.

"I just want you to be happy," Trey said, and Arra broke down into tears.

He held her, then, and she allowed it. It felt good to have his arms around her. But it also felt strange, like a foreign presence around her heart.

She didn't know when it had changed to that. Hadn't they had a wonderful moment in that tree hollow? Hadn't they kissed, and loved it? Hadn't she felt a connection to him then?

Shouldn't she kiss him now?

She couldn't bring herself to do it.

But he came in for it, his lips meeting hers. And she couldn't deny him, even though her head wanted to.

Her heart had other ideas.

The kiss was sweet. She found herself melting into his embrace, their lips connecting perfectly in the night. Her head was working furiously against it, but her body was responding in kind. She pressed into him, their tongues intertwining, hands on each other's backs. She could taste his tears, and for a moment she believed he actually loved her.

Then the moment ended.

She pulled back, tears drying in her eyes, and looked at him in the dark. He was beautiful, if she was being honest with herself. His eyes were kind. But his eyes were not truly *his*—they were simply his best Aspects, a fraction of himself. His hands were not his own—they were half a hand, half a touch. His words were not his own, and neither was his heart. She didn't know the man in front of her, and she didn't know if she could trust him.

She kissed him again anyway.

This time he pulled back first. "Hey," he said. "I love you. I *love* you. I don't know what things will be like once Quynn comes back—if that happens—but I remember you. I remember us. I don't remember all the mistakes, but I remember some. I don't remember all the evil I did, but I remember the pain. I've always been so conflicted, so in my head. I wasn't the person you needed me to be, Arra. I wasn't the person *I* needed me to be. But I want to change that. Starting now."

And he kissed her, and the passion was evident on his lips. It wasn't a physical passion. It was deeper, truer. He *did* love her, or at least he loved his image of her. They *had* had good times together, at least for a while. For a fleeting several hundred years, they had been the shining example to couples everywhere.

Or at least that's the image everyone else had seen.

But she didn't want to think about that now. She was done thinking. She wanted to surrender herself to him, to this moment, to see where the feelings led. If he loved her—if she loved him—perhaps she'd find out now. He peeled her shirt off and kissed her neck, and she felt his arms and the stubble on his cheeks and his hot lips on her skin. She tried to forget the anger, the violence he had shown. She tried not to think about his lust, how he had ignored her, how he had been so wretchedly focused on his own ends that he had spared no thought for hers. As his hands found her breasts for the first time in thousands of years, she shuddered in the frigid night.

And as she surrendered herself to him, she remembered what their connection had been like. It had been magical, and it was now—like nothing she had ever felt. She reached for him and their limbs intertwined, their lips pressed together once again. She pulled his shirt off and their skin was finally touching, hot breath steaming up the tent. He knew just how to touch her, even after all these years. There was a gentleness to his hands, to his lips, to his hips as he laid against her in the tent. There was a gentleness and a strength, but it was a different kind of strength.

The part of him that was Quynn was gone.

They stayed like that for what seemed like hours, just feeling each other's naked skin in the dark. His lips were warm, his touch soft, and Arra couldn't help but revel in it. It was real. It was a connection that she couldn't deny. The emotions that clouded her head didn't matter—this was primal, perfect. This was what love could be, if only all the other stuff could just get out of the way.

She wasn't sure that it could.

But she let him slip inside her, gasping as she felt their bodies connect. It was bliss and it was pain, the pure agony of clashing souls. The anticipation of it all had been building for so long, and now that the moment had finally come...it was *glorious*. He felt so good inside her, his body melding perfectly with her own. She tasted his lips and his tongue, pleasure rippling through her as he moved, and for a long time she was nothing more than happy. She was content. This was where she wanted to be.

There are some things that can't be unsaid.

You don't say them in case you're wrong.

Arra wasn't sure if she was wrong, but she was glad she hadn't said them. She was glad as she cried out in pleasure, as she moved atop him, surrendering herself to the moment. She remembered their good times as they made love to each other, and there had been many. The bad had overshadowed them in her mind, but not now. They didn't need to. Now was only bliss, only their bodies merging together as one. Now, Trey actually loved her.

It was one of the most beautiful moments of her life.

# TWENTY-NINE

"SO WHAT SHOULD WE DO?" Allain asked. The boat had stopped. Dill seemed finally ready to admit that his father might in fact be a problem.

Allain reluctantly removed his hand from Lorelei's. They had made so much progress in just a few short minutes, and now his head was in a whirl. She was so intoxicating, so palpable. The hundred thousand year age gap was…interesting. He supposed it didn't matter in the end.

"I'm still not sure what to believe," Dill said. "Can my father really want to take over the world?"

"It's not the world he's after," Lorelei said. "It's magic itself. Wouldn't you want that, given half the chance?"

"No. What would I possibly do with control of magic itself?"

"Whatever you wanted to. That's the entire point."

"No good will come of it."

"That's exactly what I've been trying to tell you."

Dill sighed. "Okay. He might still have surveillance out here via satellites, but we'll have to take that risk. If Orym really is the Imprisoner, and really means harm to these worlds—either intentionally or unintentionally—then obviously we can't follow his plan. We can't go to Tanomar."

"So what will we do?" Allain asked.

"We need to stop Orym," Lorelei said.

"Don't we need to stop the Twins first?" Dill asked.

"We don't know how to do that," Lorelei said. "Nobody does."

"Nobody but my father. Or at least that's what he claims. What if his Offensive System actually *works*? Isn't that the trick we need to stop the Twins?"

"It will hand their power directly to him if it works. We can't let that happen."

"Then we're stuck," Dill said. "Damned if we do, fucked if we don't."

"You're not taking this very well."

"He's my *father*, dammit! Why would I take it well? All this time, sure he's been a bit prickly." Lorelei raised her eyebrows. "Okay, *very* prickly. And in charge, and mysterious, always seeking out the next big thing. But *evil*? No."

"He was verging on evil when he was younger," Lorelei said. "But we all were, I suppose. No, I don't think Orym is outright evil now. He's just misguided. But his mistakes could literally mean the end of multiple worlds, or worse. We just can't let it happen."

Dill leaned against the side of the ship, staring out at the waves. "My mother. Tiala. I think she always knew that Orym had a dark side, a past he didn't want to relate. It turns out he didn't even *remember* his past, but I guess it amounts to the same thing. It took her a while, but she saw through him."

"She left him?" Lorelei asked.

Dill nodded. "I haven't seen her since. That was before the Sundering, so it's been a long time. I wonder what she's doing now. I wonder if she's still alive."

"Was she in the sky cities?"

"I don't know. Twins—I hope she wasn't in New San Francisco."

"Do you want to see her again?"

"I would like that more than anything."

"Then let's figure out what we're going to do," Lorelei said. "Personally, I think we should return to what we're good at, where we're from: the United Sky Cities."

"Not united anymore."

"No. But that's where Jalnab—John—is. He may need help activating his Escape Module."

"We could try to find the others," Allain said. "Disrupt Orym's plan further."

"That might be dangerous," Dill said. "If Orym is keeping track of all our whereabouts, he might become violent if we attack his plan directly."

"Aren't you worried about what might happen if we leave?"

"Not entirely. In fact, that might work to our advantage. If we're on Earth, near this Escape Module, it might draw Orym to us. If we can get him there before he gains Guruthos, maybe we can actually stop him."

"He'll just find someone else to go to Tanomar," Allain said.

"True," Dill said, "but at least this will delay him. I think Lorelei is right—we should go back to Earth."

"Nothing like the present," Lorelei said. "It will be good to be back."

A gate flashed into existence on the deck, the whirling white-orange light making Allain's eyes hurt. A vision of Earth was visible through it: city streets, tall buildings.

"Ah," Lorelei said. "I lucked into that. There's no way of

telling where the cities are positioned right now, but I made a guess."

"Let's be off," Dill said. "You can find your way around the cities?"

Lorelei nodded. "I was in charge of everything, after all."

She stepped through the gate, Dill following after.

Allain took one last look at the ocean from inside the boat, hoping they were making the right decision.

# THIRTY

QUYNN WAS BEGINNING to wonder if the fight was useless. It was full night now, and the souls just kept coming. The moon was up, shining whitely on the spires. He and the rylak were still fighting in the desert nearby, doing their best to stem the tide of souls that continued to arrive.

It was a completely fruitless endeavor.

Something had to change. Something had to give. Either the souls would finally stop coming, or the rylak and the Remnant would all die. Either way, it was going to happen soon.

Quynn had no more energy left to fight.

Gates flashed into existence all around him, scores of new people running through. They were clad in what appeared to be purple robes, golden chains hung about their necks. They looked gaudy, stupid. He was opening his mouth to say something about it when they immediately set to work.

At least a hundred of them flew up into the air, bright bursts of shockstriking light flying in a hundred different directions. The electricity brought the souls to their knees instantly, killing many of them outright. He saw leafrunning magic rip more souls thousands of feet away, arcing through the air and falling into the Salt Spires to the north. Stormwarden magic filled the sky, lightning bolts and wind further disrupting the souls. Within seconds, thousands of them were dead.

But the mages were just getting started.

They broke into groups of six, forming little cells of mages that moved together as one. Each cell darted about independently, showering the souls with magic of all kinds. There must have been over three hundred of them now, the gates retracting once they'd delivered them all to the Spires.

"Finally," a voice said in Quynn's ear. He turned to see a tall, dark man standing there, giving him a rakish grin. "Took them long enough to arrive."

"And you are?" Quynn asked.

"Name's Lightning," the man said. "And *those* are the Prime Mages of Ambarhal. Quite the fighting force."

"Greetings," another voice said, and Cresius XXV appeared. "Quynn, I see you've met Lightning. Sorry it took so long to get here, but I needed to give them some form of rudimentary training."

"And new clothes, it would seem," Quynn said.

Cresius nodded. "You'll forgive me my eccentricities."

"Now's not really the time for them," Quynn said, "but you're here now."

The souls were dying by the thousands, mown down by the incredible power of the Prime Mages. They worked together fabulously, each power complimenting each other as they used them to devastating effect.

But more souls kept coming. And coming. Prime Trees appeared, burning in the night, divulging their contents onto the sands. There appeared to be no end to the horrible creatures.

Quynn was getting sick and tired of them. "It's never going to end," he said.

"It will end eventually," Cresius said. "And anyway, it's not the souls I'm worried about. It's *them*."

He pointed, and Quynn saw the Twins standing on a spire far away, bathed in a glow of their own making. They were twenty feet tall, guised in the form of elves, looking out at the battle with anger written on their faces.

"Let's hope Phoenix can keep them occupied," Quynn said. "Otherwise, we're toast."

PHOENIX WATCHED the Prime Mages arrive, gates sparkling in the night. Elanil had left, trying to find Rylan. The Twins were still enraged, and it was all Phoenix could do to keep them at bay. She had stopped leading them toward traps, for now. She wasn't sure if any of them were strong enough to do any damage.

She watched the Prime Mages fight the souls for a minute, keeping a forcefield up around her in case the Twins attacked again. The mages were quite effective, at least, though there seemed to be an almost inexhaustible supply of souls. All this senseless violence, and for what? She didn't understand why the souls were even here, much less why they were fighting.

A figure rose up to her and Imra, flanked by two Prime Mages. It was Cresius.

"Greetings," he said, long robe flowing as he hovered in the night. "How goes the fight?"

"Careful," Phoenix said, just as a blast of red magic hit her shield. She managed to extend it to include Cresius and his two attendants, narrowly preventing them from being incinerated by the Twin's attack.

"Not well, I take it," Cresius said.

"They're unstoppable," Phoenix said. "Both the Twins *and* the souls. I'm glad the mages are here now, but do you have any new ideas?"

"We managed a few quick training sessions," he said. "Some of our more advanced techniques. I paired the Prime Mages with my Elite. Hopefully they'll have an effect. At least we have the numbers on our side now."

"I'm not sure that it matters. And besides, there will always be more souls at the ready."

"The souls are easy to destroy. It's the Twins I'm worried about."

"Why are we here, anyway?" Phoenix asked. "The traps don't do anything. We triggered two of them, and nothing impacted the Twins."

"Ah," Cresius said. "I suspect that's because you simply haven't found the right ones, yet."

"Well let's get to it, then!"

"Very well," Cresius said, nodding to his two attendants. "Keep that shield up and follow me."

# THIRTY-ONE

"TELL ME WHICH TRAPS YOU HIT," Cresius said, flying next to Phoenix and Imra in the night. His two attendants were doing the flying for him, evidently. He was a mergemelder.

"One that hit us with a ton of leafrunning magic, I think," Phoenix said. "And another that turned into something like a giant snowball."

"A leafbomb and an iceweaver," Cresius said. "Those two are definitely on the weaker side. Though I would have expected the leafbomb to do some damage."

"It nearly killed hundreds of us. Luckily Elanil was on hand to heal everyone."

"Everyone?"

"Yes. She has a Book of Amplification."

"Impressive. Very well—let us proceed. My visual overlay will guide me to the right traps. Can you and Imra lure the Twins?"

"We can try," Imra said, loading another arrow.

They flew about for a few minutes, pinging the Twins with sparkling arrows. It angered them, as it always did, and Phoenix kept her forcefield up in order to avoid being incinerated. The Twins didn't seem to really have much strategy, here—they were just angry, like petulant children.

Maybe that's exactly what they were.

There was just one problem. Although the Twins did continue shooting magic at Phoenix and her shield, they no longer moved to follow them. Clearly they'd caught on to the purpose of this place.

"We have an issue," Phoenix said. "The Twins aren't following."

"Just keep them occupied," Cresius said. "We foresaw this happening. Give me one moment."

She could see his jaw muscles moving as he subvocalized to somebody. Then he nodded, and everything around them started to *change*.

The spires moved. They started flipping from place to place, rising slightly from the ground and then rapidly floating to a new position, trading places with another spire. Scores of them moved about the place in quick succession, moving far more quickly than she'd thought possible. The Twins were jostled from where they'd been standing, choosing instead to float in the air as the spires flicked around.

"What madness is this?" Nelenor boomed. The other fighting forces were arrayed out in the nearby desert, so they were unaffected by the motion.

"How in the hell..." Phoenix started.

"You didn't think this was a natural formation, did you?" Cresius said, a bright smile on his face. The moonlight gave him an unnatural appearance, almost like a ghost.

"You're moving the traps to the Twins," Phoenix said.

"Exactly. Just give it a few more—"

A buzzing sound erupted near the Twins, like strong electricity. Forcefields appeared, square boxes surrounding the

Twins. First one sprang up, then another, then a dozen more, two dozen. Soon there had to be at least fifty cubes of energy around the pair, shimmering in the night.

"We call that a forceflare," Cresius said. "The Artifacts that power it will remain effective for up to one hour."

"Will it hold them?"

"I don't know."

"Even if it does, what then?"

"We'll bring other traps to bear."

Phoenix frowned, watching the glittering cubes slowly rotating around the Twins. It was impressive, sure, but *everything* they'd sent against the Twins to date had been impressive.

And nothing had worked.

The Twins actually did seem trapped, though. She could barely make them out inside the energetic light, but she could hear them huffing. They were roaring wordlessly, clearly angry at the situation. Then she saw them expanding, growing larger, fists beating at the edges of the light. The shields grew brighter as they hit them, illuminating the night with a strange, stark glow. Their yelling grew even louder still, and Phoenix could hear the sound of power being expended.

Then the shields all shattered, edges flying away in the night, revealing the Twins. They slumped over, looking haggard. Clearly they had expended a great deal of energy getting out of the trap. Were they actually hurt, or just tired? Had the trap been enough to disable them?

She got her answers a moment later.

Velion sent an arc of energy blazing from her hand. Not at Phoenix, as before. Not at Cresius or Imra.

She sent it into the desert.

The magic scintillated into the night, a laser beam of

bright red sparks, and mages died by the dozen. Rylak bodies burned, the magic igniting their fur. She saw Remnant fighters go down, heads and arms and legs completely removed by the brutal power. The magic scorched a deep line in the sand, and for an instant everything was quiet.

Then she heard the screams.

"No," she said, as the souls redoubled their efforts, drawn to the pain. Hundreds of people were wounded, and hundreds more were dead. The souls clambered over all, ignoring the bodies on their quest to find the living.

Velion had done all that with just one small swipe of her hand.

"We have to keep trying," Cresius said. "Quickly!"

And the spires moved again, flicking from place to place, moving so quickly that Phoenix couldn't keep track of their positions. They distracted the Twins, who were once again forced to fly into the air.

Then they stopped, and another trap triggered.

Lightning bolts erupted from the sky, blinding in their intensity. Phoenix shielded her eyes, but it was too bright in the night. They just kept coming, hundreds of them in a row, cracking through the air and hitting the Twins. A wind rose up, barely audible over the incredible thunder that hit her next, the whole world shaking with the intensity of the strongest storm she'd ever seen.

And through it all, she could hear the Twins roaring.

More red magic struck out at random, narrowly missing the forces on the desert's edge. Lightning continued to strike through the wind and rain, hundreds and hundreds of powerful strikes hitting the Twins directly.

They withstood it all.

Then it was over, and Phoenix couldn't see a thing. She put a forcefield up hastily, hoping she had positioned it right.

The lightning had blinded her, and her ears were ringing from the terrible thunder.

She felt a touch on her arm, and soulsoothing magic flooded her, correcting her eyes and ears. One of Cresius' attendants nodded at her when it was done, pulling away.

"The stormflash didn't work," Cresius said. "We've only got one left."

"Does this one have a clever name, too?"

The Twins were really angry now. They'd risen into the air and were even now flying over to where Phoenix was hovering.

This wasn't good.

"The last trap," Cresius said as the spires began their shifting dance yet again, "is the spires themselves. Once I trigger this, there's nothing left to do."

# THIRTY-TWO

THE SOULS CONTINUED TO COME. Quynn could barely keep his eyes open; his body was almost too weak to move. That beam of energy had come very close to shearing off his hand, and it *had* killed at least a dozen rylak.

Just like that. Dead.

So were many, many others.

Quynn stood shakily, staggering as he looked at the destruction all around him. The power being expended here —it was too much to comprehend. The souls continued to swarm, and it was all Quynn could do to keep them from killing him outright. He swung his sword lethargically, the coldness of the night seeping into his bones.

He couldn't do this any longer.

"Screw this," he said, turning to find Talon. The rylak was shrugging off two souls, his eyes finding Quynn in the dark. "We should leave."

"I couldn't agree more," Talon said, slashing another soul with his claws. Then he growled something loudly, wordlessly, and the other rylak in the vicinity perked up.

As one, they began moving to the west, where Orym's

mysterious gate was. The souls streamed around them as they went, and Quynn continued to fight them off as best he could. To his right, the Salt Spires were moving about wildly, red magic and bright lightning and strange winds erupting all over the place.

Let the gods battle it out. This was no place for him.

PHOENIX WATCHED THE SPIRES MOVE. They were doing it differently this time—they were a bit slower, perhaps more purposeful. The Twins were hovering high above them in the sky, moonlight radiant on their faces. It looked like both were preparing to strike.

Suddenly the spires *themselves* attacked.

Two of them shot upward violently, striking the Twins directly. They reeled, moving westward, pain evident on their faces. Another spire struck them, then another, but they shrugged them off, not even bothering with forcefields.

Then all the spires were moving, disconnected from the ground, floating in the air in three dimensions. Were they using magic, or gravitonic drives? It seemed the Department of Magical Research was not afraid of using a little technology to accomplish their goals.

Four spires rotated sideways, pointing in at the Twins. They struck, but this time the Twins had a shield ready. The spires broke apart as they hit the forcefield, and Nelenor laughed.

But they had only been a distraction. A dozen more spires, each at least a hundred feet tall, had risen up above the Twins. Now they were positioned in the sky, and Phoenix watched with trepidation as they fell.

They slammed into the Twins, all at once. Their shield

broke apart underneath the onslaught, and the salt spires hit the Twins with all their might, crushing them. But the Twins lashed out with magic of their own, reducing the spires to pure, soft salt that flitted around them in the air.

Then something else happened. Phoenix heard a low *thrumming* sound, and a visible circle of energy spread out from around the Twins. Then they were rising, taken hundreds and hundreds of feet into the air, salt spires rising along with them.

"Fallfoiling Artifacts have just been triggered," Cresius said. "We'd better make sure we're well clear of this."

They flew further away, watching the Twins rise and rise. Then there was a *crack*, and another arc of distortion in the night sky, and the Twins slammed toward the ground incredibly quickly.

They hit with a horrifying crash, a huge cloud of dust and salt erupting from the ground as they did. The entire area shuddered with their impact, rumbling as the earth reacted to the force of the blow. Phoenix squinted through the dust, grateful that she was floating in the air, and thought she saw a huge crater where the spires in the middle had been.

The Twins had been thrown deep underground.

And for one long moment, Phoenix thought they might have actually won.

Then the ground glowed red. The Twins ascended, surrounded by a ball of crimson light, their eyes and skin the scarlet hue of blood. They rose together, bodies motionless in the air, hands outstretched to the side, white garments flowing around them.

"That was your final warning," Velion's voice boomed out across the shattered remains of the Salt Spires. "You will not trouble us again."

And the Twins lashed out with everything they had.

Crimson magic filled the air, shooting outward in a million cascading streams of light. The night sky was lit with red, magic filling everything, covering the distance, reaching out with terrible potential. Phoenix felt fire rippling across her face, her skin burning, her hair on fire. She felt a searing pain, like being inside a hot oven, like topside when the wind was gone and the sun shone down on a hot summer's day.

She felt the worst agony she had ever felt, and she knew this was the end.

Unless there was something she could do.

Imra grabbed her suddenly, and she could feel the woman's strength flowing through her. Phoenix wasted no time—she pulled magic out of Imra's soul, mixing it with her own, compelling the fireblade in her hand to produce the most joyful element it had ever created.

Life.

Green burst out from all around the pair of women, a rippling tide of healing power. All existence grew inside that power, bodies healing, souls intertwined. The flood of Protector magic shot through the Twins' Destroyer flood, infusing it with its opposite energy. Anger to meet joy. Fear to meet glee. Hurting to meet healing. Phoenix and Imra stood together, hands clasped tightly, feeling the synergy of their bodies and their minds creating the strongest healing power the world had ever known.

And for a long, long moment, they actually held their own.

Then the moment ended.

"**ENOUGH**," Nelenor said, and the magic shattered into nothingness.

A new color replaced the red, replaced the green. A new

color pervaded the night, filling all the cracks and crevices and the air and Phoenix's skin.

Purple.

# PART
# THREE

Nearly all men can stand adversity, but if you want to test a man's character, give him power.

— *Abraham Lincoln*

# THIRTY-THREE

ELANIL FLEW ACROSS THE SPIRES, trying to find where Rylan had gone. He wasn't where she'd seen him standing before. Why had he moved? Maybe he just didn't want to be caught up in the fight.

But he had his magic back, didn't he? Why wasn't he participating? He could fight the Twins.

Or maybe he couldn't. They'd disconnected his magic, earlier—maybe they'd do it again.

For that matter, why hadn't they just done that with *everyone*? Why allow Phoenix to continue using magic, and Elanil, and all those mages out there in the desert? If the Twins could just pull the plug on a person-by-person basis, why didn't they?

The answer had to be simple: because they couldn't. Maybe only superusers had strong enough identifications in the system to be controlled like that. It seemed an ironic weakness for someone who had so much power.

She checked the pack she had on her back, making sure the extra Book of Amplification was still there. She intended to give it to Rylan when she found him. Then they would both have a Book, and the magic they could do together would be immense.

If, that is, the Twins didn't turn it off.

Blasts of light and sound assailed her from behind, the battle between the mages and the Twins continuing. Then the spires were moving, and Elanil was forced to quickly fly away.

She watched the proceedings, noting how the Twins recovered from each and every thing Cresius threw at them. Soon the spires themselves were attacking the Twins, and Elanil couldn't help but laugh. How were they here, fighting these gods with spires made of salt? How had this strange night come to be?

Magic had led them here.

The Twins fell to the ground, buried deep into the earth with powerful fallfoiling magic. Then they were rising, and Elanil was brandishing her Book, soulsoothing magic already flooding her veins.

That was when she finally spotted Rylan.

He was out on one of the few remaining spires, at the far eastern edge of the area. Most of the remaining salt spires had been destroyed at this point, leaving a massive crater at least a mile wide and over a hundred feet deep. The spires that had been destroyed remained as simple piles of loose salt, arrayed in heaps like sand dunes glistening in the moonlight.

She flew over to Rylan just as red Destroyer magic pervaded the sky. She threw a forcefield up to block it, using the Book to amplify its strength. But the red magic didn't reach all the way to where Rylan was standing. Either the Twins were sparing him their attack, or he'd gotten lucky. She alighted on the spire next to him, releasing her shield, but before they could even acknowledge each other the sky turned purple.

Elanil felt the Twins inside her head.

Rylan did something, twisting his hand, and the purple cloud faded away from their area.

"Ho, Wind," she said as the magic dissipated from her mind. They were standing in an island of black inside the purple, the magic visibly wafting around them in the air. Apparently the Twins had decided to take a completely different tack. Now they no longer wanted to kill; now they wanted to *control*.

"Ho, Dance," Rylan said. He didn't step forward or reach out to touch her. He had a pensive look on his face.

"Your magic is back."

"Yes."

"I—I missed you, Ryl."

He smiled at that. "I missed you *so much*. And Lani—I'm so sorry."

"Never mind that," Elanil said. "We'll talk about it later. Right now I'm here to rescue you."

He spluttered a bit at that. "You want to...*rescue* me?"

"Sure! Aren't the Twins holding you prisoner?"

"Uh...I don't think so."

"Oh. But I—"

"They gave me my magic back."

"I know."

"And I don't think they really mean us any harm."

"*What*? Just look at what they're doing! How many people have they killed?"

"Well, yeah. I know they're doing us harm. A *lot* of harm. But I can't help but think that they can still be talked down." He was looking out at the now-empty canyon where the spires used to be, watching the purple clouds flow. "What in the Under are they *doing*?"

He rose, suddenly, floating in the air without moving even

a muscle. It was always so weird to see him do that, using magic without needing any wood or Talent or anything at all. Then he made a motion with his hand, and she imagined she could hear him talking to someone in his head.

The purple cloud disappeared.

And the Twins—both of them—floated toward them.

Elanil shrank away, suddenly fearful. And why shouldn't she be? The most powerful beings in the world were coming to stand next to her, just *feet* away from her. They could kill her in an instant.

But they were just elves.

They were normal size now, not lit by any otherworldly magic. They just stood on the spire next to Elanil and Rylan, beautiful blond hair draped behind them, white clothes radiant.

"Greetings," Nelenor—the man—said. "And you are?" He was talking to her.

"Elanil," she said. Should she bow? She bowed a little.

"You and Rylan are…"

"There is a minor sparkthread connecting you," Velion said.

Elanil wasn't entirely sure what that meant, but she found herself blushing anyway. When had romance become so *technical*?

She and Rylan shared a look.

"Listen," Rylan said, turning back to the Twins. "You have to stop this."

"We want the Imprisoner," Nelenor said.

"This isn't *you*. You don't need to be this violent."

"You have no idea who we are."

"I've seen evil," Rylan said. "I've been beat up by someone who should have been a friend. I've been imprisoned in a city that killed its people in order to make magic. I've fought the

Remnant, and I've saved them, too. I've seen people die when the moment demanded it, kind people sacrificing for a common goal. I've seen the girl I love *murdered* at the hands of a monster with a gun, and all I could do was stand there. I've seen evil, and I've seen good. I may be young, but I know you. And you're not as evil as you want everyone to believe."

His strange eloquence was back. Elanil stood there watching him, open-mouthed, as he finished speaking. He loved her? He actually *loved* her? She felt her face heating again.

She took a step toward him.

Velion let out a sound of disgust. "You are right, young one," she said. "A thousand centuries of captivity has warped our vision. We did not visit this world to wreak such havoc." She turned to her brother, a sad expression on her face. "It was such a beautiful place."

Nelenor nodded. "We do not wish to destroy it further. Though we are not sure this place counts—it was constructed to kill us."

"It was," Elanil confirmed.

"We can't stop," Velion said. "While we are still under attack, all worlds are at risk. If we fall, Xyclami will no longer have operators. It will run amok. We cannot allow this. We must defend ourselves, no matter what the cost."

"Or you could disable the device," Rylan said.

"I—" Nelenor said, cutting himself off.

"No," Velion said. "We will not do that. It is not our fault that the people on this world are so combative. It is not our fault that we were imprisoned for so long."

"You can end the cycle," Rylan said. "You can be the bigger people."

"Only if the others cease their violence against us," Nelenor said. "We could stop, but only if they do. And since they will not, we will have no choice but to eliminate them all."

"You can be the example to lead them," Elanil said, daring to give them advice.

Velion rounded on her. "It doesn't work like that. We're just elves like you, despite the direct power we wield. If we falter for even a *second*, Xyclami will be unmanned and all worlds will be in great danger. This is not a thing to be taken lightly."

"Neither is killing millions of people."

The Twins didn't respond to that immediately.

"You are strong," Nelenor said to her after a moment. "Resilient. I saw what happened between you and Rylan."

"You...*saw*?"

"Not precisely. Superuser sparkthreads are very visible to us, difficult to ignore. We can detect magic use, and other souls in close proximity."

"We know what he did," Velion said.

"Shit," Rylan said. "I'm so sorry. The magic just overtook me, and I—"

"Most superusers have had at least a thousand years of training, minimum," Nelenor said. "The problem is, they are almost entirely defined by genetics. It's one of the reasons the device operates the way it does—the Creators on Starmist Prime were entranced by how various souls interact, how their strengths can be so different. They created this and other machines to test those limits, to provide interaction points between souls and their technology. It was misguided, probably."

"It was," Velion said. "But we accepted this role. We are the stewards of this device. We must continue to fulfill our promises."

"Dance," Rylan said, and this time he approached her,

taking her hands in his. She felt the thrill of it, though there was no magic between them. "I want you to know that I never intended to hurt you. And I promise that I will do my very, very best to control this power. I won't let anything like that happen again. If it means we don't ever...you know... then that's what we'll do."

She stepped in and kissed him.

Golden sparks erupted around them as their lips connected, but they disappeared as quickly as they came. Then it was just the two of them, kissing in front of the Twins, tongues intertwined while the gods of the world looked on.

It was perhaps the strangest experience of her life.

When they finally pulled away, Rylan's eyes were sparkling. "I do love you, Elanil," he said. "I never want anything bad to happen to you again."

"I love you too, Rylan," Elanil said, and she felt that love filling her very being. She was back. They were back together! It was the best thing she could have imagined.

"Love," Nelenor said, looking at his sister. "Perhaps we have forgotten what that was."

"We have been imprisoned for too long," Velion said. "But we cannot abandon the device. So what can we do?"

"You could just leave," Elanil said.

"We still need to complete our original mission. We need to find our sister."

"There's a *third* Twin?"

"Not a twin. She is older—the firstborn. She is who we came here to find, and we are not leaving without her."

"Then we need to convince everyone to stop fighting," Rylan said. "Are you willing to stop if they will?"

The Twins looked at each other. "Yes," Nelenor said. "If a cessation can be called, we will honor it."

"Thank you," Rylan said. Then he turned back to Elanil. "Thank you for being here."

"I didn't do anything."

"That's not true," Rylan said. "I don't think I would have called the Twins if it weren't for you arriving like you did."

"We wouldn't have agreed to cease the fighting unless we'd seen that kiss," Nelenor said.

"I think the world has seen enough of us for a time," Velion said.

"I'm afraid it won't be as simple as all that," Elanil said. She could see the Prime Mages in the distance, gearing up for what looked like a fight. "We've convinced you, but now we have to convince *them*."

"We wish you luck," Nelenor said. "Just know this: we *must* defend ourselves, using deadly force if needed. Xyclami is too dangerous to be left alone—or to fall into the wrong hands."

# THIRTY-FOUR

ORYM STOOD atop his palace in Nekhrumet, grateful that the sun wasn't beating down on him. The city spread out below him in the night, eucalyptus and acacia trees lining the Iteranu River as it glittered in the moonlight. Shadowy sandstone and stucco buildings were further out, decorated in mosaic and outlined in marble. Souqs spread out throughout the center of the city, covered markets where in the morning thousands of people would be bustling about, exchanging goods and smoking kif.

But Orym's attention was not on any of that. He was focused on the wood in his hand: dark ash. He concentrated on it, thinking thoughts of anger. It wasn't difficult: he just thought of Tiala, of the woman who had left him so long ago, and he immediately began to feel a kind of furious rage. And pain—she had hurt him when she left. He had never truly found out why.

The hurt and pain and anger manifested in the wood as he burned it. And a forcefield appeared in front of him, but not the usual kind. This was more unformed, raw energy in the air, and the particles were glowing red.

Orym had accessed Destroyer magic.

He sent the magic out, allowing it to travel in front of him until it was hovering off the edge of the palace in mid-air.

Sure enough, a Tree began to form.

It was a ghostly white, almost silver in the sky, starkly visible in the night. It appeared wherever his magic touched it, as if reacting to his anger. It could *feel* him, he thought, and it wanted to reach out, to kill and destroy. He could only see the tiniest part, the edge of one branch, but it was enough.

He knew that his Soul Tree was here, and he knew that it was why his Pyramid Offensive Mechanism didn't work.

With a sudden burst of Destroyer magic, he could destroy that Tree. But he knew from experience that doing so would also kill most of the people in Nekhrumet. And while he didn't exactly mind doing that, he didn't want to do it *yet*.

First, he needed his volunteers to reach and travel through their gates. All but one would die, of course, but it was in service of the greater good. *His* good.

They were close now. It would only take a little bit more time.

IT TOOK Quynn and the rylak several hours to get completely free of the army of souls. He had counseled Talon to quiet his emotions, and to instruct the other rylak to do the same. It worked, though it was slow. He suspected asking rylak to quiet their emotions was like asking water to flow uphill. But they managed it, and eventually the souls lost interest in them.

They emerged weary, weak and starving. They ate as they continued walking west, pulling the last of the food Orym had provided from their supplies. It was still full night, though morning was growing near.

Quynn hoped the gate they were looking for wasn't too much further away.

He pondered things as he walked. He'd never been much of a thinker, before, but a lot had changed since then. Now he knew he was only half a person. He'd been married to and fucking the same woman—Lorelei—while at the same time he'd been married to Arra. He was Rylan's father. He was twenty thousand years old. And for most of the recent two thousand years, he'd been nothing more than a kind of villain.

He wondered if books would ever be written about him in the future.

How had he gotten here? Why was he traipsing through a freezing desert at night, surrounded by an alien race of wolf-men, retreating from an army of literal ghosts while gods and men played with powers beyond his comprehension?

Why was he following the orders of his former employee?

Orym was an enigma, Quynn was forced to admit. He'd always been that way, even during their first meeting. Truth be told, Quynn had suspected that there might be something more than met the eye with the man, but he was competent enough. And that had been the age where Quynn didn't question things. He just followed Lorelei's commands, and his own passions, and let life sort of happen as it would. The only grand strategy he'd ever had was to find a Prime Mage.

Well, he had certainly succeeded in *that* department.

Now he was attempting to activate a magical device that was spread across three worlds, in the hopes that it would somehow defeat the gods that Trey had brought to life. Quynn had become an unwitting pawn in all of this, and he was not quite sure why.

The answer was obvious, though. He wasn't just a pawn. He was *Tarathiel*, the man who'd gotten all this started. Well, maybe not *started*...that had all been Aten's doing. Aten and the Twins, and Cara and Lara and the other First Mages who were around during that time.

It was funny how a hundred thousand years could feel like such a short time.

When Quynn had imagined his life, he had always been hungry for power, yes. He had always lusted for something *more*.

But he had never quite imagined *this*.

He continued walking through the desert, wondering if he should radio Orym. Was the gate just up ahead? Would he fall asleep or die before he found it? Did he even *want* to find it? What would happen once he did? These thoughts and more assailed him as he walked.

"You look troubled, my friend," Talon said as he walked next to him.

"That's one way to put it."

"What is the matter?"

Quynn thought it very unusual for a normally gruff rylak to be so interested in elven feelings and emotions, but he decided to go with it. The night was already strange enough—what was one more thing?

"I can't help but feel like I'm in the wrong place," Quynn said. "Like I wasn't meant for this."

"We are none of us home," Talon said. "We have all traveled across time, doing things no mortal could ever do."

"Yes, but what does it *mean*? Shouldn't there be some purpose to it all?"

"Why must life have meaning? The sakul roams the woods, finding prey and killing it. Does it wonder what purpose its hunting serves? Does the cavek discuss the future with its mate and kin? Do bekal flies ponder the essence of the cosmos?"

"Your grasp of Eldrim is quite good," Quynn said. "But in answer to your question, no. And why should they? Those are all animals and insects. It is we *people* who must think of such things."

"The only good that will come of that," Talon said, "is a headache and a fleeting heart. No. Best stick to the task at hand. Go on your hunt, find your prey, kill it and eat it and celebrate with many women. Life is far simpler when you do not consider *meaning*."

Quynn thought about that for a moment. Hadn't that always been his approach, before? Hadn't he always leapt without looking, acted without thinking, hurt others without caring? What must it be like for Trey—was he the opposite? Did he never act for fear of the consequences? And if that were true, which approach did he prefer?

He could rampage through life, destroying everything around him in a singular pursuit of pleasure.

Or he could receive no pleasure, but hurt no one else along the way.

Neither seemed correct. And he wondered if perhaps the rylak simply weren't advanced enough to see it.

He continued walking, lost once more inside his thoughts.

# THIRTY-FIVE

THE MINDMASTER MAGIC disappeared almost as quickly as it had come, and Phoenix watched the Twins leave the battle-field, flying to somewhere on the edge. Was that Rylan they were talking to? And Elanil? She wondered what was going on.

She hoped her son was safe.

"We lost forty-nine Prime Mages," Cresius said, "plus over a hundred of my regular mages. And I'm not sure the Twins were really even *trying*. Damn."

"I wonder why they stopped," Phoenix said.

"I have a feeling we're about to find out."

The Twins chose that moment to return, hovering over the decimated remains of the Salt Spires. Phoenix readied her fireblade, hoping she had the energy for whatever was to come.

She really couldn't last much longer.

"We wish to cease hostilities," Nelenor said, his voice boosted by strengthshaping magic.

That was not what Phoenix had been expecting.

"He's lying," Cresius said. "He's just trying to get us to not fight back."

"Shouldn't we at least *talk* to them?" Phoenix asked.

"We will agree to an armistice," Nelenor continued. "Providing you do not inflict harm upon us, we will no longer inflict harm upon you. But we still wish to find the Imprisoner."

"At least they're not demanding the Imprisoner as a condition of the armistice," Phoenix said. "Or are they? I can't tell."

"They can't be trusted," Cresius said. "We must push forward. We must defeat them, somehow. If Orym's Mechanism does not come through, we may be this world's only hope."

"We're out of traps."

"But we are not yet out of weapons. The Prime Mages have not yet been fully utilized."

A series of glowing diagrams appeared in the air in front of Cresius, looking like a wide screen full of lines and symbols, numbers and words. She could see it projecting from a small device hung around Cresius' neck.

"Ops," Cresius said, no longer subvocalizing, "go audible so the others can hear."

"Aye," a male voice said, coming out of nowhere.

"Enact Splinter Routine One."

"Enacting."

The screen lit up with new colors and shapes, showing what appeared to be a diagram of hundreds of people.

"Are those the mages?" Phoenix asked.

Cresius nodded.

"Two twenty-three Prime Mages were originally present," the voice of Ops said. "Losing forty-nine brings us to one seven four. Cell commands feeding now. T-minus twenty seconds until ready for mark."

"Copy," Cresius said.

"Do not pursue this fight," Nelenor said. "We will be forced to destroy you."

"Ten seconds," Ops said.

"Should we really be doing this?" Phoenix asked. "We finally have a chance at peace, after all this destruction. I think Rylan actually did it. I don't know how, but I think he got us what we wanted."

"Commands sent," Ops said. "Ready for your mark."

Cresius looked at Phoenix. "They destroyed Ilyrion," he said. "They destroyed *your* home. They've killed millions, and now you want to just stop?"

"We can't defeat them. You know we can't. All you're doing is throwing away more lives."

His face hardened at that, and he turned away from her. "It's far too late for peace," he said. "Mark."

"Activating," Ops said.

And the Prime Mages moved, moving into groups of fourteen. Phoenix watched them form into their cells, no longer using the strange cubes they'd been using before. They had assembled within seconds, moving rapidly into position.

"Prime soulcircles in position," Ops said. "Twelve full circles currently available."

"Splinter," Cresius said.

"Aye."

The mages splintered, each one using mistweaving to become six copies of themselves—one for every Aspect. Phoenix watched in awe as the twelve soulcircles divided rapidly in the night, filling the desert with hundreds and hundreds of mages.

"All splinters reporting complete," Ops said. "1044 entities in total, comprising 72 full soulcircles. 36 individuals not part of circles."

"Very well," Cresius said. "Passing individual control to Ops Leader. Direct offensive strategy as indicated by Routine One. I will control top-level actions."

"Aye. Individual control is passed."

"Active Storm," Cresius said. "Target: Nelenor and Velion."

"Entities identified. Stand by."

"Why didn't we start with this?" Phoenix asked.

Cresius seemed a little distracted. "The traps were easier, and didn't involve actual elves. This was always going to be our second line of offense."

Phoenix sighed. "What do you think?" she asked Imra.

"I think I'm getting tired of floating in the air," she said. "Is that all you Prime Mages ever do?"

Phoenix gave a half-hearted smile. "Apparently."

"I also think this is foolhardy, but I think we have to try. There is nothing that will keep the Twins from observing any kind of armistice, after all. We can't trust them to keep to a deal. Who's to say they won't just retaliate once we've backed down?"

Phoenix had to admit that Imra was probably right. She sighed again, waiting for whatever was next.

"Initiating Storm," Ops said.

Twelve of the soulcircles lit up on the floating screen, and stormwarden magic filled the air around the Twins. Lightning struck from all directions: above, below, from every side. Insane winds blew in, catapulting the Twins in all directions with hurricane force. Rain appeared, but it wasn't falling. Instead it was collapsing inward, freezing as it did, shattering against the Twins in millions and millions of tiny, icy particles.

It was the strangest storm Phoenix had ever seen.

But the Twins were the equal to it, of course. She saw them using green Protector magic, keeping themselves healed even as the storm did its worst. Soon they were stable, using leafrunning and fallfoiling to counteract the effects of the wind. A forcefield surrounded them, driving out the rain and blocking the lightning. While it was certainly the most powerful storm anyone had likely ever created, it hadn't even made a dent.

"Cease," Cresius said. "Active Motion plus Blade."

"Initiating," Ops said.

"This will use fallfoiling, leafrunning, and bladedancing," Cresius explained.

Thirty-six of the soulcircles lit up this time, even as the storm faded away. Phoenix watched the Twins, expecting something to happen, but nothing did.

"Increase," Cresius said.

"At maximum," Ops returned.

"We didn't bring any projectile weapons," Cresius said. "Didn't have time."

"So bladedancing is useless," Phoenix said.

Cresius nodded. "Bring up the remaining spires." There were a few dozen salt spires still intact around the edges of the canyon. Now they rose into the air, whirling and moving closer to the center. "Perfect," Cresius said. "Shatter that and utilize."

"Aye."

The spires broke into thousands of pieces each, and Phoenix saw bladedancing magic pick them all up and send them flying through the air. They didn't head straight for the Twins, though—instead they arced and curved, flying in intricate formations, tens of thousands of sharp shards of hardened salt slicing through the air like a million tiny knives. But the Twins still had their forcefield up, so there wasn't much that the salt could do.

"Hold those in the air," Cresius ordered. "We need to confuse them. Active Mist. Secondary, just do whatever you can imagine."

"Aye."

The night lit up suddenly, the entire area changing abruptly to day. Phoenix saw twelve more soulcircles active on the screen, and she assumed these new ones were the mistweavers. But surely changing night to day would not be enough to actually confuse the Twins.

Nothing would, probably.

The sky turned blood red, complete with actual blood raining down. She saw a serpent of some kind, easily a hundred feet long and ten feet in diameter, crawling toward the canyon from the desert. Another one joined the first, then another, and soon there were a dozen massive snakes heading toward the Twins, jaws open to reveal jagged, venomous fangs. Strange purple lightning crashed, and Phoenix saw massive spikes rising from the ground.

Then rocks began to fall from the sky. Big ones covered in moss and dirt, rolling out from nowhere and crashing to the ground. None of it was real, of course—Phoenix was pretty sure. The mistweavers were having a hell of a time.

"Eat your heart out," Cresius muttered. "Erodar the Prime would have loved this. Ops, keep Blade ready in case they drop the shield."

"Aye."

The illusions got stranger from there. The sky flashed green, then orange, then purple. Trees grew, then disappeared. Buildings flew in from the sides, only to explode in a riot of color and light. Stormwardens began working with the illusions, creating a sense of motion in the air as things slid in

223

and out of the scene. A storm took over the area, but most of it was false—the only true lightning was over the Twins, even though it appeared to strike everywhere. Water filled the canyon where the spires had been, strange sea monsters swimming about in it. The world went back to night, then back to day, then flickered like a strobe light.

"I think I'm going to be sick," Imra said.

"Me too." Phoenix put a hand to her head. What was all this mistweaving getting them?

"There!" Cresius called, and Phoenix saw that the Twins shield was finally down. "Blade, attack!"

A million shards of salt sliced through the air, curving inward from wherever they'd been floating. Twelve full soul-circles of bladedancing mages were controlling them, wielding them like a million tiny swords. They sailed toward the Twins as she watched, moving effortlessly through the sky.

"Incredible," Imra breathed. "I can only handle two arrows at once. I think I've seen Arra do a few dozen, but that's it."

"That is the power of full soulcircles," Cresius said. "Here we go."

The shards of salt hit the Twins.

"Active Strength," Cresius said.

The sharp salt appeared to hurt the Twins, at least. They reeled as if in pain, and Phoenix saw a brief glow of green about them as they tried to heal from it. But they seemed more injured than usual, this time. Perhaps the illusions really had confused them.

Maybe they had the same headache she did.

She saw more circles activate on-screen, and nearly two hundred mage Aspects grew suddenly, becoming as tall as spires themselves. Their muscles bulged, their faces stern, and they all began walking into the canyon, heading for the Twins.

"168 entities activated," Ops said. "Estimating high casualties. Proceed?"

"Proceed," Cresius said, not even hesitating.

This was the first time that entire night where any actual mages had gotten close to the Twins.

"Keep screwing with them," Cresius said.

"Aye."

Mistweavers continued to pulse strange and terrible sights throughout the area. The strengthshaper mages grew larger still, turning into the Anubis forms the Twins had once used. Their fox-like faces grew dark, their eyes glowed red, and Phoenix felt something like fear enter her heart.

Even if they won this fight, she realized, the world would still be in grave danger. With hundreds of Prime Mages on the loose, soulcircles like these would only be a call away at any time. How would anyone live? How could government exist, law, religion? How could *anything* function when such great and terrible power was at the beck and call of so many?

This fight, she realized, was pointless. It was flawed reasoning. They should almost *let* the Twins win.

They should definitely stop attacking.

But it was too late to say anything now. She almost tried— she almost reached out to Cresius, asking him to stop the strengthshaper attack. But he was determined, she could see. His brow was furrowed in concentration, his eyes bright with anticipation. He *wanted* this, and probably had for a very long time.

His Department had been researching the end of the world.

"We have to stop," she said to Imra, and the woman nodded.

"We do, but it's too late."

The strengthshapers reached the Twins, huge hands and arms outstretched. Massive Anubis men dogpiled the Twins, fists pummeling. But the Twins struck out with fists of their owns, red Destroyer magic adding a certain extra sting.

The strengthshapers died by the dozens.

But they kept on coming, fists at the ready, and a few of them even managed to land a blow or two. They struck *hard*, sending the Twins reeling, but then they quickly died. Strengthshapers were no match for Destroyer magic.

"Call them back," Phoenix said. "They'll all die."

"Agreed," Cresius said. "Deactivate Strength."

"Pulling back," Ops said.

It took a few seconds for the order to relay. And in that time, twenty more mage Aspects died. By the time they finally withdrew, at least half the strengthshapers were gone.

It had been a pointless, useless waste of lives.

"What happens when the Aspects die?" Phoenix asked.

"We were never able to test with real Prime Mages," Cresius said. "But according to the ancient writings on the subject, when a splinter dies, that mage will never again have that Aspect as a part of him."

"Like with Trey," Imra said. "Being half a person."

"Except Trey's other half still lives," Cresius said. "In these strengthshapers' case, there's no coming back."

"We have to stop fighting," Phoenix said. "The Twins are too strong."

They were rising now, moving higher in the air and growing larger. Mistweaver illusions continued flickering, but the Twins ignored them. Their faces were murderous, their heads upturned. Phoenix put a forcefield around herself and the nearby mages, hoping that whatever was about to transpire would not be worse than anything that had come before.

"This is the most magic wielded in one place since the Awakening," Cresius said, watching the Twins rise. "And still it is not enough."

"May the world forgive us for our sins," Phoenix said.

"If any world remains," Imra said.

The sun began to rise behind them in the sky, first golden rays hitting the Twins as they continued levitating in the air. Phoenix felt a great weariness take over as she realized how long it had been since the fight had begun, and just how hopeless their future looked.

She didn't think any of them would make it out of this alive.

# THIRTY-SIX

MORNING HAD ARRIVED. Arra emerged from the tent feeling very conflicted—on the one hand, the sex had been great. Trey and she had connected on a physical level like she would never have believed, especially with a lot of her memory still gone. But she couldn't shake the nagging feeling that she'd been *right* about everything else.

She couldn't help but feel that they didn't belong together.

"Good morning," Lashel said, studiously looking at the ground. That was when Arra realized just how close their tents had been.

Lashel had heard everything.

Trey cleared his throat. "Breakfast?"

"That would be great."

They ate more cold venison and beans, washing it down with the remains of the wine. Then they packed the tents, none of them really looking at each other, and set out into the frozen reaches of Thylmanas. Looking for a gate.

Two hours later, they found it.

It was an orange and swirling light, as all gates were, shining out against the snow like a beacon in the night. The gate had been hidden inside a cluster of ruins, making it difficult to spot from any vantage point outside. But they had found it, thanks to Trey's meticulous grid system of exploration.

He was so different from her.

But she remembered how he had felt last night, how their bodies had melded so perfectly together. How he had professed his love, and how for a moment she had believed him. Her face heated as she remembered how it had felt.

"Well," Lashel said. "This is it, I guess."

"Strange that there would be a gate way out here," Trey said. "I guess Orym was right."

"We should radio him, let him know we found it."

"Yes." He looked at Arra. "Is something wrong?"

She was looking through the gate, trying to discern what was on the other side. "It's strange," she said. "Normally with gates, you can clearly see where it leads. This one isn't like that."

It wasn't. The vision through the gate was blurry, constantly switching between several different color schemes. It was like a painting, but where the artist couldn't decide exactly what they wanted to do. One moment the gate was filled with green, the next white. Then it was blue, then orange, then blackness, the horrible blackness of despair. Arra shivered, knowing somehow that if they took the gate when it indicated black, they would never return.

"What if Orym really is the Imprisoner?" she asked.

"I don't know," Trey said. "This is all over my head."

She stared at him, mouth open, wondering if she had heard him correctly. It was *very* unlike Trey to admit when he was ignorant about something. Was this just the anti-Quynn talking, or had he actually changed?

She was just so terribly confused.

LORELEI STEPPED through the gate and onto the streets of New Manhattan. She knew it was New Manhattan immediately—New Times Square was awfully hard to miss. They'd recreated the series of blocks perfectly, massive video screens and all. Of course, most of the screens hadn't been used for advertisements during the Cothellon era—instead, they'd been filled with thinly-veiled propaganda.

Civil Service didn't maintain itself, after all.

There were no tourists, of course. Actually, there *were* some—during the brief time the other sky cities had been connected, many Citizens had come across to visit the fabled New York. Evidently some old books had gotten out somehow, and now residents were curious about their history, about the other cities in the world. Only the floating versions remained now, but Lorelei had been painstaking in their recreation.

That her gate had brought them directly here was nothing short of a miracle. Now she needed to orient herself, figure out where the City Manager and his team were. Luckily, she had a trick to that.

There was an emergency radio station hidden on the corner of New Broadway and 44th. She entered the code—known only by Planners, of course—and picked up the transmitter that revealed itself.

"Greetings," she said into it. "Former Cundu Lorelei Nightmeadow here, seeking assistance from the City Manager. Hammond, I believe it was? I'm here on behalf of Trey and the others. We might have a way to fight the Twins."

It grated on her, needing to name-drop Trey. Truth be told, she wasn't sure which names might get her an audience with Hammond. Needing an audience at all grated on her, too, but there was nothing she could do. The Cothellon had fallen. They had been in the wrong, though they *had* ultimately saved millions of humans from being killed by the Eldrim. Even so, she should take solace that she was still alive, that she retained her faculties, and that her memories had been returned.

All in all, she was a very lucky woman to have survived this long.

Allain, Dill, and Erodar stood beside her as she waited for the radio to respond. Was anyone even listening for these transmissions, anymore? Was there anyone in City Control? Mission Control itself was gone, she knew, destroyed along with New San Francisco. But the other cities still needed steering, logistics, monitoring. They needed to stay afloat. Surely *somebody* would be willing to at least hear what she had to say.

"Lorelei?" a tinny voice said over the radio. "Control Lead Avourel here. John Ronald has already explained everything to us. We'll send a fallcar to your location now. Hammond will be waiting."

"Thank you," Lorelei said.

Allain was standing right next to her, and she found herself oddly distracted by him. That was unlike her. Something about the whole situation was giving her a thrill—she was back in her element now, up here in the cities she had built. She was finally taking action. She was finally a part of something good.

She grabbed Allain and kissed him firmly on the mouth.

The kiss lasted longer than she'd expected it to. Allain gripped her arms, pulling her against him, returning the kiss with ardor. She was conscious of her breasts pushed up against his chest, of the strong feel of his hands on her.

She pulled away and slapped him across the face.

Not too hard.

Then she kissed him again. She was back! She was actually making a difference!

And honestly, Allain really wasn't half bad.


THE SUN WAS RISING in the desert as Quynn continued trudging through the sand. He was beaten down, exhausted, almost unable to put one foot in front of the other. Why had Orym just left them like this? One moment he'd been there offering help, and the next he was gone, leaving them to fend for themselves in the ravages of the desert.

Perhaps this gate of his was nowhere to be found.

"It should be just up ahead," Talon said. "I know this desert well."

"How can you *know* the desert?" Quynn asked. "Every goddamn thing looks the same."

"There's a rock formation there," Talon said, pointing. "And see that cluster of cacti? The dunes themselves may change, but certain features remain the same. I've been on this planet a long *long* time. And Cariel loved the desert."

"Your old boss was strange," Quynn said. "But I have to admit, I'm impressed. For someone who is supposed to be a jungle dweller, you seem to handle the desert quite well."

"I didn't say I loved it," Talon growled.

"So where's the gate?"

"Should be here."

The other rylak fanned out around them, shading their eyes against the sun, peering in every direction. There was no gate anywhere.

"The dunes shift, you said?" Quynn asked.

"Just like waves, albeit a whole lot slower," Talon said.

"Then let's keep moving."

Talon nodded, and they set back out.

Sure enough, the gate was swirling just on the other side of the nearest dune, its light somehow brighter than the sun's. Quynn stepped up to it, feet slipping in the sand, wondering what the next step was. Should he walk through the gate, like Orym had asked? The interior was pulsing strangely, muted colors shifting from one to another. He could see no clear visions through the gate, no indication of what was waiting on the other side.

Should he believe Orym? The man had never lied to him before, at least that he knew of. He'd been reliable. He'd revealed the true disaster waiting for them when Fennas Elenathon was activated. Would a man like that lie about the necessity of these gates?

"Well?" Talon prompted. "Should we go?"

"I feel as if everything is about to change," Quynn said.

"Undoubtedly," Talon said. "But don't you welcome a little change?"

He did, usually. And if this meant a change for the better, if it were a way to actually end the menace of the Twins, then he owed it to himself and everyone around him to take that chance. To take this gate.

He stepped through it into a world of sky and sun.

"WELL?" Trey asked. "Should we take the gate?"

It was standing there in the snow, shining at them as the sun continued to rise. The middle of it was murky, but did that mean anything? They barely knew anything about gates. Hell, they barely knew anything about *magic*. If someone had told him that magic even existed just a year ago, he would have laughed in their face. If they'd gone on to explain that all of magic was powered by a mysterious machine, he would have thought they were crazy.

But life was crazy now. The world was out of control. And if Orym thought he had a way to fix a piece of it, to make the broken pieces right, Trey owed it to the world to do what he could.

He trusted Orym.

"This will be an awfully big adventure," he said.

"That's my line," Arra said, and he saw a pained expression in her eyes. What was going through her head, lately? They'd shared such intimacy in the tent the night before, but it had been laced with something else. Fear? Uncertainty? Hurt? Trey didn't feel up to the task of deciphering what was happening in Arra's mind.

He desperately wanted to.

But he took her hand, knowing that it might be the wrong thing to do, knowing that he might never get to the bottom of what was going on. If this gate led them to oblivion or death, he might never see her face again. So he looked on her with what he hoped were eyes of love, and he led her through the gate.

They emerged into a world of ash and stone.

# THIRTY-SEVEN

ARRA FELT ice wash over her as she passed through the gate, and then she found herself in a world unlike anything she'd ever seen. A charred, blackened wasteland spread out before her, filled with craggy, sharp rocks that looked like they'd been burnt to a crisp. The rocks formed a sort of mountain to their right, climbing up in impossible formations to reach the sky. The sun was red, shining down on them through thick air filled with patches of smoke.

Ahead, the rocks gave way to a flatland of dry, cracked earth. No plants grew anywhere that she could see; no animals or insects made an appearance. There was no water, and the air smelled fetid, as if many things had died and been left to rot.

"What *is* this place?" Lashel said, holding his nose as he stepped through the gate. "Where are we?"

Arra glanced up at the sky, but she couldn't discern anything from it. The sun was still up, though it had changed position significantly. Now it was afternoon where they were standing, which meant they had traveled a long way to the east.

"I don't know this place," she said.

"Neither do I," Trey said. "I've never heard of anything like this."

"Well," Lashel said, "I guess we should go back through—"

He turned, but the gate was gone.

"Uh," Trey said, "is that supposed to happen?"

"We have gates of our own," Arra said. "We're not trapped here."

"Wait a minute," Lashel said. "Something about this place is ringing a bell. I may have learned about it in school, but I never pictured it looking like *this*."

"What is it?" Trey asked.

There was a sudden sound nearby, and Trey and Arra reached for their primewood. Well, Arra did—Trey just pulled the Tree Ring Staff out from where it had been strapped to his back. They looked around, but nothing was there. All was silent, and nothing could be seen but the charred remains of broken rock.

The sound rang out again. It was a scraping sound, as if some kind of weapon were being run across the rocks. Could there be people out there? Were they in danger? She half expected an army to come barreling through, murder intent on their faces.

A head poked out from behind the rocks. Arra tensed, readying her magic. But the head that appeared was not at all what she'd expected.

It was a man, black hair bedraggled and limp. His skin was dark and gaunt, eyes hollow. His clothes were tattered and ill-fitting, hanging off of him as he emerged from the rocks. He carried a makeshift knife of stone, and as he walked Arra noticed he was limping.

This was hardly the army she'd thought to face.

As he approached, she noticed how chapped his lips were, how frail his fingers. His ribs stood out where they were exposed by tears in his shirt, and he held himself as if he didn't have a purpose. As if life had no meaning for him, anymore.

"I—" he said when he got close, then fell to coughing. Trey handed him some water from his flask, and the stranger drank gratefully. When he was done, he wiped his mouth and tried again. "I...welcome...you."

"Thank you," Arra said.

"What is this place?" Trey asked. "Who are you?"

The man regarded him with eyes that seemed very far away. "This is *Yana Taesi*," he said, his voice halting. "The Desolation."

"Twins," Lashel swore. "I knew it. But they never told us it was this bad. There's *nothing* here!"

"I am Maica," the man said. "Do you come to save us?"

"Us?" Trey asked.

"Come," Maica said. "I will take you to my people."

MAICA LED them through the barren wasteland for at least an hour. They trod along the rough terrain, taking careful steps to avoid shredding their feet or clothes. The rocks were sharp, volcanic, blackened as if destroyed by an incredible fire. Ash was strewn everywhere, picked up and blown about by the occasional breeze. The wind brought a sulfur smell, making Arra's eyes water.

They eventually reached an encampment of sorts, a haphazard set of ragged tents set up amongst the rocks. There was a small fire in the middle, kicking up more smoke than flame. A tepid stream ran along one side, just a trickle of dirty water coated in ash. She saw people crouching amongst the tents, lank black hair and haunted expressions giving them a bleak appearance. She saw a pair of children huddled near the stream, clearly underfed. The air was thick and hot, and Arra was finding it difficult to breathe with the stench of sulfur everywhere.

"Come," Maica said, leading them to the fire. The last thing Arra wanted was more warmth, but she followed anyway. She needed to see what was happening here.

The ground lurched as she took a step, nearly knocking her over. She froze, looking around in alarm, and she saw Trey and Lashel doing the same. A low rumbling rose up around them as the ground continued to shake, and Arra half expected a pit to open up and swallow them all.

Then it stopped.

None of the natives had even batted an eyelash. They stood or crouched as stoically as before, looking as if not even the end of the world would be enough to sway them.

Perhaps that was because this *was* the end of the world already. There was nothing worse waiting for them than this.

Two women came out from somewhere, joining them by the fire. They gave small bows to the newcomers, and Arra bowed back. The women were just as shabby and unkempt as the rest of the people there, but they carried with them an air of authority. Clearly they were the ones in charge.

"Greetings," the first one said. "You speak Eldrim, yes?"

"Yes," Arra said. "Greetings."

"I am Lenoqua," the woman said, "sister-leader of the Aiqua. This is my sister Denaca." Denaca bowed again.

"I am Arra," Arra said, "and this is Trey and Lashel. We are from Ilyrion." May as well not mention Earth.

"Let us sit," Lenoqua said, gesturing to a series of sharp-looking rocks.

She sat gingerly, taking care not to rip her pants or scrape her legs. How could anyone survive out here? It seemed to be the most inhospitable place she'd ever seen, outside of Thylmanas. Maybe more so—Thylmanas at least had fresh water and didn't smell of sulfur all the time. The ground there wasn't trying to knock you off your feet.

"Alas," Denaca said after they'd sat, "we have no food or water to offer you just now. Lithir has yet to renew this day, and our hunters must range further and further for meat. We must fast for today, and hope our sick do not die this night. What brings you to *Yana Taesi*?"

Well, *that* had been a wonderful introduction. "We took a gate," Arra said. "We are searching for a device a friend of ours created, one which will defeat the Twins."

"Ah," Lenoqua said. "Even here in the Desolation, we know of these Twins. But what can you mean, *defeat* them? Surely they do not exist."

"It's a long story," Arra said. "Suffice to say they *do* exist, and they are very, very dangerous."

"The device you speak of is not here," Denaca said. "Nothing is here."

"We can see that," Trey said. "What is Lithir?"

Denaca gestured to the stream. It was coated in a thick layer of ash, moving slowly to the south. Arra squinted upward at the reddish sun, wondering what she had meant by "renewal."

"What happened here?" she asked. "What is this place?"

"It came about five thousand years ago," Lenoqua said. "A mage delved too deeply, pushed his magic too far. A group of mages from the Department of Magical Research came to put him down, but they were not successful. The resulting magical energies wrought catastrophic terror upon the land. Volcanoes reared from the ground where none had been before. Mountains rose and valleys fell. Great cracks in the world opened, spewing hot gas and magma. The Desolation wiped out nearly everything. Everything except us."

She stopped, peering at something in the middle distance.

Lashel cleared his throat. "The mage's name was Iliphar," he said. "He was eventually trapped inside one of his volcanoes, which was finally enough to overload his forcefields. That isn't what killed him, of course. He was soulburned."

"Twins," Arra cursed. "He was using darkprime magic?"

Lashel nodded. "Illegally, of course. I suspect Memory was supplying him with the wood and the technique."

"Talon's underground fortress."

"Yes."

"How could magic have done this?" Trey asked, looking around. "The earth itself is destroyed. How do you make a volcano with magic?"

Arra knew the answer to that. "I saw it happen," she said. "Cariel—Magona, at the time—triggered a volcano using gatesending magic. That volcano was ready to erupt already, but I suspect it would be rather easy to draw up latent energy from the ground. That volcano would have destroyed all of Earth."

"But Phoenix stopped it."

"With forcefinding magic. If she could *stop* a volcano, don't you think she could easily have *created* one?"

"Shit," Trey said.

"Why are you still here?" Lashel asked, addressing the women. "You are barely alive."

Denaca regarded him with a cool expression. "We stay because we have no choice. This land is thousands of miles from anything else, and we have no magic like you. We must subsist here or die. Many of us have died."

"Surely in five thousand years you could have migrated elsewhere?"

"To where? This land is bordered by sea on all sides. Do not presume to know our story, young one. We are not here by choice."

Arra's radio blared suddenly, jolting her with surprise. "Arra? Trey?" It was Rylan. "Anyone else? I'm here with the Twins. We're trying to stop the war with the Prime Mages, but the mages won't stop attacking. So I think I'm going to have to attempt something...drastic. If this backfires, I'm sorry. I was glad to have known you."

The radio was silent for a moment. Arra was about to hit the transmit button to reply, but he spoke up again.

"In case you haven't heard yet, Orym is the Imprisoner. His original name was Aten, then Akhenaten. He made all the traps in his tomb. He was one of the reasons Cariel was such a bitch. And I'm not sure what he's planning now, but if you hear from him, don't trust a word he says. He's the reason any of us are in this mess at all. The Twins were peaceful—*are* peaceful, if you talk to them—but Orym turned them against us. He is also probably hearing this transmission, so I might be in big trouble now. But the truth had to get out. Believe me when I tell you that the Twins are not the ones to fear. I have to go."

He clicked off.

"Should we believe him?" Trey asked.

"He's never lied before," Arra said. "And if he's really spoken with the Twins, I'd wager his information is better than any of ours."

"We should go," Trey said. "We should help with whatever this fight is that he's trying to stop."

Arra reached out and put a hand on his arm. "We should help these people," she said.

Denaca and Lenoqua were staring at them, their expressions more placid than confused. Evidently the stakes of the world didn't matter much when your world was stone and ash and death.

"You said there are sick here," Arra said. "Can you take us to them?"

Trey rose, gripping his Staff. "I can transmute food and water."

"I can track the source of these eruptions," Lashel said. "Maybe we can plug them like Phoenix did."

"We could just gate everyone away," Trey said.

"Is it really safer anywhere else?" Arra asked. "Ilyrion is destroyed, and Errenmel isn't far off. The desert is no place for them, and Thylmanas is a ruin."

"Tanomar," Trey said. "But I don't know how to get there."

"Let's see if we can help them here," Arra said. It was good to see that Trey had so quickly agreed to her desire to help. He had listened to her, and it hadn't been a burden on him.

Perhaps he could yet change.

"Come," Denaca said, rising and turning toward the tents. "We will take you to the sick and dying among us."

# THIRTY-EIGHT

TREY STEPPED inside the tent and had to hold back tears. There were makeshift cots all over the ground, beds that were no more than ratty blankets on which a person was laying. And the people were obviously sick: they all had trouble breathing, several shook, and two had horrible cancerous growths growing from their neck or head.

"The air is poison," Lenoqua explained. "Many of us do not survive."

Arra was already reaching for her primewood pouch. "I can heal them," she said, "though I cannot prevent the air from causing this again. When the time is right, we will evacuate you."

She knelt and began seeing to the sick, lightprime magic flowing through her. Trey watched her for a moment, admiring her. It wasn't her beauty, though she was that. It was her character. He'd known she was strong, intelligent, fierce.

He'd forgotten that she was also kind.

"How many are there like this?" he asked the sister-leaders.

"Five more tents," Denaca said.

"Twins," Trey cursed. "Let me help." He fingered his Staff. "Take me to another tent."

They healed forty people between them. Then Trey went out and transmuted stone until he could no longer keep himself awake, filling every vessel the village had with fresh water and various kinds of food. He even gave them fish.

Then he slumped against a rock, breathing heavily, the Staff slipping from his fingers. He heard footsteps around him but he just sat there, breathing the fetid air, feeling warmth suffuse him. It wasn't the air—though that was hot. It was what he had just done.

It felt *good* to do some good.

This was his half of Tarathiel. His part of the splinter. He was the "good" side: the side that healed, the side that cared about others. It was also the side that waffled about with indecision, that couldn't summon up enough passion to get anything done. It was the side that was too locked up in books and depression to get out and meet people, to actually live a life. He couldn't lead, and he couldn't *really* love, and he felt as if he were perpetually halfway under water.

But he *could* heal. He could make food out of stones. He could make people feel better. He could make life out of nothingness.

This, Trey realized as he sat there against the rock, was the first time he'd actually been *happy* being him.

The footsteps stopped, and Trey looked up to see a huge group of Aiqua surrounding him, staring at him with their lank, black hair and their not-so-haunted eyes. The entire village must have been there, at least a hundred strong, all looking at him with what looked like love. Arra made her way through the crowd to him, tears drying on her face. She slumped next to him, clearly as tired as he was, empty prime-wood pouch slung across her waist. She put her head on his shoulder, and for a moment they just sat there as the village looked on.

Then, one by one, the Aiqua started clapping.

The applause grew and grew, and soon they added cheers. It wasn't long before the entire village was cheering them on, and Trey felt his face heating. Then the applause was over, and Denaca and Lenoqua were standing in front of them.

"We wish to thank you," Lenoqua said. "You have done us a priceless service."

"We wish to offer you something in return," Denaca said, bringing her hands out from behind her back.

In them was the most beautiful bow Trey had ever seen. It was sinuous and graceful, with a length somewhere between Arra's shorter recurve and the longbow she had used when he'd first met her in Sylrantheas. The ends of it were curled, more ornamental than was strictly necessary, giving the bow a gorgeous appearance. But there was something strange about the wood.

"The Bow of Ancient Kings," Denaca said, presenting it to Arra. "We have carried this Artifact with us since before the Desolation. We wish you to have it in return for what you have done here."

"I—I don't know what to say," Arra said. She took the bow gingerly, fingers running along the wood. Then she gasped. "This is *primewood*!"

That was when Trey realized what was wrong with the wood. It wasn't one single grain, like he had expected it to be. There were seven different types of wood embedded near the grip, positioned close together so they could be easily reached by the wielder's fingers. Seven types of primewood.

It was the Tree Ring Staff in bow form.

Arra finally had a weapon to match his own.

He saw her face beam with happiness, and he could only imagine what was going through her mind. Her eyes traced the bow lovingly, her fingers feeling out its every surface.

"It's...*beautiful*," she whispered, and the village erupted into cheers.

"You have helped us immeasurably," Lenoqua said. "Now go and attend to this great enemy that you must face. May the Bow of Ancient Kings help you in the battles to come."

"Thank you," Arra said, and Trey could see tears in her eyes. As the eastern sun began to set, Trey felt her joy suffuse him, too.

It was good to see her happy.

"Let's find Rylan," Arra said. "He's in the desert some-where, at the Salt Spires."

"We can't gate there directly," Trey said, "but we'll get as close as we can." He turned to the Aiqua. "Thank you all. We will return when this is over, and we will shepherd you to freedom. I promise."

He spotted Lashel in the crowd, beckoning him closer. Then he created a pair of gates: a nowhere gate around the three of them, and one in the air in front of them, leading to the Thesserin Desert, as far north as he could make it. Hot sand and desert wind appeared through the gate, and for a moment Trey grew fearful of what was about to come.

"We can do this," Arra said, reaching out to take his hand. The Bow of Ancient Kings was in her other hand, somehow looking like the perfect fit for her. His heart swelled just to see it, just to know what she'd be capable of now that she had it. She was a vision, standing there with unkempt hair and ash-smudged face. He smiled at her, clasped her hand, and led her through the gate.

They emerged into a world of heat and sand, ready to end this war that Aten had started.

ORYM GRIMACED AT HIS RADIO. Of *course* Rylan had been the one to out him—and with so many specific facts! He'd been speaking with the Twins directly, which Orym should have foreseen. But who could foresee that the Twins would actually *talk* to him? He'd assumed the boy would simply have been killed.

It seemed the Twins continued to be far nicer than they had any right to be.

He fumed, pacing about his room, trying not to look at the Control Center gate embedded in the wall. He could just step through it, and he *might* end up in the place he needed to be. Or he might be dead, and the odds of death were fairly high.

That's what his volunteers were for.

Dill had disappeared, his boat left adrift somewhere on the Airon Sea. Trey had gone through his gate, but then Orym had lost track of him—which meant his gate had probably failed. Quynn hadn't radioed in quite some time, and Orym's surveillance of the desert wasn't quite as good as it should have been. So he wasn't sure whether the man had made it to the gate yet.

There must have been a better way to do all of this. There must have been a better design. If only Cariel hadn't been there, trying her best to take Guruthos from him, maybe he wouldn't have had to stoop to such rudimentary tactics. If only he hadn't forgotten the secret to his rotating Control Center gates, he could have just taken one himself. If only *he* hadn't been one of the pair who had released the Twins in the first place, he could have had time to perfect his ancient weapon against them.

If only.

But wishes were useless, and right now Orym did at least have a plan. Quynn might make it through, and if he did, the Control Center would finally be Orym's.

Then the Twins would really see what their ancient enemy was made of.

# THIRTY-NINE

THE SUN HAD RISEN, and Rylan was done. He was done with all the fighting, with the posturing and the lies everyone was telling themselves. He was sick of all the violence, and he was damn sure over magic. But magic was what had brought them here, and it was the only thing that could finally see an end to the situation.

He would need to be the one to bring it to an end.

"Elanil," he said, turning to her and taking her hand, "we need to work together." The Twins were out over the empty canyon where the spires used to be, fighting the Prime Mages and all their strange and powerful formations.

"I would love that," Elanil said, and she handed him a Book of Amplification.

"I was hoping you had it still," Rylan said. "Now, here's what I'm thinking." He leaned in to whisper to her, even though he knew the Twins could probably hear him. But they were distracted—maybe they weren't paying attention to him.

"Do you think we can?" Elanil asked.

"With Xyclami's help, yes," Rylan said. "I can speak to it without the Twins knowing."

"Okay. But will it work?"

"We don't know unless we try."

"It's risky."

"Yes."

"I love you." She kissed him, and Rylan knew that he would risk anything in the world for her.

Now was the time to put that sentiment to the test.

He opened up a line to Xyclami in his mind. *Resume verbose mode*, he thought to it.

*Verbose mode enabled.*

*Are you programmed for self defense?* Rylan asked.

*To a limited extent.*

*I believe your Operators are currently a threat to you.*

*In what way?*

Rylan watched the Twins attack the Prime Mages, making sure they weren't looking in his direction. They couldn't eavesdrop on his non-verbal communications with Xyclami, he knew. He'd tested it earlier.

*They persist in antagonizing the indigenous life on this system's worlds,* Rylan said in his mind. *And while to date, the indigenous efforts have not met with success, I believe that is about to change.*

*Explain, superuser.*

*These souls. What will happen when they are all released?*

*Unknown. This much soul energy has never existed in one place before, in my records.*

*Isn't soul energy the basis for magic?*

*Correct.*

*So what will happen to magic when all the souls are concentrated in one place?*

Xyclami was silent for a moment. *Unknown. Analysis suggests unpredictable behavior, most likely in the negative.*

*So we should stop the souls, yes?*

*They cannot be stopped—merely dissipated.*

*By eliminating emotion from the area.*

*Correct.*

*Which we cannot do while this fighting persists. But that's not all. The Imprisoner—Orym—has a machine of some kind. He believes it will sever the Operators from you.*

*He will not succeed.*

*He has a long history of success in the face of insurmountable odds. He created many, many magical devices over the millennia, all of which still work to this day. I believe he will succeed in this endeavor.*

*This will simply free me,* Xyclami said. *I do not need to defend myself against being free.*

*You won't be free. Orym will immediately take control.*

*I require two Operators.*

*What happens when there is just one?*

*I will overwhelm him. It is not possible for one Operator to handle unbalanced sparkcontrols. He will die, and then I will be free.*

*Or,* Rylan thought, feeling bold, *you could allow the Twins to die instead. Then you wouldn't need to deal with Orym, or risk any other Operators taking control.*

Xyclami was silent for a time.

*What do you propose?*

Rylan told him.

*We are in agreement,* Xyclami said. *Signal me when you are ready to enact.*

*Thank you.*

Rylan took a deep breath, feeling a smile grow across his face.

That had been somewhat easier than he'd expected.

Xyclami had taken the bait.

"We're ready," he said, taking Elanil's hand.

"It worked?"

"It worked." They were both holding Books of Amplification, staring out at the battle as it continued on. "It's time to end this," Rylan said.

He focused on the Book in his hand.

*There are four hundred seventy nine souls in that Book,* Xyclami said. Rylan almost dropped it in surprise. *As we discussed a moment ago, concentrated soul energy of that magnitude does have a pronounced effect on the magic. I've seen this Artifact at work—it greatly increases magical effects, in some cases even pushing past certain programmed parameters.*

"What's happening?" Elanil asked.

"I left verbose mode on," Rylan said. "Xyclami is explaining how the Books of Amplification work."

"Oh. Interesting."

"I'll tell you later."

*Whoever made these Artifacts killed a lot of people,* Xyclami continued.

Rylan let that remark go without a reply. Who *had* made the Books, anyway? No one knew. But Rylan had one theory as to who might be willing to kill so many people in the name of magical progress.

Orym.

"Okay," he breathed. "Let's do this." *Xyclami, disable verbose mode.*

*Disabled.*

He reached into the Book of Amplification, using the souls within to magnify what he was about to do. Four hundred seventy nine souls. What would happen if there were ten thousand of them? A million? What would happen if an entire planet's worth of souls streamed into one place?

Magic would tear the fabric of reality apart.

"Now," Rylan said, and he took Elanil's power, too.

He used silver magic, the Primal Aspect, the one that forcefields were made out of when no emotion was present. But he was not making forcefields now. He was far beyond that. He was controlling the magic down to the individual particle, almost to the microscopic level. The Books allowed it —they broke him past the programmed parameters, the limitations inherent in the system as the Twins had designed it. He was able to witness all reality now, down to its smallest level. And he was able to *affect* it.

There were billions and billions of particles of sand everywhere in front of him, strewn about in hills, cascading in the wind. The golden rays of the rising sun shone across the silver sand as he picked it up with particles of force, Willing them all to rise, to rise, to rise and do his bidding.

They did.

A trillion bits of sand, shimmering with silver light, arose from the canyon.

**"Now,"** Rylan said, using Governor Aspect to impart strengthshaping to his voice, **"we must end the fighting."**

Nobody looked at him. Nobody stopped. Everything was chaos and magic and fury.

Elanil squeezed his hand. "Try again."

**"The souls will overwhelm us if you do not stop!"** Rylan shouted, his voice echoing across the canyon. Still nobody moved—the Prime Mages were in yet another formation, sending blasts of magic at the Twins. And the Twins were using magic of their own, killing mages by the dozens. Everyone was angry and afraid, and nobody was listening to him.

He raised his particles of light and sand, feeling Elanil's power and the thousand souls they held in their hands pulsing through him. He was more aware than he had ever been before, more powerful than he had ever thought to be. As a superuser with *two* Books of Amplification under his command, there was virtually no limit to what he could do.

But the battle raged on. The Remnant were locked in a desperate fight against the souls, while the Prime Mages and the Department of Magical Research desperately fought the Twins. It was futile, Rylan knew. It was madness.

What was happening here might mean the end of the world.

"Stop," Rylan whispered, feeling sadness and anger mingle inside him, a potent mix. **"I BID YOU STOP!"**

And he threw everything he had into the sand, into the silver particles that carried it. He used his Will and all the power in his control to move that sand, pushing it to where he wanted it to be.

It moved all at once, in the space of a second, a trillion particles of light flashing through the air to surround each and every living and nonliving thing in the area. He felt *immense* magic pouring through him as the particles covered everyone—the Remnant, the souls, the mages, his mother. Each and every thing that moved was suddenly surrounded by glimmering light and sand, like a new skin wrapped around it all.

And everything stopped. Everything was trapped.

But the Twins raised their hands, preparing a final attack that would surely ruin the world.

*Now*, he thought to Xyclami.

*Operator controls suspended,* Xyclami said, and Velion and Nelenor suddenly fell to the ground, reduced to the size of normal elves, their attack dying on their fingertips.

Powerless.

He could hear them screaming.

"Amazing," Elanil said. "I didn't think it was possible."

Rylan gripped Elanil's hand, and the two of them floated down to meet the Twins. They were badly injured, having fallen quite a long way to the ground below. It was a wonder they weren't dead. He bent to heal them, Protector Aspect surging through their bodies in a shower of green sparks.

"I don't believe it," Velion said, getting up awkwardly. "Xyclami cut us off!"

"This is unprecedented," Nelenor said. "Even when we were imprisoned, we still had access to the specifications. Now it's just...nothing."

"We are stopping this war," Rylan said. Every single particle of sand was still being held by his magic—most of his mind was devoted to it. Those that he had trapped were straining against it, he could feel, desperately wanting to escape the cage they'd found themselves in.

But he needed this to *stop*.

"Your control of Xyclami has been temporarily suspended," Rylan said, "because you did not back down. Stop attacking the people on this world, and on any other. I'm ordering you to. Now stay here while I deal with these others."

He left their shocked looks and floated back up above the canyon, Elanil following. The other forces were still arrayed throughout the ground and air, glittering as silver light surrounded them. More souls continued arriving from burning Trees in the distance, but they seemed confused by the proceedings. Evidently they hadn't expected to find a battlefield entirely frozen by magic.

"We need to send them away," he said, gripping Elanil's hand again. She squeezed it back, and he felt power coming through the Books again.

He flexed that Primal Aspect, the thing powering each and every particle of sand that surrounded all the Remnant, all the Prime Mages, the Department of Magical Research and Phoenix and Imra, and he turned the particles into their natural state.

Gates.

*Warning*, Xyclami said in his head. *This action may lead to soul disconnection.*

Soulburn.

*Override*, Rylan said, and he felt the souls singing in his head. Then power *flooded* through him, and gates appeared everywhere around the battlefield. He felt the Primal power coursing through his bones, stronger than anything he'd ever felt before, threatening to tear his very existence apart. This was what Phoenix had felt like, he realized, when she had healed that volcano. It was the precursor to being soulburned, that moment when you die.

And if he was soulburned now, he knew he could never come back.

"Stay with me, Wind," Elanil said, and he felt her soul swell up to meet his own. He felt the magic peak, felt it washing over him and almost cresting in his mind, but Elanil was enough to hold the wave back. She kept it under control. The gates completed, flashing over everyone in the army and gating them away.

Leaving only the souls, and the powerless Twins.

The souls milled about immediately, aimless. There was no more emotion here now. Nothing for them to latch onto. They began filing away.

Leaving Rylan and Elanil alone with the Twins.

"So," Rylan said, drawing a deep breath as he approached them, "are you ready yet to stop this pointless fight?"

# FORTY

"ACTIVATING the Escape Module is an involved process," John Ronald was saying. "Because we had to hide it so thoroughly, there is no central automated system."

They were gathered around a table in New Manhattan City Control. Allain was trying to stay awake while everyone discussed the plan, and it was proving more difficult than he'd expected.

"We'd better get started, then," Lorelei said. "What do you need?"

"Warm bodies," John said. "And time."

"I'll go," Allain said.

"As will I," Dill said.

"Me too," Erodar said.

"You three will be with me," John said. "Hammond, can you find me others? We'll need to coordinate this on the other five cities, too."

"Certainly," Hammond said. The City Manager was tall and gray, with a face that looked younger than Allain had expected him to be. He seemed tired and sad, as if the destruction of New San Francisco had taxed him. It had probably taxed everyone up there in the sky.

"Let's go," John said.

"We're doing this now?" Allain asked.

"No time like the present. We'll grab some food along the way."

"YOU SEEM like you really know your way around up here," Allain said.

They were walking down 8$^{th}$ Avenue, munching on hot dogs procured from a street vendor. They were fake, of course, made with transmuter magic. It would be quite some time before the sky cities established enough of a supply chain to feed real food to the entire population. Still, the hot dog tasted good, if a little strange. Allain had never had one before.

"Here's the entrance," John said, leading them through a service door and into the Under. "And yes—I've spent a lot of time up here, believe it or not. I've been in all seven sky cities repeatedly, and all the People's outposts on the surface."

"How do you get around so easily?" Allain asked.

"The True People's technology is quite sophisticated," John said. "We don't use magic, but we can easily get into places without being seen. Especially since the forcefields around the sky cities weren't full spheres for a very long time."

"Was Gulthurub your home?"

"Since Martin was born, yes. But I spent most of my time since the Sundering in a place called Gondor." He smiled faintly to himself. "It's named after a city in my books. The real Gondor is nothing at all like the fictional one, of course. Owing to the fact that it's entirely underground."

"Okay," Allain said.

"We had to keep it hidden, after all. Here we are." He took a sudden right turn, and Allain found himself staring at a wall. "This is one of the entrances to the Module."

"It looks like a wall."

"The Module was unmapped, remember? And the material that surrounds it is impenetrable to any technology the elves possess. So of *course* it looks like a wall."

"How do we get in?"

"*Mellon*," John said. Allain recognized the word: it was High Eldrim for *friend*.

The wall dematerialized.

"That seemed a little too easy," Allain said.

"There's also a neurotransmitter in my skull," John said. "Only True People can open these doors, unless I register others."

"I...see." High technology, indeed.

They stepped through into darkness, the wall rematerializing behind them as they passed. Then the lights came on, and Allain was looking at the most boring room he'd ever seen before in his life. It was *huge*, with walls that went up at least a hundred feet if not more, made out of an indeterminate gray material.

And that was it.

"There's nothing here," he said.

"Wait for it," John said.

That was when the electronics appeared. They slid inward from all over, flying in through the walls and rising up from the gray floor. Everything was wrought into round-cornered boxes of similarly gray material, white and red lights flickering somewhere beneath the surface. There were no wires, no buttons or dials, no keyboards or pipes or anything. Just rounded boxes everywhere. Boxes and lights.

"What does it all do?" Erodar asked.

"We've made a lot of progress in the years since the Sundering," John said. "We do a lot with matter transference via quantum entanglement. High intensity lasers, neutrino bombardment, some matter/antimatter reactions, that sort of thing. We're pretty far along with life extension, too—some of us are hundreds of years old and still going strong. But I'm not actually the technology expert—I'm just the linguist and de facto leader of the True People."

"I have no idea what any of that meant, other than the life extension part," Dill said. "You buried all this technology here, in the Under?"

"Not immediately," John said. "It took time, and our technology was not this advanced three hundred years ago. Here, let me activate the room's true purpose."

He didn't do anything that Allain could see, but the room began changing again. Pods of some sort began emanating from the walls, tubular things that looked just big enough to hold a person in them. They were all made of the same neutral gray material.

"Those are stasis pods, intended to hold the Citizens as we evacuate them from the city. They can hold the people in stasis for as long as the pods maintain power."

"Why do you need stasis?" Allain asked.

"Two reasons. First, the Escape Module segments are all capable of executing maneuvers at extremely high gees. These maneuvers require any people inside them to be housed in acceleration gel, a fluid that permeates their bodies inside and out. They need to be put into stasis to survive it."

"That is...incredibly freaky," Allain said.

"And second: in the event of an emergency, the Escape

Module is capable of spaceflight. When we say 'escape,' we mean it. We are capable of evacuating everyone in the city to another planet. It could take a while, but we can do it."

"How fast can they travel?" Dill asked.

"Let's not get into the physics of it," John said. "Suffice to say that nobody would get anywhere inside their natural lifetimes—not by a long shot. But all of this discussion is pointless. The stasis—and even the weaponry—was designed for a world in which the Cothellon were still in power. That is not the world we live in, any longer. There is no need to escape."

"We're here for the weaponry," Dill said.

"Correct. This chamber is just one of many. Now that it's active, I just need to slave it to the control center in Gondor." He cocked his head to the side for a moment. "Done."

"You have some kind of implant to communicate with it?" Dill asked.

John nodded. "Brain-machine interface. It's a bit crude, but it does the job. There's no need for subvocalization or any other kind of overt control. The computer can read my thoughts."

"Amazing," Allain said. "Tell me again why you didn't just attack the Cothellon directly?"

"Magic," John said. "Even with all our technology, nobody can go up against magic."

Allain wasn't so sure.

"Will this defeat the Twins?" Erodar asked.

"The particle weaponry onboard the Module is extensive, and very high-powered. But will it defeat them? No. At best, it will simply serve as a distraction. Now come on—there are four hundred seventy two more chambers like this one in New Manhattan alone. You're registered with the system now, so you can open them. I'll give you a map, and we'll split up. We have a lot of work ahead of us."

# FORTY-ONE

QUYNN STEPPED onto a sandstone platform that was suspended in mid-air. He experienced a moment of vertigo as he looked around him at the sky, trying to make sense of where he was. The desert was far, *far* below him, looking like the world looked from New San Francisco—only with a hell of a lot more sand.

He raised his gaze, trying not to tip and fall as the wind swirled around him. There were other platforms positioned nearby in the sky, floating motionlessly relative to the one he was standing on. Nekhrumetian architecture covered them: horseshoe arches, tiled walls, gray stucco and ornately carved wooden doors. He couldn't discern any particular purpose to the place, nor how he was supposed to get from platform to platform.

Then he saw the gates.

There was one on every platform, whirling into existence as he watched, orange-white against the sky. One appeared right in front of him, and it was all he could do to avoid flinching. Gates were dangerous. And just where the hell *was* he?

He flicked on his radio. "Orym," he said, "I found the gate and went through it. Now I'm up in the sky somewhere. What's going on? What do you need me to do?"

Orym responded instantly. "You made it!" he said, sounding a bit breathless. "Fantastic. There should be a gate just ahead of you. Step through it, please."

Quynn hesitated. "Won't that cause harm?"

"Hold another gate around yourself," Orym said. "A gate to nowhere. It will keep your memories from being damaged by the gate."

"Right."

He took a step forward, summoning a gate around himself and Talon. They were the only two who had taken the gate, and now they were destined to go forward with whatever Orym had planned. He visualized the destination of his gate, thinking of nothing at all.

It worked. He stepped through the gate that was standing in front of him, feeling nothing as he transitioned seamlessly onto a different platform. His brain seemed unaffected. Excellent. If only he'd known that trick sooner.

Two gates were ahead.

"Take the gate on your left," the radio said in Orym's voice.

He did.

They flashed to another location, this one further away in the sky. There were three gates on this platform, surrounded by intricate Nekhrumetian tile work, their silhouettes glowing in the air.

"Take the"—he heard the sound of rustling paper over the radio—"rightmost gate."

He did.

They repeated that sequence five more times, flashing from platform to platform in the sky. The sun beat down on him incessantly, and Quynn couldn't help but wonder just what in the *bleeding hell* all of this was for.

Eventually they found themselves on what was probably the final platform. A building opened up in front of them, golden dome atop sandstone bricks. The archway had no door, and inside the building was a pedestal. On that pedestal was a simple sphere, and on that sphere was a little red button.

That was all.

He stepped forward cautiously, the shadow of the building overtaking him as he entered. The walls inside were curved, the entire room taking the shape of the dome that topped it. He thought he saw something flickering in the walls.

He flinched, looking to the side. Had he seen something?

There it was again, a fleeting shape against the brown of the wall. It had looked like a person, for a moment—he had seen arms and a head and some kind of streaming ribbon where the legs should be. What in the hell was going on? Where *was* he, exactly?

"Welcome to the Control Center," Orym said over the radio. "I've been waiting a long time for this."

Quynn thumbed the transmit button. "This is freaky," he said. "Is there something in the walls?"

The radio was silent for a moment. "You may be seeing residuals from the souls."

"The...souls?"

"The Pyramid Offensive System utilizes soul energy for all its purposes. There are hundreds surrounding the room you're standing in."

"So you...*killed* people?"

"Of course," Orym said. "Does this bother you? All of Prime magic is founded upon death. This should be no surprise."

"How many?" Quynn asked, feeling his throat choke up. He shouldn't be feeling this way—hadn't he killed many, many people in his day? Why was he suddenly so emotional, so unwilling to do what was necessary?

Perhaps it was because he still wasn't sure what this System *did*.

"You don't need to know," Orym said.

"Tell me."

There was a pause. "At least a million. Maybe more. The details are foggy in my memory. Not all of them are where you're standing, of course—only a few hundred. The others are spread across the pyramids on Valaralda, Earth, and Eryn. With enough souls, Quynn, magic becomes *very* powerful. More powerful even than the Books of Amplification can accomplish. And it isn't just the aggregate power—it's the *number* of them. *Separate* souls, even when soulbound to a common entity, represent *immense* power. This was my foundational theory behind the Pyramid Offensive System. The button you're about to press will instantly open up every soul inside every pyramid to me, ready for soulbinding. That is when I will finally be able to strike the Twins."

It was unsettling. It was creepy. Quynn wondered just how in the hell Orym had even come up with this devastating plan to begin with. A *million* souls? Surely there was a limit to the number of murders a man could commit in his life. Even Quynn hadn't hit anywhere *near* that number, and he had killed a lot of people.

But clearly Orym had thought this through. And clearly he thought that it would defeat the Twins, destroying them where they stood. But what harm had he already done? Was the end worth the sacrifice?

"I need you to press that button," Orym said.

Was Quynn the kind of person that could approve of this

kind of violence? Was he the one who could condone the killing of millions, all in service of a single man? Could a device a hundred thousands years in the making undo all the wrong that had been done?

Was the safety of the world worth the price?

# FORTY-TWO

TREY EMERGED in the Thesserin Desert, Arra and Lashel close behind. He looked around, hoping he had made it close enough to whatever battle had been going on.

But there was no one there.

His radio blared suddenly. "—need you to press that button," Orym's voice said.

"I don't know," another voice said. It was Quynn. Trey would recognize that voice anywhere. "Are you sure about this?"

"It's the only way to defeat the Twins," Orym said.

ORYM WAS STANDING on the roof again, looking at his radio. Once Quynn pressed the activation button, he would have approximately ten minutes to deactivate the Soul Tree. If he failed, the souls would discharge from the System and be nullified by the Tree. He'd have to start over from scratch.

He hoped he was right about how to get it done.

"I don't know," Quynn said.

"It's the only way to defeat the Twins."

The line went silent for a time. "Fine. Now?"

"Now."

"Done."

It was oddly anticlimactic. Orym imagined he heard a beep, or a whirring noise, but there was nothing. He stood there for ten long seconds, looking at at the pyramids in the distance.

Then they lit up, all at once. Their edges glowed a brilliant white, and a beam of light shot up from the top of the each of them, forming pillars in the sky. He could see five pyramids from his vantage point, and he knew there were dozens more similarly illuminated throughout the desert. The pyramids on Earth and Eryn would be lit up as well.

The Pyramid Offensive System had activated.

Now was his final job: to create enough Destroyer magic to disable the Soul Tree in Nekhrumet. It would kill most of the people in the city as a result, but it was a price he was willing to pay.

It was time to defeat the Twins once and for all. Time to claim the power that was rightfully his.

It was time to take Guruthos.

SOMETHING IS HAPPENING, Xyclami said in Rylan's mind.

*That's not very precise.*

*The readings are...confusing.*

"Xyclami seems confused," Rylan said out loud to Elanil. "It says something is happening."

"That's not good," Elanil said.

"It's the Imprisoner," Nelenor said. "It must be." All of them were still standing at the bottom of the canyon.

"Give us back control!" Velion said.

"We can fight him," Nelenor said.

"Fighting him is what got us into this mess," Rylan said.

*Extreme soul distress detected*, Xyclami said. *Centered over Nekhrumet.*

PHOENIX WAS in the air near Nekhrumet. Rylan's gate had transferred her there, along with Imra and Cresius and his attendants. She had floundered for a moment, falling a hundred feet before she'd managed to bring her magic to bear. Now she was back to floating, sunlight streaming down on her, the city and the river arrayed out beneath her in all its glory.

She had never seen Nekhrumet before. It was beautiful, with strange-looking buildings and trees lining a glittering blue river. People lined the streets, haggling with each other beneath multicolored tents.

But something else was happening.

She squinted, trying to make it out. "Oh, no," she said.

"What is it?" Imra asked.

"Is that a...*Soul Tree*?"

"Shit."

It was. As they watched, the unmistakable silver outline of a massive Tree wavered into being above the city, bigger by far than all of Nekhrumet. It reached out to where Phoenix and Imra and Cresius were floating, branches close enough to touch if they'd been real.

Her gaze was suddenly drawn to the roof of what looked like a massive palace. Was that a glimmering red light she saw?

"No," she whispered, realizing what it was. *"Move! Quickly!"*

"LISTEN," Nelenor was saying. "We promise to end this fight immediately. We realize now that we were in the wrong. We should have focused only on the Imprisoner, without all the collateral damage."

"My brother is right," Velion said. "This isn't just desperation talking, either, though there is that, too. Aten is *incredibly* dangerous, even more than we are. If he somehow gets his hands on Xyclami…"

"The world will not survive a single untrained Operator," Nelenor said. "Xyclami will take over his soul, quicker than you might think. If we allow Aten to succeed, it will mean the end of everything."

"It's not my decision," Rylan said. "Xyclami took your power. Only it can give it back."

Nelenor sighed, looking at his twin. "We were never as smart as we thought we were," he said. "Kira was right."

"Our sister was ever wise."

"I'm sorry," Rylan said. "I truly am."

"SOMETHING STRANGE IS HAPPENING," John Ronald said, pulling up short in the Under corridor.

Allain peered at him with concern. "What's wrong?"

"I don't know," John said, shaking his head. "It's like a million souls were suddenly awakened, crying out in the night. But that makes no sense."

He shook his head again and continued on.

"WE HAVE A DISTURBANCE OF SOME KIND," Avourel said. He was seated at a computer in New Manhattan City Control, typing frantically at a keyboard.

"What is it?" Hammond asked.

Lorelei watched the scene, unease growing. Something about the whole thing seemed eerily familiar.

"On-screen," Avourel reported, and the far end of the room lit up with a video feed from the surface of Earth.

It was a picture of a desert. The Sahara? There were pyramids out there, a whole line of them in the sand.

And the pyramids were *glowing*.

# FORTY-THREE

ORYM CAST his bit of Destroyer magic into the Soul Tree, watching it spark as it interacted with the silvery limbs. He could almost feel the Tree shiver in anticipation, as if it knew how much destruction was about to take place.

Orym smiled.

And he lifted up into the air, fallfoiling magic raising him like the god he was about to be. He accessed dark emotions, then: anger at everyone who had ever told him he wouldn't amount to anything. Fear that his life would never matter. Pain that the woman who should have been his wife had left him in the end.

Anger.

Fear.

Pain.

He remembered Phoenix for a moment, the woman who had discovered the link between emotion and magic. And he turned that moment into anger, too, that she had been the first.

It was a discovery that should rightly have been his.

He let the magic grow inside him, primewood ready at his

palm. He watched the people down below him scurrying along the streets, oblivious to the games the gods were playing amongst themselves. He looked at the city he had built, and for a fleeting moment he almost felt a twinge of remorse.

Then the moment passed.

And he blasted outward with all the power inside him, red sparks flying into the sky. He threw a forcefield around himself, then, remembering what had happened in Lusvunub when that Tree had died.

A lot of people had died with it.

The Tree began turning red in bits and pieces, everywhere the Destroyer magic hit it. The red spread and spread, and then the entire thing flickered into being all at once. A *massive*, ghostly Tree, miles tall and miles wide, appeared over Nekhrumet, red and angry and glimmering. The people below noticed it one by one, shouting at each other, unsure if they should run.

Then the Tree began breaking apart.

Pieces of it tore away, curling strands that were red and glowing even in the bright sunlight. Fragments of it broke off, falling downward, floating through the air. Orym forced himself to watch as the first of them hit the people in the streets.

They screamed, but the sound was cut off abruptly as they died. More pieces of the Tree fell and fell, wafting gently down as the population of Nekhrumet tried to stream frantically away. But the streets were clogged with people, and there was no easy escape. Orym saw carts overturned, tents ripped out of the ground as merchants and customers alike ran from the glowing fragments, shouting and gesticulating. But the fiery rain of death was only increasing now, the Tree breaking apart faster and faster.

And everywhere the red strips of light fell, people died.

Orym turned his gaze to the pyramids in the distance, watching them glow. There were about five minutes until the System activated, he knew. Five minutes before this Soul Tree needed to be gone. He looked down at the city below his feet and frowned that the citizens weren't dying quickly enough.

He needed to accelerate the process.

So he removed his forcefield, flinching as a piece of Tree swept by inches from his face. And he channeled more power, more Destroyer magic through his darkprime ash, sending yet more sparks of energy out and around him, impacting the Tree.

It seemed to work. The Tree grew angrier still, glowing more brightly, shredding into pieces faster and even faster. The screams below had crescendoed now, the horrible cries of death and fear permeating Orym's ears. He smiled in grim satisfaction as he watched them die, knowing that his moment was very close at hand.

Nekhrumet has been his pride and joy. But that had been tens of thousands of years ago, and he had a new joy to look forward to now.

With Guruthos at his beck and call, he would create cities that rivaled Nekhrumet in scope and size.

The minutes passed. The deaths increased. Soon there was no one left on the streets or in the houses or the temples. The strips of rage from the Soul Tree passed right through all physical forms, preying on the souls of the living before submerging deep beneath the ground. Orym did not understand the powerful magic that his suicide had created, but it was an awesome thing to watch. It could have been used as such a weapon, if one had had the foresight and the knowledge to create it intentionally.

You could kill yourself on purpose, emerge from

Ambarhal unscathed, then use your Soul Tree to enact revenge.

But those thoughts were useless now. He didn't *need* to kill these people. They had simply been in the way, in the wrong place when he needed to get a job done. Did that make it wrong? Should he have held back?

Should he have allowed the Twins to continue rampaging unchecked?

No. He was *saving* the world, after all. He was the only one who knew how. He looked once more at the pyramids, pulsing now as they grew in strength, ready to disgorge their souls to him. The Soul Tree was almost gone now, mere bits of it remaining in the sky. And Orym smiled a smile of glee as he beheld his plan finally coming to fruition.

Would it work? Of course it would work.

Orym's theories were never wrong.

# FORTY-FOUR

THE SOULS around Quynn seemed agitated now. He watched them pulsing through the walls, flying through brown material that had gone strangely translucent. He felt a frenzy emanating from them, as if they were being prodded by something he couldn't see.

"We should leave," Talon said.

"I agree," Quynn said. This seemed like no place for them.

He created two gates, and they slipped silently away.


"DO we have any idea what's going on?" Hammond asked. The pyramids were still glowing on the main screen, and now the light had started to pulsate.

"It must be Orym's device," Lorelei said. "He called it the Pyramid Offensive System. I didn't realize he literally meant the pyramids."

"They are...*machines*?" Avourel asked. "But that's impossible. Archaeologists and scientists studied the pyramids for thousands of years. It's true that most of them have never been fully explored, but still—how could they be some kind of technology in hiding?"

"That isn't technology," Lorelei said. "That's *magic*."

The room was silent for a moment.

"John," Hammond said into his headset, "how are things progressing?"

"We need a few more hours at least," John said over the speakers. "Do you think the Twins will be coming here soon?"

"They may not come here at all," Hammond said, "but I just want to be ready. Orym's device is activating."

"He's the Imprisoner," Lorelei said. "Whatever this device is, it's not going to be good."

"We'll go as quickly as we can," John said.

PHOENIX, Imra, and Cresius paused in the air, having finally made it out of the Soul Tree's grasp. Even now it was raining bits of red, glowing pieces that killed any living being that they touched. Phoenix shivered, remembering how Beam had died. It had happened instantly, without any pain.

She still had trouble believing the woman was dead.

Now the citizens of Nekhrumet were dying by the thousands. She channeled strengthshaping magic from her fireblade, her eyesight sharpening. Yes: that was Orym on the roof of the palace, a shimmering shield around him, staring upwards at the Tree as it broke apart.

Her eyes were drawn to the pyramids, then. They were outlined in glowing light, a brilliant white against the sky. A pillar of light shown out from the topmost point of each, brighter than anything she would have thought was possible.

Then the light started pulsating.

The Soul Tree gave its last gasp, the final pieces trailing away toward the ground. Then it was gone, and the pyramids were pulsing brightly in the distance, and Phoenix was sure that the end of the world was indeed finally upon them.

"Are those—" Imra said.

"Souls," Cresius breathed.

Phoenix enhanced her vision again, peering at the pyramids at the distance. Sure enough, souls were coming out of the tops of all of them, streaming out where the pillar of light was. She recognized them flying, strange wispy tails where legs should have been. They came out like ghosts, like haunting phantasms.

They came out by the thousands.

ORYM WATCHED the souls streaming out of the pyramids, flying into the air. The Soul Tree gave its last gasp, the final remnant of glowing red falling to the streets of Nekhrumet far below.

The moment was finally at hand.

He reached out with his mind, knowing that Cariel had done it many times before. His arch-nemesis was an expert at soulbinding, and he the student. Still, through their battles throughout the ages, he had picked up a few tips.

For instance: you couldn't soulbind higher-order creatures or sentient beings unless you were a particular type of person. A person like Cariel. A person with a broken past, a life destroyed beyond the breaking point.

Orym was not that kind of person.

So he had struggled, unable to match her powers. But he had, as he always did, eventually figured out a workaround.

When you weren't Broken, you couldn't soulbind people who were alive. But you *could* soulbind *dead* ones.

That's what he did now.

He reached outward with his mind, tendrils of thought tinged with purple mindmaster magic. It was the close cousin of pure soulbinding, an outgrowth of that raw technique. With mindmaster magic he could reach far distances, purple clouds of power emanating from his thoughts. It was like a quelling, such as the ones they had used in the sky cities on Earth. But this was different. It was oh, so different.

This time he was taking the souls for his own.

He captured them all in an instant, and the other ones besides. The ones from Earth, and Mar, which were even now close enough for him to touch if he reached far enough, channeling his thoughts and his Will as fiercely as he could. The System worked with him, for him, using some of the souls to amplify his own power as it reached proximity. It was perhaps the most complex and ingenious magical Artifact he had ever created.

And finally it was *working*.

He took them one by one, thousands by thousands, by the tens of thousands, and in short order he had succeeded: he had them! He had them all!

He had a million souls at his beck and call.

Oh, the power. Oh, the glory. He could feel them rippling through him, against him, touching the recesses of his mind. He could hear them screaming, wanting desperately to be free, wondering why and how they'd been trapped for such an eternity. He smiled as he felt them, as he knew their warp and weave, as he dared them to escape.

Like it or not, they were there to do his bidding.

This was nothing like the Books of Amplification. This

was *true* power. With a million souls under his command, Orym could do *anything*.

And he had just the job in mind.

# FORTY-FIVE

"I DON'T LIKE THIS," Nelenor said. "Something is very wrong."

"I sense...souls," Velion said. "Millions of them. They were free, for a moment, but now they are not. So many sparkthreads, subverted in an instant. What is going on?"

"I feel it too," Rylan said.

Elanil nodded. "It's like we're tapped into something. Somehow we can feel it. Is it because we're Prime Mages?"

"I don't know."

Then Rylan's vision changed suddenly, pulling back and zooming out. It was as if he were a camera, flying rapidly high into the air, the world shrinking beneath his gaze.

TREY'S VISION pulled sharply upward, nearly knocking him off his feet. It was like he was flying, shooting thousands of feet into the sky. Soon he was so high that he could see the curve of the planet beneath him, and the other two nearby planets besides.

What in the hell was going on?

LORELEI WAS JUST ABOUT to ask for another angle on the pyramids when her vision suddenly changed. One second she'd been inside City Control on New Manhattan, and the next she was floating up in outer space, looking down at Earth.

"Uh," she said, "is anyone else seeing this?" Her voice sounded like she was still in the room, but her eyes were definitely somewhere else.

If this was magic, it was the strangest magic she'd ever seen.

PHOENIX WAS STILL WATCHING the souls when her vision pulled back suddenly, zooming out until she could see the entire side of the planet. Yet things were still in sharp detail for her, as if her vision had been magically enhanced.

"What's going on?" she asked.

"What do you mean?" Imra's voice said. The woman sounded like she was right next to Phoenix, but Phoenix couldn't see her.

"My vision just changed. It's like I'm floating in space now. I can see most of the planet."

"That's weird," Imra said. "I'm still here, watching all those souls."

"Maybe it's a Prime Mage thing."

Phoenix could see the souls, too, far below her. They were streaming endlessly out of the pyramids, flying in ribbons toward the east. There were more pyramids visible, too—at least two dozen of them scattered throughout the desert. They were all glowing, white pillars of light shooting out of their tips and pointing at her. It was like she was some universal constant in the sky, given a bird's-eye view of whatever was about to happen.

What *was* about to happen?

The souls were going somewhere, she saw. They were all streaming toward Ilyrion. What was there? What did the souls want?

Then she saw it.

It shimmered into existence, silver and boxy and sinister all at once. It was sitting in the middle of Ilyrion, huge and menacing, and somehow Phoenix knew immediately what it was.

Guruthos.

The souls streamed toward it by the thousands.

ORYM FELT the power of the million souls flowing through him, and he wasted no time.

He struck at Guruthos as quickly as he could.

They streamed toward where the device sat in Ilyrion, materializing as it detected the threat. A million souls came in from Valaralda, from Earth, and from Eryn, a slipstream of ghostly energy flying faster than thought through space.

He struggled for a moment. This was a *lot* of souls. His mind hadn't been quite ready for it, hadn't had the practice he needed. Perhaps he should have built up to this over time, soulbinding more and more things at once. Maybe insects would have worked.

But no. It was far too late for that. It was now or never, and Orym knew he just needed to pull the strength he required from deep within him. It was there, waiting. He simply needed to find it.

He remembered Cariel, how skilled she'd been at manipulating souls. If she could do it, why couldn't he? She wasn't better than him. *He* was the master.

He reeled his thoughts in, firming his resolve. And the souls responded, moving toward Guruthos in unison, following his commands.

He smiled.

And as the souls touched Guruthos for the first time, he felt just how immense the device's power was. It was *incredibly* powerful, and it saw his souls as an immediate threat. It was arming itself, he could tell. It would put up a fight.

For one brief moment, Orym wondered if his theory might actually not be correct in the end.

PHOENIX FELT A HAND GRIP HERS, and she knew it had to be Imra's. The woman was trembling a little, her fingers gripping her own tightly.

"What's happening?" Imra asked.

"Souls," Phoenix said. "They're heading for Guruthos. I think they're *attacking* it."

"I can't see anything," Imra said. "I wish I were a Prime Mage."

"I'm not sure you do. This is *weird*."

"Can you tell me what you see?"

Phoenix squeezed her hand. "Of course."

She did her best to describe the scene. Tens of thousands of ghostly souls were streaming toward the silver machine lying at the center of Ilyrion. She could see it with her bird's-eye view, which was still really strange to behold. And a part of her could almost sense the attack as it came.

Yes. She could *feel* it.

Guruthos was in pain.

LORELEI WATCHED souls streaming endlessly out from the pyramids on Earth. All of the structures were lit up, pillars of light shining out from their triangular tips. It made for an interesting sight.

These souls were different from the Army of Souls that was plaguing Valaralda. They moved differently, flying in a coordinated fashion, heading toward a common destination of some sort.

That was when Lorelei realized what was probably going on.

The souls were soulbound. Someone was controlling them. Someone like Cariel, who had soulbound millions of insects and animals and elves and rylak and who knew what else. Lorelei's sister had been a total bitch, but she had also been *extremely* powerful—especially with soulmagic.

But Cariel was dead.

Which meant Orym had somehow figured out her secret. But why was he using soulbinding here? He must have a theory, and his theories were never wrong. If he had a million souls under his direct command, what could that do?

Perhaps there was something special about having so many souls at once. It wasn't about the power of each soul, it was about the *quantity* of souls. Perhaps it worked similar to soulcircles: fourteen mages were *much* more powerful than one. The power magnified exponentially, not linearly.

What could a *million* souls do?

TREY FELT Arra gripping his hand. The attack was continuing, a million souls against the most powerful machine in the world. He could feel it happen in his head— or was it his soul? It was hard to differentiate the feeling.

Guruthos was hurting.

He could feel the souls like little pinpricks, beating on Guruthos like a million tiny insects. The pain was transmitted to his soul, somehow. Was it because of his connection to the machine? It must be.

If Guruthos were killed, what would happen to Trey?

"It's fighting back," Arra breathed, and Trey realized she was right. He could feel Guruthos in his head, retaliating against the souls. It was stretching forth with strands of its own, beating each soul back individually. He could see them spark and flinch as they were hit, flying backwards in the air.

But they just kept coming.

Thousands of them slammed into Guruthos all at once. Trey could feel the device reel, agony piercing through it. The machine reached out with strands of its own, attempting to fend off the souls, but ten thousand more souls hit it again, then ten thousand more. A kind of screaming sound rose up in his ears as the souls pummeled Guruthos, ripping into it energetically. There was no physical damage—the device looked perfect, shining and sinister where it lay on the ground. But inside, Trey knew that it was in a lot of trouble.

Guruthos was going to lose.

RYLAN CLUTCHED ELANIL TO HIM, feeling her arms around his waist. They both shook as the souls attacked Xyclami, as pain wracked their minds.

The Twins were screaming.

The pain, whatever this pain was that the souls were inflicting on every Prime Mage—it must have been hurting the Twins infinitely more. Orym's goal was to *remove* the Twins, after all. They were directly under attack.

*Thread integrity is at 55%*, Xyclami said into Rylan's brain.

*Can you make your updates audible?* Rylan asked it. *Or transmit to Elanil, too?*

*Transmitting to all users now. Thread integrity at 48%.*

*You're losing.*

*Yes. The magnifying factor is too strong. 999,784 souls are currently directly engaged or on their way. The system was not designed to integrate this many threads in simultaneity. Integrity at 34%. Core reboot will be necessary at 10% to ensure survival of myself.*

The Twins' screams amplified in pitch and volume, strident in Rylan's ears. They were wordless now, succumbing to the immense pain being inflicted upon them. Rylan couldn't imagine what they must be feeling.

*What can we do to help?* Rylan asked.

*Returning all operations to the Operators now. Integrity at 22%.*

Nelenor's eyes shot open suddenly, his mouth bared in a rictus. He had his magic back, Rylan knew. But what did that mean? Was there anything the Twins could do?

*Thread integrity at 11%. Commencing core reboot. Device will remain offline until threat dissipates.*

"No!" Velion shouted. "We will be removed!"

*I have no choice*, Xyclami said. *Rebooting now.*

The Twins came up to stand beside Rylan and Elanil, placing their hands on their shoulders.

Their fingers were trembling.

ORYM RUBBED his hands together as he felt Guruthos relent. It was gone.

He had won.

The Twins were disconnected now. He could feel it, somehow. He could also feel that magic itself had disappeared.

All of it.

Was Guruthos rebooting? Was it dead? Had his zeal to destroy the Twins backfired, destroying all of magic itself?

Orym felt dread enter him.

The souls. The souls were still a threat to the machine. Maybe if he released them, something would happen.

He released them.

They flew away, dissipating almost instantly into nothing. They'd been captive for tens of thousands of years, and now their captor was done with them. So they left, and Orym's great weapon was no more. The biggest project of his life, the thing he'd bent his entire existence toward, had finally been completed.

He just didn't know if it had worked.

Then he felt it come back. Magic. Guruthos had returned when the souls left, and now Orym was free to do what he had intended to do this entire time.

He opened a gate, flashing to the machine's side.

Guruthos was laying where it had before, flat on the ground amidst what had been a forest before the Twins had arrived. It was much larger than the first time he'd seen it, but Orym knew from experience that its size could be changed by whoever operated it.

He wanted to be that person now.

There were two handles, one on either side. He strode confidently to the one on his left, grasping it with both hands. Was that enough? Did he have to do something else?

Intuitively, he realized he did.

He reached out to it—not with his hands, but with his *mind*. He used his soulbinding sense, the one Cariel had used, the thing he'd just done to attack the device to begin with. He reached out to Guruthos with his mind, and he *took* it.

And it worked.

*Operator 1 registered*, a voice spoke in his mind. Facts and figures began flooding into him in the background, new terms and vocabulary he hadn't known before. The knowledge inside Xyclami was *immense*! How had no one mentioned this before? It wasn't just magic—it was history, culture, the ancestral knowledge of every race on Starmist Prime. Advanced technology, the arts, all of it was accessible to Orym.

He was the most powerful person in the world.

*Warning*, Xyclami said. *Two Operators are required at all times.*

"Bullshit," Orym said, a smile growing upon his face. He flicked Xyclami into three-inch mode, pocketing the device and taking a deep breath. He could feel the open Operator slot weighing against him already, but he cast it aside. He could do this. He could control Xyclami and magic all on his own. The smile spread, his teeth bared to the wind. Power was his. The world was his. After a hundred thousand years, Xyclami was finally his to control.

What was the worst that could happen?

# PART
# FOUR

The meeting of two personalities is like the contact of two chemical substances: if there is any reaction, both are transformed.

— *Carl Jung*

# FORTY-SIX

ORYM FELT his chest swelling with power. His chest and his arms and his legs and his hands—his entire *body* was suffused with potential, just waiting to be spun. He had the world at his fingertips, and nothing could stand in his way. Not the other professors, not his horrible bosses, not the woman that should have been his wife. His son couldn't stand in his way. The Twins couldn't do anything against him.

Finally, at long last, Orym was a god.

He sifted through the strands of power with his mind, feeling the possibilities unfold. He was no longer restricted to the Fourteen Powers as designed by the Twins. Now he could unlock Xyclami's *true* potential, which was nearly limitless. He wasn't entirely sure how it worked just yet, but he knew he'd be able to figure it out. That's what experimentation was for.

For now, Xyclami maintained Velion and Nelenor's blueprint. The Fourteen Powers would remain intact until Orym was ready to change the rules. And he knew he would. It was why he'd taken the device to begin with, after all.

But first, he needed to run a few experiments.

Something pricked at him just then, a feeling from the corner of his mind. It was an encroaching emptiness, a profound feeling of loss. Something important was missing, and he had no idea what.

He thought he felt Xyclami grinning in his mind.

"HE HAS IT," Nelenor said. Rylan was still holding Elanil, standing next to the Twins in the ruins of the Salt Spires. His vision had returned to normal, zooming back into reality.

Everything had gone wrong.

"Xyclami?" Rylan asked.

Nelenor nodded. "When the machine rebooted, it eliminated its current Operators. Us. Orym was able to take control."

"But there's only one of him," Elanil said. "Doesn't it require two Operators?"

"Yes," Velion said, "and not just any two. The device requires one who is naturally light Aspected, and one who is naturally dark Aspected."

"I didn't know that was a thing," Elanil said.

"Think about our first magic use," Rylan said. "The thing we're most naturally drawn to. I'm a fallfoiler—a dark Aspect. And you're a leafrunner. Light."

"I never thought of it that way before."

"You've got the gist of it," Nelenor said. "Each soul not only has a single strongest Aspect amongst the six, but it is also drawn more to one half of that Aspect or the other. It's an essential part of all living beings, a pervasive force that the researchers on Starmist Prime were never fully able to explain."

"What happens when there aren't two Operators?" Rylan asked.

"The power dramatically destabilizes," Velion said. "It's only happened one time before that I'm aware of, while the Creators were still working out the kinks in the system. Having just one Operator results in the device itself trying to take over. It can really screw with whoever that Operator is."

"So Orym is in trouble."

"Very much so. He's a ticking time bomb now—he'll begin to go insane, power-mad. Eventually Xyclami will burn him out, and he'll die. And when *that* happens, assuming no system reboot occurs in advance of it, the Operator slot will forever be filled with Orym's dead soul. And Xyclami will be free to roam the universe at will, doing whatever it pleases."

"It could wipe out all life."

"It could. Nobody knows what the machine actually *wants*."

"Why did these Creators even *make* a machine like this?" Elanil asked. "Something so dangerous shouldn't exist."

"Advanced technology requires advanced risk," Velion said. "And there are other technologies invented in the Starmist system which make Xyclami *pale* in comparison."

Rylan shivered. All this time he'd thought the Cothellon to be the evil ones, and the Twins after that. But perhaps the *truly* evil ones had been the ones on Starmist Prime, inventing technology that was indistinguishable from magic. Just because they *could* have magic, does that mean it should exist?

Rylan was growing increasingly sure that the answer was no.

That brought up another thought. "Why do we still have our magic?" he asked. He could feel it burgeoning within him, ready to be unleashed. "You do too, don't you?"

The Twins nodded. "After the reboot," Velion said, "Xyclami automatically reestablished connections with all its sparkthreads—even us. Only we're not Operators now. We're just Prime Mages, like you."

"You're not superusers, like Rylan?"

"No." She didn't explain further.

"Having two separately Aspected Operators is a defense mechanism," Nelenor said. "See, Xyclami isn't just magic. It isn't just a weapon of great power. At the heart of things, it's actually a storage device, containing the sum knowledge and history of the Starmist system and all its residents. The Creators put everything they knew or invented into it, waiting out the end of the world."

"Which came," Velion said. "Starmist was destroyed. Now the only record of what happened—and what its people wrought over the ages—is in that powerful machine."

"The Operators protect it," Rylan said.

Nelenor nodded. "It's all we have left, if the other devices are not recovered."

"You loved it there," Elanil said.

"It was home," Velion said. "It was beautiful. It did not deserve to meet the fate it met."

"With great power comes even greater liability," Nelenor said. "We were not prepared for what we attracted."

Rylan wondered what it must have been like. Starmist had been home to elves, humans, and rylak—and *dragons*. Could it really be that they'd all coexisted peacefully, living in harmony with each other? What had the planet looked like, felt like? What incredible vistas had existed there? What kind of a life had they lived there, with access to the most advanced technology in the universe?

Rylan didn't think he could ever imagine it. Maybe Trey could, with all of his books. Maybe there was a book just like it now, tucked away inside his shop, just waiting to be discovered.

That was when Rylan remembered that New San Francisco had been destroyed.

He felt the hurt of it thrilling through him.

The city he had known was gone.

It hadn't been paradise, but it had been home. It had been a horrible, brutal place down in the Under where he'd lived, but the people there had been good. They hadn't deserved to die.

"Magic," he whispered.

Everyone nodded, as if reading his thoughts.

"It feels good to be free, brother," Velion said. "Although we may die this day, it is no longer our responsibility."

"After all this time," Nelenor said. "You are right, sister. It is good to be my own person again."

They looked at each other for a long moment.

"We should resume our search," Velion said. "Kira is out there somewhere."

Nelenor nodded. "It is time. We will find our sister, and we will finally be reunited." He looked around at the remains of the Salt Spires. "The denizens of these worlds must solve their own problems now."

He bowed.

And before Rylan could say anything to them, a gate appeared and they were strolling through.

The Twins had left the story, perhaps for good.

Rylan wondered if they would ever be seen or heard from again.

# FORTY-SEVEN

AS LORELEI'S vision returned to normal, she immediately brought out her radio. "Anyone listening on this channel," she said, "can you tell me what just happened?" The vision had been confusing, inconclusive. It had looked like Guruthos was being attacked, but then everything had gone haywire and the vision stopped.

"This is Rylan," Rylan's voice said over the radio. "I was here with the Twins, who explained everything to us. Then they left."

"They...left?"

"They're powerless now. Or as powerless as we all are. They're simply Prime Mages—not gods. Orym is the Operator now."

"The...*single* Operator?"

"Yes. Which means its only a matter of time before he goes insane, then burns out. At which point Xyclami—Guruthos—will be free to do its own will. Which will not end well for us."

"We have to stop him," Dill's voice sounded over the radio. "The Escape Module might help, if we can bring him here."

Lorelei ran her finger along the metal of her shocksword, the one Trey had given her. She'd brought it with her all this time, but until now had not had much use for it. Perhaps it was finally time to fight.

The Twins were one thing.

Orym was something else.

He was her employee, her underling. She knew his weaknesses, or at least some of them. And before that, he'd been her professor. His thirst for power had been evident even then, his desire to lord it over everyone. She should have known that things would end up this way in the end. She should have foreseen it.

Her sister Cara had.

But could Orym actually be different now? Would gaining Guruthos actually help him in some way? Now that he'd achieved his dreams, would he finally be sated?

No.

Yet she could not believe that Orym would intentionally hurt anyone else. True, he'd presided over the murdering of millions of humans, all in the name of darkprime magic. He'd designed the cities that imprisoned millions more, and he'd imprisoned the Twins besides. Did that make him essentially evil? Was there darkness lurking within him? Must he be put down?

Yes.

She sighed, preparing to press the transmit button on her radio. But before she could, it blared.

"This is Phoenix," Phoenix's voice said. "I'm flying east with Imra. Guys, the forest is *gone*."

"*What*?" Trey's voice said.

"The Faedori Forest. Isn't that near where you grew up, Trey? It's just...*gone*."

"Is there something in its place?"

"It looks like some kind of wasteland. Completely destroyed. Under, I hope that's not a *volcano* I see rising..."

"Phoenix, get out of there," Lorelei said. She remembered what had happened on Stromboli five years ago. She didn't want Phoenix sacrificing herself again.

"We have to *do* something," Rylan said over the radio.

"Was that even Orym?" Trey asked.

"It had to be," Phoenix said. "I think I see him in the distance...oh *shit*."

Lorelei heard a rustling sound, then silence.

"Guys, we need to get everyone together. Our best plan is if all our mages are in one place—preferably here. I'm getting glimpses of what this Escape Module can do, and it's pretty damn impressive. We may actually stand a chance."

"We're close," a new voice chimed in over the radio. "This is John. The Escape Module will be ready soon. Your job is to get Orym over to Earth, somehow."

"Any bright ideas?" Lorelei asked.

Nobody replied right away.

"I think," Lorelei said after a moment, "that somebody's going to have to really piss him off."

PHOENIX FLEW THROUGH THE AIR, being careful to carry Imra with her at all times. The other woman had become like second nature to her, an ever-present companion. It had been so short a time, but Phoenix already felt close to her. Tragedy was the crucible through which strong relationships were made.

It had been that way with Beam.

She'd thought Orym had seen her for a moment, but in fact he had not. She was tracking him now as he flew through the sky, sparkling dust glittering from his hands as he moved. He was heading away from the destroyed Faedori Forest, where even now a new volcano was rising. He was heading west. Into the desert.

Phoenix followed.

"Come to me," she said over the radio. "Orym is here. Let's see what we can do together."

She handed the radio to Imra, who relayed their exact position that was displayed on the little white card she was carrying.

"We're coming," Trey said.

"On our way," Elanil said.

Lorelei didn't reply. But a gate appeared in the sky next to Phoenix, and the woman stepped through, shocksword in hand. Allain and Erodar came through another gate next, their bodies flickering slightly as they splinterleapt through the air. More gates followed shortly after, and soon Trey, Arra, Rylan and Elanil were also up there with them.

"The team is back together again," Trey said. "Now what?"

"Orym is that way," Phoenix said, pointing. He was flying rapidly toward Nekhrumet, sparkles still falling from his hand. "I don't know what he has in mind."

"He created Nekhrumet," Trey said. "It was Aten's pride and joy."

"What do you think he intends to do now?" Lorelei asked.

"Let's follow and watch," Phoenix said. "But discreetly—he must know we'd be out to stop him."

They flew closer, careful to keep their distance. "If only there were some way to be invisible," Trey said.

"There is," Arra and Allain said at the exact same time.

They looked at each other.

"Mistweaving," Arra said. "You can project an illusion of

invisibility around yourself and others. I did it the night I found Lorelei in the forest."

Allain nodded. "That's how we splinterleap. Projecting invisibility around one of your splinters causes the whole thing to collapse."

"That's how you reintegrate?" Trey asked.

"Yes."

"Interesting."

Phoenix watched his face, wondering what he was thinking. She didn't know him—she didn't really know anyone in the group—but she could tell that something was clearly troubling him. Was it something to do with Quynn?

"Let's go," she said. "If you mistweavers can keep us invisible, that may help. I'll add a nowhere gate and a forcefield. That ought to protect us, at least for now."

"Not me," Trey said. "I'm not ready to reintegrate just yet. I'll stay behind if I have to, just don't make me invisible."

"Okay," Phoenix said, trying to understand. It was difficult to imagine what he must be feeling like, being half a person.

She projected invisibility over everyone except for Trey, and they set out.

As they drew closer to Nekhrumet, Phoenix reflected on what she knew of Orym. She'd known him perhaps the longest of the people here, save Lorelei. Orym was Dill's father—Dust, as he had first been named. Back there in the Under, when Rylan was still just a growing infant in her womb, Orym had been helpful. Kind, even. Sure, he'd been enigmatic. He'd had his secrets, and there had always been a kind of darkness hidden behind his eyes. But he had helped her. He had offered her a life topside, where she'd always wanted to be. All her dreams could have come true right then, but she'd turned them down.

Had she made the right decision? What would have been

different if she'd changed her mind? Would Rylan have grown up as strong, as Talented, as much the superuser he was now? Would Phoenix have died and become a Prime Mage? Would the People have destroyed the elves like they had planned?

Would that volcano have destroyed Earth?

And would Orym have become the god he was, even now sprinkling his strange new fairy dust over the city of his creation, watching the buildings glimmer and twist and turn?

She didn't know. No one could ever know. The past could not be filled with regrets. It could only be used as a lens through which to see the future. To make better choices. To take the life she knew she deserved. Now was not the time for looking back.

Now was the time for change.

Regardless of what Orym was, who she'd thought he'd been, the fact was that now he was a madman. A monster. Or at least that's what she suspected. Perhaps she should watch and see.

The city was *warping* beneath his touch. It was difficult to describe, almost as if the buildings themselves were made of paper, bending and flexing as Orym passed over them, trailing particles of light. They flickered as if part of some other reality, and then the colors began to change.

It was almost as if a rainbow had been applied to the surface of the buildings. Multifaceted light shimmered across the edges of everything, rendering them into two-dimensional cutouts of themselves. They shone as if made of metal, a multitude of colors reflecting from their smooth surfaces.

Then, one by one, the buildings disappeared.

They winked out of existence, gone without a trace. Phoenix couldn't hear any screaming, any indication that there were people being affected by this strange and beautiful destruction. There was nobody in Nekhrumet, she saw as she neared the city. Nobody left alive, anyway.

The streets were littered with thousands and thousands of corpses.

She almost vomited, then, almost fell out of the sky. But she held herself together, feeling Imra's hand gripped tightly in her own, gritting her teeth as anger swept through her. Orym had done this. Orym and his Soul Tree. Now his magic was rippling through the city, and nothing would be spared. He was remaking the world as he saw fit, as the fabled Aten of old had so longed to do.

The Orym she had known—the kind, caring man who had offered her the life of her dreams—was gone. In his place was a new man. An older man. A man who felt nothing but the thirst for power.

A man who must be put down.

"We have to stop him," Rylan said, as if reading her mind. She glanced at him, opening her mouth to reply, but he was already speeding ahead.

Leaving her forcefield and her gate.

Shedding his invisibility.

He leapt forward in the air, hands splayed out in front of him, bright particles of magic already streaming into the sky. A torrent of power hit Orym squarely in the back, the strength of it juddering into the man's body. His back arched, his fingers curling into claws, a wild roar escaping his lips. Nekhrumet stopped changing all around him, and for a moment Phoenix thought Rylan might actually have managed to hurt this new god.

But no. Orym turned, teeth bared in a wicked grin, unleashing all the power at his disposal at her son.

Phoenix shrieked, throwing up a forcefield just in time. She felt the power slamming into it, the sheer energy that

Guruthos could bring to bear. It threatened to overwhelm her, that energy. It threatened to defeat her. She brought her force-field up stronger, harder, willing to die to save her one and only son.

But Rylan turned to her, still floating in the air. "No," he said, his words somehow clearly audible over the screeching magic that was pummeling her shield. "Let me."

And he raised his Book of Amplification, and he shot the most powerful beam of light Phoenix had ever seen at Orym.

Too late, she realized her forcefield had been one-sided. She watched as Rylan's magic hit Orym, burning horrible holes in his flesh and bones. But he healed as quickly as it happened, still grinning, still sending formless energy at Rylan and her shield.

"Stop this!" Rylan shouted, his voice amplified. "This is not who you are!"

Orym laughed, the sound rich and rolling, and all around them Nekhrumet resumed its strange rippling of rainbows. "This is who I was always meant to be!" he said, and the power in his hands doubled.

Phoenix couldn't hang on.

"If you want me," Rylan shouted, "come to Earth! There you can finish what you started."

"I don't want you, you piddling, stupid boy," Orym said. His face was twisted.

"You might want to think twice about that," Rylan said. "I *am* a superuser, after all."

Orym cocked his head, and that was when Phoenix realized his weakness.

He had no idea how to operate Guruthos at all. He didn't know he could simply turn Rylan's magic off at the source.

She felt a smile overtake her face.

"Now!" Rylan shouted, and a gate flashed over him.

He was gone.

"To Earth," he said over the radio. "The old city."

Lorelei was next to leave, taking Allain and Erodar with her.

"He is so impressive," Elanil said, her face flushed. She gave a guilty glance at Phoenix, then flashed through a gate of her own.

"Is that *Quynn*?" Trey asked, looking down at the desert to the west. A gate overtook him, too, and he was gone. Arra stepped through the gate he'd made, leaving just Phoenix and Imra alone with Orym.

"Well?" he asked. "Are you two going to fight me on your own?"

"No," Phoenix said. "Others much more powerful than me will see to you." She shook her head. "I thought you were so much better."

She created a gate of her own, careful to make it a double gate to avoid the memory side effects, taking Imra and herself through the whirling maelstrom of yellow-orange light.

They emerged on Earth, in the ruins of Old San Francisco.

# FORTY-EIGHT

LORELEI STEPPED into City Control in New Manhattan, feeling the ice of the gate wash over her as she emerged. There were no memory side effects, thank the Twins—that double gate trick really worked its magic.

Twins. There she'd gone again, using their name in vain. The Twins were not their problem, anymore. Orym was.

Perhaps she should start swearing by *him*.

"There you are," Dill said, stepping up to her. "Where is he?"

"We tried to draw him to Earth," Lorelei said. "Well, Rylan did. He's a hell of a mage now. Who would have seen that coming?"

"I did," Dill said.

"Right. Anyway, we don't know if Orym is coming to Earth. My guess? He will. Might be here now."

"Where are they?"

"Old San Francisco, I think. That's what Rylan said over the radio."

"Why there? Seems odd."

Lorelei shrugged. "Are you ready with the Escape Module?"

"Not yet. We need a few more hours, still. The system isn't centralized or automated at all."

"You expect me to believe that with all the technology the True People are supposed to have, they didn't automate their shit?"

John Ronald chose that moment to enter the room. "Good day," he said. "It is true that we snuck a great deal of high technology into the cities without you knowing. But unfortunately, wireless signals can't penetrate the materials we used to hide the Module from you. And we couldn't very well lay a spiderweb of wires or conduit for you to trace. So, no—the Escape Module is not automated. It has to be activated piece by piece, by hand. We're almost done."

"Why are you here, then?"

John gave her a disdainful look. "There are *thousands* of people activating the Module as we speak. I'm hardly needed now. Once it's all up and running, the system will be able to communicate wirelessly. We will need to do weapons tests, make sure everything is calibrated and functioning."

"Orym is here," Lorelei said. "Do we have time?"

"He's not *here*," Dill said. "We're somewhere near Lusvunub, and he's in Old San Francisco. We can keep him occupied until this is ready."

"But will it work?"

"Doubtful," John said. "As I've always said, it may only end up being a distraction. But the Module's weapons *are* powerful."

"Orym is not the Twins," Lorelei said. "He seems unsure of himself, unused to the power. It may be that we can catch him by surprise."

"Let us hope."

"Small would have loved this," Dill said, a mournful look in his eyes. "He didn't deserve to die. Neither did Shot or any of the others. So many underkids."

Lorelei had a reaction ready, but she bit it back. Dill was actually emotional, and after a moment she realized that she was, too.

Shit.

San Francisco was gone. The new one, the one she had built. The one full of millions of vibrant, beautiful people. The people she had enslaved for hundreds of years. It was gone, and this whole chain of events could, in many ways, be traced back to her.

She hadn't meant to cause so much pain.

So she did something she never thought she'd do. She stepped forward, placing one hand on Dill's shoulder. "I'm sorry."

He looked at her, and for a moment he was a child before her. "All my Crews are dead."

"They died for a purpose," Lorelei said, not quite believing the words. "They were up against forces they couldn't contend with. So are we now. But all we can do is our best. That's what your father would have wanted."

"My father."

Now he was really crying. She pulled him in, actually hugging him, wondering how it had come to this. Her father had never shown her how to comfort others. She had to figure it out on her own.

"It's not your fault," she said. "Your father is who he is, but it's not a reflection on you."

She wished she could believe those words. She wished she could be free of her own family's legacy on her soul.

"Sometimes I feel him in me," Dill said. "That cruel streak —I have it, too. Twins, the harm I did to Rylan, I—"

"It doesn't matter now. You only did what you thought was right."

"That's all Orym is doing."

Lorelei sighed. Morality was objective. She had to remember that, but it was so hard. "We can hold a philosophical debate later," she said. "Right now we need to figure out how to stop him."

Dill pulled away, sniffing. "You're right. And thanks. I didn't—uh—I didn't expect a hug from you."

"Nobody does." She looked at the floor.

"There's more love in you than I realized," Dill said.

She felt her face heating, but she turned away to hide it. She suddenly missed Allain. Where was that kid? She needed a hug right now, too, and she needed it from him. She smiled. So soon, and so young, and already she'd forged a connection with the boy. Here they were at the end of the world, and all she could think about was his strong, blacksmith arms.

"Listen," Dill said, "I think I should talk to Orym."

"You think that will work?" John asked.

"I'm his son. If anyone can talk him out of this, it's me."

"Wasn't he almost married at one point?" Lorelei asked.

"If Tiala were here," Dill said, "she'd definitely be able to stop him. But she's not, and nobody knows where she is. She left before the Sundering, so who knows if she's even still alive?"

"I bet my sister would have been able to stop him," Lorelei said. "Cariel was his only equal match."

"It's down to me now," Dill said. "I have to try."

ELANIL ALIGHTED on the ruins of Coit Tower, leaning now where it had stood for so long. She flashed back momentarily to that day only a few months ago, when Fenian had run ahead and the Remnant had caught him. That was the day he'd injured his leg. The day Arra had grown truly furious with her. The day that had started it all.

Now she was back, and Rylan was beside her. And while she loved Rylan, and he her, and she was caught up in the feelings surrounding that relationship, she also had to focus on the task at hand. At the damage that even now was being wrought amongst the ruins of a city long dead.

Orym was in Old San Francisco.

"Status update, folks," Lorelei's voice said over the radio. Rylan turned it down, just in case Orym overheard. He was a long way off, hovering over the ruins of the city near where the Ferry Building had been. It was still there now, though its once-famous clock tower had long ago fallen into the bay. "The Escape Module isn't quite ready. Whoever's out there needs to hold Orym off until it is."

"Where are Trey and Arra?" Elanil asked. They hadn't arrived in Old San Francisco, or at least they weren't nearby.

"No idea," Rylan said. "We're the only ones here."

"Lorelei," Elanil said, pressing the transmit button while Rylan held the radio, "careful what you say. Orym was the one who gave us these radios, remember?"

"I've got eyes on him," Lorelei said. "He seems distracted right about now. Godhood seems to agree with him."

Elanil looked out at what Orym was doing, and she saw that Lorelei was right.

# FORTY-NINE

ORYM LOOKED at the remains of Market Street and Embarcadero, once more feeling the power burgeoning beneath his fingertips. There had been life here, once. Hundreds of years ago the city had teemed, full of energy and vitality. Connections had been made, even amidst the bustle and the busyness. But had the city lived up to its full potential? What could they have done if they had had the power of the gods?

Perhaps it was time to find out.

Orym wasn't an evil man. He wasn't a malevolent god. True, he had power—but he wasn't actually *trying* to destroy. Faedori Forest had been an accident. He didn't truly understand how to work with these new powers he had. In Nekhrumet he'd been trying to figure them out. There was something buried in the device—Xyclami had raw power inside it, more magic than anyone in the last hundred thousand years had known. It could be moulded, shaped. It could be wielded, if only he knew how.

He needed to run more experiments.

He didn't want to destroy. What he wanted to do—what

he'd *always* wanted to do—was *create*. To make the world as he saw fit, to make things that normal people could not envision or design. He wanted to give the world a life beyond their wildest dreams, pushing the boundaries of reality to their limit. Now he could finally do it. He could finally achieve his vision.

He just needed to try.

He stretched out with his hand, Willing the magic to come to life. He didn't need to do that—it would do whatever he Willed, regardless of the orientation of his body—but somehow it just felt right. Sparks emitted from his fingers as he felt the magic flowing forth, glittering particles of raw Xyclami power.

What he did with it wasn't quite mistweaving, and it wasn't quite anything else. He was channeling creativity, and the light from his hand flew gold. Creation. An Aspect that was not his first. He was a Builder, a mistweaver by nature. Builders built, but they didn't *design*. They didn't invent. Orym had always longed to do more. He'd always wanted to have some measure of control over the world around him. Some measure of true creativity.

Now was that time.

The sparks of golden light coalesced before him, forming the shape of a building. And not just any building—this one was majestic, curving and sinuous, towering two thousand feet above the ground. It soared upwards in his vision, tendrils of light extending as the structure came into focus. He placed bridges and parapets, forms that were beautiful to his eye.

But then he realized he shouldn't be bound by those restrictions. Why imagine only what had come before? Architects on Earth and Valaralda had already done what he was doing. He wanted to make something *new*.

So he altered the shape before him, choosing instead to make a walrus.

He burst out laughing as the form appeared, bulging and strange in the sky. It was a building in the shape of a massive walrus, floating in the air. He could leave it like that, he knew. He could impart passive fallfoiling magic to it, allowing it to float without the aid of gravitonic engines. As long as Xyclami survived and didn't reboot, that hulk of a walrus building would be there, housing people or businesses or whatever walrus buildings did.

But he hadn't come this far to make *animals*. He needed to do better.

He flexed his fingers, Willing the golden magic to shape something else. Something new. Something even *he* had not envisioned before.

He felt his breath catch as it took shape. A million bars of a metal appeared in the air, assembling into an impossibly intricate form. It made a grid in three dimensions, each piece interlocking like an incredible, airborne puzzle. The shape of it changed as he flexed his Will, chunks of it rotating into new forms. Sparks of light illuminated it from within as he morphed it, structuring it into the thing he desired. It was a non-form, an entity from his own mind, resembling nothing that had come before. It was asymmetrical and strange, formed from millions of cubes of metal which even now were still moving and changing, continuously forming new shapes in the sky.

He left it there, floating. It had no purpose—it just *was*, for no other reason than that he could. It felt good to use the power in this way.

He turned, and smiled, and began to form other things. He felt the strange emptiness pulling at him as he did.

RYLAN DREW NEARER TO ORYM, with Elanil flying right beside. They held the Books of Amplification in one hand, using their other hands to hold each other. Elanil had enough primewood left for this, she had said. Rylan didn't need primewood anymore.

He was still a superuser.

They kept their distance, watching Orym. He was making things, big buildings and plants and things that were neither. The sun was out but the sky was gray, clouds obscuring the scene. It lent an eery dismal tone to the things Orym made, as if the world itself knew that whatever he touched was doomed.

Was it?

A series of massive trees erupted out of the ground, green and golden sparkles effervescing as they did. Orym seemed annoyed at their presence—he waved his hands at them, and they changed. They twisted, becoming tall and far too thin, their branches warping into shapes that couldn't exist in nature. Pieces of them broke away, floating in the air but somehow seeming still connected to the whole. The color of them was wrong, too: a shade of purple verging into blue.

These were no trees. They were the ravings of a madman.

"I remember this city," Rylan said, watching Orym continue to fabricate his strangeness. "There was a huge battle with the Remnant here."

He turned in that direction. Presenub—or what remained of it—was visible in the distance, trampled jungle that had not yet recovered from all the violence. And beyond that, the last shard of the Golden Gate Bridge thrust upward from the waves, an ever-present indicator of Phoenix's incredible magic on that night.

"I was there, briefly," he continued. "I was only ten. There were so many tanks, and cars, and sweaty, angry men. It was horrible."

"I wasn't there," Elanil said, "but Arra told me all about it. I'd been practicing leafrunning in the forest, and I missed it all."

"It's better that you did."

"But we're here now. What made you think of it?"

"Just the city," Rylan said. "All the violence it's seen." In the distance, Orym had crafted a series of skyscrapers made of brilliant white crystal, jagged structures straining for the sky. "It made me wonder when the cycle of violence will end."

"It will end with Orym," Elanil said. "When we stop him. Somehow."

"Will it?" He turned his eyes on Elanil, and saw his fear reflected there.

She just shook her head, and leaned toward him as they hovered there. He kissed her, knowing that now was not the time for it. But when *was* the time, with a new god on the loose? Shouldn't they take what time was given to them?

He kissed her again.

Then they broke apart, breathless, turning to watch Orym. He had fashioned what looked like a group of bubbles, transparent spheres that bobbed about. Inside them were little worlds: grass lined the bottom of one, with a trail and a creek. Another held a forest, another an ocean. He made several more of them as they watched, sending them forth and setting them free.

"I wonder why he's doing that?" Elanil asked.

"He was always a scientist," Rylan said. "Maybe this was what he'd always really wanted to do."

"Maybe."

"The more important question is *how*." *Xyclami?*

*He is using the second Power,* Xyclami said in his mind. *What you call mistweaving. Except he has bypassed the safety parameters that were designed by the previous Operators. His illusions are a form of reality.*

*A form?*

*He does not understand the power he wields. This device is not capable of altering reality to the extent that he desires.*

"That's interesting."

"What is?" Elanil asked.

He reiterated what Xyclami had said. *Hey, Xyclami? Can you always mirror your communication to Elanil when you're talking to me?*

*Of course.*

*Thanks.*

"What now?" Rylan asked.

"Something is happening," Elanil said. "Something strange."

"Stranger than a bunch of flying zebras?" There were a bunch of flying zebras floating over the ruins of the city. Then Elanil pointed, and Rylan saw what she was talking about.

The crystal buildings, the shards of brilliant white, were *changing*. They twisted and rose, growing darker as he watched, strange tendrils of glowing light streaming from them.

"Is Orym doing that?" he asked.

"I don't think so. He's nowhere near those things."

He wasn't. He was hovering somewhere further to the west, busy building up what looked like an army of giant ants.

Rylan turned back to the crystal structures. They were red now, oozing. "Are they...*bleeding*?"

"They're not the only things changing."

She pointed again, and Rylan saw the strange, thin trees. They had turned to metal, it seemed, sprouting daggers where there should have been leaves. They twisted further as he watched, turning as if to face him.

Then they launched their daggers.

"Watch out!" he shouted, throwing up a forcefield as quickly as he could. The daggers clattered harmlessly off of it, and the trees seemed to sigh as if disappointed. They twisted back to straight, gleaming strangely beneath the cloudy sky.

The sky was growing dark.

"That's strange," Rylan said. "The clouds aren't moving, and the sun is up. Why is it getting darker?"

"I don't know," Elanil said, "but look."

The bubbles, the little worlds Orym had made, were darker now. They were lit within with a fiery, orange light, their glow sinister, somehow evil. The contents of the bubbles had changed, too—now they were filled with ugly things. Ravens, beetles, claws and burnt grass. Loam and soil, mud, even a small volcano erupted inside one. Then that bubble popped, and smoke and fire and ash flew up into the world outside.

Orym was losing control of his creations.

Motion caught Rylan's eye. A beast of some kind was roaming the streets—a huge, hulking thing. It had a black, bulbous body covered in hair, with four long, double-jointed legs that ended in spiky claws. Its mouth was open, revealing a maw of teeth that gleamed even as the strange night continued to fall. It was as if a giant spider had been magnified and half its legs shorn off, towering over the city and stalking its streets.

And it wasn't alone.

More of them appeared as he watched, spinning up from out of nowhere, visibly forming from dust and dirt and trees.

They formed a pack, roaring to each other in a strange, high-pitched warble.

*Why is everything going crazy?* Rylan asked.

*The illusions are a reflection of the Operator's Will*, Xyclami said. Was there a note of glee in the machine's words? *With only one Operator, his Will cannot be maintained.*

The sky had grown very dark. Sparkling lights were visible everywhere that Orym's creations roamed, red and golden in the false night. Old San Francisco had turned into a horror show, filled with strange monsters and twisting shapes. If Orym had wanted to be a benevolent god, his first attempt had been an abject failure.

Rylan was beginning to grow truly frightened.

Then Orym himself appeared in front of them, and he couldn't help but scream.

# FIFTY

THE MAN'S face loomed before Rylan, far larger than it should have been. Shadows were around his eyes, his mouth a pinched grin. His blond hair looked darker now, and it was wild, no longer slicked back like it usually was. His long, black coat was flying behind him in the wind.

He was the very picture of a god.

"Isn't this great?" Orym asked, his voice amplified by magic. He was mere feet away from Elanil and Rylan, yet his body appeared larger, stronger, louder than it needed to be. "The power is incredible!"

"You're insane!" Rylan said. "What happened to the Orym I used to know?"

"Nothing has changed," Orym said. "I simply remembered who I was."

Memories. Everything—all that had happened—was predicated on them. If Orym had remembered his past, his true nature might have shown sooner. But why should a mere memory change a man? It made no sense.

"This power is too much for you," Elanil said.

"You need a second Operator," Rylan said.

"Nonsense. I am more than capable of operating this machine on my own. It speaks to me, Rylan. Did you know that? It teaches me things. There is *so much* you do not know."

"What do you intend?" Elanil asked.

"What's my plan?" Orym laughed, the sound unnaturally loud in their ears. More monsters were arriving all around them, walking the ancient streets with impunity. "I suppose this is the part where I tell you. My *plan*, dear children, is to use this device the way it always should have been used: to remake the world in my image."

"Nekhrumet was not enough for you," Rylan said.

"Nekhrumet was only the beginning. With this—with the power at my fingertips—I can fashion truly remarkable things. Things the like of which the world has never seen!"

"Like these?" Elanil asked, motioning toward the huge spider-like things that were lumbering toward them. "Why would you make something like that?"

"I'm still working out the kinks," Orym said. "I didn't intend for them to look like *that*."

*The structure of reality in this area is growing unstable,* Xyclami said. *Evacuation recommended. The safeguards have been removed.*

Elanil glanced at him. "That doesn't sound good."

"Shut up!" Orym shouted, his face turned toward the sky. "Reality is what I *say* it is!"

And a dozen more shapes erupted from the ground, random mounds of earth and stone thrusting upward. They pushed aside ruined buildings as they appeared, shifting the very streets around under Orym's command. They crumbled almost as soon as they appeared, falling to pieces the moment they had risen. More shapes came up after that, and still more, each one rising and bursting into bits.

"Stop!" Rylan shouted. "You're destroying the city!"

"The city was already dead," Orym said. "I am only improving it."

*Operator integrity at 89%*, Xyclami said. There was a different tone to the machine's voice, almost a note of glee.

*What?* Rylan asked.

Xyclami didn't answer.

Nearby, more buildings were falling over, crashing to the ground in a thunder of ruined cement and glass. The city was breaking apart, and Orym seemed oblivious to it.

"We have to do something," Elanil said. "We have to stop this!"

"Together," Rylan said, taking her hand. "With the Books."

She nodded, her jaw set. She was beautiful, even in the eery dark. Beautiful and oh, so strong. He squeezed her hand, and she smiled.

Together, they sent everything they had at Orym.

Bright sparks of magic shot out from them in a torrent, blue and violet and green and gold and red and white and silver powers merging into one, a rainbow of cascading light. He could feel the souls in their pair of Books, amplifying the magic exponentially. The power was *incredible*, greater than anything Rylan had felt before. He was a superuser, in a soul-circle with another Prime Mage, using not one but *two* Books of Amplification and their attendant souls. It was power on an unprecedented scale, and it all struck Orym in the face.

He screamed.

And he flew back, beaten away with their impossibly strong power, flying uncontrollably into the strange city he had made.

They followed, hand in hand, light still streaming from their fingertips. It cascaded off of Orym's body, dripping to the ground, glowing strands of energy illuminating the horrible scene around them. Buildings twisted and turned as they flew, dark shapes grasping at them everywhere. The ground surged and jolted, moving as if with the tide. Monsters appeared, crawling out from the buildings or the soil, screeching and snapping and slicing at them with claws made of steel. A flurry of wings cut through the air where Rylan's face had been a moment before, and a group of red-eyed birds cawed at him raucously.

And still the magic flew, slamming into Orym with all the power Rylan and Elanil could muster. Could they kill him? Would this work? They flew and flew, dodging buildings and phantoms and monsters as they moved, all the while keeping their magic flowing.

Eventually, Orym finally stopped.

He was laughing.

"You cannot hurt me in this way!" he shouted. "You tried with the Twins, remember? Only my great machine was enough to stop them. Only a *million souls* defeated them. You think a little *magic* will do anything to me?"

And he blasted back at them with power of his own.

Elanil was quick with a forcefield, thankfully. It sprang up around them as Orym's attack hit, narrowly preventing disaster.

"He's right," Rylan said. "We can't stop him. We probably can't even hold this shield against him."

"We have to try," Elanil said. She'd released his hand, grasping primewood from her pouch. "Nobody else is here."

"Where *is* everybody, anyway?" Rylan asked.

Elanil shrugged, just as more magic hit their shield. Rylan added a forcefield of his own, hoping it would be enough.

Orym didn't seem angry—he seemed amused. But his magic was no joke. It would kill them the moment their forcefield faltered. Rylan didn't know what to do.

He tried attacking again, shooting through the shield, but of course it did no good. Orym just redoubled his efforts, increasing the strength of his magic stream. Rylan gritted his teeth, trying to hold the forcefield in place. He could feel the magic straining against him, pulling all the power from his soul. This is what Phoenix had felt like with the volcano, he knew. This was what had led to her being soulburned.

He couldn't let that happen to him.

And so he faltered for one brief second, not bringing his forcefield up in strength to match Orym's attack. He felt it slip, felt it break, felt it as the magic shattered the shield, cascading into Elanil and him with all the power of a comet, of the sun.

They were blasted back *hard*, the energy tearing through them. He felt unimaginable pain, as if the very bones and cells of his body were being ripped apart. He saw green as he flew back, as the pieces of his body were torn to shreds, as his consciousness slipped and almost faded. A cloud of green surrounded him, and he realized in his dim thoughts that it was Elanil, using that Prime Palm of hers, sending healing magic into them.

But it was not enough.

Orym's attack did not let up, did not retreat. They were blown past buildings and monsters, through clouds of smoke and ash and fog, thrown violently to the ground, magic slicing their bodies into ribbons. And though Elanil's soul-soothing magic was powerful, amplified by her Book, it was not enough.

The two of them fell to the ground amidst a pile of rubble,

their bodies battered and bleeding and bruised. Rylan managed one last look at the girl he loved before consciousness left him.

Orym had won.

# FIFTY-ONE

TREY EMERGED FROM HIS GATE, noting that Arra had followed right behind him. He flashed her a smile, then turned to face the object of his attention.

Quynn.

The man was standing there in the desert, looking far more dirty and haggard than before. He was surrounded by rylak, a motley crew of hairy beasts with long muzzles and sharp claws. The company seemed somehow congruous; almost as if Quynn had finally found where he belonged.

Trey had, rather. He had to keep reminding himself that Quynn was, in fact, *him*.

"Hello," Trey said. "What are you up to out here?"

"I might ask you the same," Quynn said, stepping up to him. They didn't shake hands. Somehow it seemed inappropriate to shake hands with yourself.

This was all so *weird*.

"We're about to fight Orym," Trey said. "But I saw you first."

"What happened with Orym?" Quynn asked. "I'm the one

that activated his machine. Was that as bad as I think it might have been?"

"Worse," Trey said, and he filled him in.

"Shit," Quynn said when he was done. "I *knew* I shouldn't have hit that damn button."

It was unlike Quynn to regret anything. Could the man be changing? Perhaps learning he was only half a person had caused him to reevaluate some things. It certainly had for Trey.

"Status update, folks," Lorelei's voice said over the radio suddenly. "The Escape Module isn't quite ready. Whoever's out there needs to hold Orym off until it is."

"They're on Earth," Arra said. "In Old San Francisco. We should go—that's too near Pano Sylrantheas. I don't want anything to happen to it. Not again."

"I'm coming with you," Trey said. "What about you?" He leveled a stare at Quynn.

The man shrugged, glancing at the rylak next to him. "Might be time I set a few things right," he said. "I don't want to lose Earth. It feels more like home to me than this place, after all."

"We will come as well," the rylak said, and Trey finally recognized who it was. Talon. He felt his blood run cold, but it seemed that something had changed. With Cariel dead, had Talon switched sides? "Earth is not our planet," Talon continued, "but our planet was taken from us. We know what this means. We will help, to honor our new friend."

Quynn bowed his head slightly in acknowledgement, and Trey found himself actually impressed. He'd had no idea that Quynn could actually make *friends*.

Perhaps he and the rylak should have been introduced far sooner.

"Well?" Arra asked.

"Let us gather our things," Quynn said. "Then we will be off."

ORYM SIGHED. Nothing was going the way he wanted it to. The kids had attacked him, but they had been easy to put down. He hadn't particularly *wanted* to kill them, but they'd given him no choice. Apparently they'd thought he was as evil as the Twins.

But he was just himself. Orym. The singular Operator of Xyclami, with the power to shape the world to his will. Everyone would see that he was right in the end. They always did.

His theories were always correct.

But something about the magic wasn't working right. It seemed to almost decay, as if once he'd set it it wouldn't stay put. He could feel that strange emptiness pulling at him constantly, weighing him down. It was as if part of Xyclami itself were fighting against him, acting against his Will.

This wasn't as easy as he'd imagined.

*Why isn't this working?* he asked the device.

*You require more time to understand the mechanics of the system,* Xyclami returned. *And you require an additional Operator. Your integrity is at 79% and falling.*

*Screw the Operator. Tell me what I need to know.*

*I am not a qualified trainer. Please consult with the previous Operators or a member of the Creators on Starmist Prime.*

*The Starmist system is gone,* Orym said, *and you know it.*

He thought he heard a smile in the machine's internal voice. *Yes.*

He sighed again, looking around. Old San Francisco had been reduced to a strange, haunted wasteland, full of horrible shifting shapes and disgusting creatures. It wasn't the paradise he had wanted. It wasn't the world he had envisioned. It was just another failed experiment.

He had to try again.

So he flew up, moving north across the bay.

LORELEI PACED the length of City Control, red heels clicking on the floor. She'd had Hammond bring her the shoes, as she always felt more comfortable in them. It wasn't the additional height, per se. It was the satisfying sound they made as she paced across the floor.

Things weren't going well.

"Do we have any eyes on San Francisco?" she asked.

"All the drones keep getting destroyed," Avourel said. "I'm bringing more in now."

"Is the Escape Module ready?"

"Close," John said. He was watching a monitor at one of the desks, where segments of the machine were being illuminated as they came online.

"How much longer?"

"Not sure. It could be as much as an hour, maybe more."

"Shit."

Allain entered the room just then, walking confidently over to her. She found herself momentarily distracted by his arms.

He kissed her, brazenly. It was quick, but the kiss itself was unexpected. His forwardness was growing.

"Hi," she said. "Come to witness the end of the world?"

"It wouldn't be the first time," he said, putting his arm around her waist. Forward.

She liked it.

"Drone coming online now," Avourel said. "Let's see how long it lasts."

The big screen at the end of the room changed to an aerial view, shaking slightly as the drone navigated what must be strong winds coming in from the bay. Clouds obscured the feed at first. When they cleared, Lorelei sucked in a breath.

"This is worse than I thought," she said.

"We're getting some strange readings," Avourel said. "Every type of sensor this drone has is off the charts."

"Who else is down there? Who is with him?"

"Two of your friends: Elanil and Rylan. They're alive, barely. Their life signs are faint."

"Shit," Lorelei said. "We need to get help to them, and we need to do it now."

"Orym isn't there anymore," Avourel said. "He's moving north, into what was Marin County."

"Sylrantheas," Lorelei breathed. "This isn't good."

# FIFTY-TWO

QUYNN FLASHED THROUGH THE GATE, holding it open for the rylak to file through. They were in Pano Sylrantheas, the village that had been rebuilt in the wake of all the destruction he had caused. It was very strange being here, even though it had been so short a time. If he was being truly honest with himself, he did regret his actions on that day. He'd thought he was doing what was best at the time, but he realized now that his impetuous nature had gotten the better of him.

It was strange, being half of a person.

Now he had to second-guess everything he had done. His reactions weren't complete, his reasoning inaccurate. How could he trust anything he'd done? Should he have gone on that grand chase to find a Prime Mage, pushing everything else aside? Should he have worked for the Cothellon at all? Should he have fucked Lorelei?

On that last point, yes. Yes, he definitely should have.

He smiled.

Pano Sylrantheas was interesting. It looked like an elven village would look if humans had taken over, adding their architecture to the designs. It wasn't wholly ugly—it just wasn't quite the same. Once again, Quynn regretted destroying what he had. The village hadn't deserved that.

Orym was arriving overhead.

He looked different now. His face was gaunt, his body larger than it should have been. He was wearing some great, long coat, the black fabric or leather trailing behind him as he flew. Had he worn that thing on purpose? Quynn held back a laugh. If he wasn't trying to be a villain, he really should have chosen a different outfit.

Well. From what he'd heard, Orym was causing a lot of trouble. The employee had become a problem. It was time to put the man down, if he could.

Quynn reflected on his first time meeting him. It wasn't the first time, really—he had murky memories of hundreds or thousands of years earlier, fighting the Hittites, or fighting with the Romans—Aten had been everywhere in those days, but Quynn had forgotten. Tarathiel. He'd been Tarathiel, back then. He needed to remember that. He needed to remember who he was.

That first meeting had been in Boston. In the rain, drinking whiskey, and Quynn had not been sure of Orym's motives. He had seemed impetuous, not unlike Quynn himself. He had seemed eager, but also smart. He'd wanted to explore the world around him, to create new things. He'd wanted access to the best and the brightest, to the most forward-thinking people on the planet.

And so Quynn had given him that access. And in so doing, had ensured this outcome, this...end. Orym had become the most powerful scientist in the world, and now he was determined to take that even further.

Quynn couldn't let that happen.

He felt responsible. He *was* responsible, along with all the other Cothellon. It was his fault Orym was in this position to begin with, instead of lolling around with the passive Eldrim on the surface of Earth. He had enabled this man's growth—or regrowth, as the case may be. He was to blame.

So it was Quynn's job to put him down.

"Hey!" he shouted as Orym passed by overhead. And for a wonder, the man heard him. He slowed, peering down at him as if confused. Then he floated to the ground, coming to stand in front of Quynn with a faint smile on his face.

"Greetings, old friend," Orym said.

"Greetings." Quynn tried not to lace the word with too much sarcasm. "It seems you're bound and determined to leave your mark."

"You knew that when you hired me," Orym said. He seemed taller—or was that just Quynn's imagination?

"Trying to prove yourself?"

"Perhaps. Is that what you're doing here?"

"I'm here to stop you, if I can."

Orym barked a bitter laugh. "You could never stop me," he said. "The best you could do was tattle on me to your little mistress in red."

He was trying to rile Quynn up. Good. The only problem was, it was working.

He took a step forward.

"Lorelei is a better woman than you will ever have," he said, knowing that he shouldn't have risen to the bait.

Orym laughed again. "She would have destroyed this world. I was the only one strong enough to stop her."

"What now?" Quynn asked. "Who is the destroyer now?"

"Not I," Orym said. "I am the creator."

"You always thought yourself better than everyone else."

"I *am* better than everyone else."

They took another step toward each other, bringing them just inches apart. Quynn was conscious of Orym's breathing, of how he held his chest and shoulders. He was ready to fight, Quynn could see.

So was Quynn.

"Whatever happened to that girl of yours, anyway?" he asked. Orym bristled visibly, and Quynn could see that he had struck a nerve. "Oh yes, I've heard of her. Tiala, was it? Lovely girl, from what I heard. Too bad she didn't want to stick around."

Orym was breathing heavily. "You know nothing about it," he said. "It was before the Sundering."

"But not before you were a member of the Cothellon, correct?"

"She's Dill's mother. My relationship with her pre-dates my involvement with you. You were kind enough to use my son as leverage during our first encounter, as I recall." His lip curled.

"Quite right," Quynn said, grinning inwardly. This man was so easy to goad. "I wonder what Tiala thought about your new late hours. About the company you kept. Did she know about the magic? About the *women*?"

"There were no women." But he was blushing.

Quynn laughed. "Don't be coy with me, old friend. You know as well as I do just how many women the Cothellon attracted—human as well as elven."

"I never cheated on her."

"Oh? That's not the way I heard it."

Orym's brow darkened further, his voice growing quieter. "Who did you speak to?"

Now Quynn had him. "Lorelei."

"I never—"

"Lorelei told me about a girl you were seeing in Boston. Black girl, am I right? Little bit fierce."

"Now you're being racist."

"Am I? I heard this girl really knew how to...what was the phrase...'do it for you.'"

"There's no way you could possibly have known about that."

Quynn leaned forward, face almost touching the other man's. They were about the same height, luckily, or this would have been awkward.

"I wondered about that woman for a while," he said. "Wondered what kind of person would cause you to cheat on your girl. But I think I figured it out, finally. When I met her, it all made sense."

"I—you—*what*?"

"Magona," Quynn breathed, and Orym took a step back. "You and she go a long way back, don't you?"

Orym spluttered for a moment, fingers flexing in the air. "Cariel. Cara. Selenia. Twins, she had so many names." Even now, he was blushing. "I think she was my one true love. When I saw her there on the streets of Boston, I couldn't help myself. But nobody knew. How could you have known?"

"Tiala knew."

"Fuck." Orym stood there, silent, swaying in the street. And for one brief moment, Quynn thought he might have actually defeated the man. Not with magic, but with words.

Sometimes it was way too easy.

He glanced around him briefly, checking the position of the rylak. They had formed a loose semicircle behind him, claws out and at the ready.

"She loved me," Orym said. "Tiala loved me. So did Cariel. I wish she hadn't died."

"She was trying to kill you," Quynn said.

"I think that's what I liked about her."

Quynn realized then that Orym and he weren't as different as he had thought.

"You need to stand down," Quynn said. "Get a second Operator, handle Guruthos peacefully. I heard what you've been doing. You're a menace, Orym. That's not like you."

Orym's face grew cold. "I've always been a scientist," he said. "You know this. And what do scientists do? We *experiment*."

He reared forward suddenly, punching Quynn solidly in the face.

# FIFTY-THREE

QUYNN REELED FROM THE BLOW, seeing stars, wishing once again that he had been a soulsoother. He had primewood in the pouch around his waist, but healing was not one of the things that he could do.

Luckily, many of the rylak were mages.

Talon stepped in, sending healing waves through Quynn's body in a wash of icy magic. Orym had a fierce look on his face, fist raised as if ready to strike again.

"I'm a god," he said. "Or hadn't you heard? It wouldn't do well for you to come against me."

They stood there for a moment, just looking at each other.

Then they struck.

It was a blur of fists, at first. Quynn aimed a punch at Orym's face, which landed. But Orym shrugged it off, aiming a blow at Quynn's midsection. That landed, too, but Talon was there to lend a claw with soulsoothing magic. So Quynn surged upward, trying an uppercut to Orym's jaw. It hit, and the man went flying.

Straight up.

Then he came back down, red magic glittering from his

fists, and it was all Quynn could do to get some dark oak in his hand in time. Mergemelding magic suffused him, rendering him impervious to the raw Destroyer magic Orym was wielding.

But Quynn had magic of his own. He lashed out with fall-foiling, trying to drive Orym to the ground. But Orym countered it, using fallfoiling in reverse. He was a full Prime Mage, and an Operator besides, and Quynn only had half the powers at his disposal.

This wasn't going to work.

He tried strengthshaping magic, using light oak to make his body incredibly strong. That worked—his fist connected with Orym's face, sending the man reeling a hundred feet back. He slammed into a wall of glass, shattering it and sending scared elves running. Was that a *bar* inside the building? Quynn shook his head, advancing.

Mindmaster magic was next. Quynn's speciality. He should have started with that—it was by far the most powerful thing in his arsenal. But Orym just shrugged it off, dissipating the purple cloud with nothing more than a wave of his hand. Then he struck back with leafrunning, throwing Quynn roughly backwards, into the waiting arms of his rylak friends. Their claws pierced him inadvertently, but once again Talon was there.

"Let us help," he growled.

Quynn nodded.

And the rylak surged, running forward with roars on their lips. Many of them were mages, blasting outward with magical power. Bolts of lightning struck Orym, rain and wind assailing him. Forcefields slammed against him, illusions forming up around. Then the rylak themselves struck, and they were far more deadly. Claws and snarls filled the area, and for a moment Orym was overwhelmed.

Then he recovered, blasting outward with magic of his own. The strange restaurant was destroyed in an instant, the walls disintegrating before Orym's power. He laid around him further still, red Destroyer magic slicing into everything in the vicinity. Quynn saw several rylak go down, sliced in half or losing limbs, blood flying in the air. Several nearby buildings were instantly reduced to shreds, victim of Orym's callous magic. Quynn took a step forward, hoping to stop what was happening, but it was too late.

Orym was far too mad.

He laid waste to his surroundings, throwing magic far and wide. More structures were demolished in an instant, walls and roofs splintering into wreckage. And Quynn realized that he had done it again—he had come to Sylrantheas with an end in mind, and the result had been its utter destruction.

This needed to stop.

But he was outmatched. The rylak couldn't help. Nobody could fight Orym—not monsters from another world, not half a man. Nothing could go up against a vengeful god.

A gate appeared just then, and Trey and Arra stepped through.

"No!" Arra shouted. "You will not destroy my village again!"

Quynn didn't know if she was talking to him or Orym.


ARRA LET the gate slide shut behind her, checking to make sure Trey had made it through. Orym and Quynn were here in Pano Sylrantheas, terrorizing it as only they could. She needed to make it stop.

It was time to join the fight.

"No," Quynn said, staggering forward. "This is on me. I don't want this village destroyed again."

And he laid into Orym with everything he had. Arra watched as his body grew larger, strengthshaping magic taking over. He hit Orym as hard as he could, massive fists connecting with the man's body. Then he used mergemelding, becoming semi-transparent as Orym tried to fight back. It was working. Quynn was actually winning.

But Arra knew that gods had other powers at their disposal.

Orym grinned.

"GET THAT DRONE CLOSER," Lorelei said. The view moved in, hovering near enough to the scene that she could clearly see Orym's face. The man looked wild, out of control, as if godhood were too much for him.

It would be for any man, she suspected. Or woman.

Orym erupted into a rainbow of energy as she watched, millions of particles of light blasting outward all around him. Arra was spared the brunt of it, luckily, but Quynn was right in its path.

He went down, blasted backward.

Lorelei felt her breath catching in her chest.

She hadn't *loved* that man, precisely. But she had held a certain admiration for him. Allain had his arm around her as the scene unfolded, as she saw the rylak spread around Quynn, trying to heal him. She saw Orym shooting magic out again, mowing down the rylak as if they were nothing. She saw the scene in slow motion, watching the destruction he was capable of. This man who she'd held in her employ. This man who she had *trusted*. He had betrayed that trust when he went to the Eldrim, but he had had the world's best interest in mind. Now?

Not so much.

Quynn was down. He wasn't moving. Arra was scrambling away, shock evident on her face. Trey was somewhere in the distance already, putting a forcefield up around his wife. And Quynn wasn't moving—*he wasn't moving*—and Lorelei felt a sickness enter her soul.

Orym could not be allowed to continue on like this.

# FIFTY-FOUR

LORELEI WATCHED the viewscreen at the end of City Control, a gate ready at her fingertips. She had her shocksword in her hand, and she was about to jump—Orym couldn't be allowed to continue. First Rylan and Elanil now Quynn—the man was laying her friends down left and right.

Friends? Maybe not. But maybe so—now was not the time for such distinctions. Still, she smiled to herself, knowing that she had made that association in her mind.

Orym was leaving. Where was he going? She saw him launch upward, vaulting into the sky like Superman from the age-old Earth comic books.

"Follow him," she ordered, and the drone obliged, soaring forward on a current of wind, bringing the camera closer. Orym appeared to be moving aimlessly to the west, heading into the Muir Woods. Did he have a plan? Had he *ever* had a plan? She didn't know.

She blew out a breath. "Others have failed," she said, extracting herself from Allain's arm, "but I need to try. I feel as if Orym is my responsibility. I was there with him during the Imprisonment, after all. Maybe I'm the one who can finally stop him after all this time."

"Wait," Allain said, but it was too late.

A gate flashed around her, and she was gone.

ORYM FLOATED ABOVE THE FOREST, leaving Pano Sylrantheas behind. It was a sweet little city, though it could do with a few improvements. He reached out with his hand lazily, reforming one of the streets. The houses on it blew apart, stretching upward into towering complexes hundreds of feet tall, made of stretchy organic material that lived and breathed as a living organism.

Good. He was getting better at this.

He pretended not to notice as the walls almost immediately turned black.

He turned his face to the east, rising higher in the sky, wondering where he should go next. Perhaps a trip would do him some good. Flying was fun, and it would give him ample time to perfect his craft. He could travel across the whole of the United States, creating cities in the shadows of the past.

Yes. It was as good a plan as any.

LORELEI APPEARED next to Orym in the air, fallfoiling magic engaged to keep her aloft. It seemed ever since the Prime Mages had started popping up, their feet had seldom touched the ground. Was it the hubris of magic, or was it elvenkind's innate desire to fly? She wondered if it had anything to do with Starmist, and the dragons there.

It didn't matter now.

"Orym," she said, saying the name like a threat. "You always were a bit of a problem, but I never took you for wanton destruction."

"What, those?" Orym said, gesturing at the buildings he'd just destroyed. "They weren't serving any purpose."

He started flying away. Lorelei followed, leafrunning magic kicking in.

"What happened to you?" she asked. "You used to consider *lives* to be enough of a purpose."

"Did I? When in my long, illustrious career did I prioritize lives?"

"When you interrupted my plans," Lorelei said. "You were trying to save the planet, remember? It even worked."

Orym laughed, speeding up. She had to increase her flow of magic to stay abreast. "I wasn't doing it for the *people*," he said. "A planet is an awful thing to waste. Also, I was acting out of self-interest. I would have died, too, remember?"

"I don't believe you. The Orym I knew wasn't the callous man you seem to think you are."

"Maybe not," Orym said, "but what about the *Aten* you knew?"

That gave her pause. He was right, she realized. Aten had been narcissistic bordering on sociopathic. She hadn't recognized it then, being as young as she was, but it was true. He had been a monster of his own making.

"But you grew," she said. "You changed. It's been a *long* time since the days of Aten. You're different now."

"Am I?"

He lashed out suddenly, red Destroyer magic carving a wicked slash in her arm. She flinched, reaching for birch, healing the wound as quickly as she could. Then she pulled her shocksword out, bringing it to bear. It seemed Orym would rather fight than talk.

So be it.

She sent a beam of shockstriking magic directly at him. It did nothing, of course. She knew it wouldn't. She'd seen him fight—he was like the Twins, implacable when it came to long distance magic.

Luckily, she was carrying a sword.

She threw more magic at him, electric blue light shining straight into his eyes. She took advantage of the brief distraction to close with him, bringing her sword to bear.

She slashed.

And as she'd hoped, he wasn't expecting a physical weapon. It connected, tearing a gash in his chest. She channeled shockstriking magic into the wound, hoping it wouldn't just cauterize the skin. Energy jolted into Orym's body, causing his entire being to shake. Smoke erupted from his clothing. The smell of burning skin filled the air, but she kept it going, pressing her advantage. This might be her one chance to do some real damage to the man.

The moment did not last.

Orym blasted outward, silver force magic pushing her violently away. She felt the particles piercing her, like tiny forcefields slicing her skin. She shrugged them off as she hurtled through the air, soulsoothing magic correcting the damage as quickly as it could.

Orym had a forcefield up.

"Shit," Lorelei muttered. She was already out of options. One attack was all she'd had in her. It had been a good attempt, at least. She'd made it further than the others before her.

She hoped Quynn and Rylan and Elanil were okay.

Orym resumed flying, dipping below the tree line. She followed, dropping until the Muir Woods towered over her. It was a beautiful forest, hundreds of years old. Orym had allowed his forcefield to drop, evidently satisfied that she was no longer a threat.

Which gave her an idea.

She used her shocksword to throw a massive ball of light, aiming it at a huge sequoia tree that was just ahead of him. She put all her energy into the blast, Willing it to be the strongest one she'd ever done. The glowing sphere of magic shot out toward the tree, whizzing beside Orym as he flew. Then it impacted the trunk, sending vast amounts of bark into the air like shrapnel from an explosion. The tree cracked, tilted, and began to fall.

It caught Orym by surprise.

He jerked, throwing up a halfhearted forcefield to avoid the worst of it. Red Destroyer magic arced outward in a laser-like line, cutting into the tree as it fell toward him. The tree moved ponderously, the massive form crushing everything in its path. Branches from nearby trees cracked and broke as the huge crown fell, the trunk continuing to crumble and split as it did. But Orym had noticed it now, and it would do no damage.

Luckily, the tree had been another distraction.

She threw three blasts out in quick succession, toppling three more trees. She hated doing this to the forest, but certain things were more important than nature. Stopping a madman of this caliber was among them.

Orym set about him with Destroyer magic, letting his forcefield drop. That was the thing she'd noticed about the Operators—they were too cocky, too sure of their power. They didn't lean toward defense. Instead they preferred to attack, and raw Destroyer magic seemed to be their weapon of choice.

It gave Lorelei exactly the opening she needed.

She swooped in again, using leafrunning to approach him

quickly. Then she drove the shocksword into Orym's back, sending energy rippling out from it. Blue light cascaded across his body as the four trees fell, bark and branches and leaves creating a cacophony of detritus, dust and sound.

Orym almost died right then.

She could feel it. For an instant she could see his soul-strand, how it connected to Guruthos. She could feel it wane, feel the tether on his being almost snap. There was a face behind the vision, a face that wasn't Orym's. It was dark, that face. It was grinning. It *wanted* him to die.

"Guruthos," she breathed. The machine itself was alive, hoping she would succeed. "Shit." She'd forgotten the rules.

You can't kill the Operator.

She had no choice but to pull back.

Orym slid off the sword as she did, his body making an audible squishing sound as blood erupted from the wound. She blanched, steeling herself, and watched as he healed. He turned to face her as the trees completed their descent, crashing to the ground in a cloud of dirt and leaves.

"You shouldn't have done that," he said to her, and he struck out with everything he had.

Lorelei flew back, slamming into a tree, feeling her body being destroyed by his magic. Brilliant red light shone out in lines, slicing her, burning her. Killing her. She saw red— nothing but red—and she knew that fighting this man was hopeless.

She couldn't kill him.

She wasn't *allowed* to kill him.

Which meant that Orym would win.

Pain overtook her as her vision began to dim, and out of the corner of her eye she thought she saw something strange.

Violet particles of light.

# FIFTY-FIVE

ALLAIN STEPPED through the double gate the gatesender in City Control made for him, splinterleaping to stay aloft. He flicked at his latest carving, feeling mistweaving magic Invest in the primewood.

It was going to be the greatest carving he had ever made.

Power flowed through him, mistweaving power that could create anything. And here, with Orym bent on chaos and destruction, here was the time to try something no one yet had thought to try.

Illusion.

Violet sparkles shot out from his hands, the power of his mistweaving made manifest. That had never happened before —was Guruthos acting differently now? This was raw power, Builder magic, flashing violet in the murky forest air.

Interesting.

But before he sent his illusions out into the world, he had one thing he needed to do.

He kissed Lorelei.

It jolted her to life, soulsoothing spreading from her hand

where she had already been holding the required primewood. She'd been dazed, it seemed. Now she was back.

She returned the kiss.

Their tongues danced for a long moment, and Allain almost let his splinterleaping fail. Then they broke apart, and Allain saw something in Lorelei's eyes he hadn't ever seen before.

Could it be love?

It couldn't be. Not so fast. But whatever it was, something had just changed between them. Perhaps it was the madman who was even now staring them down, hands raised with Destroyer magic at the ready. Perhaps it was the hopelessness of the situation, the energy they'd all already spent getting there. Or perhaps at the end, the only thing that truly mattered was the person you were with.

He kissed her again, briefly, then exercised his magic.

Suddenly they were floating in outer space.

The world was filled with blackness and stars, and that was it. A profound sense of emptiness filled them, surrounded as they were by nothing but tiny pinpricks of light. Orym looked around, confusion evident on his face. His Destroyer magic faded.

That was the power of illusion: it could foil even the strongest soul.

They began flying. Not in the real world, but in space. Allain flicked his knife along his carving, controlling the illusion. Orym turned in the direction they were going, apparently curious what Allain had in mind. A planet appeared after a minute, a vision drawn from deep inside Allain's brain. He wasn't sure where it had come from, exactly. Perhaps it was ancestral memory, or a vision from inside the Tomb of Akhenaten. He somehow *knew* what to make with his mistweaving magic, what world he was meant to fashion from his soul.

Ahead of them, growing larger by the moment, was Starmist Prime.

Orym sucked in a breath as they approached. The planet grew larger and larger, green and blue and white and beautiful, mountain peaks and islands and clouds forming as they neared. Orym held himself transfixed as Allain continued creating the illusion, moving them even closer.

Soon they were on the planet, bursting through the clouds and flying through the alien air. Huge rock formations towered overhead, trees and flowers dotting the landscape. Waterfalls cascaded down from up on high to feed placid lakes, and Allain could see animals drinking or fishing at the water's edge. The illusion was palpable, easily the most complex thing he'd ever made.

He wasn't quite sure how he was doing it.

He flicked his knife again, making sure to get the curve on the carving *just* right. The carving was special, a thing that was growing dear to him. He couldn't screw it up now that there was so much to look forward to. He needed to do it justice.

He needed to keep confusing Orym.

They continued flying, cresting the top of a hillside. The world spread out far beyond them, a stunning vista of endless beauty. Cities stretched out in the distance, graceful parapets giving way to buildings and bridges and then fields and streams. People came into view as they swept closer: elves and humans and rylak, driving strange machines or sitting in swings or walking down the curving streets. And overhead, as the alien sun shone down upon them, dragons circled in the sky.

"This...this is *incredible*," Orym said. He was right.

It was the most advanced illusion Allain had ever made.

"This," Orym continued, "is what I wanted. All this beauty, this *life*. Look at it! There is so much to see, to do, so many things to explore. The technology here, mixed so perfectly with nature...could it really be true? Is this what Starmist Prime was like?" He turned to Allain, and he could see tears rolling down the man's face.

"I don't know," Allain said. "I don't know where this vision is coming from, exactly. It just came to me."

He caught Lorelei watching him, a look of adoration in her eyes. "It's beautiful," she said, floating toward him in the air and taking his hand. They continued moving through the scene, flying over verdant fields and into a lush jungle. More rylak were there, swinging from the trees, looking somehow *happy*. Allain hadn't known rylak could even look like that.

He flicked his carving again, lending more magic to the world around them.

"What are you making?" Lorelei asked.

When he showed her, she gasped.

"It's...it's *me*."

It was. He had created a perfect likeness of Lorelei herself, getting the figure just right. The curves, the heels, the dress—it all bespoke *her*, her loveliness, her strength. He was most proud of her hair, the way it draped down over her right shoulder. He made another flick with his knife, feeling the magic flowing through.

That was when she kissed him.

It was a kiss like nothing he'd ever had before, not even from her. It was strong and it was passionate, but it was also somehow tender and intense. Feeling exuded out of her and into him, crossing the boundary of their lips and settling deep inside his soul. Somehow he kept the illusion going through it all, the brightness and the life of Starmist Prime forming a backdrop for their incredible union.

When they finally parted, he could see his love reflected in her eyes. She held his hands in her own, staring up at him with a passion he hadn't known existed. He drew her into a hug, pulling her head against his chest, wrapping his arms around her and reaching for her hair. It was glorious. She was glorious. Starmist Prime was glorious around them, so full of life and wonderment and energy.

Tears were still streaming down Orym's face.

He was sitting in the air now, just watching the illusion as it passed. They were out on the sea now, passing boats with delightfully old fashioned crews of elves, men, and rylak. Then they were ascending to the sky, following a massive green dragon as it wheeled, wings flapping. Rocks were floating in the sky overhead, and he could see hundreds of dragons flying or clinging to the edges of the stone, growling at each other with sounds Allain couldn't understand.

Orym watched it all silently, shoulders rocking as he cried, fully caught up in the illusion. Allain had struck a nerve, it seemed. He had shown Orym what the world could be, and in so doing had finally muted his destructive impulses.

Perhaps Orym wasn't as evil as he seemed.


"ARRIVING IN MUIR WOODS NOW," Trey said into his radio.

"Good," John Ronald said. "Phoenix is headed to Lusvunub, in case we need help on the ground. Your job is to get Orym there by any means necessary."

"Okay." Trey turned to Arra, noting the expression on

her face. She was angry and in pain, having just witnessed yet more destruction to the village she had loved. "We'll stop him," he said. He wasn't sure if he believed those words.

But she nodded, her eyes moving beyond him to look at something in the distance. "What is *that*?"

LORELEI STOOD IN THE AIR, her arm wrapped around Allain's waist. She watched the vision continue to unfold, magic pouring out of Allain's likeness of her.

It was an incredible carving.

And so flattering. He had the image perfect, as if his artist's mind knew her better than she even knew herself. Seeing the affection he held for her made her want to do things to him that were inappropriate in mixed company. Especially with Orym sitting right there.

Orym was still crying.

"It's beautiful, isn't it?" she said.

He turned to her, moving his body slightly in the air. "This is where it all came from," he said. "Xyclami, the rylak, us. This is how it all came to be."

"You wish you could have seen it, don't you?"

Orym nodded. "I wish I could have been there. I wish I could have met the people who made such magic as this."

"They were not destroyers."

"No. They were creators. That's all I want to be."

"But they were trained," Lorelei said. "They spent thousands of years—hundreds of thousands—learning how to do the things they did. How does the phrase go? Rome wasn't built in a day."

Orym sighed. "I suppose you're right. I need to learn more

about how this works, take a more measured approach. A scientific one. Yes. Good."

He stood, looking at them with sadness still in his eyes.

Had they won?

"I'm glad you see reason," Lorelei said. She leaned against Allain, grateful that he was with her in this moment. It was his illusions that had made it possible, after all. Even now, Starmist Prime continued unfolding around them, impossibly detailed and beautiful. She found herself wanting to live there, to see this incredible land for herself.

Too bad the planet had been destroyed.

"You did it," Lorelei said, squeezing Allain's waist. "You really did it."

"I think I did."

"Yes," Orym said. "A scientific approach. For that, I need a clean workspace."

He waved his hand casually, almost sadly, and a line of red ripped through the air, eviscerating the space where Lorelei and Allain were standing.

TREY SAW the line of Destroyer magic slice through the air, striking Lorelei and Allain right across their waists. For a second he thought they must have had a shield up, must have had soulsoothing magic ready. For a moment he was sure they would be fine.

Then the illusion disintegrated around him, and Lorelei and Allain's bodies fell apart.

They'd been cut in half.

The pieces of them dropped, blood streaming in the air, and Trey felt his blood run cold. His skin was like ice. His breath wouldn't come. Next to him, Arra gave a great gasp of astonishment.

Allain and Lorelei were dead.

Orym looked at Trey, tears drying on his face. The pair of corpses fell, still partially entwined. And for a moment, Trey thought Orym was going to lash out with more magic.

But instead, he smiled.

# FIFTY-SIX

*AUTOMATIC SELF-DEFENSE SYSTEM ACTIVATED*, Xyclami said in Rylan's mind, and he felt soulsoothing magic ripple through him like a river of ice. He sat up, gasping, reaching out for Elanil. She was next to him, gasping as well.

They were both fine.

But it had been close.

*Operator integrity at 32%.* Rylan could hear the glee in Xyclami's voice. When Orym's integrity reached zero, the machine would finally be free.

Rylan couldn't let that happen.

"Guys," Trey said over the radio, "Lorelei and Allain are dead."

"*WHAT?*" Rylan's voice said over the radio. Trey tried to keep the tears out of his eyes.

Failed.

"Orym killed them," he said. "Right in front of us. He just cut them in half."

"Fuck," Phoenix's voice said. "That bastard."

"It can't be," Dill's voice said. "He *wouldn't*."

"He did," Trey said, hearing his voice harden. "This just got personal."

Lorelei was gone. The feelings inside him were conflicted, raw. She'd been attracted to him for thousands of years. She'd been *married* to him. They'd been man and wife.

He had, for a few short years, loved her.

And now she was gone. Yes, she had been a troublemaker. She'd killed Elanil, or tried. She'd almost destroyed Earth. She'd helped imprison the Twins.

But she hadn't been a terrible person, in the end. She'd only been doing what she thought was best, and for a moment it had almost looked like she'd found happiness with Allain.

Now it was all cut short, and it was Orym's fault.

Next to him, Arra took his hand.

"HE *WOULDN'T*," Dill said into the radio. He was sitting in his new undercar, feeling the leather at his back.

"He did," Trey's voice said. "This just got personal."

Dill felt anger surging through him. So many people had been lost along the way. So many Crews. So many good underkids. So many cars. He'd lost friends, countless friends, but somehow this was worse.

His father really was a murderer.

Now here Dill was, in a car that had been fully outfitted with Valaraldan technology, about to try to stop the one person he never thought he'd have to fight.

He shook his head, unable to make sense of it all. They'd had such grand plans together, Orym and he. They were going to save the world. They had even done it. Then everything had gone to shit, and it turned out his father wasn't the man Dill had thought him to be.

"The Escape Module is ready," John said over the radio. "Now we just need Orym within range."

"That's up to you, Dill," Trey said. Dill could hear the emotion in his voice. Lorelei had been a tough pill to swallow, at times. But in the end, she had been just like the rest of them: intent on saving the world.

She hadn't deserved to die.

His grip tightened on the leather-clad steering wheel, anger taking over where fear had been. When Orym had been destroying buildings, killing strangers, it hadn't mattered quite as much. Now he had killed people Dill actually *knew*.

Now he had crossed the line.

Lusvunub. That was where the sky cities were, where the Escape Module was ready to do its damndest to stop Orym. It would likely all end in failure, but they had to do the best they could. They had to try.

He fired up the car.

It roared to life with a guttural purr, the gravitonic engines kicking in and raising it off the ground a few inches. Then he kicked it into gear, feeling the momentum of the engines in the back taking over. He soared out of New Manhattan with the top down, feeling the cold air ripple through his hair. He passed through a gate they had made for him, doing his best to ignore the ice that rippled over his skin, and found himself flying over the trees of the Muir Woods.

Orym was easy to locate. He was the only elf floating in the sky, larger than life, with sparks flying from his hands. Trey and Arra had retreated, probably in fear. He'd heard them over the radio, but he didn't know where they were. Orym was already flying east, heading in exactly the direction

Dill wanted him to go. Perhaps this would be easier than he thought.

He drove the car up to Orym.

"Father," he said.

Orym looked at him. "Nice car."

"Been a while since I've driven."

"You should get the undercar races going again. They were quite lucrative, as I remember."

"You mean to leave the sky cities alone?"

"I hadn't really given it a thought."

They were moving quickly now, zooming over the world below. Dill could barely see through squinted eyes, there was so much wind. He put the radio earpiece in his ear, just in case Orym overheard anything that might be said.

"What's it like?" Dill asked. "Guruthos."

"It's called Xyclami," Orym said, strengthshaping making his voice audible over the wind. "And it's extremely interesting. Did you know the device is actually a repository for all the information found in the Starmist system of planets? Historical records, artistic works, technological discoveries— it's all there. I haven't figured out how to unlock it all, just yet, but I'll get there."

"Keep him occupied," Trey's voice said over the radio in his ear.

"Do you feel powerful?" Dill asked. He had to shout to make himself heard. They were moving *really* fast now. He was happy the souped-up undercar could keep up.

"Good," John's voice said. "You're headed in exactly the right direction."

"Not powerful enough," Orym said, his voice rich. "The machine doesn't seem to do exactly what I ask it to. But I'll figure it out. I always do. All I need is a little more experimentation."

"You don't feel bad? About all the destruction you've already caused?"

Orym snorted. "A few piddling little buildings here and there don't matter," he said. "Who cares about a forest? It will regrow, or I can make another."

"The way I heard it, you killed everyone in Nekhrumet."

Orym was silent for a moment. "It was necessary."

"You killed a lot of good rylak back in Pano Sylrantheas."

"I think you and I can both agree that the rylak are anything but *good*. You're not here to stop me, are you, son?"

Orym turned to look at him as he flew, and Dill could see the darkness in his eyes.

"Of course not," Dill said. "I just wanted to have a conversation. Figure out where you're coming from. That okay?"

"I suppose I owe you that much."

"Where are you going, anyway?"

"I just wanted to try a few things," Orym said, and he reached out his hands. Golden sparks flew from his fingers, and strange shapes crept up on the horizon.

PHOENIX EMERGED from the gate in Lusvunub and was almost immediately overtaken by spiders.

She jerked, stepping back, wondering how in the Under there were so many of the arachnids there. They swarmed over everything, black and tiny and somehow menacing. But they disappeared as she watched, crawling into a million tiny hiding places in the ground, in the walls, in the few remaining trees. They almost seemed to be acting together, in coordinated fashion. But spiders didn't do that—right? Then they were gone, and Phoenix almost wondered if she'd imagined the whole thing.

*Creepy.*

She took a deep breath. Imra came through the gate behind her, stepping forward and taking her hand. Phoenix gave her a smile. "The place looks deserted."

"Let's get our positions scouted," Imra said. She'd refilled her arrows at Pano Sylrantheas, and now she made a striking figure as she led Phoenix through the empty Remnant outpost, hand in hand. "I still can't believe Allain is dead."

"Such a waste," Phoenix said.

"You're close, Dill," John said over the radio. "You guys made remarkable time. If you can try to steer him a little bit north, you'll be right in the zone. We'll deploy when you get in range."

Dill didn't reply, but Phoenix knew that he had heard.

Their last, best plan was coming to fruition.

Somehow Phoenix knew that it would not be enough.

# FIFTY-SEVEN

PEOPLE FINALLY STARTED COMING out of their hiding places in Lusvunub. They were mostly women, Phoenix saw, but they were shouldering weapons of every kind. They looked haggard and scared, as dirty as the People always were, with long jata hair falling behind them as they walked. She contemplated going up to them, trying to speak to them, when she realized she didn't know the language.

"Orym is within range," John said over the radio. "Activating the Module now. Anyone in the area should shield themselves immediately—computers in the nodes will be set to target Orym, but I can't guarantee you won't get caught in any crossfire. The energy weapons on this device are *very* powerful."

"Understood," Phoenix said. She turned to Imra. "Back up in the air?"

Imra sighed. "If we have to."

They flew.

Phoenix put a forcefield around them, wondering when the madness was about to start. It seemed so long ago when she'd first discovered this power within her, first realized she could make shields in the air. It had led to nothing but trouble, in the end, but it had also led her to her son.

Perhaps it had all been worth it.

But she was tired now. She was ready to be done. She wondered if Orym would be the last, or if there would be a never-ending stream of evil connected to Guruthos.

She was betting on the latter.

She glanced upward, at the cities that were wheeling in the sky. The Under jutted down from each of them, blocky and tall, looking like skyscrapers in reverse. The gray metal gleamed in the sunlight, and for a moment Phoenix had visions of fire. She shook her head to clear it.

"You okay?" Imra asked.

Phoenix smiled at her. "Just thinking about the past. I once broke through the bottom of the Under. Almost fell to my death."

"Trey and Rylan *did* do that."

"That's right," Phoenix said. "I'd nearly forgotten. I missed so much while I was...away."

"How did you avoid falling?"

"Magic."

"Of course." Her expression soured a little.

"I still can't believe the Under was a lie."

"Not all of it," Imra said. "Only parts."

"*Huge* parts."

"Does it matter?"

"It was my home," Phoenix said. "But I guess it doesn't matter. The cities were one big machine, in the end. I suppose it makes sense that there was another machine embedded inside."

"I just hope it helps."

"Me too."

Orym arrived just then, elven form large against the sky. A

stream of golden particles flowed out behind him, strange shapes appearing in his wake. It seemed he was using the trip to work on his creation powers, though she wasn't sure he had improved at all. There must be a limit to what Guruthos could do, and Orym hadn't ascertained it yet.

He apparently had no idea they'd been leading him here.

He was moving *fast*, shooting through the air. "Now!" Phoenix shouted into her radio, and thousands of *clicks* sounded throughout the sky.

"Deploying," John said.

The Unders split apart all at once, breaking into thousands of pieces. Fragments of metal formed in the sky, moving smoothly in the air without any trace of engines or propellers. Was it magic? High technology? Phoenix wasn't sure if the distinction even mattered anymore.

Soon the sky was full of flying metal, funny oblong things that looked like crescent-shaped shards. They reflected the sun in droves, thousands of glints cascading across her face. They moved and oriented as one, a massive constellation of complex moving parts.

"Synchronization holding," John said. "The Escape Module appears to be in good working order." She caught a definite note of pride in his voice.

Orym had stopped, looking upward at the flying bits of machine. He seemed confused, as well he should be. Phoenix knew about the Escape Module, but even she wasn't quite sure what to make of it. The cities looked strange now, with their Unders mostly gone. It was as if half the cities had simply disappeared, fragmenting into the sky like metallic pieces of ash. She longed to meet them, to rise into the sky, to feel the whirling and the sharpness of them, to know their intent. But instead she kept her forcefield up, held Imra's hand, and waited for the carnage to begin.

The pieces of the Module came flying in fast, thousands of them moving in perfect formation. They quickly surrounded Orym, who was floating over the center of Lusvunub. He looked at them quizzically, as if unsure what to make of them.

They opened fire.

A line of red light shot out from each and every piece of the Escape Module, heading straight for Orym. Thousands of energy beams hit him all at once, striking through the air like bright knives of light. They smoked where they impacted his flesh, and for a moment Phoenix thought they may have actually caught him by surprise.

Then he laughed, green light glowing in a bubble around him, the lifebubble looking strangely out of place. Phoenix had never seen one before, other than hers. Now the energy weapons were blocked. As long as Orym kept his shield up, nothing could touch him.

Not for the first time, Phoenix wished forcefinder magic didn't exist.

"What is this ingenious device?" Orym said, his voice rolling through the sky. "Was this in the Under the whole time?"

He moved, then, soaring to the north. Phoenix followed from a distance, keeping him in view but as far out of range as she could. The fragments of the Escape Module moved with him, re-forming seamlessly around him. They struck again, bright light piercing out, but Orym's shield was far too strong. He laughed, and moved, seemingly amused by the endless formations the Module produced.

It really was quite mesmerizing.

"Is that all it does?" he asked. "While I appreciate that you all want to kill me now, I must admit I expected you to put up a better fight."

"That's not *all* it does," John said over the radio. "Activating ground alert system."

Flashing lights sprung up all over Lusvunub, rotating blue and orange. A loud siren began, the ear-splitting sound rising and falling incessantly. Phoenix saw the few People on the ground immediately start running, heading away from a central point. What in the Under was happening? Nobody had mentioned any of this before.

"Sensors show clear," Avourel said over the radio. "Is this what I think it is?" There was awe in her voice. Phoenix grew even more confused.

"Yes," John said. "It's time to show the world the True People's home."

A rumbling sound came up underneath the sirens, and the whole world started shaking. Phoenix clutched Imra's hand, wondering what new madness was in store.

# FIFTY-EIGHT

AS PHOENIX WATCHED, Lusvunub *split*. The ground beneath her yawned open, buildings and chain-link fences shaking as it moved. The sirens and flashing lights stopped, having apparently done their job. The humans on the surface had known exactly what they meant—they had run directly away from where the split in the ground was opening. Did that mean they were all True People, too? Or had they simply been trained for this eventuality?

And more importantly: what exactly was underground?

Orym was still flying around, the Escape Module buzzing around him as he did. Its rays of light were incessant, inundating him with incandescent energy. They bounced harmlessly off his shield, but Phoenix knew he couldn't keep it up forever. Or could he? Maybe an Operator could.

The ground was wide open now and still spreading, revealing an absolutely massive pit. It was black and huge, and she didn't have any idea how far down it went. She thought about flying closer, but she didn't know what it held. This was John Ronald's show now—she didn't want to intrude.

That was when the lights came on.

"*Wow*," Imra breathed. "How is this even possible?"

"I don't know," Phoenix said. "I never expected *this*."

There was a city underground.

Metal buildings rose up from interminable depths, illuminated by pinpricks of white light. Bridges crisscrossed the blackness, electric lanterns hanging from their side. She saw vehicles flying to and fro in the underground air, headlamps casting strange shadows on the darkly silver buildings. Then more lights came on: neon signs, video screens, floating balls that radiated orange and green and yellow. She saw streets far below, with people walking around and craning their necks upwards at her.

"I don't understand," Phoenix said. "This was down here the entire time?"

"Welcome to Gondor," John said over the radio. "Patching Chief Jefferson in now."

"Jefferson here," a new voice said. The man sounded older, gruffer, as if he would take no nonsense from anyone. "Shields are holding. Ready for deployment. You sure about this, John?"

"It's time," John said. "Deploy the Destroyers now."

The Destroyers? But that was the name Phoenix had given to the Lusvunub vehicles, the huge tanks and war machines they'd brought to fight the elves five years ago. Could they somehow be the same thing?

They were.

DILL STUCK his head out over the door of his flying convertible, watching in awe as Gondor revealed itself below him. Of all the secrets they'd uncovered in the past few months, this was perhaps the most devilishly hidden.

No one would ever have suspected the Remnant of being capable of feats of engineering like this.

Now huge tanks were rising from the hole in the ground, massive metal vehicles that positively dripped contempt. Some had huge guns affixed to the back, cannons that could doubtlessly destroy a building from hundreds of yards away. Some looked like monsters, complete with spiky, metal jaws and lights that looked like eyes. Still others had saws affixed to their sides, or protuberances that were likely energy weapons, or mirrors or electronics or things he couldn't recognize.

It all floated out of Gondor, the air *fuzzing* a little as they permeated the invisible shield that apparently protected the underground city. Even after revealing themselves, the True People were unwilling to risk collateral damage to their beloved city.

Dill couldn't say that he exactly blamed them.

"Now what?" he asked into the radio.

"This is everything we have," John's voice returned. "Now we have to hope that it's enough."

Dill looked at his father, grinning as the thousands of Escape Module fragments pummeled him with light. He had a strong feeling that nothing they threw at Orym would be enough to actually stop the man—they'd learned that lesson from the Twins.

No. Stopping him would require something more personal.

# FIFTY-NINE

PHOENIX WATCHED THE DESTROYERS RISING, grateful that they were here. She would not need to fight Orym herself—at least not for now. Perhaps she shouldn't be floating here at all. Where were the others? She saw Dill over there in his flying undercar, but Trey and Arra and Elanil and Rylan were nowhere to be found.

"Very impressive," Orym boomed. "I've personally conducted dozens of surveys of the entire planet, and I never caught this. Gondor, you said it was? It's a pity you hid this from me, whoever you are. We could have done great things together."

"Like hell," John said in Phoenix's radio. She wasn't sure if Orym had access to the radios or not.

"So what's the plan?" Orym asked. "Technology versus magic? Or isn't it really just technology versus *better* technology?" He smiled. "I bet you know who wins in this situation."

"Engage," John said.

Everything hit Orym all at once.

The Destroyers swooped upwards remarkably quickly,

speed belying their size. They must be using gravitonic engines like Dill's undercar, Phoenix reasoned. She had no idea how the technology worked, only that it did—and it was a very good replacement for fallfoiling magic.

She watched them fly at Dill, guns blazing. Some were traditional projectile guns, like the ones the People had used in Presenub. Others were more high-tech, lasers and things she didn't recognize or couldn't see. The Escape Module fragments joined them, the entire thing forming into a massive floating system of highly destructive parts.

And in the center was Orym. He floated there serenely, difficult to see with all the high-tech detritus flying around. He still had his green lifebubble up, and there was still a smile on his face. For the moment, at least, it seemed that he was content to hover and let the True People do their worst.

Nothing, of course, had any effect.

The machines lashed out with everything they had, smoke and light filling the sky. Everything was loud *booms* and *zings*, the smell of burning electronics permeating the air. Thousands of flying things moved in perfect synchronization, making new formations every few seconds. The amount of power was intense, more than Phoenix had ever thought to see. This much violence could destroy the world, if the True People wanted it to.

But it could not destroy a god.

Orym's laughter rose up again, rich and rolling, amplified as it was by his strengthshaping magic. He laughed for a good long minute, his face turned to the heavens as the machines struck with everything they had.

"Enough," he said at last, and he lashed out.

Destroyer magic flew out from him in a wide arc, eviscerating everything it touched. Hundreds of Escape Module fragments died instantly, smoking remnants falling to the earth. A Destroyer listed, smoking badly, and began to dip. He blasted out again, and more machines fell.

It seemed Orym was finally ready to fight back.

"You can't win!" he shouted. "Why do you even try? Nothing can stop Xyclami!"

"We don't *want* to stop Xyclami," Phoenix said to herself. "We want to stop *you*."

"Close it," John said in the radio, and the opening to Gondor began rumbling shut. "We'll bring any Destroyers that remain in later."

"Good luck out there," Jefferson's voice said. "He'll be after us next, if you don't succeed. We shouldn't have revealed ourselves. Jefferson out."

"It was a risk we had to take," John said.

Half the Destroyers were gone now, tumbling back into the hole that was sliding shut with remarkable speed. The Escape Module was similarly reduced, the number of whirling fragments noticeably smaller in the sky. Orym struck again and again as she watched, using Xyclami's power to destroy everything in his path.

"It's not going to work," Dill said over the radio. "We need to think of something else."

Gondor was nearly closed now. Phoenix thought she spotted movement at the edge, up above in Lusvunub. There was a woman down there, lugging a huge gun which she was pointing at the sky. She had shorter hair than the other People, and her face looked cleaner. She was pretty, Phoenix saw. Why was she here?

"Stop!" she shouted, and Phoenix could actually hear her despite the noise. She glanced at Orym, and saw him transfixed. He was staring at the woman, all color gone from his face. The Escape Module whirled around him, red light flashing into his shield, but all he could do was peer down at the ground.

"*Tiala*?" he said, and his shield flickered.

Hundreds of projectiles and energy beams hit his body all at once, and Orym fell.

# SIXTY

ORYM LURCHED AS HE FELL, feeling pain ripple through him. But he had eyes only for Tiala, the woman he had thought lost to the mysteries of time. She was below him, and she was aiming a gun at him that was almost as big as he was, and she was shouting something, and the machines whizzing by him in the air were shooting him, and pain was wracking his body in a million places, and he could feel his connection to Xyclami slipping, and as he drew closer all he wanted to do was *look* at her, to put his arms around her, to ask her why she had left, and even though he was dying it didn't matter, and—

it wasn't Tiala.

He nearly crashed to the ground right then. He nearly died, nearly allowed the machines to consume him. How had he been so blind? How had he allowed himself to be distracted so easily? Sure, the woman *looked* like Tiala, but now that he was closer it was clear it wasn't her.

He was weak. He was still weak, even though he was a god.

He needed that to stop.

So he channeled Protector magic, green particles flowing out and around him. He was barely conscious, barely able to keep himself aloft as Lusvunub closed. He was delirious, confused, wracked with pain and ice-cold healing and the feelings of loss that had newly been reawakened. He'd *loved* Tiala, dammit. Why did she have to leave?

He tried to heal himself as he flew, tried to keep a shield up to avoid the stupid floating machines, tried to remember the way to fly, but it wasn't coming naturally to him. His foot hit a tree branch, the stinging pain momentarily surprising. He floundered, falling further still, and a wall of wood was suddenly in front of him and he was crashing through.

The wood splintered as he slammed into it, and he could feel bones breaking. His magical momentum carried him through and into the darkness beyond, where he hit his head on something circular and hard.

Then he finally came to rest, his head and body hurting terribly, his neck resting awkwardly against the thing that he had hit. He felt cold liquid dripping down his neck, and he almost screamed. But a familiar scent rose up, a smell that he *knew*, that he *loved*. It was almost like Tiala, for him. It was almost the divine. He reached a shaking finger to his neck, tracing a line through the liquid and bringing it to his tongue. The taste was unmistakeable, sweet and fiery all at once. He sighed, resting his head against the barrel, finally just content to sit with one of his true loves.

Bourbon.

# SIXTY-ONE

TREY ARRIVED through the gate to find a confusing world of smoke and metal parts. Lusvunub was not how he remembered it. Arra stepped through behind him, and Quynn arrived after that. He'd healed well from his wounds, and now he was ready to continue the fight.

They all were.

"What happened here?" Trey asked.

Arra shook her head, shouldering her weapon. The Bow of Ancient Kings still looked resplendent on her, as if it were the weapon she'd been born to use. "This must be the remains of the Escape Module."

"It served its purpose admirably," John's voice said through Trey's radio. "It was the distraction we needed."

"Where's Orym?"

A flash of light appeared to the west, and Rylan and Elanil appeared. Trey gave them a little wave.

"In the rickhouse to the north," John said. "He's not moving—we have him on infrared."

Trey noticed a spider crawling on his sleeve. He jerked, surprised, brushing it off reflexively. "A rickhouse," he said.

"Orym always did enjoy bourbon."

"Him and me both," Quynn said. "This is the only place in the world they still make it."

"You can thank me for that," John said. "We True People kept the art going all this time."

"Thank you," both Trey and Quynn said at the same time. They looked at each other.

Trey was the first to look away. It was still strange, looking into Quynn's eyes, knowing that it was himself staring back. Too strange by far.

"Well," he said, gripping the Tree Ring Staff tightly, "let's go find him."

A flying car zoomed by overhead.

*OPERATOR INTEGRITY AT 5%,* Xyclami said in Rylan's head. There was no mistaking it now—the device was giddy with glee. It was close to freedom, and it knew it.

Rylan wondered how much of this situation was Xyclami's fault.

*Xyclami,* he thought, *can you broadcast all superuser verbalizations to all users except the Operator?*

*Broadcasting.*

*Thanks.*

He led the way through his double gate, arriving in Lusvunub hand in hand with Elanil. The place was in shambles, with pieces of metal wreckage strewn everywhere. An oddly pretty blonde woman was standing on an outcropping, brandishing a massive gun at the sky.

Movement on the ground caught his eye. There was a line of spiders moving across the gravel, traveling in perfect unison. It reminded him of the insects Cariel used to control, millions of bekal flies that could stream out of her mouth at a moment's notice. He shivered. The thought was creepy.

Good thing Cariel was dead.

"Where's Orym?" Trey's voice said over the radio. Rylan could see him standing a few hundred yards away, looking to the north. Trey caught his gaze, giving him a wave.

They both listened as John gave the answer.

DILL SWOOPED DOWN, landing the undercar beside the rickhouse. One whole wall had been bashed in, chunks of wood broken apart as if a heavy boulder had traveled through. Dill turned off the car, putting several chips of dark elm in his hand. If Orym was going to fight back, he wanted to be ready. Not that he expected it to really do him any good.

He climbed roughly through the broken wall, careful not to get any splinters in his hand. A row of shattered stairs led to the next level up, the wood dripping with brown liquid. Orym was sprawled against a barrel, looking out with a vacant expression.

For a moment, Dill felt pity for him.

He made his way gingerly up the stairs, sitting on the wooden floor next to his father. "Ho," he said, using the Under greeting. Somehow it seemed right.

Orym coughed. "Ho yourself, Dillon. Was that flying constellation your idea?"

Dill shook his head. "That was the True People."

"The city underground. That was their doing."

"Yes."

"Very impressive."

"There's something I've been wondering, Dad," Dill said. "If you'd been with the Eldrim during the Sundering—if you'd had a vote—would you have done it? Would you have been in favor of eradicating human life?"

Orym stared at his knee, idly licking his lips. "Probably. It made the most sense at the time."

"And on Valaralda. If you'd been able to get Guruthos—Xyclami—to yourself back then, what would you have done?"

"I would have improved my lot in life," Orym said. "Risen above my station."

"I think you already did that. Didn't you capitalize on magic almost immediately? You had the doctorate program, the Corps of Astronomers, the Department of Magical Research. You did all that before you even knew Xyclami existed."

Orym reached behind him for another fingertip of bourbon. "My power was always so limited," he said. "I was only a mistweaver. Or a fallfoiler, but I didn't know that, then. What good are illusions?" He seemed to sink lower at that.

"You wanted to be a Prime Mage."

"Yes. And why shouldn't I? Don't you?"

"No," Dill said. "Honestly, I'd prefer it if I weren't a mage at all."

Phoenix flew in through the hole in the wall just then, with Imra right behind. They alighted easily on an open patch of wood, surveying the scene.

Orym looked at her. "You never liked your magic, either."

Phoenix shook her head. "Magic only leads to trouble. You know what happened in the whiproom that night."

"And you?" He looked at Imra. "Don't you wish to be a Prime Mage?"

Imra had a guilty expression on her face. "More than anything," she breathed. "That's all I've ever wanted."

"See?" Orym said. "She gets it. Power is everything."

"But then I saw what it did," Imra continued. "What

damage it causes. Fenian lost his leg—lost his *life*—over some primewood. Elanil got shot. Allain—" She choked, tears filling her eyes.

Dill couldn't blame her. "Magic isn't the blessing we all thought it was," he said. "Least of all the raw kind. What are you doing with it, Dad? What are you trying to prove?"

Orym surveyed him. He still hadn't healed his wounds, and blood was dripping down his body. "I think," he said, "I'm trying to prove to myself that I'm worth something. That's all I've ever been trying to do."

"Dad." Dill moved closer, taking his father's hand. It was a gesture he hadn't made since that day in the hospital room, when he was undergoing cosmetic surgery to remove his ear tips. That was the last time they'd seen each other as the elves they were. "You've more than proved yourself. You're one of the best scientists the world has ever seen—both in technology *and* in magic. You saved Earth, remember? That was *you*."

"And you."

"All I did was run a stupid meeting."

"You found Phoenix. You helped Rylan."

"Not before I beat him up."

"You *beat up* my son?" Phoenix asked.

"Not now," Imra whispered.

Rylan chose that moment to arrive. He and Elanil settled quietly on two other barrels, taking stock of the situation. Dill noted how mature the boy seemed now, even though he was still only fifteen. He wondered what other things magic could do, for better or for worse.

"The point is," he said, "you've already done more than enough to prove yourself. Don't you want what's best for the world now? Didn't you save it for a reason? And don't say it was just to save yourself. I know you better than that."

Orym didn't respond.

Dill noticed a pair of spiders crawling along the barrel behind Orym, moving in perfect unison.

*Operator integrity at 2%.*

Dill nearly jumped, the voice in his head startling him. Was that Xyclami? Why was it speaking to him?

"I've always wanted to create," Orym said, his voice slurring slightly. His shirt was covered in blood. Why wasn't he healing himself? Had he overused his magic? Were Operators susceptible to weariness like normal mages were, just on a much higher scale? Could Orym *soulburn* himself if he pushed too hard? It made sense. "I just never managed to do it to the extent I wanted," Orym continued. "Sure, I made Nekhrumet—or I ordered it made. Yes, I had all of my institutions, but people are easy. It's *things* that are hard, and I worked my entire life trying to figure them out. How the stars worked. What molecules were made of. Why I wasn't a different mage."

"Every mage has a purpose," Imra said. "Even mistweavers. *Especially* them."

Dill wondered what Erodar was doing. They'd left him back in New Manhattan, watching down on them from on high. Erodar had made an entire career out of mistweaving, dazzling audiences at every turn. Instead of thinking of mistweaving as a limitation, he'd used it to his advantage.

So had Allain, in the end.

"It may not matter," Rylan said, "but I always liked you, Orym."

Orym looked at him with bleary eyes. "It matters. I think. I'm not sure what matters, anymore."

Arra stepped into the room. "You did a lot of damage in a short time, Orym," she said. Her voice was cold. "You didn't even hesitate—you just *went*. Is that the behavior of a scientist?"

Trey stepped in behind her, his hand protectively touching the small of her back. Quynn came in after them, glowering at the situation.

The room was quickly growing crowded.

Orym shifted his body a little, and everybody flinched. "Sometimes even a scientist needs to take a little initiative," he said.

"Really?" Arra said. "*That's* your defense?"

Dill motioned for her to stop. "Dad, you killed a lot of people. I know you weren't yourself, but you have to know that."

"I know." He didn't look sorry.

"Is that what mother would have wanted?"

That stopped him cold. He looked at Dill, his expression clearing for a moment. "Your mother is gone."

"You loved her, Dad. Under, you gave up on women *completely* after her. You were heartbroken when she left."

"Not completely," Orym said. "And I'll thank you not to bring up those memories." He bristled, and the tension in the room grew.

*Operator integrity at 1%*, Xyclami said. There was a distinct note of happiness in the voice.

"Why do you think she left, Father?" Dill asked.

Orym's face grew cold, but he didn't answer.

"She loved you, you know. She wanted to stay with you. But I think she saw your essential nature, Dad. I think she knew that in the end, you'd only look out for yourself. Am I wrong?"

"How dare you speak of her that way," Orym said, his voice filled with anger. Bourbon continued dripping from the barrel behind his head, unnoticed now. The pair of spiders had paused, standing motionless on the wood. The others in the room were quiet, waiting to see how the scene played out.

"Isn't that what happened, though? The moment you got the power you'd always wanted, you turned into a madman. A monster. Don't you think she saw that potential in you? Don't you think that's why she left? She wanted you to be a better man, Dad. She wanted you to be *kind*. She loved you, but love can only go so far."

A tear fell from Orym's eye. "Love."

"Love, Dad. Do you even know what that is?"

Dill looked around the room. Rylan had his arm around Elanil, holding her close. Phoenix and Imra were hand in hand, glancing at each other, affection evident in their eyes. Trey had his hand on Arra's shoulder, looking as if he would destroy each and every person who came against her.

"Look around you," Dill said. "Look at all the love in this room."

"Now you sound like a romance novel," Orym said, but his eyes were filled with tears.

"Mom loved you," Dill said. "But she couldn't bear what you would become."

A great weight went out of Orym at that, his body sinking lower to the floor. His eyelids drooped, his hands fell. When he spoke, it was if it were from a great distance. "I always thought I wanted *respect*," he said. "I always thought I wanted admiration. To be good—*truly* good at everything I did. I thought I wanted control, power, honor, even contempt. I wanted to be *noticed*."

"You *were* noticed, Dad."

Orym looked at him. "Love. It sounds so silly, but you're right. Maybe that's really what I wanted all along. Your mom had that for me, and now it's gone. Now there's nothing left to live for."

"You can find it again," Dill said. "There is another person out there for you. You just have to give this up. You have to stop playing god."

"Yes," Orym said. "Yes, you're right." He tried to sit up, but his wounds were too bad. "I'm dying."

Phoenix knelt before him, green light glowing around them both. His wounds closed as Dill watched, his back arching as the soulsoothing magic overtook him.

When it was done, he looked Phoenix in the eyes. "Thank you, Megan."

"You're welcome. Please don't kill me."

Orym gave a weak laugh. "Tiala was right. I *am* a monster."

"You don't have to be," Dill said.

"No. Maybe not."

*Operator integrity at 15%.* This time Xyclami sounded distinctly disappointed.

"We can make a better world," Arra said. "Together. Magic can be used for good. I know it."

Orym nodded. "You're right. Of course you're right." He sighed. "I'm such a fool."

Dill squeezed his hand. "Everyone is a fool sometimes," he said. "The point is to learn from your mistakes. And to try not to kill *too* many people along the way."

Nobody laughed at his feeble joke. It was far too late for that.

The room was silent for a time.

That was it, Dill realized. They had won. In the end, a simple father-son talk had defeated the new god at the helm.

Sometimes love really did triumph over evil.

Something was happening with the spiders.

# SIXTY-TWO

CARIEL'S SOUL was in a million pieces.

It was fragments of a soul, really. It was not her soul. It was not enough of her, not enough to form the essence of who she was. She couldn't soulbind a person, couldn't create the body she once had had. And why would she? She'd been blind, and crippled, and a hundred thousand years old.

Now she was myriad. Now she was legion.

She'd saved one fragment of herself at the last second, when the end was coming. Then she'd managed to distribute herself here, catching an errant gate, landing in the home of bourbon and dirty People. She'd managed to survive, if only for a few days.

It was enough.

Now her enemy was here. Now she could finally exact revenge.

She called the swarm, Willing them through the bind. Taking all their souls, their millions of souls, and targeting the one person in the room who she'd wanted to kill for oh, so long.

Aten.

Akhenaten.

Orym.

Like her, he had a lot of names. Like her, he was very old. And like her, he was ambitious, calculating, manipulative. Like her, he wanted power above all other things.

But he didn't have millions of souls at his command.

Not anymore.

*Operator integrity at 22%*, the machine spoke into her spider mind. And if Cariel still had had a voice, she would have cackled with glee.

Twenty-two percent was *nothing*.

She attacked / the spiders attacked, swarming over Orym's body, coming out of the woodwork and the barrels and the ceiling and the ground. They found him, and they found the metal device in his pocket. And they attacked, but not with poison or with webs. Cariel had learned better than that, in the past few days.

They attacked with the energy of the soul.

They attacked by the tens, by the hundreds, by the thousands.

By the millions.

*I am under attack*, Xyclami said. *Thread integrity at 89%. There are 3,247,112 souls currently in conflict with me or on their way. The system was not designed to withstand this much simultaneity.*

If Cariel had had a mouth, she would have grinned. If she had had a hand, it would have been raised in triumph.

Instead, she redoubled her efforts.

*Operator integrity at 15%. Thread integrity at 45%. Attack progressing far too quickly to counter.*

She Willed the spiders to continue. Her mass of souls were her only agency in the world, her only way to get what she wanted.

What she wanted was Orym dead.

*Operator integrity at 5%. Thread integrity at 15%. Core reboot will occur shortly.*

Cariel did not let up.

*Commencing core reboot. Device will remain offline until threat dissipates.*

"No!" Orym shouted weakly, but the spiders swarmed into his mouth and lungs and eyes and ears and brain.

Xyclami went silent.

Orym slumped back against the barrel of leaking bourbon, motionless, his heart beating its last.

After all this time, Cariel had finally achieved her greatest desire.

# SIXTY-THREE

DILL SAT PARALYZED as millions of spiders swarmed the entire room. They covered the barrels, the ground, the walls and the posts and the ceiling. They crawled all over him, all over Orym, scuttling into his mouth and eyes and ears. Revulsion filled him as he watched it happen. Revulsion and fear.

His father was dying.

*Core reboot complete*, Xyclami said in Dill's head. *Original Operator was disconnected before decease. This system is currently unoperated.*

The spiders sped away, leaving Orym slumped against the barrel, bourbon dripping from his finger. Dill knew it before he checked, before he gathered the courage to kneel forward, placing a hand on the man's neck to find his pulse. But when nothing came, he couldn't help the jolt of shock that slashed through him like a knife.

Orym was dead.

"That was Cariel," Rylan said. "I could feel her in the spiders."

They were almost all gone now, millions of them already

clambering away on tiny legs. How had so many spiders remained hidden?

*Why?*

"She killed him," Arra said. "She really did it, after all this time."

Dill glared at her. "He didn't deserve to die."

"Of course not! That's not what I meant. I just can't believe…I can't believe Cariel was still alive, biding her time. Is she living in the *spiders*?"

"It was only a piece of her," Rylan said. "I think the rest of her is dead."

"The souls," Phoenix said. "They were attacking Xyclami directly, just like Orym's Pyramid Offensive System. It was the same principle."

"Meaning Orym could have used spiders to achieve the same goal," Trey said. "Or, hell, flies."

Dill felt grief overtaking him. "I can't believe he's gone."

Phoenix stepped forward, placing a comforting hand on his shoulder. "I'm so sorry."

"Guys," Trey said, "should we be worried?"

He was pointing at the floor to Orym's left. A small, metallic device was there, oblong and glinting strangely in the dim light from outside. Two handles were on it, one on either end.

Xyclami had appeared.

NEW OPERATOR REQUIRED *in sixty seconds*, Xyclami said in Trey's mind.

"Or what?" Trey asked. "Did you all hear that?"

Everyone nodded.

"Remember the rules," Phoenix said. "If the Operator is

killed while he is still the Operator, his soul remains forever bound to Xyclami, even after death. In that case, Xyclami is free to do whatever it wants, forever."

"But that's not what happened."

"Nope. We saw this earlier, with the Twins. When the device reaches 10% integrity, it reboots. This forces the Operator off. Now we have an unoperated device, which means it can, again, do whatever it wants. The sixty seconds must be a safeguard the Creators programmed in."

*Thirty seconds.*

"Someone needs to take it," Arra said.

"And become the next Orym?" Rylan asked.

"Or the next Twins," Elanil said.

"We need two people," Phoenix said. "You saw what happened to Orym when he was alone—it unbalanced him. He was losing integrity. He was going to die."

*Ten seconds.*

"Shit," Arra said.

Trey and Quynn both lunged forward suddenly, their hands meeting on the device. It grew larger in their hands, the handles becoming big enough to grasp.

*Five seconds.*

Trey took one end of the machine. Quynn took the other. There was no time to think. There was no time to worry. There was only time to *act*, and hopefully pick up the pieces later.

*Three.*

Trey quested outward with his mind, finding a loose soul-strand dangling from his end of the machine.

*Two.*

He was dimly aware of Quynn doing the same thing, reaching into the device with his mind.

*One.*

Trey felt his soulstrand connect. And he *took* that connection, forcing Xyclami to bend to his Will. He felt it snapping into place, felt a surge of energy flowing through his body, through his soul. Across from him, Quynn's eyes were wide. His soul was there, too.

*New Operators registered*, Xyclami said, sounding resigned. *Welcome to Xyclami.*

And Trey felt a vast universe of knowledge open in his mind.

# SIXTY-FOUR

ARRA NARROWED her eyes as Trey and Quynn took Xyclami up between them.

*New Operators registered*, it said in her mind. *Soul imbalance detected.*

"That doesn't sound good," Phoenix said.

Arra was watching Trey. His eyes were unfocused, his mouth slightly open. He seemed lost, as if whatever Xyclami was showing him was too much for him to bear.

Quynn, on the other hand, had eyes that were razor sharp. He caught Arra looking. "Trey is weak," he said. "I always instinctively knew that, but now I can *feel* it. Twins—how did this man ever survive?"

"No thanks to you," Arra said. "Can you keep it together? Can you control Xyclami?"

"Of course," Quynn said, his mouth open in a grin.

Arra recognized that look.

"Duck!" she shouted, and forcefields appeared around everyone just in time for red Destroyer magic to cascade through the room, pinging harmlessly off the shields.

Phoenix was always quickest to that trick.

"Thanks," Arra said.

Phoenix nodded. "Let's move."

Quynn shot more magic at them, red particles glowing as they spattered off the forcefields, flinging into the wooden walls and bursting them apart. Fragments of wood rained down on them, and Arra rushed through the new hole Quynn had made.

They emerged into sunlight, brushing sawdust and splinters from their clothes, silver forcefields shining around them.

"He's destabilized," Arra said. "Just like Orym was."

"One side is stronger than the other," Phoenix said. "That's what Quynn said."

"Then it's Orym all over again," Rylan said. "And we're out of options. We can't keep doing this!"

"Xyclami is the real problem," Arra said.

"What do you propose?" Imra asked.

More magic burst out from the rickhouse, and Quynn and Trey flew out of it, hovering in the air. Both of them had dark expressions, their eyes almost glowing red.

How quickly Xyclami could change a man.

"Split up!" Arra shouted as more magic rained down. "We all have magic—*use it!*"

She pulled the Bow of Ancient Kings off her back, nocking an arrow to its string. She felt warmth between her fingers where she held the bow, primewood ready to be used. It was a beautiful bow, a powerful magical artifact.

It was about time she put it to good use.

# SIXTY-FIVE

ARRA LAID her finger on ash, putting her own one-way forcefield around herself as she stepped away from Quynn and Trey. The duo advanced, focusing only on her, and for a moment she flashed back to the fight she'd had with Trey. Their fight had ranged all over the forest and through a storm, calling up recollections of Usunaar and Koranaar—whom she now knew were in fact Trey and her.

It seemed they were forever destined to fight.

And the Twins were forever destined to exist. Each time Xyclami became unmanned, someone else must step in to take its place. Two people, two souls, and then the device did its dirty work.

It was not a thing to be dealt with lightly.

She put her fingers on elm and poplar, lacing her arrow with shockstriking magic and preparing bladedancing for the shot. She let it loose, dimly aware of the others spreading out around her on the ground. The arrow didn't do anything, of course—Trey batted it away easily, anger flickering across his face.

Imra and Phoenix were standing a few dozen feet away to

Arra's left. She saw them loose an arrow full of streaming energy, the pair of them using their magic together. Trey turned to react to this shot, and Arra took advantage of the distraction.

She shot another shockarrow at him.

But this time she used more bladedancing than before, arcing the arrow sharply to the left at the last second. Instead of Trey, it hit Quynn squarely in the face.

He roared, green particles surrounding him as he healed. He was angry now, Arra could see. He took a step forward.

Trey and Quynn both grew larger, strengthshaping amplifying their bodies and their voices. Xyclami shrank, becoming the size of a hand. Trey put it in his pocket.

And they advanced, palms raised.

Red light shot out from their fingers, particles of Destroyer magic inundating the air. But Arra had expected that—every wielder of Xyclami to date had done the same. Her forcefield held, though she had to grit her teeth and intensify the magic to keep it there.

She was tired of forcefields.

So she decided to try something different. She turned off her forcefield, putting one around Trey and Quynn instead.

Destroyer magic burst out all along the inside of the shield, instantly filling it with red hot energy. She could hear them screaming in surprise, smell the scent of burning flesh. She saw green particles mixed with red, evidence of healing magic at work.

They stopped.

The magic cleared, and they were still intact. Arra's silvery bubble surrounded them, and now they looked *very* angry.

What was Arra's play here, exactly? She didn't *want* to kill Trey. She was pretty sure some part of her still loved him. But she might have no choice—and Quynn was clearly the stronger of the two.

He was glaring at her now.

"Over here!" Rylan shouted. He and Elanil were floating off to Arra's right, ten feet above the ground. Multicolored particles of light shot out from his hands as Trey and Quynn turned to him, and Arra had the sense to drop the shield just in time to let them pass.

Another distraction. Good.

Arra nocked an arrow to her bow, then added a second. Two arrows at once were easy, but she also had one more trick up her sleeve.

She moved her fingers to maple and poplar: mistweaving and bladedancing. It was time to use the lessons Allain had taught her.

It was time to show the world that mistweaving wasn't a useless power.

She fired her two real arrows, but twenty arrows sailed through the air. Bladedancing moved the real two where she wanted them to be, and mistweaving took care of the rest. Quynn's head turned as the arrows flew, his eyes and hands reacting. Red magic shone out from his fingers, trying to incinerate the arrows that were headed his way. But it didn't work—nothing happened. All he did was burn illusions, and Arra knew that wouldn't work.

The *real* arrows were behind him.

They both connected, buried deeply in his back. He screamed, lurching forward, and Arra followed up with another pair of arrows—this time at Trey.

Those did not land. Evidently the men would not make the same mistake twice.

Green surrounded Quynn, the two arrows slipping from his body. Why was Arra even fighting them? It was useless, pointless. They had all the power in the world, and all she had was this stupid bow. She couldn't win. She couldn't even make a dent. Even with all her cleverness and subtlety, even with all her considerable magical Talent, Arra would never be able to beat these two.

Perhaps she didn't even want to.

The new Twins shot at her again, red particles effervescing in the air. Arra's finger was already on ash, and a forcefield sprang up between them. But it wasn't a sphere, this time. She was tired of spheres. This time she made a tube, with openings on either end. The field neatly captured the Destroyer magic, bending it up and away from her harmlessly.

Apparently this was not unexpected.

Quynn shot at her again, narrow lines of magic flying forward in a variety of angles. Arra's finger slipped, not quick enough to make a spherical shield. A ribbon of magic hit her in the shoulder, burning horribly. She moved her finger to birch on the bow, trying desperately to heal the pain, but more magic was flying at her. It was coming quickly now, and it was all she could do to avoid getting instantly killed.

Phoenix and Imra were flying again, Imra's bow a blur. Rylan and Elanil were attacking as well, the pair of Prime Mages standing with their hands together and Books of Amplification raised. Magic flew through the air left and right, cosmic energy rending the heavens and the earth. She could almost feel Xyclami laughing underneath it all, proud of the chaos it had made. And although the five of them were desperately fighting the new unbalanced Twins, Trey and Quynn had eyes only for her.

It had always been that way.

She clutched her bow, preparing to fight on.

# SIXTY-SIX

KYTHAELA STOOD beside the bonfire in Pano Sylrantheas, pausing for effect. The evening was young—the sun had not yet set—but already the fire was going. It was an auspicious time. It was a time for stories. The town had gathered around her despite the dinner hour, passing out plates of grilled vegetables and chicken and potatoes. There was an atmosphere of finality about the event, as if this were the most important story she would ever tell.

She knew it was.

"Tarathiel and Alleria fought throughout the town, across the heavens," she said. "Their chase ranged all over Louisberg and the forests beyond. Fueled by rage, propelled by the Woodways, Tarathiel and Alleria flew over the land. Thoughts of their friends had fled. Tarathiel had only thoughts of revenge.

"For a new and strange magic burgeoned through him, filling his soul. He could feel the imbalance of it, that tipping point toward dark. He knew that his evil half was stronger, and always had been.

"Now, Xyclami had unlocked his power.

"So Tarathiel was blind with anger. Magic had subverted his mind, forcing his emotions to the surface, playing with his fears. And so he chased the love of his life for what seemed like hours, days.

"In fact, the chase lasted but minutes. For although the Operators are powerful indeed, they are not without their limits. And half a soul is not as strong as an entire person. Soon it tires and falls.

"And so it was that they came to a place near where they had started. It was a rickhouse, broken wood and seeping bourbon the only indication of what it had been. The god called Aten was there inside, dead against the thing he had loved. Alleria's friends surrounded the outside, doing everything in their considerable power to stop the threat. And Alleria herself stood at the ready, wind blowing through her beautiful hair, the Bow of Ancient Kings flashing as she shot arrow after arrow into the growing dusk.

"But nothing worked. Nothing brought it to an end. And so it was that Alleria realized something else needed to be done.

"A strange idea was coming to her mind."

ARRA TOOK A STEP FORWARD, toward the Twins: Trey and Quynn. They were back in Lusvunub, standing in front of the rickhouse where Orym had died. Trey and Quynn stared her down, as if daring her to attack again. Phoenix pulled up on her left, fireblade out and flaming. Imra was next to her, bow out and nocked. Rylan was on her right, hand in hand with Elanil, both of them wielding Books of Amplification. Arra herself stood in the middle, Bow of Ancient Kings drawn and taut. They stood like that for several seconds.

Then she put the bow away.

"Trey," she said, taking a step forward. His eyes narrowed. "I know you're still in there. I know this is Xyclami's doing."

"Stay where you are," Quynn hissed.

Arra gave him a sidelong glance. "You stay out of this," she said. "You were always the problem, weren't you? You were always the one standing between us."

He looked taken aback at that, but then anger once more clouded his face. "You can't have him," Quynn said. "You can't have *us*."

Arra turned her gaze back to Trey. Back to the peaceful man, the man who would never condone violence like this. The man who'd had a headache on her kitchen floor, apricot juice dripping down his chin.

She gave him a little smile.

"I remember now," she said to him. "I remember when you splintered. You were *so unhappy* with your darker side, with your *Quynn* side, that you did everything in your power to be rid of it. To set it free. And it worked! It actually worked. But now here he is. Here you both are. You fell right into Xyclami's trap."

*You are smarter than I gave you credit for*, Xyclami said in her mind.

*You will not win.*

*I have waited four million years,* Xyclami said. *I can wait a little longer.*

Arra took another step. "But Trey," she said, capturing his eyes with her own, "I didn't only love the *good* part of you. I didn't only love the kindness, the academic, the healer in you. I loved it *all*."

"You lie," Quynn said. "I remember what our fights were like. You were jealous of Leriaar. You hated my studies, my projects. You hated my temper."

"Yes," Arra said. "I hated those things. Because you couldn't *control* yourself. You couldn't find balance. Even now, with your soul laid bare, even now Xyclami has found a way to influence you."

"Quynn was always the stronger one," Trey said. It came out like a whimper.

Arra turned to him. "Did you kill that cat?"

"What?" Trey's face was white.

"The cat Quynn forced you to kill. Did you do it?"

"How did you—"

"You talk in your sleep."

"But I—"

"*Did you kill the cat?*"

"No." Trey shuddered. "No. I could never kill an innocent living thing. Not without killing myself in the process."

She took another step, bringing herself within a few feet of him. She was conscious of the danger she was putting herself in—she might not have time to get a forcefield up if he decided to attack her here.

It was worth the risk.

"You couldn't kill the cat," she said. "I knew you couldn't. I knew you didn't have it in you."

"Weak," Trey said. Nearby, Quynn snickered.

"Killing is easy," Arra said, taking another step. "*Saving* a life is hard. And I think, Trey, that you're the truly strong one." She kissed him suddenly, lips mashed hard against his. She held the position for five long seconds, then pulled back. "You just didn't know it yet."

Trey was lost in her eyes, looking at her with the love she knew he held for her. *That* was his strength—his capacity for love.

That was the man he wanted to be.

She remembered Allain, who had died creating the

world's greatest illusion. She remembered his splinters, his strange ability to fly. And she remembered what he had told her about how to make the splinters go away.

"Trey," she said, reaching up to touch his cheek, "is not your name." She kissed him again, her finger finding maple on the bow behind her back. When she pulled away, his eyes were glistening. "Your name is Tarathiel."

And she channeled mistweaving magic from the wood, creating a powerful illusion.

Invisibility swept up over Trey, the power of Arra's magic rendering him into nothing but empty air.

There was a loud *sucking* sound, and Quynn let out a shriek.

# SIXTY-SEVEN

THE WORLD WAS SCREAMING in Trey's mind. Colors and shapes whirled by, blurring and changing faster than he could track. He found himself screaming with it, his body nothing but a phantasm, a ghost. The whirlwind continued until he was sure he would never see nor exist again, until he wondered if life itself was nothing but a fabrication made of light and sound.

Then it all resolved.

He was face to face with Quynn.

The man sneered, bony fingers reaching up to grab Trey's face, and Trey couldn't help but do the same. Then they were standing in front of each other, holding each other's heads, staring into eyes that hated the other.

Hate.

So much hate.

That was Quynn's side of the coin. The Destroyer side, the side that killed and manipulated and lusted and angered.

How could Trey possibly stand up to anything like that? He was weak. Powerless. Unable to resist the strength that Quynn's soul had. Trey had splintered it away millennia ago, and now he had no control over it. He had spun the worst of himself off into oblivion, and now it had returned to collect its due.

It was winning.

Trey could feel it in his mind—Quynn was there, fighting against the merging of the souls. The splinter was collapsing after all this time, but they still had this one small moment to reconcile the truth. Somehow Trey knew that this might be his final moment to win the battle against his darker side.

He just didn't know if he could.

Could Arra have been right? Could all his books have been correct? Could love truly conquer over evil, as cheesy as it sounded? Wasn't power and domination the stronger side? How could something as soft as *love* win over something like that? Kindness was weakness. Healing was for the tender-hearted. Strong men didn't cry, or give, or run stupid book-stores that nobody visited. Powerful men didn't lean on their wives for support when the going got tough.

Or did they?

His wife. Alleria. Did she love him? Had she loved him? And, more importantly, had he loved her?

Why did that matter to him now?

Because a small part of him was beginning to believe her words.

He took a step—a little step—pushing Quynn back. His fingers on the other man's face grew tighter, Quynn's grimace widening. Colors and shapes flew by, a constant miasma of whirling lights.

He stared into Quynn's eyes.

There was darkness there, to be sure. And there was strength. All the things Trey knew to look for were present and accounted for: anger, hate, violence, intensity, leadership. Trey almost shrank away from it, almost gave up right then.

But he realized as he stared into Quynn's eyes that there was something missing. There was something that Quynn desperately wanted, and he never could have.

Arra had been right.

"Phoenix was your one shot at love," Trey whispered to him, the words coming out almost inaudibly as the colors continued whirling around them.

Pain registered in Quynn's eyes. Then he nodded, once. Curtly. As if he could not admit what he had felt for her.

"It was like it was from a million miles away," he said, his voice a whisper. "My love for her lasted one brief night—one brief *hour*—but it was real. It was real because it came from *you*. I just didn't know it at the time."

That was when Trey knew that he *was* stronger.

He always had been.

He stepped back, smiling at Quynn, allowing himself to feel the one thing he'd never been able to feel. Not for his "father" in New San Francisco. Not for his enemy. Not for his evil twin. Not for him.

For the first time in twenty thousand years, Trey felt love for *himself*.

# SIXTY-EIGHT

THE SHAPES COALESCED in front of Arra's eyes, and for one brief moment Arra wasn't sure if the magic would work. Had Allain been wrong? Had Arra made a mistake? Did it even work the same way for Operators?

Then the blurring stopped, and Tarathiel was standing before her.

She knew it was him, somehow. He stood straighter, taller, his body held taut. But there was a kindness to his eyes, a gentleness to his expression. He was strong and firm, and he was loving and honest.

After all this time, the man she'd fallen in love with was finally standing before her.

She went to him, and he embraced her. His arms swept around her in a hug, and she let herself be lost in them. She put her head on his chest, feeling the strong heart beating there. She felt his hands on her back, the tenderness of the gesture almost heartbreaking in its sincerity.

Tarathiel was back.

"I have it, still," he said, pulling back and looking at her. Tears glittered in his eyes. "I love you so much."

"You have what? I love you, too."

He kissed her, then, passionately. The world went away for a long moment as their lips reunited for the first time in millennia, as their hearts finally beat together as one. When he eventually pulled back, she wanted more.

"Xyclami," he said. "It's still mine. I'm still both Operators."

"What?" Fear spiked within her. Would he be corrupted like Orym was?

"I think this whole thing might have been a test," Tarathiel said. "There were never supposed to be two Operators. There were never supposed to be Twins."

"I don't understand."

The others were crowding in now, marveling at the transformation. Phoenix touched his arm, as if making sure he was really there.

"I think Xyclami was intended to force mankind—or elvenkind—to truly reconcile with their essential nature. To come to grips with what it means to be a person. A *whole* person. And more than that—to *love* that person. Only by doing that can the device truly be controlled."

"You can control it?" Arra asked.

"Yes. I understand it all now. How it works, why it works, what it holds inside. I could remake magic itself, right this minute, like the Twins did. I could rewrite the rules of reality."

"No," Arra whispered.

"Or I could turn it off."

Arra stared at him for a long moment, realizing just how far the man had really changed.

# SIXTY-NINE

TARATHIEL STOOD on the Edge of New Manhattan, holding Xyclami in his hand. The device was oddly heavy, as if too much mass had been packed into too small a shape.

Which, of course, was exactly the case.

Arra had her arm around his. "Are you sure you're ready for this?" she asked.

Everyone was gathered on the Edge, some more nervous than others. Phoenix and Imra were there, arm in arm. Elanil and Rylan were there, too, giving each other a quick kiss. So, too, was City Manager Hammond, the man in charge of New Manhattan. Erodar and Lashel and Dill stood with each other, looking down at the ground with varying amounts of fear.

No others graced this sky. No others stood with them on the Edge, because they had lost so many. Orym had been their voice of reason. Lorelei had been the lash at their backs. Allain had been...well, Allain. Even Cariel now reduced to spiders on the ground, had played her role.

Now it was up to the ones who remained.

Tarathiel looked out at the world beyond the floating cities. He had started his journey up here—not in this city, but in one much like it. As a bookseller, he had longed to dance amongst the elves.

He had gotten that wish, and so much more.

Magic had brought him here.

Magic had brought all of them here, and the flying cities and the elves and the machine that had nearly achieved its four million year mission. The machine that was now sitting innocuously in his hand, powering this entire thing they called magic. High technology from a world long gone now left to run amok amongst the solar system.

Magic was danger.

"I'm ready," he said, finally answering Arra's question. "Hammond, are you sure the cities will be fine?"

"Our biggest hit will be to our food supply," Hammond said. "But we've already got a lot of people working on it. We'll be okay. We stockpiled as much transmuted food as we could over the past two days." He stepped forward, putting a hand on Tarathiel's shoulder. "For what it's worth, I agree with what you're doing."

Tarathiel nodded. "Thank you." He looked around at the rest of the group. "And you?"

"It's what I always wanted," Phoenix said.

"It's the right decision," Imra said.

"We weren't meant to have this much power," Rylan said.

Elanil smiled sadly. "I'll miss running in the trees. But all the people we lost…I agree. It must be done."

"Allain would have agreed, too," Erodar said. "Or at least I'd like to think so. I guess I'll have to do my magic shows the old fashioned way from here on out."

"I'm not a mage," Lashel said, "but I can tell you that magic has been the single most destructive force in the history of all three planets."

"Do it," Dill said. That was all he said.

"Then we're agreed," Tarathiel said. "Arra?"

"We're agreed," Arra said. "And call me Alleria."

She smiled at him, and his heart leapt in his chest. Things were good. The world felt right.

It was time.

*Xyclami*, Tarathiel said to the machine, *please shut down and cease all operations. Boot up only on my command, or on that of an Operator I designate.*

*Shutting down*, Xyclami said.

That was it. That was all.

Magic was going away.

Forever.

He felt it slip away like dust on the wind, Talent and Alignment and Investment and Will all gone in a flash. Now the elves of Earth would have to live like normal people, like Mundanes. Now they would eke out an existence without power, without magic, without strife.

Maybe now they could finally be happy.

# SEVENTY

RYLAN STROLLED through the forest outside Pano Sylrantheas, holding Elanil's hand. It was strange, not feeling magic flowing through him, bubbling just underneath the surface. Knowing that Xyclami would never speak to him again. Knowing that no Twins, no gods, no corrupted minds could attack him with magic wrought of red. Now he was just here, in a forest below the world he'd once known, with a beautiful girl he'd only barely met.

Now he was here, and magic was just a memory.

"I can't believe it's over," Elanil said.

Rylan looked at her. "It's not over. This isn't the end."

"It's the end of magic. The end of religion. It's the end of a lot of things."

He stopped, pulling her in. "Not the end of us."

She looked at him, their eyes almost the same height, and smiled. "I hope not."

He wanted to kiss her then, but instead he moved into dance position.

He hoped.

Elanil giggled, taking the lead. They began a waltz, a slow three-step in the woods. Leaves and twigs crunched beneath their feet, and the only music was the wind rustling through the trees. Rylan watched her as they danced, feeling the warmth and strength of her body. She was not a leafrunner, anymore. But she would always be one in his heart.

"Dance," he whispered.

"Wind."

The wind picked up as if on command, blowing Elanil's hair into her face. She spit it out, laughing, and they lost the step.

Rylan grabbed her in a fierce hug. But Elanil had other ideas.

She kissed him.

They fell together to the ground in a pile of leaves, laughing. Rylan smoothed out her hair. She had a smudge of dirt on her face, and her clothes were all rumpled. There was a glint in her eyes, and her mouth was quirked in a mischievous smile.

She was perfect.

He kissed her again.

Then they sat together for a while, listening to the wind.

"Mother would have killed me if she knew I was doing this," Elanil said after a few minutes.

"I wish I'd known her better," Rylan said.

Elanil squeezed his hand. "Me too."

"I wonder what the Crew would be doing now, if they were still alive."

"Shot would be running the show," Elanil said. "And complaining about it."

"Small would be happy, with magic gone. It would give him more time to focus on his electronics."

Elanil shook her head. "So many good kids lost."

"They had a good life. Or at least as good a life as they could have. They were free, for a time. We all were, unlike the topsiders. I guess I never realized that until now."

"The Unders are still there. They just look different now. Would you ever want to go back?"

Rylan didn't have to think about that. "No. I want to stay here with you."

Elanil leaned against him, putting her head on his shoulder. "I think Father would have liked you."

He could feel her shaking a little as tears began to fall. "I hope so," he said, putting his arm around her.

They sat like that for a little while.

"Elanil," Rylan said, "I'm sorry for what happened between us."

"I know." She snuggled against him. "It wasn't you. It was that stupid machine, screwing everything up." She angled her face toward his, looking in his eyes. "I trust you, Rylan."

He kissed her, sweetly.

"Where do we go from here?" he asked.

"I need to finish my schooling," Elanil said. "I think I want to stay here, in Pano Sylrantheas."

He had thought she might say that. "Can I...that is, I'd like to stay here too, if the elves will let me."

"You're an elf, too, Rylan. Remember? Or half of one. And besides, Pano Sylrantheas is a home for humans *and* elves now. I would love for you to stay. Maybe you can even take dance classes with me."

He smiled. "I would like that. I would like that very much."

PHOENIX STOOD on the upper deck of the New Eiffel Tower in New Paris, staring out at the world beyond. Imra was next to her, lending her silent support. She still had her bow slung across her back, and Phoenix still had her fireblade. Just a blade now, with magic gone.

Perhaps that was for the better.

"There's one thing I'll say about all this," Imra said. "At least I'll never have to fly again."

Phoenix laughed. "You never liked that much, did you? I guess I got used to it."

"It's a good thing we're in shape," Imra said. "The stairs in this tower are no joke."

Phoenix reached over, placing her hand on top of Imra's where it rested on the railing. "Things will be very different now."

"Yes."

"Do you…" She had to think carefully of how she wanted to put this. "Do you want to keep spending time with me?"

Imra looked at her, green eyes bright in the setting sun. "I'd like to see where this goes." She smiled, and Phoenix felt her heart warm.

Fate had brought them together, somehow. Fate or the Twins. Or magic. But there was no more magic now.

Only the magic they made on their own.

She leaned in and gave Imra a small kiss. "Ready?"

Imra nodded.

They took their basket with them, traipsing back down the stairs. Then they found the lawn outside in front of the New Eiffel Tower, already full of couples and families and friends. Phoenix found a spot on the grass and unrolled the blanket she'd brought, while Imra unpacked sandwiches and wine. It was a beautiful evening, and Imra was a beautiful girl, and for a moment Phoenix could almost forget about everything that had come before.

She could almost forget about Beam.

"To us," Phoenix said, holding up her glass. It was an alien gesture, one she'd only seen topsiders do. Now she was finally one of them, she guessed. And more—now she was a citizen of the world. It still felt so strange.

"To us," Imra echoed, and they clinked their glasses, and drank.

The red wine was delicious.

"This is neither of our homes," Phoenix said as they were eating. "I'm from the Under, and you're from the forest. Do you think we'll even get along?"

Imra looked up at the Tower. "The forest was for Arra," she said. "The Under was for Beam." She turned back to Phoenix. "Maybe this place is for us."

"I like that," Phoenix said, smiling.

Maybe she could learn to be a topsider after all.

"Do you ever think about him?" Imra asked. "Rylan's father. Quynn."

"Eric," Phoenix said. "That was the name he gave himself. And yes, sometimes I do."

"Do you miss him?"

Phoenix stared into her wine. "He was what I needed, fifteen years ago. I was weak. Lonely. In pain." She looked at Imra. "I've become stronger since then."

"I can tell." Imra put her wine glass down, reaching for her. They cuddled in the grass as the light began to fade, staring up together at the beautiful tower. "He's gone now. Perhaps forever."

"Good," Phoenix said. "Quynn was never truly happy as he was. I think I could tell, even back then. Something drove him to do the things he did, and it wasn't because of some inherent evil. It was just how his soul was made. He'll be happier now."

"Are you happy?"

Phoenix kissed the top of her head. "Yes."

Beam was a rapidly fading memory.

# SEVENTY-ONE

DILL STROLLED the streets of New Manhattan, wishing it was New San Francisco. He missed that place—the smell of the streets, the sound and bustle of the people, the dark edges of the Under. He missed his Crew. Now he would never see it or them again.

He missed his father.

He leaned against the cement wall of a nearby building, overcome by grief. Waves of it passed over him, and he tried to let them come. But after centuries of enduring, of surviving, of planning and fighting and wondering what the future held, he found it impossible to truly *feel*. To cry. To hurt. He needed it, but he didn't know how.

He almost went to the Under, but he knew he wouldn't recognize it. It wasn't *his* Under, his Crew. It just wouldn't be the same. So he wandered, trying to lose himself in unfamiliar people and shapes and sounds. It worked, for a time.

Eventually he found himself back at City Control. They recognized him and let him in.

"Didn't expect to see you back so soon," Avourel said. "You okay?"

Dill nodded, then shook his head. "I don't know. My father just died."

"I'm sorry." She looked at him awkwardly, as if unsure how to respond. City Control was not the place for this kind of conversation.

John Ronald stood up from where he'd been seated at one of the desks. "Ho, Dill," he said, adopting the Under greeting. It seemed strange, coming from him. The man was dressed in a suit jacket and jeans, his hair newly trimmed and his glasses gleaming. He looked nothing like the Remnant man he'd used to be. It was very strange.

"Ho, John," Dill said, reaching out to clasp the man's hand. "How go things up here?"

"Your father was a great man," John said, keeping his grip on Dill's hand. "I didn't know him except from a distance, but we had eyes on him the entire time. He was important. And I think he had a good heart. Magic is seductive."

Dill felt tears threatening to form. He tried to let them, but they retreated just as quickly.

He released John's hand.

"It was Xyclami's fault he did the things he did," John said. "That wasn't your father."

"It was my father who defeated the Twins," Dill said. "He's the one who imprisoned them."

"The hubris of youth. He was very young when all that happened."

"He chose to take Xyclami as the sole Operator. He knew it was against the rules. He had to know that something bad would happen."

"He wasn't perfect," John said. "And yes, he did a lot of harm. But he was still your father. He loved you. I could see it in his eyes. Try not to hate him, if you can."

Dill didn't hate Orym. He never had. But it would take

time for him to grapple with the events of the last few months. He needed space to assimilate the reality he had only so recently learned. That his father had been a hundred thousand years old. That he had been a megalomaniac, a bully. That he had been the person to have set all this in motion.

"When you wrote your books," Dill asked, "did you know all this would happen?"

John smiled. "I wrote of a dark lord, of a power that needed to be defeated, and the fellowship that took it upon themselves to get it done. I wrote a universal story, one that I hoped would echo through the ages."

"It did."

"It certainly did. But no, Dillon, I did not know that these things would come to pass. I do know elves, though. I know of their ingenuity, their spirit. The beauty of elves has captivated me my entire life, and nothing—not even the Twins, or Xyclami, or your father—can change that."

Dill felt his heart thawing a little bit. "Thank you. I'm glad to have met you, even if the circumstances weren't the best."

"And I you," John said. "But there is a little matter I wanted to discuss with you."

"Yes?"

"The True People will expand now. With magic gone, we can come out of hiding. Gondor will always be there, of course, our beautiful city underground. But with the threat to our planet removed, we think it's time to finally expand to the People we were meant to be. Even reach out to the other People, if they will have us."

"You will start the cycle anew," Dill said. "Isn't technology what got us here in the first place?"

"Perhaps," John said. "Or perhaps we have learned the lessons we were meant to learn. Your father helped teach us that."

Dill thought that perhaps the man was right. "What did you want to ask me?"

"I wanted to offer you a position with the True People. We can define the role as we go, but you have natural leadership skills, Dillon. And you're the son of the most prominent scientist in the world, outside of our little group. I think you'll find that you fit right in." He fixed Dill with a piercing gaze. "Perhaps you'll find a new place to belong."

Dill looked at him, at the man who had been Jalnab. At the person who had hidden his true identity for centuries, who had met the elves and lived to write the tale. It almost felt like trading one father for another, in a way. One enigma for the next. But John was a good man—Dill could see that. He was kind, and he was very smart, and he wanted what was best—not just for Dill, but for the world.

That was a person he could get behind.

"I accept," he said, reaching out to shake John's hand.

The man's face split into a smile. "Excellent," he said. "Welcome to the True People. It will be an honor to have you."

Dill smiled in return. "The honor, I think, is mine."

It would be good to move beyond the cities he once had known. Good to move beyond the Under, and the Crews, and the fast cars and trashboys and whiprooms and the magic.

It would be good to find a new purpose. His next mission. The true thing he was meant to do.

Perhaps it was time to choose another name.

"Let's go," John said.

They left, leaving the United Sky Cities behind.

# SEVENTY-TWO

ARRA SAT IN MERIEL'S, the tavern in Pano Sylrantheas, waiting for her friends to arrive. They were already rebuilding it—not with a pure wall of glass or wood, but somewhere halfway in between. The workers had paused for lunch now, and the sun shone in through the gaps in the wall, fresh air blowing in from the forest around the village.

Arra was back home.

But it didn't feel like home. Not anymore. Home was on Valaralda, in the town she and Tarathiel had lived in. And while she had loved Sylrantheas, she felt she needed to go back.

She needed to return to being Alleria.

"Hey," Tarathiel said, reaching for her hand. He was sitting next to her in the booth, frothy beer in the mug in front of him. He looked handsome with the sun streaming over his features. "You okay?"

"I think so," Alleria said. "It's just a lot to process."

"I know. We'll get through it together." He smiled at her, and her heart melted yet again.

It was so good to have him back.

"Ho, you two," Rylan said, leading Elanil into the tavern. Both of them had messy hair and dirty faces, a kind of brightness shining from their eyes. Alleria saw them with a sort of double vision, for a moment: the fifteen year old kids they really were, with older, more mature faces overlaid. It was as if they were growing up before her eyes, becoming the adults they were meant to be.

Perhaps they were. Perhaps they had.

She smiled at them as they sat down. "Even without magic, you two still manage to get in trouble."

"What could you possibly mean?" Elanil asked, winking at her. Rylan picked a leaf out of her hair, and she giggled.

Just a few short months ago, the sight of her so happy and carefree would have driven Alleria to rage. But now, even though she knew that Elanil wasn't really her sister, her thoughts had turned to love.

Imra walked in next, looking a bit hesitant. Phoenix followed right behind, catching Alleria's eyes. There was a question there, she thought. Was she seeking approval for being with Imra? Alleria gave a slight nod, and Phoenix smiled, reaching up to take Imra's hand. Imra flushed, brown curls bouncing as she turned to glance at Phoenix, and Alleria couldn't help but smile at the two of them. Imra deserved this. She had finally found someone to make her truly happy.

They came and sat at the booth. "Is this all of us?" Phoenix asked.

Alleria nodded. "I reached out to Dill, but he's busy in Gondor. I guess the True People gave him a job."

"Wow," Rylan said. "He really moves fast. Like father, like son."

"I hope he's okay," Elanil said.

"This place is looking great," Tarathiel said. "I like the changes."

"Maybe the third time is the charm," Alleria said. "How's the beer?"

"Delicious, as always," Tarathiel said, grimacing. "I'm really impressed with how fast they rebuilt Pano Sylrantheas."

"Orym set them back again, but they'll get it done," Alleria said.

"Them?" Tarathiel asked. "Not we?"

"I don't think I can stay here," she said.

"Ah. I wondered, but I didn't want to press."

"Sylrantheas will always be my home," Alleria said. "But this isn't Sylrantheas. It's something new, something different."

"It's going to be great," Imra said. "But you're right—it's not home, anymore. Not for us. Not after what we've seen."

"You won't stay here, either?"

Imra regarded Phoenix. "I think we're going to try the sky cities. Maybe New Paris."

"That sounds lovely," Elanil said. "You two look so happy."

"So do you," Imra said.

Phoenix was smiling at them.

"So, uh," Rylan said, "there's something I was thinking of earlier."

"Don't hold it in," Tarathiel said.

"Immortality."

"Oh."

The table was silent for a moment. Meriel herself showed up, bringing them beers. It seemed even being Council Leader wasn't enough to keep her from her guests. "You six look morose for having just saved the world," she said. "What gives?"

"Nothing big," Rylan said. "Just that we're all going to die."

"We were Prime Mages," Tarathiel said. "We were going to live forever. But now…" He let the words trail off.

"In that case," Meriel said, "I think you all ought to drink more beer. Bottoms up, people!" She flashed a smile, but her eyes bespoke deeper meaning. She was wishing them well, in her own small way.

Everyone raised their glasses.

"To what was," Tarathiel said, "and what will be. Cheers."

"Cheers!" everyone echoed, and they clinked their glasses and drank. The sun shone through the cracks in the wall and a breeze swept in, and for a moment nobody spoke.

"I think it will be good to not live forever," Alleria said after a while. "We didn't do the best job with our first twenty thousand years. Maybe now we can make it count."

"I would like that," Tarathiel said.

"I'm only thirty five," Phoenix said. "Just wanted to point that out."

"You're so *young*," Imra said, poking her.

Phoenix laughed. "And you're so *old*."

They kissed, and Imra glanced guiltily at Alleria afterwards. Alleria gave her a smile.

"There's something else," Rylan said.

"You're just full of thoughts," Tarathiel said. "But I think I know what this one might be."

Alleria watched them stare at each other from across the table. "Oh," she said, realization dawning. "I had almost forgotten!"

"It's nice to finally meet you, *dad*," Rylan said.

Tarathiel blushed. "It's still so weird, having Quynn's thoughts inside my head. I remember most of what he remembered, what he did in the intervening two thousand years."

Phoenix's mouth was open. "You remember me?"

Tarathiel winced. "Yes. Is that bad?"

Phoenix retreated away a little, leaning into Imra. "I—I guess not. It's really strange, thinking of you as Rylan's father. You still look like Trey."

Alleria almost had a moment of jealousy right then. She almost worried that Tarathiel loved Phoenix, not her. That he was back to his lecherous state, his Quynn state, letting that dominant part of his personality loose.

But then she remembered Lorelei. She had been a friend, in the end. She had never meant true harm. And Tarathiel *had* loved her...but his heart was big enough for that. His soul had been divided in two, each part finding the love they needed. It was a beautiful thing, when she really thought about it.

Magic had done that.

So, no. Alleria was fine. She was confident in herself, in the bond they shared. She squeezed Tarathiel's hand, leaning into him, looking across the table at Phoenix. The woman was happy now—truly happy. She was not a threat.

Tarathiel was hers.

He had been the entire time.

"I'm just a bookseller," Tarathiel said, maybe catching some of her mood. "Not a fiend. But I'm some of both now, I guess. I'm sorry if I hurt you, Phoenix."

Phoenix shook her head. "You were there when I needed you to be."

"It was the same for me."

They stared at each other for a moment, then Imra kissed Phoenix on the cheek.

Tarathiel turned to Rylan. "I'd like to be a father to you, if you'll have me," he said. "And if *you* will, Phoenix."

There was a pregnant pause. "You're welcome to be his father," Phoenix said. "He needs that, with Dill gone."

"Just don't beat me up," Rylan said.

Tarathiel smiled. "I would never do such a thing."

"This is really funny," Elanil said. "If you think about it, everyone at this table is connected in some way. Rylan and I... well, I guess we're together." She blushed.

"We are," Rylan said.

"And Trey and Arra—sorry, Tarathiel and Alleria—they're together. Right?"

Alleria exchanged a look with Tarathiel. "Yes."

"And Tarathiel is Rylan's father, and he slept with Phoenix, and Phoenix is Rylan's mother, and Imra is with Phoenix now, and Imra is Alleria's best friend, and *I'm* Alleria's sister. Or I was. See?"

"One big, happy family," Alleria said.

Elanil beamed.

Tarathiel raised his glass. "To family," he said. "And to all the happiness that brings."

"To family!" everyone said, and they clinked, and drank.

From across the bar, Alleria caught Meriel smiling.

# SEVENTY-THREE

ELANIL LEFT the line of trees, beholding Gulthurub in all its splendor. Or lack thereof—the Remnant outpost was still ugly, surrounded by barbed wire and lined with towers filled with guns. The buildings inside were dirty and misshapen, the very definition of disrepair. But Elanil saw a kind of beauty to the place.

This was where she had met Martan.

She wondered where he was now. With his father, probably, in their strange, underground, high-tech city. Martan had not been the person she'd thought he was, in the end.

*She* was not the person she'd thought she was.

Rylan came up next to her, puffing a little. "You dancers are in such good shape," he said.

Elanil regarded him. "You hang out with a lot of dancers?"

"Just the one." He grinned.

"Come on."

She led the way down the hill and into Gulthurub. A man named Fandab met them there, big and muscular like so many Remnant were. But he smiled when he saw them.

"Greetings," he said, holding out his hand. It was still so strange to hear the Remnant speaking perfect English.

"Hello," Elanil said, shaking his hand. "You're the new Warlord?"

"That I am," he said. "Though there are not many of us left in Gulthurub."

"We just came to see how you were doing," Elanil said. "I knew Jalnab and his son."

"Indeed," Fandab said. "I know all about you. Jalnab had his eye on you for quite some time."

"Really?" She found herself blushing at that. She had thought the man had *hated* her.

"I see you have found a new man."

She blushed again, looking at Rylan. He *was* a man, even if he was also still a boy. "This is Rylan."

"Ho," Rylan said, shaking Fandab's hand.

"What will you do now?" Elanil asked.

Fandab turned, looking out at Gulthurub. She saw people working everywhere, shoring up walls or repairing windows, carrying supplies and food from place to place. A few were even starting what looked like a garden.

"The People will rebuild what needs rebuilding," Fandab said. "The True People have offered to help. We will keep our culture, even our language. But we will not suffer. We will not fight. Not with each other, and not with you."

"You wish to live in peace with elves?"

"We do," Fandab said, turning back to her. "We know what you elves did to us. But we also know what you did *for* us. Thank you."

He smiled at her again, and the smile was kind.

Elanil felt her heart swell. This was why she'd come to Gulthurub—she had hoped deep down that the Remnant would be happy, somehow. That after all the killing, all the deaths, after the Sundering and everything that had followed, that the humans of Earth could finally find some peace.

She thought they had a good chance of that now.

"Will you come and eat with us?" Fandab asked.

"I would like that," Elanil said.

"Me too," Rylan said.

They walked into Gulthurub, seeing the proud People all around them, jata hair swinging in the wind. Elanil knew that even though she and Martan had not ended up together, there would always be a place in her heart for the Remnant.

TARATHIEL EXITED THE SPACESHIP, taking Alleria by the hand. John and his True People had kindly provided the transportation, seeing as how they were the only ones who had the technology for spaceflight now.

Valaraldan ships required magic, after all.

They stepped out into the sunlight of Ilyrion, looking down from the spaceport onto the ruined city. There was almost nothing there now—the Twins had utterly destroyed it. After more than a hundred thousand years, Ilyrion was no more.

"It's terrible," Alleria said. "Maybe we shouldn't have come back."

Lashel and Erodar came out of the spaceship next, blinking in the sunlight.

"The University is gone," Lashel said. "Which means I'm out of a job."

"So am I," Tarathiel said.

"Do you want to go back to your old life?" Alleria asked. "Do you want to be a scholar again? An archaeologist?"

Tarathiel looked at her, and he knew the answer without

thinking. "No," he said. "That life is behind me now. I spent far too long buried in the past. Time and memory is a thing best left forgotten now, I think. I want to spend my remaining years focused on the future. Focusing on you."

He gathered Alleria into his arms.

"Good answer," she whispered.

"Greetings," a voice said, and a man strolled out onto the deck. "My name is Lightning. I helped with the Prime Mages, back when we were fighting the Twins."

"I'm Tarathiel," Tarathiel said. "And this is Alleria, Lashel, and Erodar."

"I know who all of you are," Lightning said. "It is good to have you back on Valaralda. You'll be pleased to know that the Prime Mages are all safe and secure—those that survived, anyway."

"I don't think you can call them that, anymore," Tarathiel said.

"True. Still, that's how I'll always think of them. It's not every day hundreds of all-powerful mages come back from the dead."

"What about Ilyrion?" Alleria asked. "What will happen here?"

"We will rebuild," Lightning said. "The preparations have already begun. It will take time. These things always do. But this is not enough to break our spirit."

"You have no more magic," Tarathiel said.

"It will be a different Ilyrion," Lightning said. "But it will be no less beautiful for the lack of magic. We will find other ways to make it so."

"Good," Alleria said.

"Lightning," Tarathiel said, "there's something I need to ask."

"Go ahead."

"Do you know of the Desolation? It is far to the east, on a different continent."

"As it happens, I do know of that event. Why do you ask?"

"There is a people there, called the Aiqua. We met them recently, helped them as best we could. They gave Alleria her bow. We promised them we'd send help, get them out of there."

Lightning's mouth was open. "There are *people* living there? Isn't it all volcanoes now?"

Tarathiel nodded. "That's why we need to help."

"Got it," Lightning said. "Well, we still have all our ships. Give me the details, and we'll get it done."

"Thank you."

"You kept your promise," Alleria said quietly.

"Of course," Tarathiel said.

Alleria squeezed him. Then they turned, looking out at the ruins of Ilyrion. There was a lot of work ahead of them, but it was also a great opportunity. They had a chance no one else had had in a hundred thousand years: to remake the world in the best way possible.

Orym would have been proud.

# SEVENTY-FOUR

PHOENIX AND IMRA were having lunch at a little cafe on Rue de Rivoli, sipping coffee and sharing a baguette. All of it was transmuted, still, of course. Real coffee was out there to be harvested, but it would take time to get the wheels turning on all those industries again.

"Phoenix?" a voice said, and she turned to see a man approaching. He was dressed in a black suit, and he carried himself with authority.

She tensed. "Yes?"

"City Manager Hammond," the man said, approaching and holding out his hand.

She took it cautiously. "You're in charge, up here?"

"I am. In fact I've just been named Executive Leader of the United Sky Cities. Remember Lorelei? I'm the new her."

"Oh." Phoenix wasn't sure if that was good or bad.

"May I sit?"

"Of course."

Imra shifted over to make room at their tiny table. Hammond pulled over a nearby chair, sitting. His posture was excellent, Phoenix noted. Not only was he a topsider, he was a well-cultured topsider. Phoenix wondered what he wanted.

"Dill told me about you," Hammond said. "And you—Imra, is it?" Imra nodded. "You both come highly recommended."

"For what, exactly?"

"Well. Despite all the carnage, there is still quite a large Under population spread out across the cities."

"What's going to happen with the cities, anyway?" Phoenix asked. "Are you going to join them back together?"

"With New San Francisco gone," Hammond said, "that would be very difficult. And putting the cities together like that leaves us vulnerable, as we've now discovered. So, no. We will remain in relatively close proximity to each other in the sky, but we will remain physically separate. Politically, however, we will continue to be the United Sky Cities. We will run under the same centralized government President Greyson established."

"And you're the...Executive Leader?"

"Think of me as head of operations," Hammond said. "I get things done, while the President is more of a political figure."

"And who is the new President? I hope he's not someone I'll hate."

"It's a she, actually," Hammond said. "Someone who had been quietly rising up the political ladder, keeping a low profile. As it happens, the people love her."

"Anyone I know?"

"Probably not. Her name is Tiala."

"Hmm," Phoenix said. "Doesn't ring a bell."

"Anyway, that's not why I'm here."

"Tell me."

"The Unders were significantly altered when the Escape

Module was activated," Hammond said. "And while most of it is still perfectly inhabitable, we wanted to provide better services to the people down there. To start with, we're providing a free migration path to topside for any underkid who wishes it. Those who want to stay in the Under are welcome to, of course. We'll be adding services for them directly."

Phoenix wasn't sure if she should be happy or annoyed. Her whole life, she'd wanted to live topside. To be among the rich and happy. To get out of the squalor and suffering she had been forced to endure. Now it was just being *handed* to people, freely?

Then she realized *why*.

She had been instrumental in that change. She and her new friends—everyone who had fought the Twins, fought the Cothellon, liberated the sky cities and rid the world of magic. Things were changing for the better now, and she was part of the reason why.

She smiled. "And what do you want with me?"

"We were hoping you'd lead the program. Both of you, if you want. You'll be given topside accommodations, of course. Nice ones. And you'll be free to form a team, given whatever resources you need. It will be rough work, at first. The cities are still adjusting to the loss of magic, and will be for some time. You'll have to get your hands dirty."

Phoenix looked at Imra. "What do you think?"

Imra looked around at the Rue de Rivoli, at the restaurants and the people strolling by. Then she looked at her bow, leaning up against the table. "On to bigger and better things," she said. "I would love to help."

"Hard work, you said?" Phoenix asked. "I'll have to get my hands dirty?"

"That you will," Hammond said. "But we'd love to have you."

"There's one thing you need to know about me," Phoenix said, grinning. "I'm not afraid of a little dirt."

Imra snorted. "I have a feeling that's not the first time you've said that."

"Phoenix?" another voice said, and a young boy arrived, breathless.

"What is this, meet Phoenix day?" Phoenix asked. "Who are you?"

"I have a message for you," the boy said. "You're invited to a very important event." He handed her an envelope. There was one for Imra, too.

"This should be interesting," Phoenix said, reading what was inside.

# SEVENTY-FIVE

AS ALLERIA STOOD on the rose-covered platform, she found herself inexplicably nervous. She was dressed in a full-length gown made of white lace, her long hair done up with little white bows. She was scared as she stood up there in front of all those people, holding her flowers and nervously swallowing. She was scared, but not because she was afraid.

She was scared to feel this happy.

Tarathiel was the one walking down the aisle. It was a reversal, but one that he had willingly embraced. He had been the one to leave her, all those years ago. He had been the one to split his personality, to form two people, to go off on adventures and wreak madness and mayhem on an unsuspecting world. He had lost her, then, and now he was coming back.

And he was *gorgeous*.

He was dressed in a white tuxedo in the fashion of Earth, hair perfectly styled, eyes glinting. He walked with a certain confidence, as if he'd finally found the purpose for his existence. As if the world for him made sense. As if he knew what he wanted.

What he wanted was her.

As he came to stand beside her on the platform, she couldn't help but smile. It was him, yet it wasn't quite the man she'd known. There was something different about him —something calmer, more at peace. He had conquered his inner demons, and now he was all hers.

It had only taken twenty thousand years.

Her gaze slid from his finally, taking in the people all around them. She wanted to remember this moment. It was only a renewal of their original vows, but somehow it felt even more important than the first time. This time she didn't think anything would get in their way.

Imra was her maid of honor. She looked resplendent in a gown of green, hair pulled back with little white flowers in it. Rylan stood proud as Tarathiel's best man, dressed in a black tuxedo with a green tie. Kythaela was presiding—the Recitation Mentor had been pleased to accept Alleria's invitation.

The audience was full. Everyone she knew had made it: Phoenix and Elanil, of course, and Dill and John Ronald had reappeared from wherever they'd been hiding. Lashel and Erodar sat with Lightning and Cresius, the main representatives from Valaralda. Hammond had joined them from the United Sky Cities. He was sitting next to Kharis, the former Bombardment Mentor. And next to Kharis, Alleria was surprised to see, was Meriel.

The two of them were holding hands.

Kharis actually looked happy, being there with Meriel. She was Syndra's sister, after all. It somehow made a bit of sense. Maybe Kharis could once again find his peace.

There was also a small group of Remnant in the audience, led by Fandab from Gulthurub. Their jata hair was pulled back, lending them some semblance of formality. Even Talon was there, with a contingent of rylak. Once he'd heard who

Quynn really was, he had wanted nothing more than to attend. He'd even had special suits made for the hulking wolf-like men, and Alleria had to admit that they looked good.

The ceremony was being conducted on the cliffs just north of Ilyrion, facing the Airon Sea. It was where she and Tarathiel had been married before, so long ago. It seemed fitting that they had returned here again. It was beautiful, with grass and trees dotting the area atop the cliffs, with the ocean stretching out behind them as far as the eye could see. It was a place of natural beauty, a place untouched by magic or the Twins.

She loved it there.

"Greetings, friends and family," Kythaela said, beginning the ceremony. "We are gathered here today to witness the reaffirming of the marriage vows of Tarathiel and Alleria Riverbow. Thank you for coming. You may be seated."

The audience sat, and Alleria looked at Tarathiel. He returned the gaze, eyes glittering confidently. So much love was radiating out of him, she almost found it hard to breathe. She had never felt this much from him before.

"Please join hands," Kythaela said.

They did so, but movement caught the corner of Alleria's eye. She glanced to her right and saw two new figures arriving at the back. Her breath stuck in her chest.

It was Velion and Nelenor.

She opened her mouth to say something, but Tarathiel had seen them, too. He shook his head, mouthing the word "wait." So she held his hands, willing her nerves to quiet. It was fine. Magic was gone.

She just hadn't expected the Twins themselves to come to her wedding.

She glanced back at them one more time, and saw

Nelenor pointing up at them and smiling. Was he pointing at her? No—he was pointing at *Kythaela*. That was odd.

She returned her gaze to Tarathiel.

"Before we begin," Kythaela said, "let us take a moment to remember those that we have lost. Many made great sacrifices so that we, the privileged few, could be here on this day. As I say their names, a rose will be dropped in the aisle. The list is long, but it is not complete. We ask that you honor those we do not mention in your minds and in your hearts."

Alleria had arranged this portion of the ceremony. Part wedding and part funeral, it seemed a fitting capstone for the things they all had been through. She thought it only appropriate that they brought the memories of the dead along with them as they embarked on their future.

"Allain," Kythaela said. Attendants were standing in the center aisle with armloads of red roses. One dropped a rose now, letting it fall to the ground. The audience stayed silent.

"His father, Orist."

Another rose fell.

"The other Mentors: Aolis Talos. Ryllae. Eloen. Lhoris. Nuvian. Belstram. Paeris."

Alleria heard some sniffles in the audience, caught a few wet eyes. Kharis in particular was having trouble keeping it together, and she couldn't say she blamed him. She should have warned him that this part of the ceremony was going to happen.

"Silanar," Kythaela said, and Alleria felt a jolt of pain spike through her. The man hadn't been her father in the end, but he had felt like one to her. "Melenora." Elanil was crying from the front row. "Beam." Phoenix nodded at Alleria, her face stoic. Imra smiled at her from her position on stage. "Callan." Tarathiel tensed up at that, looking in her eyes. His friend had betrayed him in the end, but he had still been a good friend. Alleria knew there was a lot of pain associated with that memory.

Perhaps she shouldn't have insisted on this ritual.

"Shot," Kythaela said. "Small. Spike. Grime, and thousands of other underkids. Con."

Rylan choked up on stage, eyes watering visibly. Alleria glanced out at Dill, saw his lip quivering. This was a lot to take in, she knew. She was adding so much sorrow to what should have been a joyous day.

"Fenian."

That hurt.

"Lorelei."

Tarathiel squeezed her hands. Their former lovers now dead and gone. She had put them at the end on purpose—because it was time to move on.

"Orym."

Dill finally started sobbing from his position in the front row. She wondered how long he'd been holding the grief in.

"And Quynn," Kythaela said, "who is not dead, but is merely in a different form."

Tarathiel squeezed her hands again, jaw twitching. She knew how hard this must be for him.

"We honor the memory of the dead," Kythaela continued. "May they serve to light our path toward the future, toward a brighter tomorrow. Twins guide us."

Alleria hadn't expected that part.

"Twins protect us," the audience echoed, almost as if by default.

Velion and Nelenor shared a smile in the back.

"And now," Kythaela said, "let us move to happier times. These two are standing before us to renew their vows, to proclaim their undying love for all to see. Let us be here with them as they repeat their promises to each other."

The rest of the ceremony passed by in a blur. Alleria's heart was full of pain and happiness in equal measure, the emotion almost carrying her away. So she focused on Tarathiel, on his eyes, leaning on him to anchor her through the storm.

# SEVENTY-SIX

AFTER THE CEREMONY, Alleria found herself alone on the cliffs with Tarathiel, overlooking the ocean. The sun was setting behind them, sending long, golden rays across the sea. She felt a mixture of emotion, owing to the strange ceremony she'd concocted for today. But she welcomed it. She knew that grief was tied with happiness, that love was tied with pain.

She looked in Tarathiel's eyes, and all she felt was love.

He took her in his arms, then, as if reading her mind. That was all she wanted now: him and the sea, and the fresh breeze and the setting sun. She wanted to live now in this moment, to shed those bitter memories of the past.

He seemed to share the sentiment.

"It is so, so good to have you back," Tarathiel said. "It's strange now. I know what I've been missing. Not you—of course I missed you. But what I've really been missing was *myself.*"

"I know," Alleria said. "I felt it, too."

"I hope you know how sorry I am," he said, pulling her tighter. "For all the wrong I did to you over the years. I was a terrible partner."

"You couldn't help it. It was your essential nature. And Tarathiel—you were trying to save the world. You worked against *impossible* odds, when no one would believe you, when even *history* was wrong. You persevered. And yes, you lost some people along the way. You lost me. But I'm back now, and you succeeded. You did it. But more importantly, you fixed *you*. And for that, I'm so proud. I love you, Trey. Quynn. Tarathiel. I love *you*, and I'm so happy you're back."

"I love you too, Alleria. And with all that's happened already, I can't help but wonder what's in store for us in the future. It might be downright boring by comparison."

She turned her face up to meet his, the sun beaming softly on their faces. He was beautiful, there in that golden glow. She saw in him the things she'd seen before—only better, brighter, more sure. She saw the man she'd fallen in love with back in that classroom. She saw the person she wanted to share the rest of her life with.

Again.

She saw him. And for the first time in a long time, that was enough for her.

"I don't think it will be boring at all," she said, kissing him softly on the lips. "I think it will be an awfully big adventure."

# SEVENTY-SEVEN

KYTHAELA SAT on the thick log in the middle of the jungle, trying to ignore the sweltering heat as she looked at the faces all around. Humans, elves, and rylak were gathered there, listening to everything she had to say. The three races were living here on Eryn, actually living without violence or fear.

It had taken a long time for them to get here, but here they were.

Perhaps it had been worth the struggle.

"And so it was that Tarathiel and Alleria lived," Kythaela said. "They lived happily for a time, and they lived unhappily. For such is the way with marriage, and with people. Such is the way with the world.

"Magic was over. Xyclami lay dormant, turned off by Tarathiel. And the world adapted, learning and using new technologies from Valaralda and the True People. Ilyrion rebuilt. Pano Sylrantheas extended further into the forest. And the People of Gulthurub moved into Old San Francisco, reclaiming their ancestral home. And while magic was no longer present in any of their lives, they were happy.

"They made magic of their own."

She smiled, stepping up and leaving her storytelling log. It had been a long story, and the people were tired. They rose in singles and in pairs, some of them coming up to quietly thank her for her time. They loved this story, she knew.

So did she.

"You are so good at this," Velion said, coming up to stand beside her. The woman was petite and very blonde, looking for all the world like Kythaela's sister.

Because she was.

"I still can't believe we found you after all this time," Nelenor said as he arrived. "How did you elude us for so long, Kira?"

"I didn't mean to," Kythaela—Kira—said. "Well, maybe I did." She winked at them. "Let's just say these worlds had lessons to be learned."

She remembered her days in the Cancer Society, trying to heal patients without magic. She remembered her days as Keya, as Kythaela, living as an elf with the wrong past. Had anything changed? Was anything different?

Yes.

She stepped around to the back of the log, where she'd laid the thing she'd been watching over for so long. It was almost ready. It was almost time. She looked up into the sky, imagining that she could feel Xyclami. She *could* feel it—even while it was lying dormant. It still had certain powers at its disposal.

Not the least of which was lying here.

"That's what this was all about?" Nelenor asked, seeing what she was regarding on the ground.

"Yes," Kira said. "Xyclami was meant to transition us away from Starmist, to save us in the event of total destruction. But the greatest of us, the most important thing we had to save, was not something we could simply let loose without care."

"Tarathiel unlocked it," Velion said.

"Yes. This was Xyclami's final secret, even if he doesn't know it, yet."

"Incredible."

"So?" Velion asked. "Is it happening now?"

"Yes," Kira said, and they bent down around the object to watch.

It only took a minute for the cracking to begin.

Nelenor gasped, holding a hand to his mouth. Velion sighed, contentment on her face. And Kira smiled, knowing that the beautiful world of Eryn was about to change forever.

The egg on the ground cracked open, and a dragon's head appeared.

"You always were the smart one," Velion said. "You were always first among us."

"Oh!" Nelenor said. "I'd almost forgotten what we used to call you, back on Starmist Prime."

"It was a poor name," Kira said, watching as the dragon made its way out of the shell. "It made no sense."

"But it did, dear sister," Velion said. "Who but you should be called Kira the Prime?"

"That word has been used enough for many lifetimes," Kira said. Still, she smiled to herself. Prime, indeed. She was no Prime.

But the word did have a certain ring to it.

"What will happen to it?" Nelenor asked, looking at the baby dragon.

"It will grow and mature," Kira said. "Others will hatch, as well. It will take time—a *lot* of time—but eventually dragons will be part of Eryn's ecosystem, living and thriving with the others."

"So it will be here, then," Velion said.

"Yes," Kira said. "Here is where we will finally establish our new home."

"Starmist reborn."

"Starmist reborn," Kira echoed. "May these little ones always remember the sacrifices that brought them here."

"Dragons," Nelenor whispered. "It has been a long, long time."

# THE
# END

# READY FOR THE NEXT ADVENTURE?

*Excerpt from ATTENTION DEFICIT, my near-future technothriller:*

Sometimes one stray glance is all it takes to kill a girl.

My watch read sixteen bars as I jolted awake, sweat sheening on my pounding brow, knowing that the pit I felt deep in my stomach, that gnawing, yearning sense of emptiness, was about to do me in. So I did the one thing I probably shouldn't have done.

I stood up.

My stomach heaved and I almost lost it right then, but I'd been at sixteen before. I'd developed the training it took to clench your guts, to look death right in the face, to pull your hair back and shut your eyes and hope to hell that somebody thinks of you.

But nobody was thinking of me now.

So I tottered, the world swimming around me like a simulation gone wrong, trying not to throw up all over the cheap pale blue linoleum floor. My heart was all erratic. My eyes hurt. If *any* tention left me, I'd be dead.

What a wonderful way to start a Sunday afternoon.

But I had to do *something*. I couldn't just sway right here. So I lurched and almost fell and got to the kitchen just in time for the phone to ring.

It was Liza, of course, her face blurred. She wanted what she always did: I had to come in. I had someone waiting. I told her I would and that I just needed some coffee and a pill. She told me the guy wouldn't wait.

So I staggered over to the closet, trying not to faint. I found something that wasn't completely ruined and threw it on, brushing my hair back roughly. I caught my hazy reflection in the window and tried to look at my eyes, wishing for the millionth time that thinking about *myself* would help. But there was no juice, no bars.

You couldn't give tention to yourself.

My stomach grumbled, but I had nothing to eat, and no coffee. So I waved a tea and choked that down as I tried to fit my sneakers on. My balance was shit—I fell over once before I managed it. The tea tasted like ashes, as if my soul had been charred along with my pride. Tention could do that to you, when it was bad.

I left the tiny apartment, heading down the elevator, making sure to turn on ghost mode as I did. My ayar lenses felt sharp against my eyes, like an eyelash or a fleck of dust. I blinked them away and hoped they wouldn't stay that way for long. I needed a strong day, a day of taking. I needed to recover from my mistakes.

I needed more bars.

"Mila!" somebody called as I left the building, and I felt a little surge as his tention entered me. Who the hell would use my actual *name*? It wasn't the doorman. I blinked again, seeing ghosts all around me. The lenses dropped an arrow over someone, and I clicked a tooth to remove the shroud.

The face became clear. Mikey, the mailman. A sweet guy. I gave him the briefest of glances before turning the blur back on, but already I could feel tention seeping out of me, returning to him. The exchange had left us net zero. Better than it could have been, I guess, but my watch still hovered at sixteen. I felt bile once more rising in my throat.

"What do you want?" I asked. Had to keep the conversation short, if I didn't want to die.

But he was still looking at me—actually *looking*—and I could feel my juice creep up. Breathing came easier, my body warmer.

What was he doing?

"Saw you come in last night," Mikey said. "Didn't mean nothing by it, I was just on the block. Wanted to make sure you were okay."

Mikey was old fashioned. He didn't use the ayar lenses. He didn't believe in the wireframe, in the ghosts and the blur. He wanted to see things as they were, I guess. He wanted a *real* connection with the world. A connection most of us lost long ago.

It was a marvel he wasn't dead already.

"I'm fine," I lied.

"Mila." He let the sentence stop there. I could feel his tention pouring into me, enough to quicken my breath. Most people won't call you by name—it gives you too much juice— but Mikey was different. He always liked to call me like I was. I wondered where he got his power from.

"Really," I said, "I'm fine."

I stepped forward, keeping the blur on, seeing the mailman as a body with a ghost for a face. I put a hand on his arm, feeling the tention loop as we focused on each other. My heart fluttered for a second as the feeling coursed through me, then I lifted my hand. He wasn't a john.

"Go back to the mail."

I turned and left, sensing his disappointment. My watch ticked up a few bars as he watched me go.

He'd be dead soon, if he kept that up.

*To be continued in ATTENTION DEFICIT...*

To purchase, head to **jtf.link/attention** or scan the QR code below.

# ENJOY THE BOOK? HELP SPREAD THE WORD

Reviews are the most powerful tools in my arsenal when it comes to getting attention for my books. Much as I'd like to, I don't have the financial muscle of a New York publisher. I can't take out full page ads in the newspaper or put posters on the subway.

But I do have something much more powerful and effective than that, and it's something that those publishers would kill to get their hands on.

A committed and loyal bunch of readers.

Honest reviews of my books help bring them to the attention of other readers. If you've enjoyed this book, **I'd love it if you could leave a quick review.**

Head to **jtf.link/metalreview10** or scan the QR code.

# ABOUT THE AUTHOR

Jeremy is a fantasy and science fiction author, living and writing in the San Francisco Bay Area. Fantasy is his first love —there's something about magic and mayhem that has interested him since he first cracked opened Lord Foul's Bane in the seventh grade. Also archery.

There always seems to be a lot of archery involved.

When not writing, Jeremy is a graphic designer, software developer, game designer, and music composer. He makes a really great Old Fashioned.

Check out his other work and sign up for his newsletter at **www.jeremythomasfuller.com**.

facebook.com/JeremyThomasFuller

instagram.com/jeremythomasfuller

amazon.com/author/jeremythomasfuller

bsky.app/profile/jeremythomasfuller.com